THE EARL'S UNSUITABLE BRIDE

LAUREN ROYAL

DEVON ROYAL

June 2021 Edition
SWEET CHASE BRIDES

THE EARL'S UNSUITABLE BRIDE by Lauren Royal & Devon Royal

Published by Novelty Books, a division of Novelty Publishers, LLC, 205 Avenida Del Mar #275, San Clemente, CA 92674

June 2021 Edition

Cover by Kimberly Killion

Learn more about the authors and their books at www.LaurenandDevonRoyal.com.

ISBN: 978-1-63469-175-8

MORE SWEET CHASE BRIDES BOOKS

~

For our father and grandfather,
Herbert Royal,
who taught us to love books

PROLOGUE

London
April 22, 1661

HE DAY AMETHYST Goldsmith was born, her king was beheaded. Now, twelve years later, his son was returning to England, and Amy wanted to see every exciting second of his triumphant procession. Without taller people blocking her view.

Unfortunately, it seemed nearly everyone was taller than she.

She shouldered her way through the crowd, her parents and aunt murmuring apologies in her wake. "Here, there's room!" Finally reaching a few bare inches of rail, she clasped it with both hands and turned to flash them a victorious smile. "Come along, it's starting!"

Hugh and Edith Goldsmith joined her, shaking their heads at their daughter's tenacity. Hugh's sister, Amy's Aunt Elizabeth, squeezed in behind. Ignoring the grumbling of displaced spectators, Amy spread her feet wide to save more room at the front. "Robert, over here!"

Robert Stanley tugged on her long black plait as he wedged himself in beside her. She shot him a grin; he was fun. Although he'd arrived just last week to train as her father's apprentice, Amy had known since birth that she was to marry him—or at least since she was old enough to understand such things. So far they seemed to be compatible, although he'd been surprised to find she was far more skilled as a jeweler than he. Surprised and none too pleased, Amy suspected. But he would get over those feelings.

She might be a girl, but, as her father always said, her talent was a God-given gift. She'd never give up her craft. Robert would just have to get used to it.

With a sigh of pleasure, Amy shuffled her shoes on the scrubbed cobblestones. "Look, Mama! Everything is so clean and glorious." She breathed deep of the fresh air, blinking against the bright sun. "The rain has stopped...even the weather is welcoming the monarchy back to England! Have you ever seen so many people? All London must be here."

"These cannot all be Londoners." Her mother waved a hand, encompassing the crowds on the rooftops, the mobbed windows and overflowing balconies. "I think many have come in from the countryside."

A handful of tossed rose petals drifted down, landing on Amy's dark head like scented snowflakes. She shook them off, laughing. "Just look at all the tapestries and banners!"

"Just look at all that wasted wine," Robert muttered, with a nod toward the fragrant red river that ran through the open conduit in the street.

Amy opened her mouth to protest, then decided he must be fooling. "Marry come up, Robert! You must be pleased King Charles will be crowned tomorrow. Our lives have been so dreary until now. But now Cromwell is gone, and we have music and dancing!" She felt like dancing, like spreading her burgundy satin skirts and twirling in a circle, but the press of the crowd made such a maneuver impossible, so she settled for bobbing a little curtsy. "We've beautiful clothes, and the theater—"

"And drinking and cards and dice," Robert added.

But Amy wasn't listening. She'd turned back to ogle the mounted queue of nobility parading their way from the Tower to Whitehall Palace. Such jewels and feathers and lace! Fingering the looped ribbons adorning her new gown, she pressed harder against the rail, wishing she too could join the procession.

"Where did they possibly find so many ostrich feathers in all of England?" she wondered aloud, then burst into giggles.

Her aunt laughed and wrapped an affectionate arm around her shoulders. "Where do you find the energy, child? You must come to Paris. Uncle William and I could use your happy smiles."

Feeling a stab of sympathy, Amy hugged her around the waist. Aunt Elizabeth had lost her three children to smallpox last year.

"We need her artistry here," Amy's father protested, poking his sister good-naturedly. "Your shop will have to do without."

"Ah, Hugh, how selfish you are!" Aunt Elizabeth chided. "Hoarding my niece's talent for your own profit." She aimed a teasing smile at her brother. "No wonder we moved to France to escape the competition."

Amy grinned. Aunt Elizabeth and Uncle William had been forced to move their shop when business fell off during the Commonwealth years. But they'd flourished in Paris, becoming jewelers to the French court, and wouldn't think of returning now.

"I'm glad you came for the coronation, Aunty. It wouldn't be the same without you."

"I wouldn't have missed it," Aunt Elizabeth declared. "Old Noll drove me out of England, so my home is elsewhere now. But heaven knows no one here is happier than I."

"Listen!" Amy cried. A joyous roar rolled westward toward them, marking the slow passage of His Majesty in the middle of the procession. "Can you hear King Charles coming? There are his attendants!" The noise swelled as the king's footguards marched by, their plumes of red and white feathers contrasting with those of his brother, the Duke of York, whose guard was decked out in black and white.

All at once, the roar was deafening. Amy grasped her mother's hand. "It's him, Mama," she whispered. "King Charles II." Glittering in the sunshine, the Horse of State caught and held her gaze. "Oh, look at the embroidered saddle, the pearls and rubies —look at our diamonds!"

Amy didn't care for horses—she was terrified of them, truth

be told—so she paid no attention to the magnificent beast himself. But three hundred of her family's diamonds sparkled on the gold stirrups and bosses, among the twelve thousand lent for the occasion.

"Oh, Papa," she breathed, "I wish we could have designed that saddle."

Aunt Elizabeth's hand suddenly tightened on Amy's shoulder. "Charles is looking at me," she declared loudly.

Amy's father snorted. "Always the flirt, sister mine."

Amy's gaze flew from the dazzling horse to its rider. Smiling broadly beneath his thin mustache, the tall king waved to the crowd. His cloth-of-silver suit peeked from beneath ermine-lined crimson robes. Rubies and sapphires winked from gold shoe buckles and matching gold garters, festooned with great poufs of silver ribbon. Long, shining black curls draped over his chest, framing a weathered face; the result, Amy supposed, of having suffered through exile and the execution of his beloved father.

But his black eyes were quick and sparkling. Some women around Amy swooned, but she just stared, willing the king to look at her.

When he did, she flashed him a radiant smile. "No, Aunty, he's looking at *me*."

Before her family even stopped laughing, the king was gone, as suddenly as he had arrived. But the spectacle wasn't over. Behind him came a camel with brocaded panniers and an East Indian boy flinging pearls and spices into the crowd. And then more lords and ladies, more glittering costumes, more decorated stallions, more men-at-arms, all bedecked in gold and silver and the costliest of gems.

Yet none of it mattered to Amy, for there was a young nobleman riding her way.

He looked to be maybe sixteen, a bit older than Robert—but she thought he looked much more mature. It wasn't the richness of his clothing that caught Amy's eye, for in truth his garb was rather plain. His black velvet suit was trimmed with naught but gold braid; his wide-brimmed hat boasted only a single white plume. He wore no fancy crimped periwig; instead his own raven-black hair fell in gleaming waves past his chin.

4

Eyes the color of emeralds bore into Amy's as he set his horse in her direction. His glossy black gelding breathed close, but she felt no fear, for the young man held her safe with his piercing green gaze. It seemed as though he could see through her eyes right into her soul. Her cheeks flamed; never in her life had a boy looked at her like that.

He tipped his plumed hat. Flustered, she turned and glanced about, certain he must be saluting someone else. But everyone was laughing and talking or watching the procession; no one focused their attention his way. She looked back, and he grinned as he passed, a beautiful flash of white that made Amy melt inside.

Long after he rode out of sight around the bend, she stared to where he had disappeared.

"Amy?" Robert tugged on her hand.

She turned and gazed into his eyes: pale blue, not green. They didn't see into her soul, didn't make her feel anything.

Robert smiled, revealing teeth that overlapped a bit. She hadn't really noticed that before. "It's over," he said.

"Oh."

The sun set as they walked home to Cheapside, skirting merrymakers in the streets. Her father paused to unlock their door. Overhead, a wooden sign swung gently in the breeze. A nearby bonfire illuminated the image of a falcon and the gilt letters that proclaimed their shop GOLDSMITH & SONS, JEWELLERS.

There came a sudden brilliant flash and a stunned "Ooooh" from the crowd, as fireworks lit the sky. Amy dashed through the shop and up the stairs to their balcony.

Gazing toward the River Thames, she watched the great fiery streaks of light, heard the soaring rockets, smelled the sulfur in the air. It was the most spectacular display England had ever seen, and the sights and sounds filled her with a wondrous feeling.

If only life could be as exhilarating as a fireworks show.

When the last glittering tendril faded away, she listened to the fragments of song and rowdy laughter that filled the night air. Couples strolled by, arm in arm. Robert stepped onto the balcony and moved close.

His voice was quiet beside her. "This is a day I'll never forget."

"I'll never forget it, either," she said, thinking of the boy on the black steed, the young nobleman with the emerald eyes.

Robert reached out to tilt her face up. Was he going to kiss her? She'd never been kissed—what a day this was turning out to be! Her heart pounded as he bent his head and brushed his lips softly, chastely against hers.

Her heart stopped pounding.

It was her first kiss; she was supposed to feel fireworks.

But she felt nothing.

ONE

Five years later
August 24, 1666

"**A**RE YOU TELLING me *you* made this bracelet? A girl? This shop is Goldsmith and *Sons*, is it not?" Robert puckered his freckled face and made his voice high and wavering. "Where are the sons?"

From where she stood by the stone oven, Amy's laughter rang through the workshop. "Lady Smythe! A perfect imitation."

"Well done, Robert." Her father smiled as he brushed past them both and through the archway into the shop's showroom.

Robert's pale blue eyes twinkled, but he stayed in character, cupping a hand to his ear. "Imitation? Imitation, did you say? I was led to believe this was a *quality* jewelry shop, madame. I expect genuine—"

"Stop!" Amy fought to control her giggles. "You'll make me slip and scald myself."

Robert's gaze fell to Amy's hands. As he watched her pour a thin stream of molten gold into a plaster mold, his expression sobered. "I like Lady Smythe," he muttered. "At least she buys the things *I* make."

"Oh, Robert." She sighed. "Why should it matter who made something, as long as we're selling a piece?"

"I'm a good goldsmith."

"You're an excellent goldsmith," Amy agreed. Although she also thought he was a bit unimaginative, she kept that to herself. "What does that have to do with anything?"

"You're a girl."

She clenched her jaw and tapped the mold on her workbench, imagining the gold flowing to fill every crevice of her design. "I'm also a jeweler," she said under her breath.

"Never mind." He walked to his own workbench and plopped onto his stool, lifting the pewter tankard of ale that sat ever-present amongst his tools.

Ignoring him, Amy picked up a knife and a chunk of wax, intending to whittle a new design while the gold hardened. The windowless workroom seemed stifling today—hot, close, and dark. She dragged a lantern nearer, but the weak, yellowish glow did little to lift her mood.

Five years she'd lived and worked with Robert Stanley, and he still didn't understand her. She couldn't believe it. She was marrying him in two weeks, and she couldn't believe that, either.

Once it had seemed like a lifetime stretched ahead of her before she had to wed. But now she was seventeen, and Robert was twenty-one, and his apprenticeship had ended. Which meant it was time for them to marry.

She'd asked for more time, but her father had refused. According to the betrothal agreement that had been signed when she was born, Robert was now due a share of the shop—and Hugh Goldsmith wasn't about to share his family's hard-earned business with a man who wasn't his son-in-law. So he'd set a date, and that had been that.

No matter that Robert thought his wife should stay upstairs and mend his clothes; no matter that he resented it when Amy's designs sold faster and she received more custom orders than he did.

No matter that she didn't love him. Not the way a wife should love a husband. Not the way it was in the French novels she smuggled into her bedchamber. Not the way she had felt, five years ago at the coronation procession, when that young nobleman's emerald eyes had locked on hers.

Never mind that she'd been but a fanciful girl of twelve at the time—she'd felt something, and that feeling was something she'd never forgotten.

She would learn to love Robert, her father said. But it hadn't happened—not yet, anyway. Not even close.

Amy sighed and lifted the plait off her neck, fanning the hot skin beneath. She'd set out to talk to her father dozens of times, to beg him to reconsider. But her courage always failed her. Since the death of her mother in last year's Great Plague, it seemed she could take anything but her father's disapproval.

When the casting was set, Amy plunged it into the tub of water by Robert's workbench. She rubbed the mold's gritty plaster surface, feeling it dissolve away in her hands, watching Robert's knife send wax shavings flying as he sculpted a model.

She scowled at his curved back. "I believe I fancied you more as Lady Smythe."

Robert turned and stared at her for a moment, then hunched over suddenly. His face transformed, taking on a Lady Smythe look. "Are you certain, madame?" he asked in that high, wavering tone. "I hear tell you've had dancing lessons and speak fluent French. Such pretensions. I don't hold with women reckoning account books, you know. Not at all." His voice deepened into his own. "Or making jewelry, either."

Amy flinched. She pulled the casting from the water and carried it to her workbench to brush off the remaining bits of plaster.

He rose and came up behind her, tilting her head back with a hand beneath her chin. "Two more weeks, and a proper wife you'll be," he said and clamped his mouth on hers.

The faint scent of his breakfast had her squeezing her eyes shut and praying for the end to this torment.

"Part your lips, will you?" he said against her mouth.

She didn't. She wished he'd use one of those newfangled little silver toothbrushes Aunt Elizabeth had sent from Paris.

Finally he raised his head. "Two weeks," he repeated.

Her eyes snapped open and burned into his. "Papa will never allow you to keep me from making jewelry." Looking down, she brushed at the casting harder.

He shrugged. "Your papa won't be here forever." His hand moved to grip her waist.

Amy's gaze flickered toward the showroom in warning.

Sighing, he wrenched away and strode back to his work-bench, back to his ale. "At least soon I'll be allowed to touch you whenever I please." Grinning, he lifted the tankard in a salute. "Two weeks."

Amy had once thought his grins shy and engaging...but of late they only made her uneasy.

The bell on the outside door tinkled, giving Amy a start. She stood and whipped off her apron. "I'll get it."

"Your father is out there," Robert reminded her. "He can handle it."

Paying him no mind, she straightened her gown and smoothed back a few damp strands that had escaped her plait. She put a shopgirl smile on her face before heading through the swinging doors into the cool, bright showroom.

"A locket," a girl at the far end of the L-shaped case was saying, smiling up at a tall gentleman with his back to Amy.

Deep red curls draped to the young lady's rather scan-dalously bare shoulders; her lavish golden brocade gown had a wide, scooped neckline Amy's father would never allow. Was she the gentleman's mistress?

The gentleman addressed Papa. "My sister would like a lock-et." He urged the girl—his sister, not his mistress—forward. "Go on, Kendra, see what you fancy."

Though the gentleman seemed determined to work with her father, Amy stepped closer, poised to turn the corner and help close the sale. Papa glanced at her, then smiled. "Have you a style in mind, or a price, Lord...?"

"Greystone." His back still to Amy, he waved an impatient hand. "Whatever she likes."

Papa cleared his throat. "Perhaps my daughter can help you decide. Amethyst, please show Lord Greystone the lockets."

She took a tray from the case and moved to set it before the gentleman's sister instead.

"They're all so pretty!" Lady Kendra exclaimed in delight.

When she bent her head to look closer, her beautiful red curls shimmered to rival the glitter of jewels in the case.

Amy's hand went reflexively to her own head, as though she could rearrange her hated black hair into something more fashionable than its serviceable plait. Resisting the urge to sigh, she lifted an oval locket with tiny engraved flowers.

"See the gold ribbons forming the bale?" As her father had taught her, her voice was sweet and confident, reflecting her certainty of both the quality of the piece and her ability to sell it. She snapped open the locket and extended it, looking from Lady Kendra to Lord Greystone. "It's—"S

Her voice failed her.

Her father nudged her, frowning. "Amy?"

"It-it's quite feminine," she stammered out, telling herself Lord Greystone couldn't be the young nobleman she remembered.

But then his emerald green eyes locked on hers—as they'd done five years earlier.

It *was* him.

The nobleman from the coronation procession, the one she'd been unable to forget. Only now he was all grown up. Her heart seemed to pause in her chest, and for a second she thought she would drown in those eyes; then she looked away, with an effort, and down to the locket she was holding.

Lady Kendra reached to take the locket from Amy. "Oh, look how pretty it is, Colin." She held it up to her bodice, turning to model it for her brother.

With seeming reluctance, Lord Greystone swung his gaze toward his sister. "I'm not sure I care for it."

"Notice the fine engraving, my lord," Papa rushed to put in. "Truly first quality."

Lord Greystone ignored him and looked back to Amy. When his eyes narrowed, Amy found herself studying him in return. Classic symmetrical features: a long, straight nose, sculpted planes, a slight dimple in his chin. His complexion appeared more golden than was the fashion.

Marry come up, he was beautiful.

When he finally spoke, his voice, smooth and deep, sent an

odd shiver down her spine. "Have you a locket with...amethysts?"

Amethysts...

She opened her mouth to answer, but the words refused to come out.

"I'm sorry, my lord, we don't," Papa said. "But emeralds would suit the lady—"

"Yes," Amy interrupted, finally finding her voice. "Yes, we do have amethysts! If you'll but wait one moment." She reached to grab the key ring off her father's belt, then turned and bolted for the workshop.

"What are you in such a rush for?" Robert asked as she jammed the key into the first padlock on their iron safe chest.

"Customers are waiting." Having removed the second padlock, she knelt on the floor and began working the twelve bolts in their complicated sequence.

Robert wandered over, wiping blunt hands on his apron, leaving streaks of abrasive gray slurry. "What customers?"

"A gentleman and his sister," she said as the last bolt slid into place, allowing her to access the final lock. She opened it with the largest key, then lifted the lid and rummaged inside.

Luckily, the locket she was after was there in the top tray. "Ah, here it is." Just seeing the piece, the shimmering gold, the sparkling gems, made her smile.

She rose and headed back to the showroom, Robert at her heels. He lounged against the archway and fixed Lord Greystone with a distrustful blue stare.

Well, she would just ignore him.

"I found it," she announced, handing the locket to Lord Greystone. She watched for his reaction even as she plunked the key ring into her father's outstretched palm.

Lord Greystone blinked at the piece in his hand. "Beautiful. It's truly beautiful."

Amy's heart swelled. "It does have amethysts, my lord, and diamonds, too."

"I can see that," he said, staring at the locket. "It's splendid."

"Splendid doesn't do it justice!" Lady Kendra's eyes had gone wide and round.

The piece had taken Amy weeks to make, so many hours she could still see it with her eyes closed. On top, a cutwork pattern of diamond-set leaves surrounded an amethyst flower. The lozenge-shaped locket dangled beneath, encrusted with amethysts and diamonds, its lid enameled with delicate violets. Swinging from the bottom, a large baroque pearl gleamed.

Lord Greystone finally looked to her father. "It's remarkable."

"*I* made it." Amy felt a flush blossom on her cheeks.

Lady Kendra's mouth dropped open in surprise. Lord Greystone's startled gaze swung to Amy, over to her father, who nodded proudly, then back to Amy. "I don't believe it. You're—"

"A girl?" She heard the challenge in her own voice.

His grin was a bit sheepish. "However did you learn to make something like this?"

Her father cleared his throat. "We hadn't much to do during the Commonwealth, my lord. I expect you were abroad?"

Lord Greystone nodded.

"Well, jewelry was much frowned upon, other than some mourning pieces. I had time aplenty to train Amy in the arts of goldsmithing." Amy's father placed a possessive hand on her shoulder. "She's a natural—even did the enameling herself."

"I must—I mean, *Kendra*—must have it."

Papa shook his head. "I'm afraid it's not for sale. It's Amy's own keepsake."

"Of course it's for sale, Papa." Amy regarded Lord Greystone with a speculative gaze. "But it's very expensive."

"I'd expect so. We'll take it."

Lady Kendra turned to him, a frown creasing the area between her light green eyes. "Are you sure, Colin?"

He looked down at his sister. "Don't you like it?"

"It's lovely, but…"

"I said I would buy whatever you chose for your birthday. I want you to have it." He fished a pouch of coins from his surcoat and handed it to Amy. "Here. Take whatever's fair. Include a chain; I want her to wear it now."

Shocked that he would leave the price up to her, Amy fumbled with the pouch. She drew out a few coins, then a few more. The materials had been costly, and the piece had taken a lot of her time—she didn't want to take advantage of Lord Greystone, but she wouldn't short herself, either.

"Papa?" Closing the pouch, Amy showed her father the gold she'd taken.

Papa nodded. "That's fine, Amy." He pocketed the coins and placed a gold chain on the counter.

As she returned the pouch to Lord Greystone, he handed her the locket. His fingers brushed her hand, and another brief, warm shiver rippled through her. She hoped no one noticed the way her breath caught.

Robert sullenly pulled a cloth from his apron pocket and moved from the archway to stand beside her. He polished the glass case as she threaded the chain through the bale on the locket, then held it up for Lady Kendra to see.

"Ooh," Lady Kendra breathed. "Will you put it on me?"

She turned, and Lord Greystone lifted her hair so Amy could fasten the clasp.

Lady Kendra faced Amy and touched the locket reverently. "Thank you so very much. I'll treasure it always."

"Thank *who*?" her brother prompted with a smile.

"Thank you, Colin," she said and turned to embrace him.

Amy bit her lip, feeling a twinge of envy. She envied the girl's shiny red curls and exquisite, fashionable gown, but most of all, she envied the way Lady Kendra was hugging Lord Greystone. She glanced down at the counter, lest Robert catch sight of her telltale eyes.

Lord Greystone ushered his sister outside, then lingered in the doorway, looking strangely reluctant to leave.

"Can…" The long fingers of one hand drummed against his thigh, then stopped. "Can you make a signet ring?"

His question came low across the small shop, to Amy, not her father.

"A signet ring?" she said with a small smile. "Of course, it's a simple matter."

Beside her, Robert stopped polishing.

"Excellent." Lord Greystone paused, frowning a bit. "I'll send a messenger with a drawing of the crest," he said at last. "And my direction to deliver it when you're finished."

Amy nodded, feeling a quick stab of disappointment that she wouldn't be seeing him again. Robert's hand resumed its deliberate circular motion on top of the counter.

"I thank you," Lord Greystone said. Then he melted out the doorway and into the teeming streets of Cheapside.

The bell rang again when the door shut. Amy stared at the solid wood until her father cleared his throat.

"I cannot believe you sold your locket," he remarked. "I thought it was your favorite piece."

"It was," she answered dreamily. "But I can make another one."

Her stomach fluttered with happiness, just knowing Lord Greystone admired her craftsmanship and his sister would be wearing her locket. And soon, *he* would be wearing her ring.

"If you ask me, it was a clod-headed idea," Robert put in with a shake of his carrot-topped head. "You'll never find time to make another locket with all the custom orders you get."

Amy and her father shared a quizzical look.

"Besides, I didn't like him," Robert added. "I didn't like the way he looked at you."

Amy lowered her gaze and brushed past him into the workshop. She'd liked the way Lord Greystone looked at her, very much.

Very much indeed.

TWO

*C*OLIN ENTERED their carriage to find Kendra seated inside, her arms crossed. "What took you so long?"

He sat opposite her and looked out the window. The door of the jewelry shop had closed, so he couldn't see the girl with the amethyst-colored eyes and the long, thick, ribbon-entwined plait.

"I ordered a signet ring," he said.

"You *what?*"

Colin could have asked himself that question. But in all his twenty-one years he'd never met anyone like the girl who had made that exquisite locket. He'd wanted his sister to own it, and he'd wanted something she'd made for him, too. "I need a signet ring, for a seal."

Kendra shot him a look of patent disbelief. "You couldn't even afford this locket." She shook her bright head. "Something happened in that shop."

"Nothing happened," he said, although he knew very well something had. And he knew the girl—Amethyst—had felt it, too. An instantaneous pull of attraction. He smiled to himself. He was glad he'd met her, though nothing would ever come of it.

But he wasn't about to admit as much to his little sister.

Unfortunately, Kendra was observant as anything, a fact that could be deucedly inconvenient at times. "I just thought it was a beautiful piece of jewelry," he told her, "and I wanted you to have it."

"Od's fish, Colin, you're the one always lecturing us about saving funds…"

He turned off her voice in his head, instead remembering the little hitch in Amethyst's breath when he'd accidentally-on-purpose brushed her hand.

"…planning for the future…"

She was completely off limits, of course. A sheltered young woman of the merchant class, for certain she was nothing like the promiscuous ladies of the court.

"And then you ordered a ring. You never wear jewelry!"

Which would suit him just fine, in truth—he wasn't that sort of fellow anyhow. But well-suited though they might be, Colin Chase, Earl of Greystone, had no intention of marrying beneath himself.

"I cannot believe you bought this locket in the first place."

Besides, he was already betrothed to the perfect girl.

"I do love it, though."

As they passed Goldsmith & Sons, he glanced out the window. He would never go back there. He couldn't remember the last time he'd set foot in a jewelry shop, and…

No, he had no reason to ever return.

"Thank you, Colin. I truly do love it."

He blinked and looked at Kendra. She was sighing, gazing down at the locket and touching it possessively.

What had she been saying?

Oh, she loved it.

"I'm glad. Shall we go buy our brother that telescope he's been prattling on about?"

"Are you sure? Ford will be thrilled." Kendra bounced on the seat, then settled her skirts about her as though she'd just remembered she was a grown-up sixteen. "Can it be from me, too? Much as I hate to encourage his scientific obsession, he *is* my twin, and I like to make him happy."

Colin gave his sister a tolerant smile, hoping the gentleman she married would have more energy than he did. "Yes, it can be from you, too. Now, where do you suppose we might find such a contraption?"

THREE

"Ring-a-ring o'roses
A pocket full of posies
A-tishoo! A-tishoo!
We all fall down."

"RELAX YOUR shoulders, if you please."

Amy looked down to the seamstress who knelt at her feet, pinning up the hem of her wedding dress. "I'm sorry, Mrs. Cholmley," she said with a sniffle.

Mrs. Cholmley glanced up, concern in her kind hazel eyes. "Reminds you of your poor mama, don't it? The children playing outside, I mean?"

Amy nodded, blinking back tears. She concentrated on the gown's wide lavender lace skirt, counting the love knots—small satin bows sewn loosely all over, one for each wedding guest to tear off after the ceremony as a keepsake.

Fifty-eight, fifty-nine...or had she already counted that one? No matter, the hot press behind her eyes was gone. Her shoulders relaxed.

"It reminds me of my Edgar, too." Mrs. Cholmley shook her head. "The song, I mean."

Amy's shoulders tensed up again. "Perhaps it's best not to dwell—"

"Roses for the rash," the seamstress went on, absently reaching for more pins. "Posies to sweeten the putrid air. The ring is…the plague-token, of course. Please, dear, try to relax."

"I'm sorry." Amy had her gaze trained back on the love knots. Twenty-two, twenty-three—

"My Edgar had a plague-token—not rosy, but black and filled with pus. He screamed so when the doctor cut into it. Lud, I still hear him in my dreams. Turn, please."

Amy obeyed, her stomach twisting into its own knot. She looked up to the window, staring at the sky, gray with the smoke from burning sea-coal.

"And your mama? Did she suffer one?"

Her gaze dropped to Mrs. Cholmley's head, which was also gray. "Suffer what?"

"A plague-token."

She bit back a groan. Would this woman never stop chattering? "We don't know. At the first sign of fever, she begged us to go to Paris and stay with Aunt Elizabeth." She rubbed her stomach, her voice dropping to a whisper. "I was in Paris. I don't know what happened to her. I know only that she's gone."

Mrs. Cholmley sighed. "Hard to believe a year has passed. It feels like yesterday they painted that red cross on my door. House after house marked for the quarantine and staffed with guards, all up and down the street. I thought I was like to meet my maker, right enough. And the death carts rattling by…'*Bring out your dead! Bring out your dead!*'" The woman shuddered and pinned. "My Edgar was buried in a plague pit. Your mother, as well?"

Amy shut her eyes and bit a mark into her lower lip. "We think so. We've found no grave." No place to bring flowers, nowhere to go talk to Mama, to tell her about the upcoming wedding and all her misgivings.

When Amy returned from Paris, it was to the heavy, sweet stench of decaying bodies. The smell had hung over the city for weeks. She'd read in the *London Gazette* that one in five Londoners had died. But that had been months ago, and London had recovered its usual bustle.

Mrs. Cholmley had apparently—mercifully—talked herself

out. Beyond the window, the children's voices faded, replaced by the ordinary sounds of busy London. Swiping the tears from her cheeks, Amy listened. Creaking wheels, animal snorts, the familiar din of grumbles, shouts, and the singsong chants of vendors.

She opened her eyes. The remembered reek of decomposing corpses became the scent of new, starched fabric. At a gentle touch on her knee from Mrs. Cholmley, she turned again.

Her fingers worked at the love knots on her dress. She wished she could tear the little bows off now—or better yet, tear the whole gown off and into shreds. Ten more days and she would be Robert's wife.

Ten days! It seemed impossible.

For six months now, her father had gone about making wedding plans, and she'd done nothing to stop him. It had given him something to think about in the wake of his wife's death, and Amy hadn't found the strength to fight him. It had all seemed so very far away.

But now her wedding day was almost here. Every morning she woke up wishing it were no more than a bad dream. She had to find the courage to call off this wedding before it was too late.

Now.

"Are you finished yet?" she asked, her voice sharper than she'd intended.

Mrs. Cholmley sighed again and stood, flexing her arthritic joints. "All done," she said, smiling in a sympathetic way that made Amy feel even more guilty. "You nervous brides." Clucking good-naturedly, she drew off the wedding dress. Amy's maid pulled her periwinkle gown from the wardrobe cabinet.

Underskirt, overdress, laces, stomacher, stockings, shoes… dressing seemed to take forever. At last Amy went down the corridor toward her father's room. The closer she got, the faster her heart beat and the slower her feet dragged.

She paused in the doorway and stared at her father's back, struck as always by how empty the room felt without her mother's presence.

"Papa?"

Her father jerked, startled. He stood slowly and turned to face her. "What is it, poppet?"

A familiar, dull pain briefly squeezed Amy's heart as her gaze dropped to the miniature of her mother, its oval gold frame cradled between her father's work-worn hands. "She was lovely, wasn't she?"

"Yes, she was." He smiled down at the picture. "You have her delicate chin and her beautiful amethyst eyes."

"And *your* unruly black hair." Papa didn't react to her gentle teasing tone. "Sometimes...sometimes I think that if you could wear out a painting by looking at it, Mama's image would have disappeared from that canvas months ago."

He looked up, offering her a wan smile. "We shared a rare love, poppet."

It was a perfect opening; she couldn't let her courage fail her again. She lifted her chin. "Papa, I...I always dreamed of a love—"

"Have you seen those ruby earrings your mother wore to see *Henry V* the week before she—she—"

Amy crossed her arms, sympathy and impatience warring within her. Impatience won. "Papa, I need to talk to you."

"I just want to see them," he said gruffly.

She knew his moods, and there was no arguing with his retreating back. Determined to say her piece, she picked up her skirts and followed him down the two flights of stairs and into the workshop.

While he started unlocking their safe chest, she tied on an apron and sat at her workbench. More to calm herself than to accomplish anything, she unfolded the sheet of paper Lord Greystone had sent her and smoothed it flat against the table. She squinted at the drawing while she steeled herself to broach the subject again.

The last bolt clunked into place, and she heard Papa throw open the lid and begin removing trays to access his private collection in the bottom. She dragged a candle closer to study the Greystone crest, listening to the soft metallic sounds of her father sifting through centuries of treasures.

She had to just say it. "Papa—"

"Mmm...I've always loved this piece."

Exasperated, she turned to watch her father sit back on his heels and hold up a pendant. It sparkled in the lantern light.

Drawn despite her low spirits, she rose and moved to him. "Let me see. Who made it?"

"Your great-grandpapa, a master with enamel. Look."

"Ahh..." Amy studied the piece, a merman, his torso consisting of one huge baroque pearl. His tail was an enameled rainbow of colors set with cut gemstones. The merman wore a miniature necklace and bracelets and carried a tiny shield and saber. The entire, elaborate pendant was less than four inches tall, including three pearls that dangled from the bottom. "It's exquisite. I remember it now."

"He was inspired by Erasmus Hornick's design book." Papa still had the treasured book, an ancient leather-bound volume from Nuremberg that Amy was almost afraid to touch. "But the workmanship was his own. He outdid himself with this one—in nearly a hundred years, no one in the family has ever been able to bring himself to sell it."

"I'm glad."

He replaced the piece and hunched over the chest, resuming his search for the ruby earrings. He was mellow, she thought. Maybe now...

"Papa—"

"Your talent came from him, you know. Through the generations. A gift—and an obligation."

She swallowed and took a deep breath. "Papa, I—"

"I know what you're going to say, Amy." His knees creaked as he stood up. "You think I don't know how you feel? It's naught but nerves. Every bride has them."

Amy shot him a hurt look, shocked that he'd known all along that she wanted to call off the wedding, yet chose to do nothing about it. Her own father.

She returned to her workbench and set Lord Greystone's ring into a clamp attached to the table.

"You bear a responsibility. Here, in this shop, our people have worked for generations, for *you*. You can do no less for your own children. And you cannot do so as a woman alone."

Amy heard her father's footsteps, then a small *clink* as he placed the earrings on her work surface.

The pear-shaped, blood-red rubies were bezel set and pavéd with diamonds on long, graceful drops. Amy's heart clenched as she remembered how her mother had protested they were too fancy, but then held her head high that night at the theater, to show them to advantage.

"Life is fragile, poppet." Papa's voice cracked. "I want to see you settled before something happens to me, too."

The rubies seemed to wink in the candlelight, a poignant reminder of her mother and her mother's expectations. Her throat closed with emotion. She had to force the words out. "Nothing is happening to you, Papa."

Looking away from the earrings, she dug in a drawer for a stick of engravers' wax and heated one end in the candle flame, then rubbed it over the top of the ring.

"This family has hoarded gold, coins, and gems for centuries —*centuries*, Amy—making certain no Goldsmith will ever suffer a moment of insecurity. The shop sold almost nothing during the Commonwealth. Could we have lived through it as we did— with servants, and nice clothes, and good food on the table— without that legacy handed down from our ancestors?"

She stilled, a sharp-tipped tool in her hand. "No." The word was directed toward Lord Greystone's ring, its hard-won shine dimmed by engravers' wax and the blur of unshed tears.

"And now that the good times have returned, we work every day to replace what we were forced to use. It's my responsibility, and one day it will be yours."

With the quick, sure strokes of an artist, she traced a reverse image of the crest into the wax, then lifted the graver. The murmur of Robert assisting two customers came through the arch from the showroom, but the workshop's silence grew tight with tension.

Papa sighed. "These marriages—they're the way our trade works. I want your word that Goldsmith and Sons will go on. I need your promise."

"Nothing is happening to Goldsmith and Sons."

Amy began engraving, meticulously carving tiny ribbons of

gold from the signet's top. She felt her father's gaze on her and knew he wanted an answer, not a denial. An answer about Robert.

The tool slowed as she focused on the ring—and the gentleman it was for. A hazy image of Lord Greystone's beautiful face hovered in her mind. He'd just looked at her with his piercing emerald eyes, and she'd felt warm all over and known that it would never, *just never*, be that way with Robert.

She hurried to finish, set down the graver and held the ring to the candle, studying the reverse crest for imperfections.

"Promise me," her father insisted. "You have a gift that cannot be wasted, an obligation in your blood. Promise me."

She dripped a shiny blob of red sealing wax onto the design sheet and pressed the ring into it. It made a perfect imprint of the Greystone coat of arms, but she didn't feel her usual surge of satisfaction.

Sighing, she turned to search her father's concerned blue eyes. "It's just Robert, Papa. He...he doesn't understand me."

"He doesn't have to understand you. You were promised to him years ago, and he knows his place. As a second son, he's lucky—very lucky—to be marrying into a wealthy family, with his wife-to-be the sole heir. Without you, Robert has nothing. He knows that. He's the right man for you—the right man for Goldsmith and Sons."

Her father didn't understand her, either. "He scares me when he touches me."

"You know nothing of the marriage bed, poppet. It won't scare you for long."

Amy's cheeks heated even as tears stung the backs of her eyes. "He wants me to stop making jewelry."

A short, harsh bark of laughter followed that statement. "The boy is feeling impotent now. Once you're wed—once he owns a share of the shop—he'll feel differently. He won't care to do without the income from your designs."

He reached for the ruby earrings and turned to put them away. She watched him gaze at the jewels, then kneel to tenderly place them in the bottom of the chest. Her fingers clenched tight around Lord Greystone's ring as the tears that had been threatening welled up, and before she could stop herself, she dropped to her knees beside him.

"Papa, look at me. Me!"

She reached for his hands and grasped them in hers, the ring trapped somewhere amidst the tangle of their fingers.

"Papa! Remember you told me I'd have a love, a love like yours and Mama's? You promised, but it hasn't happened! I don't love Robert!" She felt a tear escape and roll down her cheek as her desperate eyes implored his pained ones. "If something happened to him, I wouldn't gaze at his picture, I wouldn't—"

"Enough!" Papa stood so abruptly that Amy fell back. Never had he raised his voice to her. Now in his fear, his loneliness, he lashed out. "I loved your mother—I still do—and she's gone! I cannot work—I stare at her painting—I loved her so! Better you and Robert think straight. Not like me!" His shoulders slumped, and his voice dropped to a husky whisper. "Not like me."

She watched him draw a shuddering breath as he reached a hand to pull her up. "I'm sorry, poppet." His eyes fluttered closed and then open as he ran a shaky hand through the black tangles of his hair. "That it's come to harsh words...I'm sorry. But there's more to life than love. It will be better for you this way. You must see a bigger picture. Tradition, continuity...this is how our guild has survived for centuries."

The hard edges of the heavy ring bit into Amy's clenched fist. She blinked back the tears. Like the vast majority of betrothal agreements, hers was not binding until consummation. No money had yet changed hands. There must be another way for her that would still preserve the business. "Surely there's another jeweler..."

"Ours is a small industry. Others were apprenticed a decade ago. Many died in the plague. These matches are made for infants, and you're seventeen. It's time your future is cemented." He moved to wrap an arm tight around Amy's shoulders, as though willing her to understand, to accept the realities of her life. "Robert is a good goldsmith, a steady young man. You cannot have everything, Amy."

You cannot have everything.

The words echoed in Amy's head, summing up her destiny. She was stuck, as sure as an insect in amber.

Shrugging out of her father's grasp, she picked up a cloth embedded with reddish rouge powder and rubbed the ring absently, a final hand-polish to make it gleam. It felt solid in her hands, this thing she'd created from nothing more than raw metal and elusive inbred artistry. She could never give up making jewelry. She was born to it.

Her gaze swept the cluttered workshop. Tools, hunks of discarded wax, and half-finished pieces of jewelry littered every available surface. A thin veil of the reddish rouge powder dusted the tabletops and stained her fingertips.

This was where she belonged. And if her father said Robert belonged here as well, that was the way of it.

The fire below the oven snapped, and she blinked, then knuckled the last trace of tears from her eyes.

You cannot have everything.

"Promise me, Amy. Promise me that Goldsmith and Sons won't end with you."

"You have my promise."

"I love you, poppet," Papa said quietly.

He only wanted what was best for her. As she turned into his arms, the ring slipped from her fingers and clattered to the wooden floor.

"I love you too, Papa," she said.

∽

*I*T WAS A LONG time before she bent to pick up the ring, an even longer time before Robert came in to find her staring at it.

He stood over her. "You still working on that blasted signet?"

She looked up at him, but couldn't find the energy to summon as much as annoyance.

"It's finished," she said. "I'll have it delivered in the morning."

FOUR

"COLIN! DOWN here!"

From along the ridge where he and nine others were grappling with a huge block of limestone, Colin glanced to the path below to see his brothers climbing from the carriage and Kendra leaning halfway out the window, waving wildly.

"You're early," he called a minute later, heading down the rise. He wiped gritty palms on his linen breeches, his shirt billowing in the light wind that buffeted across Greystone's quarry.

"Early?" His older brother Jason laughed, pointing at the sky.

Colin glanced straight up and then west to where the sun was nearly setting. "Sorry." He shrugged. "I've been about since six this morn. In the woods, the fields...I reckon I lost track of the time."

"I reckon you lost your hat as well?" Kendra fixed him with a half-serious frown of reproach. "Look at you, brown as a gypsy!"

With the back of one hand, he wiped at the sweat on his forehead. "Have you come to see the renovations, or to harp on my appearance?"

"To harp on your appearance," Kendra's twin, Ford, answered for her. "But I've a curiosity to see your new kitchen. Pipes and taps...do they work due to a siphon effect, or is it simple gravity? In Isaac Newton's new paper, he says—"

"Criminy—how on earth should I know? I'm a farmer, not a scientist. They work because the mason put them in right."

"What *I* want to know"—Jason patted his stomach meaningfully—"is whether we'll find food in this kitchen."

"Oh, yes." Colin laughed. "Benchley's been slaving since dawn, I expect. Go on up to the castle, and I'll follow along shortly. Four quarrymen are down with the ague, and we've two more slabs to bring up."

～

"*O*D'S FISH, IT'S quiet here." Kendra paused before climbing from the carriage into Greystone Castle's little courtyard. "Listen." A few low birdcalls, distant bleating from the fields, a faint rustle from the smattering of trees that stood sentinel around the tiny circular drive. "It sounds like no one's home."

"No one *is* home," Jason reminded her. "Colin has only Benchley for company until the renovations are further along, and he's likely in the kitchen."

"Let's go see the kitchen." Ford urged them along. "Those pipes—"

"The food—"

"Those Chase stomachs!" Kendra laughed as they walked toward the door to Greystone's modest living quarters. "I cannot say I'm surprised that Colin restored the kitchen first."

"A fellow's got to eat," Ford declared.

"I could feed an entire village on what you three pack away in a day. Look…the door is ajar." Her hand on the latch, Kendra stopped and turned back to watch their carriage pass under the barbican gate, the driver heading out to Colin's stables. "And the drawbridge is down."

Jason's green eyes sparkled with suppressed laughter. "It probably hasn't been up in a hundred years. What would be the point? There's naught in this old place of interest to anyone."

"Something doesn't feel right."

"There she goes, leaping to conclusions again." Ford pushed

the door open and stepped inside the plain, square entry. "Egad, what is that on the floor?"

"What?" Kendra took a step back.

"Ouch!" Jason wrenched his foot from under hers. "Why do you insist on wearing those accursed high heels?" He shouldered his way past the twins. "Something spilled, is all."

Leaning down to touch one of the dark splotches, he rubbed the substance between his fingers, then sniffed and turned back to them slowly.

"It's blood."

"Blood?" Kendra squeaked.

"Don't get overwrought." Jason grinned. "I'd wager it's just one of Colin's pranks."

Kendra took another step back. "Real blood a prank?"

Ford put a hand on his twin sister's shoulder. "Perhaps Benchley butchered something outside and failed to notice it dripping when he brought it through here. Look, the drops trail under the door to the great hall, toward the kitchen. I wonder what it is? I'm hoping for suckling pig."

The great hall's door was ajar as well. Jason led the way into the gutted, roofless chamber, its pitted stone floor still scattered with rusted cannonballs from Cromwell's last siege.

"How couldn't he have noticed it dripping?" Kendra's voice was a whisper, her gaze riveted to the bloody trail. "It was pumping out here, from the looks of it." She followed her brothers, stepping carefully. "A suckling pig!" she exclaimed, her voice rising. "More like a cow, I'll warrant you. I've never seen so much—"

"The latch…" At the far end of the hall, Jason had reached for the door, then jerked back his hand. "It's covered in blood as well."

Kendra bit her lip. "Maybe we ought to wait for Colin."

"Don't be a goose." Jason kicked at the door with one booted foot, and it gave, swinging open with a prolonged creak.

They traversed the short corridor, following meandering bloody footprints. "I don't like this," Kendra muttered, gingerly picking her way past the dark red marks.

They paused at the entrance to the kitchen. "Benchley?" Ford ran a shaky hand through his wavy brown hair. "Benchley, are you here, man?"

"It appears not," Jason said unnecessarily.

Kendra pointed to one of the two sunken wells. "Oh, my heavens."

Ford glared at her. "What now?"

"Do you not hear the dripping?"

"Dripping?" Jason started toward the well, then suddenly flung out an arm. "Stay back!"

"What?" Kendra breathed. "What is it?"

"This is no prank. Ford, fetch Colin *now!*"

Despite Jason's warning, Kendra rushed forward, then let out an earsplitting scream before whirling to muffle her face against his chest.

"He's dead, he's dead, he's dead," she panted. "Benchley's dead. Oh, my heavens, Benchley's dead!"

Instead of fetching Colin, a whimpering Ford flung his arms around them both. "I can't look! Oh, please, let's get out of here!"

Squished between her brothers, Kendra turned her head and cracked an eye open, just to make sure. Bent at the waist over the crossbar that spanned the well, Colin's manservant dangled, his clothes streaked with red. More blood dripped from the sopping mass of his prematurely gray hair, echoing as it plopped into the water far below.

She moaned and promptly reburied her face.

Until, with an unnerving suddenness, mad laughter burst out behind them.

FIVE

$\mathcal{C}$OLIN'S SIBLINGS stared, dumbstruck, as he strode in and leaned over the well.

A plaintive voice resonated from the depths. "My back is killing me. Help me out of here, I beg you."

Kendra blinked. The color rushed back to her cheeks. "You lout! That was mean."

"But a good one," Jason admitted with a sheepish chuckle. "You did yourself proud, Colin."

"A fiendish mess, but worth it," Colin agreed cheerfully. He reached down to hoist Benchley up. "The looks on your faces…"

"And the screams!" The manservant's shirt was plastered to his short, wiry form. "*Oh, get me out of here!* Took everything I had not to laugh and give myself away." Laughing now, he braced his hands on his hips and leaned back, stretching his spine. "Mind you, it'll be hours of scrubbing to get up all that blood."

Colin waved that away. "I'll help, of course."

"Well *I* won't!" Ford muttered, his face distinctly red.

"I'll be going to clean off now," Benchley announced, stepping gingerly over a puddle on his way out of the kitchen.

"Hurry back!" Jason called. "We're fair starving!"

The siblings looked round at each other—and burst into peals of laughter. Even Ford joined in, after a moment.

Jason leaned against the large, scrubbed wooden worktable, his long black hair falling forward to hide his face. "I cannot credit that I fell for it," he mused. "I even said at first..." He lifted his head and gave Colin a rueful smile. "Your betrothed will be sorry she missed this one."

"Bosh!" Kendra rolled her eyes. "She would say it was a childish waste of time."

"It *was* a childish waste of time." Colin grinned. "But what on earth is wrong with that?

Ford sniffed at a covered platter. "Suckling pig," he mumbled, looking pleased as he made his way over to one of the basins and reached for a bronze tap.

Ignoring her twin, Kendra turned to Colin. "Speaking of Lady Priscilla Snobs, have you two set the date?"

"Lady Priscilla *Hobbs* and I have yet to decide." Colin scanned the shelves, looking for something he could use to clean up. "She won't move to Greystone in its present condition."

"Gravity," Ford declared, opening the tap, then shutting it again. With obvious glee, he repeated the motion. "Definitely gravity."

Kendra frowned. "She could live at Cainewood with us."

"Not likely. This family is a bit too, uh, high-spirited for Priscilla." He dropped a wad of rags on the biggest puddle of pig blood, poking at it with one booted foot. "She's an only child, you know—used to peace and quiet."

"She's a snob, you mean. Otherwise—"

"Kendra!" Jason's leaf-green eyes glared into his sister's lighter ones. "Lady Priscilla is a perfectly nice girl. More important to Colin, though, she's pretty, titled, and the only heir to an enormous fortune. If it takes her a while to get used to us, we'll just have to put up with it." He turned to Colin. "How are the rest of the improvements coming along?"

"Slowly." Colin looked up from where he crouched on the floor, mopping the last of the bloody trail. "My study and one bedchamber are finished, enough for Benchley and me to stay here and work. But for Priscilla..."

Raising a hand to his new, fashionable black mustache, Jason smoothed one side, then the other. "I imagine Lady Priscilla requires a small army of servants, as well as a proper suite and a couple of receiving rooms, at the very least." He shot Kendra a warning glance. "On the other hand, she's not going to wait for the entire castle to be fixed up, is she?"

Colin shook his head vehemently. "Good heavens, no." An incredible amount of work lay ahead; the castle had stood vacant nearly twenty-five years, ever since the Roundheads laid the great hall in ruins. "I'll warrant we'll see another quarter century before it's fully restored."

"See this lead pipe?" Ford gestured at the stone wall. "I'd lay odds there's a cistern on the roof. This second tap controls outflow—the River Caine lies downhill from here, yes?" He grinned, his deep blue eyes flashing with satisfaction. "Gravity."

"Fascinating," Jason said dryly.

Standing up slowly, Colin twisted the new gold ring on his finger, considering the magnitude of the task ahead of him. "Priscilla wishes to wed and start a family soon—as do I. Just a few more rooms..." He sighed. "Everything's so deuced expensive, and I'm spending more on farm equipment and livestock than the castle. Until the estate is in shape, it cannot generate a decent income."

"Poor Colin." Kendra walked around the kitchen, trailing a hand along the mantels of the three immense fireplaces. "I suppose I cannot fault you for wanting her and her *enormous fortune*," she said, stepping in front of Colin, who was busy lighting candles to ward off the encroaching dark. "But don't you mind waiting?"

"It's what she wants," Colin said with a shrug.

His attention finally diverted from the pipes, Ford moved to break off a piece of the fresh-baked manchet that Benchley had left on the table. "Why wouldn't he wait?" He sank his teeth into the fine white bread, talking around a mouthful. "It's the honorable thing to abide by a lady's wishes, is it not?"

When he reached for more bread, Kendra slapped his hand away. "You and your *honor*. If Priscilla Snobs had half the honor of any one of you, she'd swallow her pride, marry the man she supposedly loves, and help him rebuild his home. She can afford to live simply for a few months; it wouldn't kill her. Or she could move in with us at Cainewood, or live at our town house in London."

Colin gave another shrug. "We've already discussed all the options." One by one, he took four goblets off the shelves and set them on the table. "The town house always has people coming and going—it's no place to actually live—"

"I like living there." Kendra reached for some napkins and began folding them into triangles. "London is exciting."

"Well, Priscilla feels differently. She's a very calm person. I like that, you know. Having been dragged halfway around the world most of my life, I'm looking forward to staying in one quiet place, with my own quiet family."

She straightened the fourth triangle, then looked up. "You'll be bored to tears in no time."

"Kendra's right enough," Ford put in around another mouthful of bread. "It sounds like Lady Priscilla's main attraction, other than the aforementioned *enormous fortune*, is her talent for putting one to sleep—"

"Enough!" The word burst out of Colin like thunder. His gaze flashed around the table, resting on each sibling in turn. "Perhaps I've yet to set a date, but I *am* marrying Priscilla, and I won't have you discussing her this way any longer. I *like* her. I like her appearance, I like her demeanor, I like her background, and yes, I like her title and her fortune. She's exactly what I've been looking for, and I'm not going to let any of you ruin it for me!"

There was a rare silence among the Chase family. Colin considered his siblings might even have stopped breathing; the only motion seemed to be the candlelight that flickered against the whitewashed stone walls.

"I'll be right back," he muttered after a minute, then stalked off down the corridor to the buttery.

Though he took his time selecting a bottle of wine, the silence still reigned when he returned. Jason shifted uneasily on his feet, Ford traced aimless circles with his finger on the tabletop, and Kendra seemed to be studying her shoes.

Colin almost felt sorry for them.

"Colin?"

"Yes, Kendra?"

"Do you love her?"

He sighed impatiently and set to uncorking the wine. "Our parents were in love, and what did it do for all of us? They were very *loving* people, weren't they? They loved each other, the monarchy...we were born of their love, not because they wanted children." He looked straight at Kendra, his eyes burning into hers. "No, Kendra, I don't love Priscilla, but I do like her. And I think it's better that way."

He filled the goblets, the sound of pouring wine unnaturally loud in the tense atmosphere.

Jason took a careful sip, then set his goblet back on the table, his expression fretful. "You've thought about this a lot, have you?"

Colin's chin went up. "Yes, I have."

Jason shook his head, nearly imperceptibly. "It wasn't really like that, you know. Our parents—all of us—were victims of the times. I felt very wanted as a small child. During the fighting, I missed them terribly, and I'm certain they missed us. A pox on Cromwell!" He slammed his fist on the table, making the empty bottle dance and the wine sway in their goblets.

"I cannot miss them," Kendra said quietly. "I never knew them." She and Ford had been but one year old when their parents died. "But I've imagined them all of my life, and I always imagined them in love."

"Well," Colin began—then broke off, interrupted by Benchley's sudden return.

The small man skidded into the kitchen, panting, his freshly washed hair dripping.

"My lord, you must come!" A lantern bobbed in Benchley's trembling hand; Colin leapt to grab it before it might crash to the floor. "I went outside the walls to dump the water, and—lud, you must see it!"

"See what?" Colin asked, but the words were directed to Benchley's retreating back.

They followed him at a run, through the darkened castle and outside the turreted walls. A hush seemed to fall over the countryside as the five of them gazed toward London. At the edge of the jet-black night sky, a dazzling red glow hovered at the horizon.

Kendra's whisper shattered the silence. "What is it?"

"A fire," Jason stated grimly. "And it looks big."

"London, on fire?" Kendra's voice was tense with fear. "It looks closer."

Jason put a hand on her shoulder. "Don't trouble yourself, Kendra. It won't reach us here. It's just that the night is so dark, it seems to light the sky."

"But it looks enormous. Whitehall Palace could be burning, or St. Paul's or—our town house! Oh my heavens, what if the town house is on fire?"

By the dim light of the lantern, Jason's gaze met Colin's over their sister's head.

"We must go help," Colin said for them both.

Jason nodded. "Ford, you'll come as well. Colin, you've extra horses? Carrington will fetch Kendra home in the carriage. Let's move."

SIX

*C*OLIN PAUSED to lean and pat his skittish gelding's black, lathered neck as Jason and Ford rode ahead. "It's all right, lad," he murmured, though he knew the words were likely swallowed by the sounds of chaos that engulfed them.

"Colin!" Though they'd barely fought their way into London, Jason's voice already sounded hoarse from smoke and overuse. "Come along! We'll lose you, man!"

Usually dark and deserted at night, London's streets were alive with an appalling incandescence and a crush of displaced humanity. Colin's skin prickled with heat as he picked his way around people, animals, and debris. Bits of ash drifted down, dotting his clothes and hair. Squinting into the haze, he searched the maelstrom for his brothers.

There they were, their familiar forms near a commanding presence riding tall on a huge black stallion: King Charles with his own brother, James, Duke of York. Colin watched as the king reached into a bag flung over his shoulder and threw a handful of guineas to the workmen, encouraging them in their efforts to create a firebreak. The gold coins shimmered in the light of the flickering blaze, as though hung suspended in the thick, smoky air.

"Criminy," Colin breathed, catching up to his brothers. "Where to start?"

"Here's as good a spot as any." Jason twisted in the saddle, looking for a safe place to leave their horses. His gasp made his brothers turn.

Hands white-knuckled on the reins, Colin could only stare at the terrible splendor of St. Paul's Cathedral all ablaze.

He opened his mouth, but no sound came out.

"I was *there* last week." Ford jockeyed his horse closer to Colin, shaking his head in disbelief. "Lady Tabitha and I—we carved our names into the lead on the roof."

"They're erased now," Jason said grimly. "Along with six centuries of other signatures." The molten metal of St. Paul's roof ran down in fiery streams, the blaze rising like a torch from the sea of flames made by thousands of structures burning all at once.

Jason shook himself, then reached to touch Colin on the shoulder. "Come, there's work to do."

They wheeled to see King Charles dismount and toss his reins to a liveried groom, who led the enormous horse to a makeshift penned area crammed with aristocratic mounts.

"There's a likely spot." Jason's eyes lit with relief. They left their own horses—along with a fair amount of coin to guarantee they'd see them again—and headed down Warwick Lane on foot, jostling through the swarm of firefighters.

A bucket brigade broke apart and reformed to include them, and before he knew what was happening, Colin was accepting pails from Ford and thrusting them at King Charles. From all evidence, the king and his brother had spent the night wading ankle-deep in trenches and splashing through mud and water: their silks and laces were drenched, sooty, and scorched.

"You've been here since when, sire?" Colin yelled as the king turned to take a bucket.

"We came downriver yesterday noon." Charles twisted to pass the bucket, then turned back to Colin. "Would have ventured out Sunday, but the Lord Mayor assured me it was nothing."

"Nothing? We saw it from Greystone!"

His Majesty gave a derisive snort, then stepped from the line when James thrust a shovel into his hands.

The royal brothers trotted off into the smoke. The fire was giving Charles his first opportunity as king to play the hero in person—and he performed the part superbly, Colin mused in some vague recess of his mind, passing along another bucket.

"Help!" The cry, thin and distressed, came through the shouts of the workers. "Help! My little brother!"

A hand tugged at Colin's breeches, and he looked down at a grimy young face. "Where's your brother?" he asked.

"In a burning house!" The boy grasped his hand and, with desperate strength, yanked him out of the queue.

The next bucket landed in the dirt, soaking Colin's boots and spewing mud into the frightened boy's face. "Where?" Colin repeated.

"P-Paternoster Row!" The boy was off like a rocket, brown hair flying as he threaded his thin form through the confusion. Colin followed at his heels. Rounding the corner and skidding to a halt, the boy pointed up at a high window.

Behind the mottled glass, a pale face hovered. The child's little fingers clawed helplessly at the pane.

Accursed bad luck, the lad was trapped in one of the few houses in this old neighborhood that actually boasted glass windows. The ground floor was engulfed in flame. Black smoke billowed out, cloaking the street, a narrow, dirty alley lined with tall houses leaning forward until they nearly met their opposite neighbors.

Colin peered through the haze. Flames leapt from roof to roof, eating their way toward them.

Without thought, he bolted past another burning house to a third that seemed deserted but yet unscathed. He booted open the door and sped up two flights of stairs, coming out on the balcony.

The houses were crammed together. It was an easy leap to the balcony next door, and then once again to the one beneath the lad's window.

"Stand back!" he implored the terrified face.

Climbing onto the balcony's rail, Colin stretched toward the upper story to hack at the window with his sword. The boy disappeared into the smoke-filled room. Seeing flames lick up the far wall, Colin whacked at the window harder. But his elegant rapier blade was no match for the thick, uneven glass.

He dropped to the deck of the balcony and whirled in desperation, relieved to see Jason and Ford among a crowd that had gathered in the street.

"Rock!" he yelled, and the next second a chunk came sailing up; he caught and hurled it through the window in one smooth motion. A swipe of his blade cleared most of the glass from the sill. He dropped the sword and struggled out of his surcoat, tossing it up to drape over the frame before he jumped to catch the window ledge with his hands and hoist himself inside.

The small, towheaded child cowered against a side wall, wide-eyed with terror. Fed by the fresh air from the broken window, the blaze thundered. The fire seemed alive, a hideous monster come to devour all in its path.

Colin's lungs burned as he swept up the boy under one arm and leapt out the window. They landed hard on the balcony, tumbling into a tangled heap, Colin's surcoat twisted around one foot. Flames followed, orange and white and blue tendrils snaking through the window, threatening the wooden structure on which they huddled.

Colin unsnarled the garment and threw it over the rail to his brothers. He stood, pulling the boy up with him, and jammed his sword back into his belt. Below the balcony, several men waited, a quilt stretched tight between their hands.

"We're going to jump!" he shouted to the child over the roar of the flames.

"No!" The boy squirmed out of his grasp. "No! No!"

He snatched him back. They hadn't time to be scared of heights, but then again…

Colin's gaze focused on the quilt. Three stories, and his considerable weight plus the lad's—they'd likely not survive anyway.

Hot flames licked at his back; black, billowing smoke choked his air supply. Through tear-blurred eyes, he searched out Jason's face, far below.

"Rope!" he bellowed, the word tearing at his raw throat.

Scarce seconds ticked away while he watched his brothers

argue with a man intent on securing his worldly goods. At last they gave up and simply filched the rope from the laden cart, Ford tugging while Jason brandished his sword in the obstinate fellow's face.

A moment later, the lifeline snaked up, thrown in a wide arc by Jason.

With shaking fingers, Colin knotted it to a balcony post and pulled tight. He hauled the child onto his back, yelled "Hang on!" and they were speeding toward the ground. After sliding to the dirt, Colin seized the boy and rolled out of harm's way as the balcony fell to the street, landing with a mighty crash and a deadly shower of sparks.

Safe for the moment, Colin and the boy lay tangled together, coughing their lungs out.

"John!" The child's brother rushed forward and scooped him up. "I thought for sure you were dead!"

John dissolved in tears. The older boy hushed him as, one on either side, Jason and Ford helped Colin stand and shrug back into his surcoat.

They urged him down the street, farther from the threatening flames, while Colin in turn tugged the boys after him.

"Wh-where are your folks?" he croaked between coughs.

The older boy shook his head. "We don't know," he yelled over the deafening racket. "They told us to wait, but that was"—he tilted his blackened face to the sky—"yesterday, maybe." The smoke was so thick it looked like dusk, but the sun had risen, bathing the city in an unearthly glow.

The boy stopped walking. Clutching his sniffling brother to his side, he shoved the tangled hair from his face and fixed Colin with pleading eyes. "Can you help us, my lord?"

"I..." Nonplussed, Colin looked to Jason and Ford.

They shrugged.

"Can you help us? *Please?*" Without waiting for an answer, the boy grabbed his brother's hand, pulling him along as he shouldered his way purposefully through the throng.

Colin's gaze was glued to the children's skinny, vulnerable backs. "I'll see you at Cainewood!" he called to his own brothers before taking off after them.

He chased them through the teeming confusion of the intersection and onto Friday Street, where they ducked into a space between two buildings. Seven more children huddled there, most of them in tears.

"Davis!" a few cried in unison, running over to embrace the tall boy. They pulled little John into the center of their circle, a small island of camaraderie amongst the misery.

Colin's chest squeezed. These children could have been himself ten years ago, and Jason and Ford and Kendra. They might be commoners, not aristocrats, and lost rather than abandoned.

But the desperate feeling was the same.

Davis withdrew from the group and returned to Colin. "We all live by Ludgate," he explained breathlessly. Though tall for his age, the boy couldn't be more than ten or eleven. "We waited there together, but our folks will never find us now. We had to move, to Warwick, then we found that empty house on Paternoster, then here...but my brother didn't make it here. Oh, I thank you, my lord." He sank to his knees in the mud. "You saved my brother's life."

Colin awkwardly patted the boy's head, leaning to look into the street. "A fat lot of good it will have done if we all burn anyway," he muttered. "It's headed this way. Wait here; I'll be back."

He darted before a creeping wagon, its bed laden with a hodgepodge of household goods. With Colin's palms outstretched to press against the two horses's muzzles, the wagon ground to a quick halt.

"Hey!" the driver shouted. "What the dickens do you think you're about?"

"I need this vehicle." Colin came around and leapt up beside the man, who shook his slick, bald head indignantly.

"Folks paid good silver for me to save their belongings. I'm bound for Moorfields, for the refugee camp." The man's accent branded him from the countryside, no doubt come into London to assist the victims' flight—and turn a handy profit in the process. A simple cart had suddenly become a high-priced asset, and this was a sturdy wagon.

"Silver, you say? I'll pay gold." Colin fished a pouch from his ripped surcoat and pulled out a guinea. He jumped to the street and began unloading the wagon, suffering a pang of guilt at his cavalier disregard for others' prized possessions. But a line from one of Dryden's poems came to him unbidden: *And thus the child imposes on the man.*

Surely children's lives took precedence over men's possessions.

The driver bit on the coin and then pocketed it, climbing down to watch with disbelieving eyes.

Colin tossed him another guinea. "There's for your flea-bitten horses. And there's another in it for you if you'll help me unload. The fire's gaining."

A quick glance toward the flames had the man throwing goods off the back end, heedless of the clutter it added to the street. He grabbed the third coin, then took off at a run toward Cheapside, disappearing into the wretched mass of newly homeless.

The children clambered up into the wagon bed, their faces masks of relief beneath the tear-streaked soot. Waves of heat lashed at Colin's back, spurring him to move on.

He shrugged off his hot coat and stood up on the bench seat, plucking his damp, grayish shirt away from his body as he peered through the smoke toward the west. Priscilla lived in that direction, and his family's town house was there too, in Lincoln's Inn Fields. Thankfully, the area appeared untouched. The fire was heading north now; west was the best way out of London.

And out was where Colin intended to head—out and to his brother Jason's home, Cainewood. There was no sense searching for the children's families until the fire died down, which could be days. And there was no suitable space for them at Greystone.

He sat and picked up the reins. Traffic was unbearable, and they moved at a crawl. A quarter-hour later, they'd traversed to the next corner of Friday Street and made the turn onto Cheapside. Just three or four more streets, a little further from the leading edge of the fire, and then—

"No, Papa!" The voice cut through the roar of the crowd; a rather familiar voice, though Colin was sure he'd never heard it raised before. His fingers went oddly, instinctively to his ring. "Papa, you cannot!"

His head whipped around. There it was, Goldsmith & Sons. And the girl, Amethyst.

He jerked on the reins as her father shoved her stumbling into the street, flames thundering in the shop behind. A small trunk came out after her, then the man gestured wildly and ducked back inside. Colin saw him start up the stairs—stairs already engulfed in fire—before a blast of heat slammed the door shut.

"Papa!" The girl's wail was a knife to Colin's heart.

"Davis, take it," he barked, throwing the boy the reins. He jumped to the street, dodging cross-traffic as he made his way toward the girl. She hastened up the street in the direction her father had indicated, not making much progress, weighed down by the trunk she dragged in the mud.

They both whirled at the sound of an ominous crash. She let out an anguished scream as the roof of her home caved in, sending a column of sparks into the sky that looked extraordinary, even in stark daylight.

"Papa!" She dropped the trunk and rushed back toward the door. The gilt shop sign crashed to the street, but she lifted her skirts and leapt over it without missing a step. Colin reached her just as she grasped the door latch, but she jerked back, staring at her palm, where angry red welts were already rising. Cradling the hand, she doubled over, oblivious to the soot and ash that rained down on her head.

"Papa!" The cry was a whimper now.

Black smoke puffed out from beneath the door, swirling around her grayed skirts. She didn't move. Flames licked at the shop's windows. Good heavens, the blaze would consume her in a moment, and she wasn't moving.

Colin grabbed her good hand and pulled her toward the wagon.

"No!" She wrenched from his grasp and rushed back to the door, bunching her skirts in one hand for insulation as she reached again for the searing metal handle.

Colin couldn't believe his smoke-blinded eyes. He clutched her by the waist and yanked her back against his body.

"No!" She slammed into him and immediately lunged forward. "Papa's in there—I must save him!"

The door's paint was now blistering, writhing, bubbling. At any moment the planks would flare up. Yet she tugged against Colin's restraint, aiming a shoulder at the door, clearly intending to batter it down.

With both hands on her shoulders, he dragged her back a yard...two...three.

"No! Let me go!" She twisted and turned in his grip. Heat battered them in scorching waves. *"No!"*

"Yes!" He spun her around and, desperate, gave her a shake meant to rattle some sense into her fevered brain. "You must leave!"

"I have to save him!" Head down, she kicked at his shins. Still he hung on, jostled by the torrent of evacuees, dragging her stumbling toward the wagon as she struggled. "Let go of me!"

Jaw clenched, he stopped and took her face between his hands, forcing her eyes to his. "He's dead!" he roared over the deafening noise. "He went up the stairs, and the roof collapsed! Now come, before you're dead as well!"

A glassy look of despair began to cloud her amethyst eyes as she went limp beneath his hands. Her knees buckled. He scooped her into his arms and ran to the wagon.

After flinging her light frame up front, beside Davis, he made to climb up after her.

She stiffened, bolting straight up. "My trunk!" she screamed, pointing at the homely object. It sat mere feet from the shop, flames from the front wall reaching deadly fingers in its direction. But one look at her face convinced him he'd have to retrieve it, or she'd attempt to do so herself.

"Go!" he shouted at Davis, slapping the nearest horse on the rump for emphasis. Davis lifted the reins, and the wagon lurched, inching down the street.

The heat was incredible. A window burst as Colin raced toward the shop, the blast scattering glass and releasing clouds of smoke that seared his lungs anew. Coughing, his eyes streaming tears, he knelt to lift the trunk.

How on earth was a small trunk so heavy? He let it drop and, grabbing one handle, dragged it clunking down the rutted street to where the wagon crept along. Waving the children back, he managed to heave the trunk into the wagon bed, then ran around and swung up to the bench, taking the reins from Davis, who scrambled to join the others in the back.

"Are you hurt?" He forced the words past his raw throat. "Amethyst?" What had her father called her? "Amy?"

At the sound of her name, she looked up, her glazed eyes registering first confusion, then disbelief.

"Lord Greystone?"

Before he could respond, she threw her arms around his neck and burst into tears.

Colin placed one arm around her, gingerly and then tighter. The sobs wracked her slight body. Hot tears soaked through his shirt, wetting his shoulder.

Long, gut-wrenching minutes passed. They progressed several streets before she choked back the tears and slowly lifted her red-rimmed eyes to meet his.

Dark purple smudges marred the delicate-looking skin beneath her eyes. The fire had been burning since Sunday; she'd likely not slept for days.

"I'm so sorry," he said.

She nodded her head miserably.

"Where can I take you?"

Sniffling, she gave a vehement shake of her head. "Nowhere," she said in a trembling whisper. Her eyes filled again and threatened to brim over. "I have no one."

Discomfited, he turned back to the road. No one? It couldn't be so; surely she knew someone who would take her in. Her father had perished, true—he'd seen that with his own eyes—but what of a mother? A relative? A neighbor?

He felt her take a shuddering breath. Keeping her eyes lowered, she bunched up his discarded surcoat to make a pillow and lay down on the bench, her knees drawn up like a small child. Less than a minute later, her breathing slowed and evened out in the rhythm of sleep.

He drove on, absently smoothing the damp hair off her face, letting his gaze wander over her slumbering form draped along the length of the seat. Something vaguely unnerving fluttered and settled in his stomach as he turned onto Lothbury and headed west.

SEVEN

"**S**HE'S TOUCHING me."

Rubbing his dry, burning eyes, Colin glanced over his shoulder at the children in the wagon bed.

"He's looking at me oddly."

Colin clenched his teeth and turned his attention back to the road, where it seemed every inhabitant of London was ahead of him. A leisurely carriage ride from London to Cainewood Castle normally took about five hours, but the sun was setting, and after six hours they weren't even a quarter of the way there.

They could walk to Cainewood faster than they were moving, he thought irritably.

"She won't stop humming."

"Ouch!"

He had to find somewhere to stay before major warfare broke out. For the past hour, he'd stopped at every inn along the way and sent Davis to inquire about available lodging. Colin was beginning to believe every room in the kingdom was taken.

When Davis came out of the last one, shaking his head, Colin had briefly considered bedding outdoors for the night. But although it was warm, there was a persistent wind, and he shuddered at the thought of trying to make nine children comfortable with not so much as a blanket.

Nine children and Amy Goldsmith.

He glanced down at her grimy face. Amethyst Goldsmith—whoever would have thought? He'd left her shop two weeks ago with no intention of ever going back, ever purchasing another piece of jewelry, ever seeing her again. And now here she was, dropped—literally—right in his lap.

He could've laughed himself silly, if not for the tragic circumstances of their reunion.

She'd moved up in her sleep, and her head now rested against his leg. He smiled to himself, picturing her turning red with embarrassment if she knew. He allowed himself to touch her, skimming his fingers down her arm, encircling one dainty wrist.

Just to check that her pulse was still steady, of course—she'd doubtless inhaled a great deal of smoke.

It was quite steady.

For the dozenth time, he fervently thanked God she was alive.

When she stirred, Colin hastily withdrew. Amy murmured something incoherent, then settled back into sleep. Her long black lashes looked feathery against her ashy, tear-streaked cheeks.

Colin tore his gaze away and stared straight ahead at the congested road. The top of Amy's head still pressed against his leg. Being near her felt so very different from being near Priscilla. He'd kissed Priscilla before, but never had he felt this…flustered. Yet she was his betrothed, and she was beautiful, intelligent, exactly what he wanted—and Amy was just a shop girl he'd smiled at once.

He was more familiar with Priscilla, he decided, more comfortable. He and Amy weren't *supposed* to be touching—indeed, they certainly wouldn't be if she were awake. It was simply the excitement of the forbidden masquerading as some deeper emotion.

And he wasn't looking for emotion in his marriage. He'd told his sister as much just last night.

Heavens, had it been but a day since his family's visit to Greystone? He felt ages removed from the fellow who had gleefully pulled that prank. It seemed as though he hadn't slept in a week.

He paused before another inn and sent Davis to investigate. Scuffling sounds and a high-pitched shriek came from the back of the wagon. Colin's empty stomach complained loudly, and he came to a decision.

They were stopping here. To eat, if nothing else.

They were in luck—of sorts. Davis came running back to report that there was room in the inn. One room, to be precise. With two beds. For eleven people.

Well, it was shelter, and Colin was inclined to think there might be nothing else available between here and Cainewood. He sent Davis to claim it before someone else pulled off the road.

EIGHT

*A*MY WASHED down a bite of meat pie with ale, allowing the children's anxious chatter to lull her. Wedged on the bench between a girl of five and a boy of six, she kept her gaze on her plate and avoided Lord Greystone's eyes across the table.

She had no wish to talk—given her choice, she wouldn't even be awake. She'd managed to spend the past few hours in oblivion, casting the time away. Dreaming...warm hands touching her, soothing her...comforting. Now that she was conscious, she felt guilty for having such a pleasant dream when her father was dead.

A sudden sharp pain of loss overwhelmed her, and she struggled to force it back inside. She couldn't think about it now—it was too fresh, and she was too broken.

"Bread, Amy?" Lord Greystone's rich voice cut through her thoughts.

She slowly brought her gaze to his. "No, thank you."

"Cheese?"

"I'm really not hungry." She could see Lord Greystone eyeing her barely eaten pie, so she stuck her spoon in it.

"You have to eat." The statement was matter-of-fact, but his voice was filled with concern. "You'll fall ill."

When she dropped her spoon and lowered her eyes again,

Lord Greystone cleared his throat and rose. "I'll take the children upstairs. You stay for a bit and finish your supper. Will you wait for me here?"

Amy raised her chin and nodded up at him.

"I'll come back down for you," he promised, and took himself off, the children trailing in his wake.

She toyed with her food for the next quarter-hour, breaking up her pie, the spoon awkward in her left hand. She attempted a couple of bites, but the meat had turned cold and stuck in her throat, nearly making her gag. Gulping more ale, she pushed her plate away; she hadn't been hungry in the first place, but Lord Greystone had insisted on setting it in front of her.

When her ale was finished, she stared at the pattern in the oak table and blanked her mind until, out of a corner of her eye, she glimpsed Lord Greystone coming downstairs.

He'd cleaned up, neatly pulled back his hair, donned his surcoat. It was ripped a bit, but he'd brushed it clean of the ash and soot. His grayish shirt showed beneath the unbuttoned front. Dark stubble dotted his cheeks and chin.

Watching as he went through a swinging door into the kitchen, she ran her fingers through her own knotted hair. Earlier, she'd scrubbed the grime from her face and unraveled her disheveled plait, but found nothing with which to brush it out. Their tiny room had no mirror—she was sure she looked a sight.

Not that she cared.

NINE

$\mathcal{C}$OLIN BACKED through the kitchen door with two bowls full of sloshing liquid in his hands, some strips of cloth draped over one arm, and a jar of honey wedged between chin and shoulder.

He put everything on the table and straddled the bench beside Amy, motioning his head toward her plate. "Finished eating?"

"Yes, I am."

"May I have a look at that hand? We really should clean it."

"I suppose so," she said, offering her hand.

Colin wondered if he were up to the task of drawing her out of this dreamlike state. He had to figure out something to do with her, but she wouldn't be much help if she persisted in answering him with three-word sentences.

He glanced at her hand and winced. "Ouch!" he said with a mock shudder.

"It's not so bad."

"Bad enough." He gently placed her hand in one bowl. "We'll soak it for a few minutes, shall we?"

Her long black lashes swept down as she squinted at the bowl. "What is it?"

He smiled distractedly. "Cream."

"Cream? You mean, from milk?" She gave a slight shake of

54

her head, making her dark hair shimmer in the flickering light.

"Why cream?" she asked.

"Huh?" He shook himself. "Doesn't everyone put cream on burns?"

"I think not," she mused, drawing her eyebrows together. "Butter. In my family, we put butter on burns."

"We always use cream," he asserted. "As well as honey. I hear tell butter's no good."

"That's not what I've heard," she said dubiously.

"Well, how does it feel?"

She paused, considering, then tilted her head. "A little better, I guess."

"See?" His smile was triumphant.

Amy smiled back; the smile was shy and more than a little bit sad, but a smile nonetheless. Colin congratulated himself.

"That should do it." She started a little when he took her hand, but he pretended not to notice. While he held it over the bowl, watching the cream run off in tiny rivulets, the air between them crackled with unasked questions. Her hand stopped dripping, and he rinsed it in the bowl of water.

Her eyes closed, and he felt her relax, her hand limp as he swished it around, pulled it out and turned it over.

"Hmm…" He dabbed gingerly at her palm with one of the linen strips. "It's clean now, and a bit less red." He held it up for her to see. "What do you think?"

Her eyes popped open. "It's fine."

But she was grimacing, and the longer she looked at it, the more he felt her stiffen. Not that he could blame her. The puckered blisters were an angry hue.

"We need it perfectly dry." He dabbed at her hand again, trying not to hurt her. "There. Now the honey…" He opened the jar, dipped in a spoon, and drizzled the sweet thick substance onto her injured palm, spreading it gently with one finger.

She sat silent as he wound a fresh linen bandage around her hand, tucked in the end, and rinsed his fingers in the bowl.

"Davis is watching the young ones." Wiping his palms on his breeches, he rose. "Would you care to take a walk?"

Without waiting for her answer, he took her by the elbow.

TEN

*T*HE ROAD OUT front was noisy, crammed with an endless stream of people fleeing London. A well-worn path in back of the inn led up into gently rolling hills, and it was here that Lord Greystone guided her.

It was a cloudless night, the wind having blown every wisp over the horizon, and Amy could just make out his profile, dark against the moonlight. Aided by what seemed a million stars, her eyes adjusted to the darkness.

Twisting the gold ring on his finger—the ring she had made —Lord Greystone cleared his throat.

"How is your hand?"

"Not too bad."

"Are you right-handed, or left?"

"Right."

"It will be a spell before you can write, then."

She shrugged. "I expect so."

Lord Greystone paused, and the fingers of one hand drummed against his thigh. "Amy…"

His voice sounded too serious. She didn't want to discuss…it. Not yet, not tonight. Maybe tomorrow. Or, if she were lucky, perhaps this was all a horrible dream, and tomorrow she'd wake up back in Cheapside.

She was glad for his presence, but she wished they were back at the inn, sitting side by side with tankards of mind-numbing ale, not saying anything. If he were going to insist on talking to her, she would have to make sure the conversation stayed on safe subjects.

When the drumming stopped, she took a quick breath. "You...you're very good with the children."

"Thank you." He looked relieved. "Davis is an enormous help."

"Why are you...doing this? Caring for these children, I mean. It's very nice, but..."

"But why am I shepherding children when every other able man is still in London, fighting the fire?" Lord Greystone led her up a rise to where he'd spotted an ancient, broken stone wall. He seated himself upon a low section. "It's difficult to credit, but I've always felt a kind of...empathy, I suppose you could call it, for children who are lost or abandoned. Perhaps I would have been of more use fighting the fire, but—"

"No, not at all." Amy levered herself up to sit on the wall, angling to face him. "The children needed you. Thousands are fighting the fire; one more would make little difference."

Lord Greystone hesitated, then shrugged. "I know how those children feel. When I was small, my parents left me quite often. Most of the time, in fact. And I was lonely and scared all the time. I wasn't the bravest of boys," he admitted ruefully.

"They left you?" Amy could barely conceive of such a childhood; her parents had never left her for so much as a day.

Until today, she realized suddenly.

She felt a brief, sharp stab of grief, then pushed it down, down, far inside, like stuffing one of those new jack-in-the-box toys back under its lid.

She bit her lip. Lord Greystone was watching her. As long as she kept asking him questions, she wouldn't have to think about it. "Why...how could they do that?"

He cocked his head. "They were passionate Royalists. Cavaliers. King and country came first. We, my brothers and sister and I, were such a distant second we barely even counted."

"But...where did they leave you?"

"Oh, at home—with kind servants. They weren't cruel—they

didn't actually abandon us. But to a child…well, it felt as though they did. To me, anyway." He paused, twisting his ring again. "My brother Jason—he's a year older than I—feels differently. He's always idolized our parents, most especially our father."

"How about your sister?"

"Kendra and her twin, Ford, were so young they never knew any other kind of life. They're sixteen—about your age, I think?"

Amy nodded. "I'm seventeen. And now?" she asked. "How do they feel about it now? Your parents, I mean. Are they sorry?"

"They died. At the Battle of Worcester, fifteen years ago."

His parents were dead…just like hers. "Oh…" she started, then couldn't say anything more.

Mistaking her renewed grief for sympathy, Lord Greystone rushed to reassure her. "No need to feel sorry. It was Charles's last stand against Cromwell, and my folks wouldn't have missed it for the world. Soon afterward we were taken to Holland to live with other Royalist exiles. We were safe. After a while I realized I didn't miss my parents much, since they had hardly ever been around anyway."

He fell silent, gazing out into the endless dark rolling hills.

"Was your family Royalist, Amy? During the war, I mean?"

"No," she said slowly, pausing as she thought how to explain it. "I mean…we weren't *not* Royalist, either. We were—nothing, I guess. Papa just tried to keep doing business no matter what happened." To Amy's surprise and dismay, her mention of Papa released a floodgate of emotions. Tears began welling in her eyes. "I'm sorry," she whispered, chagrined that she couldn't control herself.

"Don't be sorry. Whether you were Royalist or nay—it doesn't signify. It seems a fine survival tactic to me."

She couldn't answer. Her throat seemed to close up, and a warm teardrop rolled down her cheek and splashed onto her clasped hands.

"Amy?" Lord Greystone probed. "Where is your mother?"

She tried to swallow past the lump in her throat. "Gone," she answered in a quavery voice. "The plague took her. Last year. She fell ill and we had to leave. We went to France, and I never saw her again."

"I'm sorry," he said softly. He moved over on the wall and placed an arm around her shoulders. "I'm truly sorry."

His voice was soft and compassionate, but she wasn't ready to accept sympathy just now. It made everything too real.

"I..." His arm tightened around her. "I don't understand. Your father, why he went back inside. When the shop was aflame."

Slow tears overflowed, quiet tears, not a storm like earlier in the day when he'd found her. They burned in her eyes and traced hot paths down her cheeks.

She was so exhausted.

"He wanted a painting of my mother." She brushed at the tears with the back of her good hand.

"A painting?" She could feel Lord Greystone beside her, shaking his head in disbelief.

"He *had* to have that picture. A miniature. He used to sit for hours, staring at it. Perhaps—perhaps he didn't really want to live without her," she said with a flash of insight that felt like a knife in her chest. "Now I have no one. I'm all alone."

He jumped down and stood before her, gripping her shoulders. "You're not alone, Amy."

"Yes—yes, I am. My parents are gone...my home is gone..."

Well, there was Robert, a little voice in the back of her head reminded her.

But there was no one to make her marry him now.

"You must have family, somewhere?"

"Only my Aunt Elizabeth." The words came out a whisper, forced through her painfully tight throat. "She lives in Paris. Last year when I stayed with her I was miserable."

"You'd just lost your mother," he reminded her gently. "You would have been miserable anywhere." With him standing and her seated on the wall, they were of a height. His eyes searched hers, an intense gray, their color neutralized by the darkness. "It's not so bad as all that."

More tears brimmed over, and she saw his brow crease in response.

"I wish I weren't alive," she whispered, dropping her head to escape his penetrating gaze.

"Never say that," he said vehemently. "It's good to be alive. Never ever say that."

Hesitantly, almost shyly, he leaned forward and reached his arms around her, pulling her to him. Her downturned face was squished against his shoulder, her body rigid with tension and uncertainty. She finally had to raise her chin to breathe and felt his cheek graze hers, warm and a bit rough. The unfamiliar sensation took her aback.

"Dear heavens," she whispered.

It was the first human connection she'd felt since she saw her father disappear into the raging inferno that used to be her home.

Suddenly, here in Lord Greystone's arms, she was far away, removed from her hostile reality, and she wished she could stay here in his arms forever. He stroked her hair, and she let him, lulled by the gentle tug of his fingers working slowly, patiently through her tangled curls. Some of the tension drained from her body. She was only half-aware of her arms snaking around him, her chin settling snugly in the crook of his neck.

Dimly realizing that his attempts at comfort were edging too far toward impropriety, Colin tried to pull back. But Amy came off the wall with him, sliding down his front until her feet came to rest on the grass, her face pressed into his shirt, her tears soaking the thin linen.

Criminy. Despite her gut-wrenching misery, he couldn't help but think how good she felt in his arms. It was absolutely...flustering.

In fact, with Amy pressed up against him, he could hardly think at all.

When she wiped her eyes and tilted her head back to look up at him, he pulled her even closer and touched his lips to hers.

The travelers rumbling by in the background, the crickets in the hills, the wind blowing past...all faded away. Like magic.

Amy was so surprised, she kept her eyes open instead of squeezing them tight as she always had against Robert's kisses. But then, this was nothing like Robert's kisses. This kiss was soft and sure, warm and welcoming. It was like a potion—she couldn't remember who she was or whether she had any problems. Lord Greystone smelled smoky and salty but tasted like the ale they'd had at dinner, only sweeter, and he was just as beautiful up close, especially when he opened his startling emerald eyes and looked straight into hers—

Colin wrenched away, his arms falling to his sides. His breathing was sharp, his nerves jangling. What was he doing?

Kissing a girl who wasn't his betrothed, that's what.

And even worse, he was taking advantage of Amy's grief, her vulnerability, her overwhelming loneliness. What on earth had come over him? He wasn't that kind of person. He'd always thought of himself as cool and rational, never carried away by impulse.

And certainly never anything less than a gentleman.

He was thoroughly disgusted with himself.

Amy stared at him, dazed, her legs wobbly.

"I'm sorry," he said.

He didn't sound like Lord Greystone, Amy thought. His voice was rough, and he did look sorry—ashamed, even.

"Sorry?" Amy's senses were still spinning. She wasn't sorry, not one bit. She'd never imagined any person could make her feel like someone else, in a different time and place, and she'd wanted that feeling to go on forever.

And, unless she was mistaken, he'd felt much the same. Surely he couldn't have kissed her like that if he hadn't. Or could he? She realized she had no idea.

"You're sorry?" she pressed.

"Well, not sorry exactly," he said in that unfamiliar rough voice, fumbling for the words. "It's just…I shouldn't have done that…taken advantage of you like that. Not that I didn't want to —oh, a pox on this!" He took a step toward her and put his hands on her shoulders, holding her at arm's length, clearly exasperated. "You're a proper young merchant girl, and you've suffered a frightful tragedy, and I mean to protect you, not—not *ruin* you." The flush rising up his neck was visible even in the dark.

His words *sounded* sensible enough. The girl Amy was yesterday surely would have agreed. But today, battered and bruised and alone in the world, she wasn't sure of anything.

Except that she'd like to kiss Lord Greystone again.

"My lord—" she began.

"*Colin,*" he interrupted. "I imagine once you've kissed a fellow, you're allowed to call him by his Christian name."

Amy blushed furiously. Still, she tried the name in her head. *Colin.* She'd never called a nobleman by his given name, and it should feel wrong. But now she thought *Colin,* and it made her feel warm all over.

"And if you were about to tell me it doesn't matter," he continued, "you're wrong. It matters a lot."

"But—"

"No buts." He shook his head. "It's late, and we're both very tired. We have a long ride to Cainewood in the morning. Let's get some sleep."

He took her good hand and pulled her toward the inn. She followed reluctantly. There was no arguing with him, it seemed.

Her hand tingled where his bare skin touched hers. She'd held hands with Robert and never felt anything at all. Even with her limited experience, she knew this couldn't be normal.

Was it not the same for him?

ELEVEN

*I*T WAS.

And Colin was quite certain this wasn't one jot normal. But it was absurd. He was betrothed, and Amy was a commoner, a girl who, as of this morning, had nothing whatsoever to her name.

He was tired; that must be it. He was very, very tired.

If his body felt like it were vibrating, that was only because he was tired.

After a good night's sleep, he'd feel differently. He'd be more himself, back in control. They'd go on to Cainewood, wait a couple of days until the roads were clear, then he'd take her to Dover and buy her passage across the Channel. They'd never see each other again.

His pride would remain intact, not to mention his future and her reputation.

They arrived back at the inn and trudged wearily upstairs, to find four little bodies bundled in each of the two beds, crosswise, and Davis curled in the only chair, snoring softly.

Colin's mouth fell open.

"You expected what?" Amy whispered. "That they'd all lie down on the floor and leave the beds to us? I'd say they settled themselves quite fairly."

"I thought they'd leave *part* of each bed to us," he complained loudly. "Greedy little monsters, aren't they?"

"Shhh! You'll wake them."

"I wish they would waken, so I could rearrange them. But you're not well acquainted with children, are you? Nothing short of a cannon blast would wake them."

Despite the sleeping evidence, Amy still couldn't bring herself to talk out loud. "I have no brothers or sisters. How should I know how children sleep?"

"I'll go downstairs and fetch some more blankets," he said, turning on his heel.

He stopped short of slamming the door behind him. Amy slumped against the wall, wondering what had made his mood change so suddenly.

She slid down to the floor and waited, her knees to her chest. Alone, the grief started creeping back. She wouldn't think about it. She'd think about the kiss...

Her lips seemed to burn at the memory.

At last he returned, two threadbare blankets in hand. "It was like negotiating a treaty," he declared, "and they cost me a pretty penny. I'd be willing to wager they're her own personal blankets." He sniffed at them suspiciously. "They smell as bad as she does."

Amy wrinkled her nose, remembering the stout, flushed innkeeper's wife and her greasy hair.

Colin began to hand her the smaller blanket, then glanced at Davis uncovered in his chair.

"A pox on him," he muttered to himself.

There was nothing for it; he was going to have to share a blanket with Amy. *Why?* What had he done to deserve all this struggle?

He covered Davis and gently tucked him in.

"Sorry." He spread the other blanket on the floor and sat on it to pull off his boots. "This is what I was afraid of."

"Afraid of?"

"We'll have to share this blanket," he explained crossly.

"Is that what you were so vexed about?" Amy's features lost some of their tightness. "Strangers sleep together all the time when inns are full. Of course, they generally have a bed," she reflected.

"They're generally the same gender," he said pointedly.

"Oh."

"Yes. Well, come then, take off your shoes." He shrugged off his surcoat and rolled it up to make a pillow. "If they're anything like normal, the children will be up at first light."

He lay down. Amy slowly removed her shoes, then joined him at the edge of the blanket and arranged herself on her side, carefully separated from him. He threw the other half of the blanket over them both.

Her tears were silent, but Colin could feel the blanket tug slightly when her shoulders began shaking. "A pox on everything," he murmured under his breath. He turned toward her and slid an arm around her waist, pulling her against him.

"Hush," he whispered, although she wasn't making a sound. "Hush. It's all right. I'm here."

TWELVE

*A*MY TRAILED listlessly behind Colin as he hustled the children to the wagon. Leaning against the side, she watched them clamber into the back, wondering where she'd find the energy to climb up herself. She felt like she hadn't slept a wink last night; barring some catnaps Monday evening and her uneasy slumber in the jostling wagon yesterday, she'd been awake for nearly three days.

"Keep an eye on them, will you?" Colin asked.

She nodded, watching his easy stride as he headed into the inn. Thank heavens he was here...

Closing her eyes, she shook her head in a vain attempt to clear it. She had to think straight, figure out a plan. While it was easier to let him take care of her, she couldn't rely on Colin. He was a tempting comfort, but a false one. She meant nothing to him.

Her thoughts drifted to last night. How could she have asked him about himself and his past as though everything were normal, as though Papa hadn't just died? And dear heavens, had she actually kissed him? And enjoyed it? Her face flamed at the memory. What kind of a daughter was she? She didn't deserve to enjoy *anything*, ever again.

She opened her eyes to see Colin returning, her trunk balanced on one straining shoulder.

"What on earth is in here?" He set it in the wagon with a decided *clunk*.

"Everything I own," she said in a broken whisper, her gaze riveted to the wooden slats, the leather straps, the brass fittings.

Papa's life's work was in there.

Colin pushed the trunk under the bench, making a hideous scraping noise. Suddenly her throat constricted and she seemed unable to breathe. The grief was bubbling up inside her. A weight settled in her stomach; a fist closed around her heart. Her eyes filled with hot, blinding tears.

It was rising, threatening to overwhelm her, and this time she couldn't stop it.

She stumbled up to the bench, but she couldn't sit upright, so she sank to the boards and covered her face with her hands. Then she let it rise up and out, the pain and the tears and the great, tearing sobs.

Her breath came in hysterical gulps. Colin stroked her hair, but she shook off his hand, though she knew it might hurt his feelings. The children were silent; she could feel their pitying gazes. She didn't care. Papa was dead. She would never see him, never hug him, never hear his voice again.

She was jostled when the wagon started moving, but the tears wouldn't stop. Wordlessly, Colin stuffed a handkerchief into her fist. Before long it was sopping wet and twisted in her hands.

The world retreated until she was a mass of wretched pain. Papa was dead; her home was gone; she had no father, no mother, no family at all except one aunt in a foreign country.

It was all Papa's fault. When he'd gone back inside their burning house, he'd robbed her of both her father and her life.

How dare he? she thought. *I hate him!*

Bolting upright, she gasped and slapped a hand over her mouth as though she'd said the words out loud.

She felt Colin's gaze, his compassion, but it didn't help at all.

When he drew her hand away from her mouth and threaded her fingers through his, she levered herself up to the bench and leaned against him, closing her eyes. The tears leaked slowly, tracing new paths down her raw cheeks. Her head throbbed; her eyes burned, hot and swollen. But no physical pain could match the anguish in her heart.

She'd been furious with Papa, to the point of hating him— and for one split second, she had really felt that.

THIRTEEN

STANDING BESIDE the wagon with one hand resting possessively on her trunk, Amy watched, dazed, as Lady Kendra led two children by the hand toward Cainewood's immense double oak doors.

The raked gravel of the drive crunched beneath their feet. "I cannot believe you did this, Colin." Lady Kendra turned on the steps to count the young ones. "Nine children! You must have had your hands full." She paused on the threshold, eyeing Amy speculatively. "Though it looks as though you had help."

Colin didn't respond, but Amy slipped him a guilty sidewise glance. She bit her lip, knowing she'd been less than helpful. She hadn't even been decent company. They'd been on the road for the better part of the day, and she'd strung no more than five words together the entire time.

But she had no time to dwell on herself now, not with Cainewood Castle before her in all its ancient glory.

The living quarters formed a U around the quadrangle's groomed lawn. She looked up, and up. Four stories.

"More than a hundred rooms," Colin said beside her, as though he'd read her mind. "Most of them closed up. Jason has years of restoration ahead." He pointed out the marks of cannon-balls in the high, crenelated wall. "Cromwell sacked the place twice."

Beyond the smooth green grass of the quadrangle, a tall, timeworn tower rose majestically. "The original keep," he explained. "I believe it dates from 1138. Cainewood's been in our family, save during the Commonwealth, since 1243."

"Oh..." Blinking, she turned and stared up at him, his bold features shadowed by the turreted curtain wall. An *enormous* castle's wall. Other than Whitehall Palace, it was the largest structure she'd ever seen.

And his family *lived here...*

The thought was amazing. Nearly inconceivable. Back in her shop and at the inn, Colin had seemed almost ordinary.

He shifted under her stare, and she glanced away, embarrassed.

He pointed again. "Beyond the keep, that's the tilting yard. Obsolete, these centuries past. Jason doesn't bother caring for it."

His wave indicated the vegetation, untamed and ankle high. Still, a tilting yard...she could picture knights of old, mounted on glittering steeds, jousting, their lances held aloft. She'd been reading an Arthurian collection—she'd left it on her bedside table. It must have burned—

"Come, Amy." His concerned voice rescued her from those thoughts. "I know you're tired. Come inside and you can rest."

He shooed the last of the children up the steps and motioned her after them, through the massive doors. The sun was setting, and she expected the entry would be dim. But a chandelier dangled from the vaulted ceiling, blazing with candles that flooded the cream-colored stone chamber with light.

In awe she moved toward the slim columns that marched two-by-two down the center of the three-story hall. An intricate stone staircase loomed ahead. At intervals along the gray marble handrail, carved heraldic beasts held shields sporting different quarterings of...

"The Chase family crest," Amy said softly.

"How did you...?" Colin set down the trunk and blinked at her. "Oh, you carved those symbols on the sides of my ring."

She smiled to herself, admiring the ornate iron treasure chests that sat against the stone walls, alternating with heavy chairs carved of walnut. Tapestries enriched and softened the effect.

"It's…impressive, no?" Colin cleared his throat. "We, uh, used to have somewhat of a fortune," he said, rather sheepishly. "Before the war, that is."

Amy looked up to the balcony that spanned the width of the hall. "I've never seen the likes of it," she admitted. "It's magnificent. The workmanship…"

"My home, Greystone, is nothing like this—take my word for it."

She didn't reply, mainly because her gaze had wandered back down the stairs and settled on Lady Kendra. From the top of her coiffed head, with her striking dark-red ringlets wired out on the sides, to the quilted slippers that peeked from beneath her mint-green satin skirts, Lady Kendra was the picture of perfection.

Amy glanced down, mortified. Her own wrinkled, smoke-stained skirts had started out lavender on Monday, but now looked a grubby gray. She could only imagine what her face and hair looked like, all dirty and disheveled. She wanted to drop into the floor.

"Kendra, you'll remember Mrs. Amethyst Goldsmith?" Colin's words prompted a small smile from Amy. Only harlots and pre-adolescent girls were called "Miss," and in light of her behavior last night, she considered herself lucky that Colin considered her neither.

A frown wrinkled Lady Kendra's forehead. "I'm not certain…"

"You met Mrs. Goldsmith last month in London," Colin reminded his sister. "She made your locket."

"Oh, of course!" Lady Kendra's face lit up at the memory. She scrutinized Amy more closely, then smiled. "It's just that I didn't expect to see you here."

Considering it was more likely that Colin's sister hadn't recognized her under all the filth, Amy warmed to her immediately. "That makes two of us, Lady Kendra. I didn't expect to be here myself."

Lady Kendra's laughter tinkled through the hall. "I suppose you didn't, at that," she conceded. "And please, call me Kendra —just Kendra. May I call you Amethyst?"

"My friends call me Amy," Amy returned hopefully. She badly needed a friend right now.

"Amy, then. Um…might I guess you'd like a bath?"

"Oh, yes," she breathed gratefully.

"And some supper," Colin interjected. "She hasn't eaten in two days," he explained to Kendra.

Amy shook her head slightly. She was certain she couldn't eat yet. "I really just want to sleep."

"Warm chocolate, then," Colin insisted.

Amy nodded acceptance.

"With brandy in it," he added decisively. "And some soup."

Amy sighed. "Perhaps some soup. The chocolate sounds nice."

The brandy sounded nice. The brandy and bed. She'd be willing to wager the beds in a place like this would be soft and comfortable.

"Well, up you go, then." Colin gestured toward the stairs. "Up you all go, in fact," he declared in a raised voice, striding over to the children huddled in the back of the hall, whispering amongst themselves. "Baths for everyone, first thing. Then supper, then bed."

There were audible groans at this announcement. "Could we not just wash up a bit?" Davis spoke for the group. "We won't really have to take *baths*, will we?"

Heading up the stairs, Amy smiled to herself. She knew that at home, Davis probably bathed twice a year, if that. Cleanliness was considered an invitation to infection.

"Oh yes, you will," Colin stated firmly. "Kendra, two at a time. And fresh hot water for each bath."

Behind her, Amy heard the children's startled breaths. Such lavish use of water was unheard of in the City. She met Kendra's amused eyes.

"Tell Cook to prepare supper—lots of it," Kendra called down toward her brother's dark head. "Then, for heaven's sake, come up and give me a hand. *I'm* not the one who volunteered to play nursemaid."

FOURTEEN

"*T*HE MEWS was over there," Colin said, pointing through the keep's glassless window.

The children clustered around him, craning their necks to see out. He felt a small tug on his breeches and looked down. Noon sunshine streamed into the ancient roofless tower, dancing on a small lad's red-gold mop of curls.

The child cocked his head. "What's a news?"

Colin smiled at his puzzled look. "A *mews*," he corrected gently. "A building where the lord kept his falcons. It was destroyed by the Roundheads in the siege of 1643."

"The same time the holes in the floor happened?" another boy asked.

"The same time," he told the child, a sturdy apple-cheeked lad. "But that only makes it more fun for hide-and-seek and treasure hunts, doesn't it?"

The boy and Colin shared a smile before the boy sobered. "When can we go home?"

"Yes, when?" another echoed.

"Today?" The smallest girl's blue eyes looked so hopeful in her angelic little face.

Colin gave one of her golden ringlets a gentle tug and watched it spring back into place. "Not today, Mary, but soon, I'm hoping." As a disappointed silence seemed to permeate the stone walls, he looked away, twisting his ring and searching for the right words of comfort.

"Did you live in this keep when you were a little boy?"

"Heavens, no!" Colin met the large brown eyes of another girl. "How old do you think I am?" She and a few of the others giggled. "No one's lived in here for centuries. The building was open to the sky long before my boyhood. Would you like to see the wall walk?"

The sound of a clearing throat rang from the doorway. Colin turned, startled.

"'Dinnertime," Kendra announced.

He frowned. "How long have you been there?"

"We want to hear another story," piped up a chubby towhead. Davis's little brother, if Colin remembered right. After a good night's sleep and cleaned of the soot and ash, he appeared a different child.

"That wasn't a story," he told the boy, then looked up at Kendra. "I was just explaining a bit of history."

"It's time for dinner now," Kendra said firmly. "Lord Grey-stone will tell you another story later."

"I will?"

"Yes, you will." Kendra shot him a diabolical grin. "You brought them here, you're responsible for their entertainment. You owe them a bedtime story, at least." She motioned to the children. "Come along, you all need to wash before eating."

"But I promised to show them the wall walk," Colin protested.

"Oh, very well, but quickly. You know how sulky Cook gets when her lovely meals grow cold."

Beckoning, Colin led them all into the stairtower and down the winding steps to the archway. The children ran out along the top of the crenelated wall, shrieking with delight.

"Not too far," he yelled after them, "and be careful!"

"Dunderhead," Kendra chided. "When did you ever know a child to be careful?"

"Never," he said with a sheepish smile.

They both turned and faced outward. Resting their forearms on top of the ledge, they gazed out over the River Caine and the fields and nearby woods. Like most medieval castles, the tower at Cainewood was built on a tall motte—a huge mound of earth. Up on the wall walk they could see for miles in all directions.

"You're marvelous with the children," Kendra said quietly.

Colin shrugged. "I remembered playing in the keep—it was so much fun. I just wanted to bring it to life a bit for them."

Kendra sighed wistfully. "I never got to play in the keep." The war had begun years before she was born, and as well-known Royalists, the Chase children had been whisked to the Continent shortly after their parents' deaths. Sadly, even that had failed to stop Cromwell from bringing his wrath down upon their family home.

But now the days of war were long over. It was peaceful up here.

"How is Amy?" Kendra asked suddenly.

"Still sleeping. Sixteen hours."

"She was exhausted." Kendra slanted him a glance. "I saw you shaking her when I walked by her chamber."

"To no avail. She'd rouse for a few seconds at most, then drop back into sleep." He shook his head. "I thought she'd be wanting some dinner. She'd eaten but a few spoonfuls of broth, though her chocolate cup was empty."

"And her hand?"

"Blisters, but no red streaks of infection, thank the Lord. I changed the bandage and applied fresh honey. I believe it will mend without incidence."

Kendra cocked her head. "You like her, don't you?"

"Of course, don't you?" he said a mite too quickly.

Her lips curved in a knowing smile. "I meant you really *like* her."

"Not like that."

She gave an unladylike snort. "I was there that day in her shop. I'm not blind, you know. I've noticed the way you care for her. Worry about her. And you put her in the Gold Chamber." The beautiful room was usually reserved for honored guests. "Colin—"

"I'm betrothed," he stated firmly.

"But—"

"No buts, Kendra. I—"

"I hate it when you say that!"

"Well, I hate it when you argue with me! As I was about to say, I know you dislike Priscilla, but I *am* marrying her. And nothing you—or Amy—could say will change my mind."

"But *why*? I've seen you with Priscilla—you don't love her, I can tell."

"I don't want to love her; I've told you that. She's wealthy, she's pretty, she's—"

"Cold."

Colin ignored that. "—she's titled—"

"As though we care about such things. We're titled, and what did it get us? Nothing! We were paupers on the Continent, dragged from Paris, to Cologne, to Brussels, Bruges, Antwerp—wherever King Charles wandered. We had no home, no one who really cared about us. People are what matters. Titles are worthless."

"But that's where you're wrong. That title kept us fed, allowed us to tag along with the court, obligated them to take us in. It was all we had, the only thing of value our parents gave us. My children will have no less—and a lot more."

"Of course they will—you're an earl, for heaven's sake! If the king hadn't granted you the title, I'd understand your view. As a second son, you'd have had to marry an heiress or else make your own fortune somehow. But Charles owed a debt to our parents, and he gave you the earldom. Your children will inherit. You have a title—you've no need to marry one."

Colin's jaw was set. "My children will have titles from both sides. They'll never know a day of insecurity."

"What a bunch of blatherskite! You're using this as an excuse to avoid caring about someone—someone like Amy. The Chases know it's what's inside that counts. We don't care about titles."

"This Chase does."

Kendra stamped her foot. "Oh, you're so stubborn!"

"No more than you are, little sister. It runs in the family."

"Hmmph!" She crossed her arms and turned from him, facing outward.

"Hmmph!" Colin did likewise, in imitation.

She burst out laughing.

But his attention was already diverted elsewhere. "Good heavens!" he exclaimed. "Kendra, look!"

She turned and squinted in the direction he was pointing. "What? I see nothing."

"*Exactly*. It's London. *Not* burning."

Sure enough, although a dark cloud of smoke still hung over London in the distance, it seemed to be lifting, and there were no visible flames underneath.

"Oh!" Kendra's voice went up an octave in excitement. "Ford and Jason are on their way home already, I'll wager."

"And I'll take the children back to London first thing in the morning. We can only pray we won't have trouble locating their families."

"And Amy? Will you return her to London as well?"

"Of course," he snapped.

He was relieved when Kendra didn't comment on his temper. "Come, our dinner is getting cold," she said instead. "Let's bring the little ones inside and deliver the good news."

He led the way down from the tower. Once in the quadrangle, the children ran ahead, racing noisily to the entrance.

Crossing the lawn more sedately beside Kendra, whose fashionable high-heeled slippers discouraged running, Colin suddenly stopped in his tracks.

"Now where am I supposed to find a story, I ask you? No one found time to tell *me* fairytales when I was little, you know."

"Oh, you'll think of something." Kendra flashed him an arch smile. "I have complete and total faith in you, big brother." Then she took off across the grass, running anyway.

FIFTEEN

*C*OLIN GENTLY tucked the bandage and set Amy's hand on top of the quilt. It looked tiny and delicate lying alone, with the rest of her buried beneath the covers. He licked a bit of honey off his finger, watching her heart-shaped face. She'd missed dinner, and now supper...he glanced behind in case his sister might be watching, then, feeling foolish, shook Amy's shoulder again.

Nothing.

He rested a hand on her forehead. Still cool, and he could tell by the rise and fall of her chest that she was breathing. He felt beneath her chin for a pulse. Nice and steady.

He sighed and flicked open his pocket watch. The children were waiting for that story he—no, Kendra—had promised them. One story, then he'd take everyone back to London in the morning. Surely Amy would be awake by then.

And by tomorrow night, his life would be back to normal.

The children waited on the drawing room's black-and-coral carpet, sitting with their backs to the fire. Weary after the strain of the past two days, their bellies full of Cook's good hot supper, they watched him walk in with eyes that were already drooping.

Their chatter died down as Colin seated himself facing them in one of the coral-colored velvet chairs. Kendra sat off to the side in its mate, her head bent to her embroidery.

The castle was cool and drafty in the evenings. Kendra hitched herself closer to the fire and struggled to thread her needle. Colin was amused to see her engaged in such a ladylike occupation. It was quite foreign to her nature, but he supposed she considered embroidery a fitting pursuit for a lady passing the evening surrounded by children.

He hoped she'd stick herself in the finger.

The children shifted impatiently on their bottoms. "My lord, what story are we to hear tonight?" Davis asked.

Colin glanced up at the carved wooden ceiling, but there was no help from above. All around the room, large gilt-framed portraits of solemn ancestors watched over him, waiting for him to prove himself a worthy entertainer of children.

When his gaze fastened on a newly commissioned painting of his king, inspiration hit. "Tonight, you will hear the story of the Royal Oak," he announced.

The children scooted forward in anticipation. Kendra looked up with an approving smile.

"After the Battle of Worcester," Colin began, "our king, Charles II, endured great hardships in escaping his enemies."

"Were you there?" Davis's little brother interrupted.

"No, I was only six at the time. But my father and mother were there."

Colin saw no reason to tell them they'd both died in the battle. They were already worried about their own parents.

"For nearly six weeks, King Charles was hiding and sneaking about," he continued. "Sometimes he hid with persons of high rank, and sometimes with those of low. He'd been declared an outlaw, you see, and he was hunted for his life. But the people still saw him as their lawful sovereign and willingly risked their own lives to save his."

"Our king was hunted?" The girl with the large brown eyes looked doubtful. "For real?"

"Yes, certainly. Cromwell wanted him well out of the way." When the girl nodded, Colin went on. "Charles rode hastily away from the scene of his defeat, in the company of a few faithful friends. Whenever they came within hearing range of anyone, they spoke French to avoid detection. His friends brought him to a lonely farmhouse where five brothers named Penderel lived. It was death to anyone who dared to conceal the king, while a great reward was offered to any who would betray him to his enemies, but these honest farmers cared neither for threats nor rewards."

"How much was the reward?" Davis asked.

"A thousand pounds."

"A *thousand* pounds?" Davis's eyes widened. "Are you sure?"

A thousand pounds was an absolutely vast sum, more than the average workman would earn in a lifetime.

"I'm sure," Colin assured him. "Charles cut off his famous black lovelocks so no one would recognize him. The Penderels dressed him like themselves, in clothes belonging to the tallest brother, for the king is over two yards tall."

"Like you?" little Mary asked, gazing up at Colin as though he were a giant.

Colin nodded solemnly while quelling a smile. "Yes, Charles and I are almost exactly the same height. He had to wear his own stockings with the fancy tops torn off, because his feet were so big they could find none to fit. And the clumsy country boots they gave him were too small, so he was forced to tramp around all day in great pain."

"Ouch!" said the apple-cheeked boy.

"Indeed. In fact, King Charles's memory of those boots is so strong that today he has the largest collection of shoes in the land, each pair made exactly to fit."

A couple of the children giggled. Colin glanced at Kendra. She was still smiling down at her embroidery. So far as he could tell, she'd yet to complete a single new stitch.

"What happened then?" an impatient little voice asked. The girl had long dark hair and gray eyes, and Colin realized with a pang that she reminded him of Amy.

He gave his head a shake as though to clear it. "I'm just getting to the good part. One day, while the king was with the brothers in the forest, Parliamentary soldiers came upon them. Quickly, Charles climbed up an oak tree and crouched amid the leaves."

"How long did he stay there?" Mary asked.

"More than twenty-four hours, a whole day and night. The soldiers were certain they'd seen more men, so they rode back and forth searching all that time."

"How many soldiers?" Mary asked.

Colin shrugged. "I don't know, sweetheart."

"How many?" she persisted.

In a quandary, he glanced again at Kendra. She looked up, biting her lip to keep from laughing.

No help there.

"Seven," he announced finally. "I'm certain there were seven."

When the little girl smiled happily, Colin tugged one of her bright gold curls. "Charles slept for a time in the tree. When he woke, the soldiers were directly under him, saying how glad they should be to catch him. Hoping they wouldn't notice him there, Charles held his breath."

Hearing the children's indrawn breaths brought him a ridiculous sense of satisfaction.

"Finally, the next day, the soldiers rode off and left him to get down in safety." Little breaths were released. "That tree, in memory of the good service it had done him, was afterwards named the Royal Oak, and if ever you go to Boscobel you can visit it," he said by way of conclusion.

"What happened *then*?" asked a boy. "How did he escape?"

Colin glanced toward Kendra, but she was smiling back down at her handiwork. "Yes, Colin," she said to a misshapen embroidered flower. "What happened then?"

"Hmmph," he said, wishing she were close enough to kick her. "The brothers were afraid the Roundheads would return when they couldn't find Charles elsewhere, so they moved him to another house, a few miles away. They had to find him a horse to ride there, because he couldn't walk that far on his aching feet. The boots, remember?"

Nine little heads nodded.

"He hid in a priest-hole in that house, and he was very cramped and uncomfortable in there."

"Because he's so tall," said little Mary.

"Exactly. Charles needed to get to Bristol to catch a ship and escape England," he continued, "but he couldn't travel in the farmer's clothes, since farmers don't often take to the roads. So they dressed him as a manservant and found a loyal woman named Lady Jane to ride behind him on a horse, posing as his employer. He decided to call himself William Jackson, and they made up a story that they were on their way to a wedding."

"Whose wedding?" Mary asked.

A smothered laugh came from Kendra.

Colin's mind raced. His gaze swept the chamber. "Lord Cornice and Lady Chimneypiece."

He would swear Kendra was choking. Not that she didn't deserve to.

He cleared his throat. "Charles and Lady Jane playacted all the way to Bristol. One day Charles's horse cast a shoe, and as he held the mare's foot for the blacksmith, he asked the man if there was any news since the battle."

Mary's blue eyes were round as saucers. "What did the man say?"

"He told Charles that some of the Royalists had been found and arrested, but not yet Charles Stuart. The Roundheads called the king by the name of Stuart."

"Then the blacksmith was a Roundhead," Davis surmised. "Wasn't Charles afraid to talk to him?"

"Not Charles. But Lady Jane, she was having a fright. And what do you suppose our good king said then?"

"What?" the children chorused.

"He told the smith, 'If that rogue Charles Stuart is taken, he deserves to be hanged, more than all the rest.'"

"He didn't," Davis breathed.

"He surely did. Charles enjoyed his jest, but Lady Jane nearly expired on the spot."

"I don't blame her," said the dark-haired girl. "Not at all."

"Me, neither," Kendra put in with a raised brow. "That prank brings to mind one of my brothers."

"Let me finish," Colin scolded. "Lady Jane breathed more easily when the shoeing was done and they could be on their way. But at Bristol they were disappointed. For a whole month, there was no ship sailing to France or Spain. So Charles had to hide about the countryside again until they finally found a ship that could take him to France. The ship was named the *Surprise*, but it's now called the *Royal Escape*."

He stood. "And *that* is the end of the story. Time for bed, children. We've a long trip back to London in the morning." He flexed his shoulders and stretched.

Applause came from the doorway behind him. He turned to see his brothers, faces and clothing black with the soot of London's fire.

"Welcome back!" Kendra sprang up to greet them, her embroidery landing unceremoniously on the floor. She hugged them each in turn. "How did you like our storyteller?"

"Watch your gown; we're both sorely in need of a bath," Jason admonished. He aimed an exaggerated nod toward Colin. "I would have liked to attend the Cornice–Chimneypiece wedding. Pity that we were too young."

"Colin certainly rose to the occasion," Kendra said. "I all but forced him into it—in a sisterly way, of course." When Colin snorted at that, she flashed him an innocent smile. "Whatever made you think of that particular story?"

"Do you not remember? We must have heard Charles tell it a hundred times on the Continent. It was all but our nightly entertainment." He looked to Jason. "You brought Ebony with you, I'm hoping?"

"We're both fine," Jason drawled. "Thank you so much for asking." He turned to Ford. "So nice of him to inquire after us before thinking of his horse."

Ford shrugged. "It's not as though we've spent three days battling flames, exposing ourselves to the dangers of falling walls and debris—"

"No, nothing like that," Jason agreed. "Nothing that would compare to the hazards of telling a bedtime story."

"Oh, that's not all he's been doing. You don't know the half of it." Kendra rolled her eyes toward where Amy slept upstairs, and Colin moved closer, intending to elbow her in the ribs.

With a laugh, she dodged out of his way. "We'll see the children to bed. You two go clean up, and we'll meet you back here with some supper."

SIXTEEN

*A*MY WOKE to the sound of low voices nearby. She kept her eyes shut tight—she had no intention of letting anyone know she was conscious just yet—but even so, she could tell from the color inside her lids that morning had arrived.

Finally.

Several times during the interminable night, she'd awakened and floated to the surface of awareness, first hearing the soft crackling from the fireplace, then feeling the persistent burning in her right palm. And then she'd remember—and immediately force herself back into the depths of slumber. Back to where it was last week, and she wasn't alone in the world, and her only worry was her upcoming nuptials.

Once, she'd sensed a presence in the chamber and slitted her eyes open, peeking through her lids to see Colin watching her, his profile dark against the light of the flickering fire. She'd shut her eyes and lain perfectly still, feigning sleep until he left. He'd sighed heavily before closing the door behind him.

What kind of sigh had it been? she'd wondered vaguely as she lapsed back to her troubled dreams. A sigh of concern, or a sigh of exasperation?

He certainly seemed to be exasperated now.

"I need this deuced business over and done with," she heard him say. "I've responsibilities to get back to."

"Well, it's not to be," a deeper voice answered reasonably. His older brother, Amy reckoned. So the brothers were back. "You'll have to deliver the children without her. You're not going to haul her around the countryside unconscious, are you?"

"Of course not!" Colin snapped.

"Shh! She might be ill, you know, if she's been sleeping this long." A younger, slightly scratchy voice. The other brother.

She heard a couple of footsteps, then a warm palm pressed onto her forehead and rested there a few seconds. Colin. It had to be. "She's not hot," she heard him say from right above her head. "And I checked her hand again last night. There's no infection."

Amy's stomach fluttered at the thought of him caring for her while she slept. Perhaps she should let him know she'd awakened...

No! He'd take her away, ship her to France, and she wasn't ready to go. Aunt Elizabeth was kind, but she'd smothered Amy with concern following her mother's death. She couldn't face that yet; she needed a few days to think about things, to come to some kind of peace within herself.

Better to pretend she still slept.

"It won't be a simple matter to find a chaperone in London right now," Amy heard Kendra pointing out. "And you cannot just plop her on a ship by herself."

"That's true," he admitted grudgingly.

"You'd better go," Kendra advised. "The wagon is packed, and the children are waiting. She's not going to magically wake up, and even if she did, it would take her too long to get ready. She hasn't eaten in two days."

"More like four days," Colin grumbled. The voices receded, accompanied by footsteps. "I suppose you're right."

"We'll have her ready and waiting when you return," Amy strained to hear Kendra say before the voices faded away entirely.

Amazingly, Amy Goldsmith woke up the minute Colin's wagon rattled over the drawbridge.

SEVENTEEN

"*I* RETURNED to take her to Dover and put her on a ship, and hang it, that's what I'm going to do!"

After three days spent weeping, thinking, and healing, Amy had approached Kendra that very afternoon and shyly asked about joining the family for supper. She'd been certain she felt ready for some human interaction.

But now that Colin was home, she wasn't so sure.

In the corridor outside the drawing room, she stood frozen in place, listening. The Chases made an incredible racket. Amy and her parents had rarely shouted at one another, but this family seemed to use shouting as their main mode of communication. Even when they'd discussed her at her bedside, she reflected, they'd shouted in whispers.

Tonight, they were none so circumspect.

"I promised her, Colin!" she heard Kendra wail. "I promised she could stay here until she's ready."

"Ready? What on earth is that supposed to mean? She's awake, she's ready."

"I'm not quite certain she's awake," Ford's scratchy, adolescent voice put in, with more than a little amusement. "She's been wandering around like a ghost."

Amy winced. Was that what they thought of her?

"She has not!" Kendra leapt to Amy's defense. "Her father just died, for heaven's sake. I promised her."

"A pox on your promises! I need to get back to Greystone. I needed to be there a week ago."

"Jason?" By the tone of Kendra's voice, Amy imagined her looking toward her brother beseechingly.

"A Chase promise is not given lightly." Jason, the voice of reason.

"A pox on you, too!"

"I agree with them, Colin. Promises aside, she's in no state for travel." So Ford was on her side as well.

"A pox on all three of you! I don't care who agrees with whom. I brought her here, and I'll take her away when I please."

"I promised her!"

"You sound like one of those newfangled cuckoo clocks, Kendra. 'I promised her, I promised her, I promised her.' Well, cuckoo all you want; I'm not changing my mind. We're leaving come morning. Where is she? You said she was coming to supper."

Amy took a step back down the corridor.

"Your arrival probably scared her into the next county!" Kendra yelled.

"You're both acting like children!" Amy heard Jason shout while she steadily backed away from the room. "Colin, this is out of your hands. Go to Greystone in the morning. I'll arrange for Mrs. Goldsmith's travel when she's ready. Kendra, go fetch her. We'll meet you in the dining room in half an hour."

Amy fled up the stairs to her chamber and was sitting primly on the edge of her bed when Kendra arrived.

Her friend stood in the doorway, frowning. "It's nearly time for supper. You're...not planning to wear that gown, are you?"

Amy looked down to her skirts. The lavender dress had been laundered and pressed while she slept, but there were a few tiny holes where embers had landed, and little gray spots where the soot had stained it permanently. She'd worn it three days straight already.

Her face burned. "I haven't another," she said to her lap.

"Wait here a moment." Kendra started to leave, then reappeared in the doorway. "Oh, Colin is back." She disappeared again, yelling "Jane!" as she went.

Wondering what Kendra was up to, Amy ran her hand down the gilt bedpost beside her for what seemed like the millionth time since she'd awakened in this beautiful room a few days ago. It wasn't the costliness of the gold that stole her breath, for gold was so soft and pliable that she could hammer a single ounce into a hundred square feet of gold leaf. But she thought the intricately carved bed looked like nothing so much as a gigantic, exquisite piece of jewelry, and—with a fresh stab of grief—she wished she could show it to her father.

All of the room's furnishings were gilt, marble, or golden brocade. Amy felt like she was living in Queen Catharine's bedchamber.

A floral fragrance suffused the air. She shuffled her smoke-damaged shoes where they rested on a plush patterned carpet of brown, cream and gold. At home, the floors had been polished wood. Her family had owned two precious Oriental carpets, but the larger one had adorned a wall, the smaller, a table. Before arriving at Cainewood, she'd never considered actually *walking* on anything so expensive as a carpet.

Kendra came back leading Jane, a plain-faced young maid with a kind smile and an armful of dresses. Kendra grabbed a yellow one from the pile and held it up to Amy's cheek. "No, too sallow," she muttered, tossing it aside. The next was peach. "Too pale." Jane handed her another, a burgundy satin. "Perfect," Kendra declared.

Before Amy could protest, her gown was removed and Kendra's dropped over her head. A rose scent wafted from the fabric. Wiggling into the dress, she inhaled the luxurious fragrance, thinking the Chases lived a different life indeed.

It wasn't *her* life, though. Her life would never feel complete without her craft. Without the thrill of working raw stones and metal into lasting bits of beauty.

Jane laced up the bodice, attached the stomacher, and tucked up the skirt to reveal a shell-pink underskirt. She plucked Amy's chemise through the slashed sleeves, which were caught together at intervals with pink ribbons. Then she seated Amy before the oval gilt-framed mirror and began fussing with her hair.

"I cannot figure out how to plait it properly." Amy tugged up her lace-edged chemise to fill in the gown's low neckline. "Our maid used to entwine ribbons somehow."

"Oh, curls are the fashion now." Kendra waved a hand. "Have you decided what you're going to do?"

What *was* she going to do? Amy stared at her reflection. Without her father to force the issue, the one thing she *wouldn't* do was marry Robert Stanley. She would have to write soon to tell him so.

"Not entirely." She sat very still as Jane wielded a hot curling iron. "Go to Paris, to my aunt and uncle's jewelry shop, is what I *should* do." She toyed with a bottle on the marble-topped dressing table. "I promised my father I'd never give up my craft...and jewelry is my life. I know no other."

"Well, you needn't leave until you feel ready. I promised you that."

"Thank you." Her eyes met Kendra's in the looking glass. "You're a good friend."

Jane tied a pink ribbon in Amy's hair and stepped back to view her handiwork. "What do you think?" She reached out and tweaked a curl.

"Beautiful," Kendra said.

Amy gazed at her reflection, touching a finger to her lips. The lips Colin had kissed. Maybe, just maybe, she would find a young man—another jeweler—in France. A jeweler who could make her feel like Colin did.

"No time for cosmetics," Kendra said with a sigh. "We're late already."

EIGHTEEN

"*W*HERE ARE they all?" Ford lifted the decanter of wine. "Kendra and Amy I can credit—girls always take forever to ready themselves. But Colin—"

Jason wrested the wine from Ford and, with a meaningful look, refilled his youngest brother's goblet only halfway. "Speaking of Colin, I think Kendra is scheming to match him with Amethyst Goldsmith."

"Huh?" Ford shook his head. "Whyever would Kendra do that?"

"I'm sure I don't know. Mrs. Goldsmith has no fortune to offer. It's debatable whether a well-to-do merchant could meet Greystone's financial needs, and now that her family's shop has burned to the ground, the question is moot."

Ford sipped. "She's quite pretty, though."

"What on earth has that got to do with it?" Jason lifted his goblet. "I know Priscilla doesn't top Kendra's list of favorite people, but for her to push this match—" He stopped and took a quick swallow of wine. "Colin, there you are."

Colin narrowed his eyes in suspicion. "What were you two speaking of?"

Ford jumped in. "We were just wondering if you'd managed to match up all the children with their families in London?"

"Yes—and no." Colin took his seat. "It seems the littlest one,

Mary, is an orphan. Her parents both died in the plague. Neighbors had taken her in, but now that they're homeless..." He shrugged. "I brought her back with me."

Jason nearly spilled his wine. "You cannot be planning to keep her?"

"Priscilla would never put up with it," Ford put in.

Colin flashed him a scathing glance. "No, I'm not planning to keep her." He turned to Jason. "I was hoping you could find her a home in the village."

"I expect I can." Jason's hand came up and smoothed his mustache, his eyes thoughtful. "But couldn't you have left her at a foundling home in London?"

"I could have, I suppose." Colin reached for the decanter. "The authorities are handling such problems. But I hadn't the heart to leave her in such chaos. Moorfields is a sad scene. The grass is littered with rescued belongings that people are wary of relinquishing, covered in ashes—"

When Kendra and Amy walked in, Colin paused midsentence and stared.

Jason cleared his throat and kicked his brother beneath the table. "Colin?"

"Um, yes." Colin's hand dropped, and the wine decanter thudded to the mahogany surface. He blinked and came back to life. "Good evening, Amy."

"Good evening," Amy murmured, not quite looking at him.

"Won't you sit down?" Jason waved his hand, and a servant began ladling soup while two others pulled out ladder-backed chairs on either side of the rectangular table, at the end where the Chase brothers had seated themselves.

Kendra craftily slipped into the chair beside her twin, leaving Amy no choice but to sit next to Colin. As she seated herself, Colin smiled and offered her wine.

In the guise of reaching for a piece of cake, Kendra leaned close to Jason. "Look at the two of them together," she whispered in his ear. "You'd have to be addlepated not to notice."

"I heard that!" Colin's face was aflame, his eyes trained down, avoiding Amy's.

Amy just looked confused.

"Colin was just telling us about returning the children to their families," Ford said a little too brightly. "It sounds a mess out there."

"It's getting organized somewhat," Colin told his soup. "Charles has arranged for public buildings to store the goods of the homeless, and provided army tents and bread, all without charge. It was impossible to get about to find anyone, but they've set up a missing persons area. I waited there until all the children were claimed—all except Mary, that is."

A frown appeared between Kendra's brows. "The curly-haired girl with the never-ending questions?"

He nodded. "I brought her back with me. If I had a shilling for every question she asked on the way here, I'd be able to restore Greystone tomorrow."

Kendra smiled. "And our town house?" She spooned up a bite of cake; Kendra always ate dessert first, in case she might not have room for it later.

"The town house is safe—Lincoln's Inn Fields was never in danger. The fire stopped short of Chancery Lane and Essex House. But the burned parts smolder so hotly, no man would venture in. The first rain started this afternoon, though—I reckon that will help."

"It rained but a few minutes." Kendra glanced out the diamond-paned windows. "I shouldn't think it would help much."

"Perchance it rained more in London." Colin shrugged. "Though with all the homeless, I suppose we should hope not..."

He was having trouble concentrating with Amy seated beside him. A rose scent drifted over from her direction. Having left her weak and stricken and sleep-shrouded, he'd been astonished when the old Amy entered the dining room.

Well, not quite the old Amy. Not precisely. This Amy was more subdued and sort of Kendra-ized, wearing a dress he recognized as Kendra's, with her hair coaxed into long, Kendra-like ringlets.

And she wore not a speck of jewelry. That separated her most from the old Amy. That, and her reserve. She seemed to be eating in a trance-like state.

But he felt the same something between them nonetheless.

"And Charles?" asked Ford.

If Colin could inch his chair to the right...

No, too obvious.

If he moved his knee beneath the table...

Ford banged down his goblet impatiently. "Colin? How is the king holding up?"

Jason kicked Colin again.

"Ouch!" Colin blinked. What had Ford been asking about? "Oh, Charles. Heavens, he's in his glory. He hadn't much time to chat, though."

He rubbed his ankle, thinking he'd deserved the kick. What was it about this girl that made him forget anyone else existed? Why could he think of nothing but touching her?

He was worse than flustered. He was...sappy!

Thank heavens he was leaving for Greystone in the morning.

Before he turned into a complete dolt.

NINETEEN

*A*MY SPOONED soup, letting the conversation swirl around her. The buzz was calming, soothing. Like layers of flannel protected jewelry, the family's chatter protected her from her own thoughts.

"Did you pay Charles a visit at Whitehall?" Kendra asked Colin.

The question startled Amy from her trance.

At Whitehall? she mouthed silently. Was this family on intimate terms with the king? She sneaked Colin an incredulous sidelong glance, then chided herself.

Why should she be surprised? The Chases lived in a castle, after all. Jason was a marquess, Colin an earl, Ford a something-or-other...a viscount, that was it. Titles all granted by Charles, Kendra had told her, explaining the unusual situation.

Colin shifted beside her. "No, Charles rode out to Moorfields. The stories of his heroism during the fire spread quickly, and those who didn't witness it are as loyal as those who did. He sat on his horse in the midst of the crowd, the ruins of St. Paul's in the background, smoke hanging over the rubble of the City, and he vowed, by the grace of God, to take particular care of all Londoners, by means of grand plans for rebuilding. Cheers went up..." Colin grinned. "Old Charles is a popular man these days."

Painted by Colin's vivid words, Amy could picture the scene

in her head: King Charles, seated tall atop his horse, addressing his adoring subjects. It was history in the making, and she loved history.

She sighed in satisfaction.

"What are these plans?" Jason asked. "Did he elaborate?"

"He issued a proclamation that all new construction should be done according to a proscribed plan, so that London would— let me see if I can remember his words—'rather appear to the world as purged with fire to a wonderful beauty and comeliness, than consumed by it' and 'no man whatsoever shall presume to erect any house or building, great or small, but of brick or stone.' I think I got the words right, but that was the gist of it, regardless."

Amy smiled to herself at Colin's precise descriptions; it had been the same when he showed her the castle. Dates, words...he paid attention to detail.

But one detail she was certain of was that he didn't want her here. He'd as much as said he couldn't wait to get rid of her. Still, she could swear she felt a warmth emanating from him, an inviting warmth that seemed to reach out and draw her in.

It was the very oddest feeling. And confusing.

"It sounds like a good plan," said Ford.

Colin nodded. "Charles also decreed wider streets so buildings on one side cannot catch fire from the other. He's appointing Christopher Wren as...let's see...'Deputy Surveyor and Principal Architect for Rebuilding the Whole City.'" He smiled at the grandiose title. "Wren is charged with drawing up a plan of boulevards and plazas and straight streets."

"Charles announced all of this?"

"He told me of Wren privately. It's not official yet. Wren was supposed to have the plans ready to submit today, and then an announcement will be made."

"A new London, rising from the ashes," Amy murmured, staring at one of the chamber's enormous tapestries, but imagining instead what this bright new city might look like.

Colin turned to her. "What did you say?"

"Nothing," she mumbled.

He looked at her with that soul-piercing gaze of his, then

cleared his throat and turned back to the others. "Did you know that Wren's plan for restoring St. Paul's was accepted by the Commission just two weeks ago?"

"And now St. Paul's is burned to the ground," Jason said with a mournful shake of his head. "If I hadn't seen it with my own eyes, I would never have believed this much destruction possible."

"Two-thirds of London is gone," Colin lamented, "and more than half the people are homeless. But, miraculously, it seems that only eight lives were lost." He put a hand on Amy's arm. "I'm sorry your father had to be one of them."

Colin's touch startled Amy out of her vision, dragged her back into the real world. She nodded, but couldn't meet his eyes. It wasn't fair. Only eight dead, and her own father one of them…

Her spoon halfway to her mouth, she paused, swallowed a swiftly rising lump in her throat, and fought back the tears. It was a losing battle. Suddenly, she rose. Her spoon clattered in the bowl where she dropped it.

"Excuse me," she apologized huskily, hastening from the room.

∾

"*Y*OU LOUT!" Kendra threw down her spoon. "This was her first supper in company."

"What did I say?"

"'I'm sorry your father had to be one of them,'" Ford mimicked in a mincing voice. "Egad, Colin, *I'm* the one who's supposed to be tactless."

"I said I was sorry," Colin protested feebly. He twisted his ring, listening to Amy's footsteps fade as she reached the top of the stairs and turned down the corridor.

"Leave Colin alone," Jason said. "He's confused enough as it is."

"What on earth is that supposed to mean?" Colin demanded.

"Just that you have feelings for Mrs. Goldsmith, and you haven't decided what to do about them."

"*What?*" Ford burst out in surprise.

Kendra snorted, rolled her eyes toward the arched stone ceiling, then focused on her twin. "You are so oblivious. If something cannot be weighed or measured, it fails to command your attention."

Colin's hands clenched. "I don't have feelings for Amy—"

"Are you lying only to us, or to yourself as well?" Kendra fixed him with a pointed stare.

He glared right back. "She's an emotional wreck!"

"So what?" Kendra asked.

"So I'm leaving in the morning, most likely before she rises, and Jason will see that she gets to France, where she will recover in peace and never see any of us again. That's what."

"Now, Colin—" Kendra began.

"Leave it be, Kendra." Jason looked at each of his siblings in turn, signaling that the conversation was at an end. Then, food being the typical Chase cure-all for most unpleasant situations, he rang for the servants. "I'm ready for that roast venison. How about the rest of you?"

TWENTY

*A*MY BIT her lip and added another crumpled ball to the small mountain of paper that was growing on the gilt dressing table in her bedchamber.

Why couldn't she get this right?

She flexed her hand. Though the blisters had healed, sometimes it still hurt if she overused it. One more try. She dipped her quill in the ink.

26 September 1666

Dear Robert,

Perhaps you already know that I lost Papa and the shop in the fire. I am devastated. I've lost everything. My entire life has changed, and I'm afraid yours as well. Please forgive me, but I cannot marry you—

"May I come in, Lady Amy?" Small fingers tapped on Amy's shoulder.

She looked up to see big blue eyes in an angelic face framed by golden curls. "I think you already have come in, Mary." Smiling, she set down her quill and let the child climb into her lap. "But I'm not a lady. Plain Amy will do."

"You look like a lady."

"But that's only because I'm wearing Lady Kendra's dress."

Mary squirmed out of Amy's lap almost immediately and flounced away to the bed.

Growing up, Amy had never spent much time with small children—at least not since she was one herself. She watched as the little girl mounted the bed steps, stretched out her arms and, with a whoop of delight, flung herself facedown on the costly brocade counterpane.

Mary was a peculiar little thing.

"I'm wearing Lady Kendra's dress, too," Mary declared, the words muffled against the golden fabric.

"And so you are!" The dress hung loose on her small frame and was hopelessly out of style. But she was thrilled with her new wardrobe. Kendra had found an old trunk filled with her childhood gowns, and Mary had worn a different one every day since her arrival. "And a lovely dress it is. Are you a lady then, Mary?"

"Nay." Mary giggled and sat up. "Are you sure you're not a lady? You live in this fancy place."

"Not really." Amy's gaze swept the gorgeous gilt chamber. "Before the fire, I lived all my life in London."

"Like me?" Mary pointed her thumb—a thumb that looked recently sucked—at her own chest.

"Just like you. In Cheapside."

"My house was in…" Her little face scrunched up as she thought. "Ludgate."

"Ludgate Hill? Then see, we were almost neighbors."

Mary's feet swung back and forth off the end of the bed. "And your mama and papa are dead like mine."

Suppressing a familiar twinge of sorrow, Amy nodded patiently. An eavesdropper would never guess they'd had this conversation at least a dozen times already. "Yes, my mama and papa are gone as well."

"And they're never coming back."

"No." She bit her lip. "They're never coming back. But I think about them all the time, so their memory lives on."

Mary jumped off the bed. "How many days has it been?" One little hand reached up to the marble-topped dressing table and snagged a silver comb. "How many days since the fire?"

"How many days was it yesterday, Mary?"

"Um..." Her tiny fingers traced the fine-etched roses on the comb's grip. "Twenty-something?"

"Twenty-one." Amy took the comb from her and faced Mary away so she could untangle her golden ringlets. "So today, how many days has it been since the fire?"

The girl raised one short finger, then popped up another. "Two. Twenty-two." Her voice was full of pride.

"Very good, twenty-two days." The comb made a pleasant swishing sound as Amy drew it through Mary's hair again and again.

"My mama died of the plague. How many days since that?"

"Oh, sweetheart, I couldn't tell you." Amy sighed. "A lot."

"More than a hundred?"

"More than three hundred."

Mary's eyes widened in the mirror. "That *is* a lot."

"Surely it is." Finished, Amy turned her back around. "And inside, it hurts a little bit less every day, does it not?"

"Maybe. A little bit." Mary's chin trembled for a second, then she picked up Amy's letter and stared at it uncomprehendingly. "Who're you writin' to?"

"Someone I knew in London." Amy set the comb back in place. "In fact, I think I'm finished."

She took the letter from Mary. It would have to do. It was blunt, but she couldn't seem to get the words right no matter how hard she tried.

Perhaps Robert would be relieved. He might think that her promised value as a bride had been reduced by the loss of the shop. He'd be free to wed elsewhere, free to find someone who could be the sort of wife he wanted.

That is, if he could find another eligible heiress in the jewelry trade...which might prove difficult. But Amy had enough difficulties of her own to be getting on with.

She lifted her quill, dipped it in the ink, and put a period after the last word she'd written. *Please forgive me, but I cannot marry you.* Mary's thumb went into her mouth as she watched Amy sign her name: *Amethyst Goldsmith*, very neat and formal.

After blotting the ink with sand, Amy folded the letter. She wrote Robert's name and his father's address on the back, then set it aside, adding no return address.

There, it was done.

And Robert wouldn't be able to find her.

"How about this one?" The thumb popped out and jabbed at another letter. "Who is this one to?"

"My aunt in Paris. I'm going to move there and live with her soon. But not too very soon, I'm hoping." Amy smiled at Mary's wet thumbprint on her letter. "I like it here with you."

"I like it here, too." Mary's rosy lips pouted. "But I wish I had a mama."

"Lord Cainewood is going to find you a new mama very soon. He promised, remember?"

The girl nodded.

"A Chase promise is not given lightly."

"What?" Her small brow creased.

"He always keeps his promises."

Apparently that was good enough for Mary. She jabbed the letter again. "What did you say to your aunt?"

"I told her how sad I am about my father." Amy rose from the dressing table and wandered to the diamond-paned window. Below, a servant hurried across the quadrangle, carrying a basket of laundry, leaving footprints in the damp grass. "Sometimes it helps you feel better to write a letter about your sadness."

"Like if I wrote a letter to Mama?"

Beside the window hung a gilt-framed painting of a woman. Colin's grandmother, perhaps. Or great-grandmother. Her clothes looked to Amy like they belonged in the previous century. "You surely could write a letter to your mama. It might make you feel better." Neither she nor Mary had paintings to remember their ancestors by.

"I cannot write."

Amy turned to the girl. "Would you like me to write your letter for you?"

She nodded, her eyes shining.

They seated themselves together at the dressing table and Amy set a sheet of foolscap on the marble surface. "What would you like to say?"

Mary stared at the blank sheet. "Dear Mama, I love you, Mama. I miss you, Mama."

Amy dipped her quill and wrote, her throat closing painfully as the words scrolled onto the page. She swallowed hard. "Anything else?"

"That's all I can think of," the little girl said gravely.

"It's a perfect letter. Would you like to sign your name?" She handed Mary the quill. With a look of utter disbelief on her face, Mary thrust it joyfully into the ink, splattering the page, then scribbled something that Amy took for a signature. For good measure, she added a very crooked heart and a pair of stickpeople that might have been Mary and her mother, holding hands. Amy was afraid to ask.

In fact, she was afraid to speak at all. When she did, her voice came out raspy. "Here, sweetheart, you can fold it."

Mary folded, and if the edges didn't line up, well, it certainly didn't matter. "Will Mama get it in heaven?" she asked.

"If you give it a kiss, she'll get it right away."

Her rosy little lips puckered and kissed the letter gently, leaving a tiny wet mark. Amy imagined it was exactly the way Mary used to kiss her mother. Tears pricked her eyes. She found her arms wrapping themselves around the girl and squeezing tight.

"Did Mama get my letter?"

"Surely she did."

"Even though it's still here?"

"Even though. There is special mail delivery to heaven."

Mary nodded. Children were so trusting. "Will Mama write me back?"

"In your dreams, sweetheart," Amy promised, needing to believe it. "When you go to sleep tonight, your mama will visit your dreams and remind you how much she loves you."

TWENTY-ONE

"*I*'VE NEVER been in a fancy carriage." Mary bounced on the leather seat. "It goes slow. Why didn't we ride a horse?"

"Your friend Amy doesn't like horses," Jason said. "We would have had to leave her at home."

"No, I want Amy." Mary jumped up and onto Amy's lap, then turned to peer across at Jason. "Did you really find me a mama?"

He angled sideways to stretch his legs in the cabin. "I surely did, Miss Mary."

"When will I meet her?"

"In a few minutes, as soon as we get to the village."

Mary's thumb went into her mouth, then slid back out. "Why does she want a little girl?"

"She lost her husband last year, and she needs someone to love."

Amy knew Clarice also needed the money Jason would provide for Mary's care. It was the perfect solution all around.

"If her husband is lost," Mary said, "why does she not just look for him?"

Amy stifled a laugh. "He died in a mill accident, sweetheart."

"Oh." The girl's legs swung back and forth, kicking Amy's

shins until she lowered a hand to stop them. "Why do big people say that someone is lost? Why can't they just say he is dead?"

"My, you are full of questions, aren't you?" Jason said.

"Will I have any brothers or sisters?"

"I'm afraid not. Mr. and Mrs. Bradford never had children of their own." Jason's hand went up to smooth his mustache, then he smiled. "That's why she wants a little girl so badly."

"Will she love me?"

"How could she not?" Jason reached to tweaked Mary's nose. "And you will love her too, Mary, I promise."

"A Chase promise is not given lightly," Mary quoted solemnly.

His jaw went slack in surprise. "What did you say?"

"That means you always keep your promises. Amy told me."

"Oh." Jason and Amy shared a smile over the girl's head. "Well, she's right, you know."

"Amy is always right." Mary craned her neck to see out the open carriage window. "Is that the village? Ooh, pretty!"

Amy's gaze went to follow hers. "Much prettier than London, isn't it? And cleaner."

"It smells nice, too. Every house has flowers."

Mary watched, rapt, as they passed several more houses and rolled to a stop before a small white cottage with a thatched roof. The coachman hadn't finished opening the door and lowering the steps before Clarice Bradford rushed out to meet them, holding a new rag doll.

Mary bounded down the steps and right into her outstretched arms.

For a long moment they clung together. Then they pulled back to give each other a considered look. Clarice reached trembling fingers to touch Mary's bright curls.

She looked to Jason, who had followed Amy from the carriage into the cottage's tidy garden. "Oh, she's beautiful, my lord."

Mary's head tilted up, then slowly went down as she took in the glossy blond plaited bun that sat atop Clarice's head, her gray eyes set in a delicate-featured face, her simple tan dress, and the plain black shoes that peeked from beneath her skirts. "You're beautiful too, Mama."

The gray eyes filled with grateful tears.

"Is this doll for me?" Mary asked.

"Just for you. I sat up all night making it." Too excited to sleep, Amy guessed. Yesterday, when she and Jason visited to propose the arrangement, Clarice had been overcome with joy.

"Thank you, Mama. She's beautiful, too. I'll name her Amy." Mary clutched the doll close as she watched the coachman and outrider carry Kendra's trunk into Clarice's cottage. Her blue eyes widened. "Do I get to keep all those clothes?"

Jason nodded. "With Lady Kendra's compliments."

"And..." Moving closer, Amy pulled something from her pocket. "Lord Cainewood gave me permission to leave this with you, as a memento of our time together. I hope it will help you remember me."

The engraved silver comb sparkled in the sunshine as Mary took it, staring at it as though it were one of King Charles's crown jewels. "Oh, my lady—I mean, Amy! I will 'member you always."

Amy lifted her up, blinking back tears as Mary's little arms wound around her neck. She hugged her back fiercely.

When Amy let go, Jason knelt down in the grass before Mary. "Will you be all right here with Clarice?"

"Yes." Her hand shot out and tweaked his nose. Jason rubbed his face in surprise as Mary scurried to Clarice's side and reached up to take her hand. "I'm home now," she said.

Amy couldn't help thinking: *When will I be home?*

TWENTY-TWO

*K*ENDRA DASHED into the library and leaned against the large globe, breathless. "Amy," she panted. "It's Colin." She paused for more air. "He's here. What are we going to do?"

Amy felt as though she'd been punched in the stomach. "Dear heavens," she whispered. "He's come to take me away, hasn't he?"

She looked up to the carved wood ceiling, her eyes tracing the intricate design while her mind wrestled with denial. "There's nothing we *can* do," she said finally, her gaze dropping to Kendra. "I'm lucky he stayed away this long—"

"You fit in here. I don't want you to leave."

Kendra's words warmed Amy's heart. She rose from the chair and gave Kendra a brief, sisterly hug. "Thank you for saying that; you'll never know how much it means to me." She sniffed back tears. "I've enjoyed every minute of my month here. But I have another life."

Kendra's brow furrowed in concern. "A life in Paris?"

"It's not so bad as all that," Amy said, remembering Colin telling her so outside the inn, after the fire. A long time ago, it seemed, but now she believed it. "As much as I love it here, this isn't my place. I'm a Goldsmith. I need to create, to cast and polish and engrave."

Indeed, her fingers fairly itched to make jewelry. Her hands clenched as her gaze dropped to the red-carpeted floor and ran along the wide decorative golden stripes, down the length of the long, narrow library to the fireplace. Kendra remained silent while Amy gazed into the distant flames, struggling with her feelings of being uprooted once again.

But she knew it was the only way. Robert must have received her letter and accepted her decision by now…and if not, well, he'd never find her in France. She'd work at Aunt Elizabeth's shop while she prepared to open her own.

She'd vowed that Goldsmith & Sons wouldn't die with her, and she meant to honor that vow.

Her trunk was gathering dust in the corner of her borrowed bedchamber, her inheritance locked inside. More than enough jewelry to stock a small shop, plus gold to pay for tools and equipment—gold that would be faithfully replaced as soon as she was able. She'd never deplete the Goldsmith fortune. Like the generations before her, she bore an obligation.

Kendra heaved a mournful sigh. "If you leave, I'll miss you."

Amy tried to smile. "Mayhap I'll hide in here till Colin leaves. Up on the balconies—no one ever looks at the books there except me. You can sneak up food and tell him I've gone to Paris."

Kendra's laugh echoed through the two-story library. "I vow and swear, for a minute there I thought you were serious." She relaxed and leaned back against the brass mesh set into the bookshelf doors, then looked at Amy sharply. "You *are* fooling, aren't you?"

"Marry come up, Kendra! Have you ever heard of anything more ludicrous?"

"Oh, fine. I'll go find out what Colin wants."

"We both know what Colin wants."

Kendra rolled her eyes as she straightened up. "*Colin* doesn't know what Colin wants. I'll just see what kind of ideas I can plant in his head." And with that cryptic statement, she left the room.

Amy plopped back onto the chair. The history books in front of her had seemed fascinating a few minutes ago, but now they'd lost their appeal. She pushed them aside and laid her head on the exquisite mosaic table, the tiles cool beneath her cheek. She would miss this family, but she knew her life was destined along another path.

You cannot have everything, she heard her father say.

She sighed and rose to go ready herself for supper. If she hurried, perhaps she'd have time to take a walk around the grounds and think things through. But deep in her heart, she knew there was really nothing to think about.

This was it. Her time was up. Colin wanted her gone, and this time he would see it done.

She had no excuses left.

TWENTY-THREE

*J*ASON HAD plenty of excuses.

In the midst of shouting at his brothers, Colin didn't spare Kendra a glance when she walked into the drawing room and settled herself next to Ford. *"She's still here?* I cannot believe it!"

"It hasn't been that long," Jason stated calmly.

"More than a month! Don't tell me she hasn't recovered enough in more than a month."

"I haven't asked her," Jason admitted. "She does seem to be getting on fine, though."

Colin stormed over to where his older brother lounged against the carved stone mantel. "You never asked her?"

"I just said so, didn't I? We've been quite busy these past weeks."

"You've been busy?" Colin's fists clenched. It hadn't been easy to walk away from Amy the first time. Now, thanks to his lazy brother, he'd have to go through it all over again. "Too busy to take a day or two to deliver her as promised?"

Jason only shrugged. "With the end of the harvest, Ford and I have been out collecting rents. It's that time of year, you know."

"Yes, I know," Colin said between gritted teeth. Jason's nonchalance wasn't improving his mood in any way. *"I've* been busy. Disposing of the harvest, looking after the livestock, overseeing the quarrying and logging operations, collecting rents, directing restoration work, working on the accursed account books—and all by myself with just Benchley for help. *You* have Ford and a battalion of laborers and servants, yet you hadn't the time to—"

"Amy's been doing my ledgers for me," Jason interrupted. "I reckon she'd be willing to help you out. She's quite grateful, you know."

Colin made his way to one of the coral-upholstered chairs and dropped onto it, defeated. "She's been doing your ledgers," he said in a dead voice.

"Oh, yes," Kendra bragged, "and she's much faster than Jason ever was. Why, she says she's just about caught up."

"That's a miracle," Colin allowed. "However did this come about?" They were bound to tell him anyway, so he might as well cooperate.

"I was showing her the portraits in the picture gallery," Kendra explained brightly, "and the door to Jason's study was open. He invited her in to look around, she asked what he was working on so hard, and that was that. She kept the books for her father's shop." Kendra smiled in a way that set Colin's teeth on edge. "She's so smart, Colin, you wouldn't believe it."

"Oh, I'd believe it all right." Yet one more thing to add to the shining qualities of Amy Goldsmith.

"She became great friends with little Mary. I reckon she's just as fond of children as you are." Jason made his way to the chair beside Colin's. He sat and stretched out his long legs, crossing them at the ankles. "I found a home for Mary in the village, with the widow of one of my men who was killed in the mill accident."

"Good." Wonder of wonders, his brother had actually followed through with something he'd asked of him. "Thank you for taking care of that."

"My pleasure."

"Ow!"

Colin turned to see Ford rubbing his arm and glaring at his twin, who had a carefully innocent look on her face. Ford cleared his throat. "We've also been discussing Amy's fine education," he announced in a stilted way, as though his words were rehearsed. "She's interested in science"—Ford was forever complaining that no one in the family shared his fascination with science—"although she prefers history. She spends hours and hours in the library."

"She does, does she?" Colin crossed his arms and turned back to Jason. "When are you taking her to Dover? You *are* taking her to Dover?"

"Of course, Colin. Whyever would you think not?"

"She should stay here," Kendra protested. "She's clever and sweet and helpful and a good friend and she has no one—just one aunt—and she fits right in with the family." Kendra paused for a deep breath and squared her shoulders. "You should marry her, Colin. We all think she's wonderful."

Colin had seen it coming. "Then you can all marry her," he suggested lightly, rising to go out the door. "I'm going to get cleaned up."

"Wait!" Kendra yelled after him.

He whirled around. "*You* wait," he returned fiercely. "I'm marrying Lady Priscilla Hobbs, or did that slip your mind somehow?" He turned to Ford. "You want Amy in the family? *You* marry her."

Ford's blue eyes widened in alarm. "I'm not ready to get married! I'm only sixteen! I want to attend university!"

Undaunted, Colin turned on Jason. "You marry her, then. You seem to enjoy having her around."

"I'm—I'm not attracted to her," sputtered the unflappable Jason. "She's—she's a bookkeeper!"

"Exactly." Colin turned on his heel and headed up to his bedchamber, shaking his head.

Sometimes his family was more trouble than they were worth. Kendra, especially.

You should marry her, Colin.

Hmmph! He'd get Kendra back. Tonight. He'd get her good.

TWENTY-FOUR

"*D*EFENDING THE castle?"

Taken off guard, Amy turned to see Colin framed in the archway that led to the keep's stairwell. He was dressed casually, in buff-colored breeches and a billowing white shirt, his hair still damp from a recent washing.

The last time she'd seen him, he'd been mentally and physically exhausted. Now the circles were gone from under his eyes. He looked relaxed and rested, and under those breeches and that shirt...

Well, he looked quite fit.

She swallowed hard, her hands tightening on the iron grille set into the keep's window. "Defending the castle?" she echoed.

His smile reached his compelling emerald eyes. "This is where the castle guard lived, and you were watching through the window."

"Oh." She blushed, feeling thick-witted for not catching the reference. What was it about him that robbed her ability to think straight? "I was just...ruminating." She glanced out the window, struggling for some relevant comment she could make. "How could they see to guard? The windows are so narrow."

"The better to deter arrows in days past." Colin moved toward her, then abruptly stopped. She thought she saw a frown flit across his tanned face. "In truth, they only lived and stored weapons in here. There used to be a level above where they took turns day and night, watching through the notches in the battlement all around."

Amy looked up at the sky, streaked with colors from the setting sun. She imagined the guards up there, pacing back and forth, clanking around in their armor. Colin's words seemed to do that to her: make her imagine other places, other times.

She stole another glance at him. His gleaming black hair was loose for a change, cut just to his shoulders, easy to manage if not fashionable. It was odd, but the color she hated on her own head looked perfect on his.

She'd been convinced that her intense reaction to his kiss, that one time that now seemed so long ago, had been an outgrowth of her grief, a method for escape. But suddenly she knew she'd been fooling herself. It seemed each time she saw him, the pull was stronger.

She took a step closer. "I can picture the knights up there when you talk about them."

"A romantic image, but they weren't knights decked out for battle." Colin took a step back and leaned against the wall, crossing his ankles and arms. "Just regular men, mostly. Each of the lord's vassals—all the men granted use of his land—was obligated to spend part of his year as a member of the castle guard."

"I've been wondering what it used to be like to live here."

"Well, Kendra sent me to find you for supper, but I can give you my famous tour on the way down."

Amy's laugh bounced around the bare stone walls and tapered off into the night as she followed him to the stair tower. She was surprised such a light, happy sound had come from her.

"It's hard to imagine living in anything so primitive as a keep today," Colin's words floated up to her, "but in the twelfth century, it would have contained the best residential lodging for the lord. In those days, others lived in the smaller towers set into the castle walls, while the rest of the people had their homes constructed against the inside surfaces of the enclosure."

When they came out on the next floor, Amy wandered to a window where she could oversee the quadrangle. "No wonder it's so big," she said, imagining hundreds of people milling below.

"The castle was like a small town, and this keep was the ultimate in luxury accommodations." He joined her at the window, accidentally grazing her arm. At least, it *seemed* like an accident. "There was a poultry yard where all the animals were kept." When he moved closer, the pit of her stomach began tingling. "Soldiers, skilled workers, servants and their families—everyone made their home within the castle walls."

Suddenly she felt giddy. His words weren't going in one ear and out the other, not quite, but she was having a hard time concentrating.

"Tell me more," she begged.

"The portcullis, that wooden iron-banded gate at the barbican over there, would be down all the time, not just at night like it is now. The drawbridge would be raised unless someone needed to leave or enter."

When Colin paused, she turned to look at him. Their eyes met, his gaze steady. "This would have been the lord's bedchamber."

"Oh." She blushed furiously and looked at her hands.

"It would have been decorated with beautiful tapestries, and the bed would have been draped with yards and yards of fabric that could be pulled together to keep in the warmth. An enormous bed, so that on cold nights they could all get in, the whole family, and nestle together to keep warm."

Though Colin's words were simply informative, his voice was full of meaning, as though…

No, it was all her imagination. He hadn't asked how she was, or anything else of a personal nature. She had to stop dreaming. He'd come only to fetch her for supper.

And to take her away.

Well, there was no sense dwelling on such a depressing subject. "Is supper waiting?" she asked.

Colin blinked before answering, and when he did, his words were clipped. "I reckon it is. We should go."

Amy followed him down the twisting staircase, but when he headed toward the courtyard, she slowed on the ground floor.

Despite everything, she didn't quite feel ready to share him with his family.

"What was this room for?"

He hesitated before turning back. "This would have been the main living quarters for the lord and his family." He was the tour guide again, his voice instructive, nothing more. "They would have eaten here, food brought to them by servants from the castle kitchens. The lord's children would have had their lessons here, and the family would have played games and received visitors here. There would have been lots of food and supplies in the storeroom underneath, in case of a siege."

Amy ran her fingers down the ancient wall. "You've a lovely home, my lord."

He shrugged. "It's Jason's, really."

She walked around the circular chamber, trailing one hand along the rough stone. "I can picture your lord and his family living here. Were they happy, do you think?"

"I imagine so." Colin chuckled. "The Chases were always a boisterous lot, I'm told."

Amy halted, startled. But of course it had been his family living here these past four hundred years; it just hadn't occurred to her before. They'd been peers for all that long. Just as her own family had been jewelers for an untold number of years. It was an intriguing thought, and a sad one, emphasizing the many reasons she and Colin could never be together.

"They're surely waiting for us by now," he said, breaking her reverie. "Shall we?"

TWENTY-FIVE

*W*HEN COLIN and Amy reached the dining room, they found the family arranged the same way they'd been seated the night before he'd left, forcing the two of them to sit beside each other again.

Colin wasn't surprised.

He took his seat, and supper was served. Conversation swirled as usual, but tonight he was the one not participating. He was so aware of Amy, he could swear he felt heat emanating from her. It had taken all his self-control not to kiss her in the keep.

She seemed different tonight. She wore a different gown, a hunter green he remembered Kendra wearing at a house party last year. Her hair was in curls again...

It was her eyes, he decided suddenly. The amethyst sparkle was back.

No one would think of describing this self-assured girl as "a wreck" now. She laughed and joked with his sister and brothers, kept up with their repartee as though born to a large, noisy family.

This large, noisy family, in fact.

Colin was startled. Amy was everything his siblings had claimed: intelligent, talented, animated, witty...beautiful...and entirely too comfortable amongst the Chases.

When she laughed again, his fists clenched under the table. He forced himself to look at his plate instead of her.

He would deliver her to a ship bound for France—tomorrow. It was clear that Jason had no intention of doing so any time soon, and it must be done—the sooner, the better.

"What do you think, Colin?" Amy asked, breaking into his thoughts.

"Pardon me?" He hadn't followed the conversation in the slightest.

"Amy has challenged you to a game of piquet after supper," said Ford.

"I just taught her last month," Kendra complained, "and already she puts me to shame."

"I'm weary tonight." Colin had no desire to match wits at a card game, most especially not with Amy. Besides, he had his plan to carry out. "I was looking forward to relaxing and listening to you play the harpsichord, Kendra."

"I played last night."

"Not for me. Please?" He sighed theatrically. "I've been locked up in my isolated stronghold for weeks, with no civilized entertainment…"

"Oh, very well. You don't need to act so miserable." Kendra sounded irritated, but her eyes danced. She dearly loved being appreciated.

TWENTY-SIX

*T*HE **FIRST** wrong note slipped by practically unnoticed, what with everyone's voices raised in rousing song and Kendra's nimble fingers flying fast. But then she hit another sour note, and another…

She paused momentarily, then resumed the tune.

Kendra rarely made mistakes. She'd been an apt pupil, training for hours upon hours while in exile, an eager student for the bored ladies looking for ways to pass the time. Just as the men had taken Colin and his brothers under their wings, putting them through fencing maneuvers until they could parry and thrust to perfection, so had the ladies put Kendra through her paces. As a result, she was quite an accomplished musician, making this night's trouble particularly frustrating.

When three more notes proved off key in less than a minute, Kendra stopped abruptly and shook her head as though to clear it.

"What's wrong?" Ford teased. "Too much Rhenish tonight?"

"I never drink too much, Ford, and you know it."

"Oh, yes, I forgot. That's Amy's problem. Half a glass and she's on the floor."

Amy giggled.

Colin looked at her sharply, then back to his younger brother. Criminy, his family knew more about her than he ever would have guessed. She'd really been worming her way in, the little minx.

He hardened his resolve to remove her tomorrow, before she insinuated herself even deeper.

"Are you tired, Kendra?" Jason inquired.

"No, I'm not tired." Kendra was clearly irritated. "I'll just start over."

Start over she did, and proceeded to hit the same sour notes. She slammed her fists down on the keyboard, exasperated.

"Are your eyes bothering you?" Amy asked.

"No. And I could play this with my eyes closed, at any rate."

"Let's just talk tonight," Jason suggested. "We haven't all been together in a long while."

Kendra heaved an impatient sigh. "No. I know I can play this —I've done it hundreds of times."

She attacked the keyboard with a new vigor and hit the same wrong notes again.

The same wrong notes.

She leapt off her bench seat and lifted the lid of the wooden instrument. Half a second later, she slammed it shut and whirled about, pointing an accusing finger at Colin.

"You! You and your pranks. Have you any idea how long it will take me to retune this?"

"However long it takes, you deserve it, little sister. 'You should marry her,' indeed!"

"Marry who?" asked Amy.

"Never mind." Colin waved her off in what he hoped was a casual manner. He grinned at Kendra. "Got you good, didn't I?"

"I reckon you did," she admitted with a wry smile.

"What did he do?" Ford walked over to the harpsichord, lifted the lid and peered inside, then convulsed in mirth.

"What?" Amy asked. "What is it?"

"He—he—loosened the strings!" Ford managed to choke out between gales of laughter. "Well, some of them. Come look."

Amy joined them at the instrument. Though she knew nothing of music, it was obvious what Colin had done. A half-dozen random strings were sagging at the middle.

"See?" Ford pressed a key causing a plectrum to pluck a taut string, followed by a key to a loose one. The resulting sound was so discordant that Amy burst into helpless giggles.

They felt so good, those unconstrained giggles. She couldn't help herself; the giggles led into peals of uncontrollable laughter.

It proved infectious. Colin joined in, and Ford and Jason, and finally Kendra, until they were all laughing simply because everyone else was laughing. One by one they stopped, dwindling into occasional chuckles, all except Amy. She clutched the harpsichord to keep from doubling over as she laughed and laughed. She didn't even know why, anymore.

Her sides hurt, and tears ran down her face.

Ford put a hand on her shoulder. "She thinks you're funny, Colin."

Amy blushed, but Colin just smiled. "I appreciate a girl who appreciates my pranks."

Amy's face heated even more. "I'll—I'll be right back," she hiccuped between bursts of giggles.

She had to gain control of herself.

Leaving the room, she wove her way through the corridor, laughing, and down the stairs, leaning against the wall at intervals. They must think I'm drunk, she thought—but she knew better. She was merely giddy from close proximity to Colin, intensified by a feeling of well-being, surrounded by laughing people who loved one another.

Maybe her family hadn't shouted, but they hadn't laughed together much either.

The laughter made her feel slightly sick, and she hugged her stomach and aching ribs. At the foot of the staircase, she gazed through tear-blurred eyes at the tall wooden front doors. The quadrangle beyond enticed her, the crisp night air exactly what she needed. She stumbled through the entrance hall and out the doors, laughing all the way, nearly tripped down the steps outside, and fell into a heap on the damp grass.

As her giggles diminished, she took delicious breaths of cold air deep into her lungs. At last she sat up, wiping the tears from her cheeks between hiccups. Placing her hands behind her on the grass, she leaned back and gazed up at the sky, enjoying the feel of the frigid air on her hot face.

Colin came into the quadrangle and crouched down beside her.

"The family elected me to check on you," he said wryly. "Better now?"

"Uh-huh." She watched a dark cloud creep slowly across the moon. "I'm sorry. I guess I made a fool of myself." She hiccuped, more loudly than she would have liked. "Excuse me."

"No excuses necessary," Colin declared chivalrously. "And you made no fool of yourself, either. To the contrary, we're all pleased to see you've recovered your spirits."

Silent, Amy continued watching the clouds gather, dark shapes against the starlit sky. She hiccuped again.

"I'll take you to Dover tomorrow," Colin said quietly beside her. "I'm sorry Jason hasn't found the time to do it."

Suddenly, the air seemed cold instead of refreshing. She shivered and sat up straight, folding her legs beneath her. "It wasn't a problem. I've been fine here."

His family's faint laughter drifted through a window. She felt a stab of pain at the thought of leaving them all; she was even growing used to their inevitable arguments. But it was only by chance that she'd been afforded the luxury of being a part of them for a while, and her time was up.

She shivered again.

"Are you cold?" he asked.

"A little bit."

He moved closer and put an arm around her shoulders, drawing her against him. "You'll catch your death out here. We should go back inside."

His heat seeped through the fabric of her dress, warming her all over. She wouldn't have moved an inch for the world. "In a minute," she stalled.

He squeezed her shoulder. "How is your hand?"

"Fine." She spoke softly, fearing he might pull away. "It healed weeks ago."

Colin took her hand to examine it in the moonlight. "Mmm," he murmured, running his warm palm over the back. "So it did."

More laughter sounded from above. Quite suddenly, his fingers came around and laced through hers, and then, to her complete surprise, he brought their joined hands to his lips and held them there.

Amy bit her lip and closed her eyes. When she felt Colin move around to kneel in front of her, she opened them to find his only inches away.

"How are *you*, Amy?" he asked in hushed tones, searching her face for the answer.

"I'm better," she whispered, overwhelmed by his intensity. "Much, much better."

"That's good," he replied, then swiftly, before either of them could think about it, he yanked her hard against him and brought his lips to hers.

She was shocked, but her body seemed to know what to do. Her arms wound over his shoulders and around his neck, her fingers meshing themselves in his thick, silky hair. His mouth was soft and damp as the grass, but his hands felt strong and rough on her cheeks. She pulled him even closer, till they were pressed together from chest to knee, leaving no space for shyness or insecurity. Somewhere in the back of her mind, she felt surprised by her daring, but the feeling faded quickly, for she was too full of other feelings.

But he must have been surprised, too, because all at once, he jerked away from her. Dizzy and thrown off balance, Amy nearly toppled over. It was lucky she was already so close to the ground. She caught herself on her hands in the wet grass, and all her newfound confidence vanished. Suddenly, she felt foolish and embarrassed.

Colin sat back, muttering an oath. "I'm sorry," he said with a sigh, running a hand raggedly through his hair.

Of course he was sorry. He didn't like her; he wanted to get rid of her. What she couldn't understand was how he could kiss her like that, feeling as he did.

She didn't trust herself to speak. Instead, she sat down and put her head in her hands. But she didn't cry. She felt too mixed up to cry.

"I'm betrothed, you know," he said suddenly.

Amy looked up. She hadn't known—nobody had mentioned it.

"Her name is Priscilla Hobbs," he continued. "*Lady* Priscilla Hobbs. Her father's an earl—she'll make a perfect mother for my children. Oh, and she's very nice," he added unconvincingly.

"Why are you telling me all this?" she asked, more confused than ever.

"I'm just trying to explain why I cannot…pay court to you."

Humiliated, she lashed out. "Pay court to me? Because of a little kiss? What an absurd notion!" Her voice rose an octave in her agitation. "I'd never expect you to marry me—you've tried to get rid of me at every turn."

"That's not true," he protested.

"It is so true," she contradicted, but the anger was seeping out of her already.

Things were as they were.

She wasn't suited to him, and there was nothing she could do about it.

"Amy," he began, rising on his knees to face her.

When she instinctively scooted backward, a flash of hurt crossed his face. She looked down, rubbing at a damp spot on her skirt.

"I'm sorry," he finally repeated.

They were silent for a while. Then Amy forced herself to look up and locked her gaze on his.

"When I'm with you," she confessed softly, "I feel things I never thought to feel. I don't know if you might feel them, too. What I do know is that it doesn't matter. You belong here, with lords and ladies and the king, and I belong in France, working at a jeweler's bench."

An inscrutable mask settled over Colin's features. He hesitated, then stood and brushed the grass off his breeches.

"We'd better get some sleep," he said in a voice devoid of any emotion. "I mean to get an early start."

His long legs carried him up the steps and through the door without hesitation. Amy took a deep breath and raised herself up, hoping her own legs would carry her.

TWENTY-SEVEN

*C*OLIN CURSED fluently, aiming a boot at the side of the carriage for emphasis.

"My lord, we'll have to stop here," Benchley concluded.

"Oh, is that right?" Colin's voice dripped with sarcasm. "I imagined we could drag along to Dover on three wheels."

Benchley usually stood as tall as possible to compensate for his deficient height, but now his shoulders hunched over and he positively drooped.

"My apologies," Colin hastened to say. Though he'd be hiring more servants in the near future—as soon as there was lodging available for them at Greystone—at this point Benchley was his valet, butler, coachman, cook, and serving-maid all rolled into one. He didn't deserve Colin's misplaced wrath. "Hang it, but I'm vexed, is all."

"I understand, my lord. I'll just take one of the horses and return with a wheel and a wright to install it. You two sit tight and eat the dinner Lady Kendra sent. I'll be back in no time."

"I think not." Colin gestured angrily at the sky. "This accursed storm is due to kick up any minute."

As though on cue, a few snowflakes drifted down from the clouds.

Benchley brushed a flake off his beak of a nose. "I fear you're right, my lord. I'm not certain I'll be able to find a wheelwright willing to come out in this weather."

The clouds that had begun gathering last night looked unequivocally threatening now. The family had tried to talk Colin into postponing this journey, but he'd been adamant. He meant to deliver Amy to a France-bound ship, and he meant to do it today.

Broken wheel or not.

The thought of spending extra time with Amy, in a freezing carriage going nowhere, was daunting. The only thing colder than the weather was her demeanor. They'd spent the first short part of their journey in total silence, in diagonal corners on opposite seats, each with their nose buried in a book.

Spending the afternoon cooped up with her here was unthinkable.

"Pay the wheelwright whatever it takes." He dug in his pouch and slapped some coins into Benchley's hand. "The one saving grace is we happen to be close to Greystone. I'll take Mrs. Goldsmith there on the other horse. When the wheel is fixed, ride on over and we'll be on our way."

Colin helped Benchley unhitch one of the matched bays and sent him off with a smack on the horse's rump. Then he climbed into the carriage and sat opposite Amy, shutting the door against the frigid air.

Amy looked up from the book she'd been struggling to read in the failing light. "Yes?" she asked in a frosty tone.

"The wheel is broken," he began.

"I surmised as much." Amy shut her book. "I heard every word you uttered, foul and otherwise."

"Benchley has ridden off for help," Colin explained anyway. "We'll ride the other bay to Greystone and wait for him there."

"How far is Greystone?"

"A mile and a half, or thereabouts."

"I'll walk."

"No, you won't," Colin declared.

"I'm not riding any horse."

He knew she was unhappy with him, but did she have to contradict him at every turn?

"I won't allow you to walk. It's snowing, and you have no cloak. You'd freeze to death before you made it halfway."

"It's snowing?" Shooting him a skeptical glance, she rubbed a circle of condensation off the window with her fist. She peered outside, wrapped the blanket tighter about herself, and leaned back into the corner. "It's snowing."

Colin looked out the view hole she'd created.

"Curse it, it's getting worse than I expected." Her mocking expression made him bristle. "It's not my fault we're surprised with a November snow. For heaven's sake, we haven't seen snow this far south in three years. How on earth was I supposed to predict such an occurrence?"

"It was cold regardless. You could have waited for decent weather before insisting—"

"I have my reasons for needing to get on with this."

"Why? So you can get rid of me once and for all?"

"No!" he said too quickly. She'd hit too close to home.

Her response was a stony stare.

"Amy...I'm sorry this happened. I've already said I'm sorry for the way I've treated you."

She remained tight lipped.

His hands clenched on his knees as he fought to control his tone. "We need to get to Greystone, and at the rate you're moving this will be a full-blown blizzard before we even get out of the carriage."

Her icy mask fell, and she shrank further into the corner. "I cannot ride a horse."

"What?" His hands relaxed, and he rubbed them on his thighs. "Whyever not?"

"I've never ridden a horse," she confessed in a choked voice. "I cannot do it. I just cannot."

"People ride horses all the time."

"Other people."

"You've never been on a horse. What makes you think you won't like it?"

"I didn't say I've never been *on* a horse. I said I've never *ridden* a horse. Papa put me on one once, in Hyde Park, when I was eight. I was up so high, and this thing under me moved, and

I screamed until he pulled me off. I swore I'd never get on a horse again."

Colin couldn't believe what he was hearing. They needed to be on their way, and now. "You're not eight anymore, Amy."

"I cannot. I just cannot. The thing is ten times my weight, it has a brain all its own—why, it could buck me off, or run under a tree and make me hit my head on a branch, or—"

"Now you're babbling." He reached for her hand to pull her out.

Snatching it back, she burrowed even further into the corner and tucked the blanket tighter. "I'm sorry. If I cannot walk, then I'll just wait here. I have a blanket, a book, and food. I'm prepared to stay until Benchley returns."

"This storm could last until morning," Colin argued, though he hoped to good heavens it wouldn't. "You're coming with me, and you're coming on the horse. I'll hold on to you. You'll be fine." He flung open the door, grabbed her hand from beneath the blanket, and pulled her up and out of the carriage in one smooth motion.

Glaring, she shivered in her blanket while Colin unhitched the horse. He watched her surreptitiously, his earlier annoyance rapidly turning to amusement. Imagine, an intelligent and educated young woman being scared of a perfectly harmless animal. Surely once she was riding, she would see it wasn't frightening.

When the horse was free, he motioned her over. "I suggest you ride astride—you'll feel a lot more secure that way than sidesaddle."

"Sidesaddle?" She shot him an accusatory glare. "There's *no* saddle."

"Up you go," he said cheerfully, his laced fingers providing a foothold to boost her.

"You go first."

"Amy," he said with an exasperated sigh, "if I get on first, I won't be able to help you up."

She huffed, then clenched her jaw and stepped onto his hands, swinging her leg over awkwardly.

And nearly fell off the other side.

Her screech pierced Colin's ears even as he leapt to right her. Seated at last, her eyes wide with fear, she wrinkled her nose. "It smells terrible."

Her skirts were hitched up in disarray, and the look on her face was so comical that Colin had to bite his tongue to keep from laughing.

"It feels warm," she reported. "And scratchy. And very *alive*." The horse took a small step backward, and she shrieked.

"It's all right," Colin soothed. "He's not going anywhere."

He turned back to the carriage, muttering to himself.

"Wh-where are you going?" she yelled after him. "Come back! You cannot leave me alone on a live beast!"

He leaned into the carriage to fetch Kendra's basket of food. "I was just getting our dinner."

After swinging up easily behind her, he held the basket in one hand and Amy firmly against himself with the other. His arm reached almost all the way around her waist.

"Better?"

She nodded. He waited until she relaxed back against him, then urged the horse at a slow walk toward Greystone.

They moved—an entire twenty feet.

"Stop!"

Colin didn't. "You're doing fine, Amy."

"No! I mean, we have to go back!" She twisted, trying to face him. "We left my trunk!"

He reined in, swearing under his breath. "Oh, no. We're not lugging that deuced trunk to Greystone. It'll be here when we get back."

"No—it must come with me," she insisted, sounding panicked. She looked up and back at him, bumping her head on his chin in the process. "I'll get it myself if I have to." To emphasize her threat, she leaned to the side as though she were determined to slide off.

Colin clutched at her. "What on earth is in that trunk that makes it so important?"

She gritted her teeth. "Everything I own."

The same answer she'd given before. He was certain she was hiding something from him, but then tears filled her eyes and he found himself climbing off the horse. He set the basket on the ground and headed back to the carriage.

"Thank you so much," she called to his back.

It was the first civil thing she'd uttered to him all morning. He hadn't a clue how he'd manage to carry Amy, the trunk, and their dinner on one horse, but he supposed it would be worth the effort, if she would act pleasant as a result.

Another shriek rang out as he stepped into the carriage. "It's moving! The beast is about to run away!"

"Pull back on the reins," he shouted.

"The what? Oh, dear heavens, it's leaning down! It's going to roll over on top of me and crush me!"

Alarmed, Colin backed out of the carriage. The horse had moved, all right—all of three feet. His head lowered, he was munching contentedly on a clump of grass by the roadside.

"Dear heavens is right." Colin hefted the trunk and made his way toward her. "Heaven save me, please."

"What did you say?"

"I said I hope you're pleased I'm saving your trunk."

When he heaved the small but heavy trunk onto the horse's back, the poor animal turned its head to look at him dolefully. Colin sighed. He found it hard to believe the lengths he would go to in order to placate Amethyst Goldsmith.

"All right." He looked to her. "Now move back so I can ride in front of you."

"In front of me? How will you hold on to me?"

"I cannot hold on to you and balance the trunk, Amy."

She tightened her knees around the horse's middle, as though she expected him to haul her off. "I'll balance the trunk."

He looked at the heavy trunk and back to her, drumming his free fingers against his thigh. The thing practically weighed more than she did. "I think not. Of course, we can leave the trunk here…"

"No," she capitulated. "I'll move."

She inched back until Colin nodded. Keeping a hand on the trunk, he leaned to scoop up Kendra's basket. "Here, you'll have to carry this."

She gazed at him dubiously, but took it and wisely kept quiet.

Still balancing the trunk with one hand, he managed to mount the horse without kicking her in the face, a feat he felt deserved her undying admiration.

She didn't even seem to notice.

"Hold on to me," he said.

"I cannot see ahead," she complained. "I can only see down. It-it's a *long* way down."

"If you'd rather ride in front, we can leave the trunk here," he suggested in the most pleasant tone he could muster.

"No, no...I'll be fine. Wait a minute, though." She pushed the handle of the basket up to her elbow so she could place both arms around him. "I'm ready," she announced.

"Wonders will never cease," Colin muttered. He urged the horse forward, torn between going slowly and freezing, or moving quickly and frightening Amy half to death.

Mercifully, he chose to freeze.

He would swear he felt Amy's heart pounding against his back, even though he was insulated by his cloak, her blanket, and both their layers of clothing. Her hands, clasped together about his waist, were white knuckled with strain.

"You have me in a death grip," he complained. "The basket handle is digging into my side."

"Sorry." Her arms loosened an entire half inch, then tightened again when the horse gave a snort.

"Are you all right back there?" he asked with a sigh.

He hadn't the slightest idea what he'd do if she weren't.

TWENTY-EIGHT

"I'M FINE," Amy ground out between gritted teeth. She wondered how long it would take to ride a mile and a half. It felt like forever already. "But snowflakes are tickling my nose."

"Feel free to let go of me long enough to brush them off."

She shook her head violently, though of course Colin couldn't see her.

"Does it still seem a long way down?"

"My eyes are closed."

That was the only way she could bear it. Even pressed against Colin's wide, warm back, she felt unsafe. Her heart skittered, and her legs were getting numb from squeezing tight around the beast's prickly body. It was ridiculous, and she knew it—even country bumpkins were comfortable sitting a horse.

But telling herself that didn't keep her from trembling.

"Cold?" Colin asked, apparently feeling her body quake.

"Yes." Better to let him think that was the reason.

"I warned you we needed to go quickly."

When the horse sped up, she yelped, and Colin scrambled to right the trunk, swearing under his breath. If she'd needed any more confirmation that she fit poorly in his world, she had it now.

Resolved to stay calm until this torture was over, she

squeezed her eyes shut tighter and began singing to herself. Perhaps by the time her song was finished, they'd be at Greystone.

"'I tell thee, Dick, where I have been; Where I the rarest things have seen; Oh, things without compare! Such sights again cannot be found; In any place on English ground; Be it at wake or fair.'"

"You've a sweet voice," Colin called back, amusement lacing his words.

He was laughing at her. If she could only get past her fear and let go of him, she might be tempted to shove him off the horse.

Instead, she continued singing.

"'At Charing Cross, hard by the way; Where we, thou know'st, do sell our hay; There is a house with stairs. And there did I see coming down; Such folk as are not in our town; Forty at least, in pairs.'"

"*Ballad Upon a Wedding*," Colin remarked. "The man who wrote it—Sir John Suckling—fought beside my father in the war."

"'Amongst the rest, one pest'lent fine; His beard no bigger though than thine; Walk'd on before the rest. Our landlord looks like nothing to him; The king, God bless him, 'twould undo him; Should he go still so dress'd.'"

"That's the groom, who is said to be Lord Broyhill. And the bride was Lady Margaret—"

"If you know the song," she interrupted, irritated into finally addressing him, "the least you could do is sing along with me."

But he didn't. There were fifteen verses to *Ballad Upon a Wedding*, and Amy sang them five times through before the horse finally stopped.

"We're here," Colin said with an exaggerated sigh of relief. "I believe the basket handle has impressed a permanent indentation between my ribs."

"Thank heavens." Amy's eyes flew open, and she blinked against the daylight. "I meant thank heavens we're here, not about your ribs."

A snort floated back, making Amy jump—but the sound had

come from Colin this time, not the horse. He unwound her arms from his waist and reached back a hand. "Here, let me help you down."

When she landed on solid ground, her knees nearly buckled under her. Taking a deep breath, she looked around. She found herself on a circular drive in a modest courtyard, enclosed on three sides by a crenelated curtain wall. The living quarters of the small castle made up the fourth side. The entire structure would fit into a corner of Cainewood.

She was enchanted.

Colin hopped down from the horse and slid her trunk to the snowy ground. He gestured at his home. "It's not like Cainewood, is it?"

"No, not at all," she said seriously. "It's much nicer."

"Nicer?" he asked in apparent disbelief.

She watched his gaze wander over the ruined portions of the wall and a huge roofless chamber that dominated the edifice. She followed along, seeing ancient weathered stones with stories to tell and a building the perfect size for one happy family.

"Yes, it's much cozier. Cainewood is beautiful, but I cannot imagine why anyone would actually want to live there."

"Try explaining that to the girl I'm marrying," Colin muttered, leading the horse to one of the posts set around the drive.

Still carrying the basket, Amy wandered back to the entrance and stared up in wonder at the massive oak portcullis gate. Outside the walls, she could see the moat was dry and had been for some time. A mosslike grass grew in its bottom, lightly dusted with snow.

"Once upon a time, it was filled by the River Caine." Colin's voice startled her, nearby. He pointed out the river in the distance. "It runs all the way from the coast past Cainewood to here. In fact, the license to crenelate was granted by King Richard II to protect Greystone from pirates who sailed up the River Caine from the sea. It was originally built by a bishop."

Amy felt her beloved history books coming alive within these walls. "How long has it been in your family?"

"Not at all, till recently. Its Royalist owners perished with no issue. Charles deeded it to me after the Restoration, when I was all of sixteen. I'm just now getting around to fixing it up."

At all of twenty-one, Amy knew. Somehow he seemed much more mature, much older. She supposed that was what came of being orphaned at six and growing up on one's own.

A ruined tower sat adjacent to the entrance, and she looked down inside it—a long way down.

"The oubliette," he explained. "It was secured with a heavy iron grille." His voice sounded mysterious and deep as the pit. "Miscreants would be cast inside…and sometimes forgotten."

Suddenly shivering, she tightened the blanket around her body.

With a grunt, Colin shouldered her trunk. "Come inside, where it should be warmer." He motioned for her to follow him down a short passageway with an unassuming oak door at its end.

He unlocked the door and entered, bending to set down her trunk. She followed in time to see him shove it against the wall with one booted foot.

"There." He glared at her accusingly. "I'm not looking forward to our riding back with it, I'll warrant you."

Her legs were still shaking, though she'd never admit it. She set the basket on the floor. "I'm not riding a horse back."

"Benchley cannot drive the carriage here with one horse."

"Then you'll ride out with him and return with the carriage. That way you won't have to carry the trunk on horseback," she pointed out.

"That's true," he conceded rather crossly. Averting his face, he turned to arrange some wood in the fireplace on the right.

The vestibule was small and square, with an open-beam ceiling of oak. An oak staircase marched up the wall opposite the entrance. To the left, Amy saw an arched door. She walked over and tried the handle.

"It's locked," Colin said, standing up. "The great hall is beyond, lacking half a roof at present."

She nodded, turning back to him. Behind him, the fire burned brightly, illuminating the dim chamber. Shadows danced on whitewashed, unadorned stone walls. The stone floor was polished smooth from centuries of use, and a fringed Oriental carpet rested in the center.

"Is this where you sleep?" Amy asked. She knew his home was mostly unrestored, and many families lived in a room this size or smaller. Perhaps he had a pallet that he put in here at night.

"Heavens, no." He laughed and picked up the basket. "Come this way."

She followed him through an open archway and down a corridor. He paused at a doorway on the left.

"This is my temporary bedchamber," he explained. "Once the great hall's roof is complete, the rest of the living quarters will be restored."

Amy stepped into the austere room. It held a wooden washstand, a dressing table with a mirror, and a large bed with a small table beside it and a chest at its foot. Carved in a twisted design, the bedposts supported a cream-colored canopy that matched the bedclothes and plastered walls. A gray stone fireplace and hearth echoed the gray stone that framed the three windows.

She wandered to a window and drew in her breath in surprise.

"You're looking behind the great hall." Colin's voice came across the room from where he lounged against the doorjamb. "It's officially called Upper Court. The main courtyard where we entered is called Lower Court."

Amy gazed into the secret space, partially concealed by a light blanket of freshly fallen snow. Come springtime, when the winter cold subsided, it would contain a beautiful garden. Placing her elbows on the wide stone windowsill, she rested her chin in her hands and stared out dreamily. Having grown up in crowded London, the thought of a private walled garden was blissful.

"I would call it Hidden Court," she said softly.

A low chuckle came from the doorway. "That's exactly what I do call it, to myself."

Amy wasn't surprised. It was the perfect name for this most perfect place. "How do you get to it?"

"Through my study, next door."

Leaving the window, she followed him down the corridor. His study contained a large scarred wooden desk with a comfortable chair; a long, plain upholstered couch with a low table before it; and some rough shelving stuffed with a few books and a lot of ledgers and piles of paper.

"Benchley sleeps here," he said, indicating the couch.

But Amy had eyes only for the glass-inset double doors in the exact center of the back wall. She went straight to throw them open and stepped into the courtyard beyond, heedless of the frosty air and falling snow.

Colin turned to start a fire, slanting a glance now and then to watch her. He laughed when she brushed snow off the plants to see what lay beneath. What a marvelous creature she was, quick to anger, but even more easily pleased. Now that she'd emerged from the cocoon of her grief, she was like a beautiful butterfly, and his heart ached with the knowledge that he could never capture her.

Finished with the fire, he turned to warm his back near the flames, watching Amy flit around his private courtyard...the courtyard Priscilla had failed to even notice on her one visit to her future home.

He shook himself. Priscilla embodied everything he required in a wife. He wasn't the sort who let fleeting emotions rule his life—he never had, and he had no intention of starting now.

That wouldn't be rational.

His betrothal was an ideal, sensible arrangement. And not only was he bound by a formal promise, but he'd spent part of Priscilla's dowry on the restorations. He saw no way out of it, and he'd be a fool to consider it at all.

Amy was right: the two of them were unsuited, and the matter was no more simple or complicated than that.

He poked his head out the door to let Amy know he was going to settle the horse and would be right back. By the time she shook off the snow and came in from the courtyard, red cheeked and shivering, he'd not only returned, but emptied Kendra's basket and laid out their dinner—cold chicken, bread, cheese, and a bottle of wine.

Everything was neatly divided and set on cloth napkins, his on his desk, hers on the low table in front of the couch. He closed the doors behind Amy and took his place behind the desk.

"Hungry?" he asked.

"Yes, famished, although it must be early still." Amy picked up her food and carried it to the carpet before the hearth. She looked over at Colin, up through her thick eyelashes, where drops of melted snow sparkled in the firelight. "It's much warmer here. Will you join me in a picnic?"

Colin knew that if he joined her, it would be for more than a simple picnic. He felt much safer behind the desk. "I'm accustomed to dining here, and Benchley there," he said with a wave toward the table.

"I'm not Benchley," she pointed out.

He gave her a considered look. "I've noticed."

A blush crept into her cheeks, and his whole being was aware of how pretty she looked framed by the light of his fire, magical in the flickering hues. He tensed.

"Do you suppose he'll return soon?" she asked.

"Who?"

Her eyes narrowed, regarding him uncertainly. "Benchley."

"Oh, him. I certainly hope so," he said, glancing out the window.

The accursed storm was building. Benchley had better return soon. Colin shuddered to think what might happen if he and Amy were left alone here for a whole night. When he'd kissed her yesterday, he'd felt as if he'd lost control, of his mind, of his body, of everything. He'd betrayed his intended bride—again— and was wracked with guilt—again.

What was happening to him? He wasn't *that* sort of man...at least, he hadn't thought he was.

He could only pray that he'd learned his lesson this time. And stay on his guard.

He wouldn't be kissing her again.

He looked back to her with a sigh. "I'm miserable at preparing anything to eat. I assume you can cook?"

"I've never tried. We always had a housekeeper who cooked. You *do* have food?"

"Of course," he answered crossly. "I live here, you know."

"Of course."

Amy grinned, suddenly realizing how happy she was. Colin's plan to deliver her to Dover was foiled for now. Despite his hope that Benchley would return soon, that wasn't likely to happen, given the weather. She'd survived the ride on horseback, and now she was alone with Colin in his enchanting castle, possibly overnight…

She felt like she'd just received a stay of execution.

Maybe he'd even kiss her again.

TWENTY-NINE

*C*OLIN **UNWOUND** himself from his cross-legged position on the floor, where he'd faced Amy across the low table and whiled away the past hours playing piquet. "So, what's the verdict?"

Amy scribbled for a few more seconds before looking up. "I won...but by less than a hundred points."

"That's supposed to make me feel better?" He smiled at the concerned look on her face. "You won all three parties."

"You won five hands."

There were six hands in each partie, which meant he'd won five hands out of eighteen.

Well, at least he hadn't been completely humiliated. He'd proven himself a sharp card player in the past. He was out of practice; he didn't have the time to spend hours—not to mention money—playing cards like many courtiers.

He was *not* distracted by her close proximity, her quick intelligence, her joyous laugh, the soft curves that weren't hidden by that modest old lavender gown.

No. He was tired. He was unlucky. He was hungry.

Oh yes, he was hungry. Where on earth was Benchley?

Tired of waiting, Colin reached for his cloak.

"I've been playing quite often," Amy said, continuing her efforts to soothe his ego.

"I thought you just learned?"

"Well, I learned recently, but I've been playing quite often."

He shrugged into the cloak. "I see." Actually, he saw plenty. For one thing, he saw Amy wasn't the sort of girl who would let him win just to make him feel good. He liked that.

"Bundle up, now," he said, holding out the blanket. When she stood, he wrapped it around her shoulders, vexed at himself when he noticed the appealing rose scent that seemed to waft from her whenever she moved.

Turning away, he took an oil lamp off the mantel and lit it.

"We're going outside?" she asked as she trailed after him down the corridor.

"In a manner of speaking."

He stopped to unlock the door to the great hall, and she followed him inside. Lighting the way, he led her along the wall, moving beneath the overhang created by the partial new roof. He took her elbow to guide her around a rusted cannonball.

"I was hoping to have this roof finished before the cold set in," he yelled over the wind. It was picking up, making a deuce of a racket. "Now, if it proves to be a snowy winter, I may as well stay at Cainewood much of the time. I won't see much progress in this kind of weather." A glance through the open roof had him shaking his head at the threatening clouds.

They were forced to brave the snow to reach another door in the center of the end wall. Once they were inside, he shut it quickly, glad for the sudden quiet.

"Storerooms," he explained, leading Amy down the short corridor with two cellars on either side. They came out into his large kitchen.

Amy looked suitably impressed. "My goodness, this is impeccably restored."

"It projects outside the curtain wall," Colin pointed out. "I suppose it made the castle somewhat vulnerable at the time it was first built, but it was a sound decision as a precaution against fire damage."

Proud of all his improvements, Colin showed her the ovens, spitted fireplaces, and wash basins with bronze taps and spouts.

After she'd expressed appropriate admiration for the kitchen, he took her down a long, unused passage to the left.

"This was the original garderobe," he explained. "It hung over the moat, a nice innovation at the time. Owing to the location, though, everyone had to go through the great hall and kitchen to use it."

Amy peeked into the rough wooden latrines. "I'm glad I'm visiting now instead of then." She'd already made use of Colin's new garderobe, twin latrines with all the modern comforts, and declared them the most luxurious cubbyholes she'd ever seen. They had water closets, newly imported from France—the first water closets she'd ever used—and pipes all the way to the River Caine.

"I'll stick with the one next to your study, thank you," she said. "It's cold over here."

"It is, isn't it? Let's take our supper and head back."

Backtracking through the kitchen and toward the great hall, Amy followed Colin into the vaulted cellar on the left, a pantry stocked with plenty of food, although not yet a great variety. Handing the lamp to her, Colin grabbed a basket and filled it with a small wheel of cheese, some carrots, apples, and a jar of—

"What's that?" Amy asked in some alarm.

"Pickled snails."

"Pickled *snails?* Surely you jest."

"I do not. They're delicious."

"I suppose I'll try them," she said dubiously, "but I have to say they look and sound disgusting." She slanted him an assessing glance. "You gentry certainly eat some strange things."

Colin laughed and led her into the vault across the corridor. Walls lined with racks held but a few bottles of wine, one of which he hastily selected. Watching Amy look around, he tried to see the cellar through her eyes. Great empty barrels were scattered about, and two long, ancient wooden tables ran down the center of the arched chamber.

"Let me guess," Amy suggested, "the taproom?"

"The buttery."

"A butter room?"

"Well, it's not where they kept the butter, but that's what it was called. Your first guess was close—this room was dedicated to brewing and serving beverages. 'Butt' is an old word for bottle."

Amy followed him out of the buttery and back toward the great hall. "How do you come to know so much about old castles?"

Colin shrugged. "They've always interested me. I spent my early years at Cainewood and the rest of my childhood in a succession of old, drafty castles on the Continent. I asked a lot of questions, read a lot of books."

He motioned with his head for her to open the door, then winced when she got a blast of cold snow in her face for her trouble. He ushered her ahead, and she held up the lamp to light their way back.

"Most people, given this land, would choose to build a new house and leave the ruined castle as a relic for their children to play in," he shouted from the swirling snow behind her. "It would probably cost less and certainly be easier to heat."

When they reached the other end, Amy opened the door and they stepped into the welcoming entry hall, warmed by the dancing fire. Colin shut the door against the wind, and the room went abruptly silent.

Setting the basket and bottle of wine on the stone floor, he turned to lock the door. "Heaven knows why I'm restoring this place; it makes little sense." Finished, he faced her. "But it's three hundred years old, and it seems a shame to just let it crumble into ruin. The walls are thick and solid—it's a good home…" He shrugged and smiled at her. "I like living here."

"That's the romantic in you, Lord Greystone," she said softly.

Romantic? No one had ever accused Colin Chase of being romantic. Charming, perhaps; handsome, definitely—the ladies of Charles's court had never been shy about telling him so. But romantic? Never.

He searched her amethyst eyes for any trace of irony. But he could see she was sincere.

She obviously didn't know him very well.

He cleared his throat, breaking the silence and tension between them. "The lunatic in me, is more like it."

She shook her head, smiling. Colin's gaze moved to her cheeks, pink from the cold, and her lips, red and slightly wind-chapped. Her curls, arranged so carefully by Kendra's maid that morning, were blown loose around her face...

He wanted to kiss her. He stepped forward.

She licked her lips. "Are those pickled snails really edible?"

He shook his head to dispel those preposterous thoughts. "They're the best. Although I've just realized I forgot to bring spoons from the kitchen."

"You needn't brave the cold. I'm perfectly willing to share your knife with you." She flashed him an odd little smile. "After all, I'm naught but a simple merchant's daughter."

Amy leaned down to pick up the wine bottle. Colin frowned at her back.

But it was as well that Amy had reminded him—for with all this talk of romance, he'd been on the edge of forgetting just who and what she was.

Clutching their supper to his chest, he turned and hurried down the corridor, back to the relative safety of his desk.

THIRTY

*T*HE KEEP WAS *built of lavender stone, cut in perfect rectangular bricks, set together seamlessly to form the tallest tower in the world. As Amy wound up the spiral staircase she paused at an arched window to look out.*

Ferocious, fire-breathing, terrifying...the dragon lumbered closer, its heavy tread making the earth shudder. She ran up and up, a burning stitch in her side, but came no nearer the top.

Papa was up there. She had to get to him.

The dragon let out an earsplitting roar, breathing its red and yellow and blue fire through a window. She pressed herself against the wall as flames raced past her up the winding steps, in a thick burning line toward the top where Papa waited.

When it seemed as though neither her legs nor her lungs would hold out for one more step, she finally reached the top—but Papa was gone. In his place sat a skeleton, and it was on fire. It reclined in Papa's favorite chair, holding an oval-framed picture, its feet bones resting on a bolster. Flames shot from its skeleton eye sockets and between its bare skeleton ribs.

The dragon's roar shook the tower. Its glittering eyes looked straight into Amy's before it bent its head and breathed fire into the stairwell. Red and yellow and orange flames burned a path all the way to her right hand. Her hand was on fire, burning brightly, and it started up her arm...

144

She screamed for help, but nobody came.

~

*I*T SOUNDED as though someone were in the castle, attacking Amy in the bedchamber next door.

His heart pounding, Colin leapt from the couch, struggled into his breeches, grabbed his knife from the desk and his rapier off the floor. Blades at the ready, he burst into the bedchamber, where Amy thrashed wildly in his bed.

Alone.

He could scarcely imagine what demons could cause such a nightmare.

He tossed the weapons into a corner and launched himself onto the bed with a force that nearly sent Amy over the other side.

"Amy, wake up!" He shook her frantically. "It's naught but a dream. Wake up! You're all right."

~

*A*MY HEARD her own cries and struggled through her fog into reality, her screams turning into deep, wrenching sobs.

"Hush, it's over." Colin pulled her into his arms. The quilt, which she'd thrown off during her nightmare, slid to the floor. She wrapped her arms around him, pressed her wet face into his warm chest. He rubbed her back through her chemise in a slow, soothing rhythm, murmuring to her all the while.

At last she calmed enough to pull away. Taking a deep, shuddering breath, she sat up and stared at her right hand in disbelief.

"It was burning…"

"Does it hurt?"

She shook her head, remembering both the real pain from her old injury and the many-times-magnified pain of the dream. But the sensation now was just the fading tingle of memory, and the hand was fine, not the skeleton fingers she'd been half-expecting to see.

"No, it doesn't hurt at all." She dropped her hand to the bed, still staring at it by the light of the dying fire. "I'm sorry I woke you."

"I thought you were being attacked." He laughed shakily and stood up. "I ran in here with my sword, ready to defend you. I'm not sure I'd have been a very effective warrior."

"Oh." She looked up, her gaze landing on his chest, which looked bronze in the shimmering firelight. A thin white scar, long since healed, made a diagonal slash across his left upper arm. She wondered fleetingly what had caused it. Her gaze dropped to his bare feet. Why, he was nearly bare, clad in naught but a pair of unfashionably snug breeches. And here she sat, wearing only her thin chemise…

In an instant, she forgot her dream. Her cheeks flushed, and she shivered. She wished she hadn't taken her gown off to sleep. Both of them were embarrassingly undressed.

"Cold?" he asked. He walked around the bed to retrieve the quilt, made a great show of shaking it out, then let it drift down upon her. The blanket seemed to embrace her as it settled. She wished it were Colin's hands instead.

He sat on the edge of the bed. "Do you want to tell me about your dream?"

She shook her head vehemently. "No. I don't want to think on it at all." She scooted down to lie flat and nestled into the covers. "Would you stay with me for a spell, though? We could talk of something else."

"I'll stay as long as you like," he assured her, taking her hand. "What would you like to talk about?"

His hand felt warm and comforting. She shrugged. "Anything."

"Would you like to talk about how much you like pickled snails?" he suggested with a teasing grin.

"I *did* like them," she protested, although they both knew that wasn't true. She'd tasted one bravely, even swallowed it without gagging, but her appetite had fallen off afterward.

Her stomach was grumbling now. "Are there any apples left?" she asked.

Colin's smile was too knowing. "I believe there are."

He left, returning from the study with a shiny red apple. When she sat up and reached for it, he pulled it back playfully. "Hungry, are you?" Grinning, he handed it to her and stepped over to the windows.

Amy took a bite and slowly chewed. She watched him peer out into the night, his hands linked behind his back.

"It's still snowing hard," he told her. "I reckon we may be stuck here through tomorrow."

"Mmm-hmm," she replied around a mouthful of juicy apple. The fruit was sweet, she was cozy, and she could think of worse fates than being stuck with Colin Chase another day and night.

"I should do bookwork tomorrow, so long as I'm here."

"Mmm-hmm." She took another crunching bite.

"What will you do?" He turned from the windows to face her.

Amy chewed and swallowed before answering. "I can read. Try my hand at preparing dinner. Help you with your bookwork." She took another big bite.

"I don't need any help."

She shrugged again. "I'll explore your castle, then."

"I'm afraid there's not much to discover." He walked over to the fire, added a log from the basket, and stirred up the embers with a wooden-handled poker. "It's small. And cold and damp."

"None of that will stop me."

Colin crossed back to her bedside and stood looking down at her with a wry smile, his teeth as white as the snow outside. "I suppose a bit of cold and damp are unlikely to deter the likes of you. So long as there's not a horse involved."

Grinning, she held out the apple core and slid down under the covers.

He put the core on the table next to the bed. "Better?"

"Much." She wiggled under the quilt, getting comfortable.

"Good." Offering her a distracted nod, he turned to the door.

"No, don't leave yet." She patted the bed beside her. "You said you'd stay as long as I liked."

With seeming reluctance, he turned back and slowly sat down. Amy reached over and took his hand. He tensed; she saw the muscles go rigid beneath his bronzed skin.

The nightmare had left her completely. The apple rested comfortably in her stomach, the room was warm, the bed was soft, and her hand tingled in Colin's. She gazed at his profile in the wavering firelight, willing him to kiss her. Just one more time. Just once more before he put her on a ship and she sailed out of his life forever.

Could she persuade him somehow? He hated her, didn't he? Or at least he didn't like her—she was naught but a bother to him, an inconvenience he needed to rid himself of. But he seemed to like kissing her, for some inexplicable reason…

She squeezed his hand, and he turned to meet her gaze.

Her heart beat faster. His eyes searched her face, and his free hand rose to wipe a bit of apple juice off her chin. His hand lingered; his knuckles grazed her cheek.

He was going to kiss her, she knew it.

THIRTY-ONE

"**C**RIMINY**,**" Colin murmured. Amy's skin was petal soft, her eyes dark liquid pools of longing. He leaned closer. He couldn't move away, not with her looking at him like that. And he knew instinctively that she'd keep looking at him like that until she got what she wanted.

The minx.

He'd kiss her just once—an innocent goodnight kiss—and then he'd leave.

When she closed her eyes, he brushed her lips with his, a mere whisper of sensation. A little sound escaped her throat, and her arms came up and around his neck, dragging him back down. She twined her fingers in his hair, her lips sweet and insistent.

"Amy," he groaned, trying feebly to pull away. But in the end he gave in. He'd never really had a chance. He was weak.

And she was heaven. Soft and eager and smelling of roses. He seemed to forget where he was, who he was…he forgot about everything but her.

It was a long while before he found it in himself to break contact. Her eyes fluttered open, deep purple in the low light. She drew a long, shuddering breath.

Using every ounce of his willpower, he pulled back. "I cannot do this."

She raised herself to place a warm, damp kiss in the hollow of his neck. Her eyes questioning, she fell back to the pillows.

She truly was a minx!

"Amy," he said, standing up, "this isn't right."

"Why not?" she asked breathily. "I *like* kissing you."

"I like it too, but we shouldn't be kissing. I'm sorry."

She struggled up on her elbows. "Would you *please* stop saying you're sorry every time you kiss me!"

"I'm sorry." He smiled innocently, and she burst into helpless giggles.

But seconds later, his smile reversed to a frown, and he turned away, looking into the fire. He ran his hands through his hair. "Amy?"

She sobered instantly. "What?"

"You understand what I'm telling you, yes? I cannot marry you, so I shouldn't be kissing you. It's not that I don't want to, love."

He stopped himself from clapping a hand over his mouth. But he couldn't stop himself from whirling around to see her expression.

Her eyes were wide and round, her mouth agape.

Love, he'd called her. *Stupid, stupid, stupid.* What had he been thinking?

He hadn't, obviously. He hadn't been thinking at all. The word had escaped his lips thoughtlessly.

He'd never been "in love," and he didn't love Amy. He was infatuated, to be sure, but that didn't mean he loved her. He hardly knew her, despite their weeks of acquaintance.

Besides, love wasn't part of his plan. Love was dangerous. It made one too vulnerable, too open to the pain of loss and betrayal. Look how much strife this mere *infatuation* was causing him! *Love* must be many times worse!

Until he could rid himself of her, he had to be more careful, put more distance between them.

"Don't leave," she reminded him, then sighed and closed her eyes.

In the dancing firelight, her face looked stunning and flawless. Despite everything, he wanted to lie beside her and wrap her in his arms. His pulse quickened at the thought of staying with her.

But he couldn't stay with her *that* way. Instead he backed up and settled himself on the chest at the foot of the bed.

He sat there until she slept, until her breathing came even and untroubled. And then he sat there watching her for a while longer before leaving.

Something in him hoped it would still be snowing hard in the morning.

THIRTY-TWO

*O*N THE MORNING, Colin brought Amy breakfast in bed, then refused her offer of help again before disappearing into his study.

She sighed. Nothing had changed there.

After eating, she quickly bathed from the washstand and donned her old gown, then decided to see if she could find clean sheets to change the bedding before she left the room. She hadn't noticed anyplace linens might be kept in the unrestored portions of the house, so she looked around the bedroom. The chamber held no cupboard, only the chest at the foot of the bed. She lifted its heavy wooden lid, and Colin's scent wafted out.

She breathed deeply, a smile teasing at her lips. Inside, his clothes were neatly folded. The suits were darker colors than were currently in fashion—hunter green, deep blue, rich brown —the fabrics fine, the decorations simple and tasteful.

One was black velvet with glinting gold braid…was it the same one he'd worn for the coronation procession, or had he grown taller since then? His shirts were very white, sewn of gossamer cambric that felt smooth and expensive beneath her fingertips. She shook one out and held it up to herself, giggling when it fell well below her knees.

Carefully she folded and replaced it, then delved beneath lace-edged cravats, tall boot stockings, and more handkerchiefs than a man could possibly use in a lifetime. To her vast relief, she found extra sheets in the bottom. And atop them, a small leather-bound book.

Gold lettering on the red cover identified it as *Hesperides, or The Works Both Human and Divine of Robert Herrick, Esq.* Inside, the front page was inscribed in beautiful, flowing script.

"March 1651. Poetry, for my son the dreamer. Your loving Mother."

Colin, a dreamer? Amy's lips curved at the thought.

She opened the book to a random page.

Gather ye rosebuds while ye may,
Old Times is still a-flying:
And this same flower that smiles today,
Tomorrow will be dying.

Words to live by, were they not? Smiling, she replaced the book and changed the sheets, folding the used ones and leaving them atop the chest. Anxious to explore the castle, she hurried to finish getting ready.

A survey of the ground floor revealed nothing of interest. Narrow slits through the curtain wall let in little light, rendering the unrestored chambers dank and dark. What was left of the furniture was draped in cloth, encrusted with layers of dust sufficient to discourage her from peeking underneath.

She paused at the closed door to Colin's study, picturing him inside hacking away at his ledgers. She hoped he was suffering mightily, although in truth she had no idea whether he had an aptitude for such work. There was a lot she didn't know about him, she admitted to herself.

Squaring her shoulders, she made her way to the entry, where the beautifully restored oak staircase renewed her hopes of finding something more intriguing upstairs. She trudged slowly up, then stopped when her gaze lit on her trunk down-stairs, still sitting against the wall where Colin had shoved it. What was left of her family lay locked inside.

She closed her eyes, rubbing her temples. Months had passed since the fire. What would her father think of the way she'd put off getting on with her life, put off reestablishing the family business she'd promised would continue?

"Oh, Papa!" Her hoarse whisper filled the entry as she lifted her skirts and bolted downstairs for the trunk, then dragged it scraping along the stone floor to the bedchamber. She reached to pull the key from her hem even as she shut the door behind her.

Falling to her knees, she worked the lock with unsteady fingers, then threw open the lid. The tray on top was lifted and dropped to the floor, the box of loose gemstones discarded without a thought. For underneath lay the real treasure: bits of her father wrapped in small squares of white flannel, pieces of his soul etched forever in his exquisite works of art.

She thrust her hands into the trunk, filled both fists with jewelry, then moved to the bed and allowed the pieces to sift through her open fingers...remembering.

THIRTY-THREE

WITH A HEAVY sigh, Colin dropped his head into his hands. His desk was piled high with receipts, his ledgers lined with numbers he'd spent the morning staring at with unfocused eyes.

In fact, he'd found himself unable to focus on anything this morning—anything except Amy Goldsmith.

He twisted the heavy gold ring on his finger distractedly. It was obvious he wasn't going to accomplish anything today. A glance out the window convinced him he wouldn't be delivering his distraction to the docks today, either.

The storm was waning, but the snow still fell steadily and the drifts were deep. His rumbling stomach reminded him it was past noon and Amy had offered to prepare dinner.

Leaving the study without bothering to don a cloak, Colin briefly poked his head into each of the empty downstairs chambers, then dashed through the freezing great hall and into the kitchen. He'd laid a fire for her earlier, hoping she'd be inspired to prepare something hot.

But she was nowhere to be found. Quick glances into the pantry and buttery also failed to reveal her presence. There was nothing bubbling in the stew pot nor any other evidence she'd been at work.

Was she lost? No, Greystone was too small to be confusing.

Hurt, perhaps? That was a possibility. Despite all the time and money he'd spent on restorations, the structure was still in bad shape; she could have tripped and twisted her ankle, or even worse.

He set out grimly to find her, back through the great hall and the ceaseless snow.

Once in the entry, his gaze swept up the stairs, and he remembered the library. Of course, he thought, relieved. Ford had told him of the countless hours she'd spent in Cainewood's library. She must have discovered his library and lost track of the time, forgetting about dinner altogether.

He took the steps two at a time, ran to the back of the upper level, and burst through the library door.

No—she wasn't here. Nor had she been here. Not a speck of the considerable dust was displaced; the titles on the neat rows of books were as obscured by grime as ever.

Amy couldn't have found this room and left it undisturbed. It was completely against her nature to ignore a room full of books, regardless of its filth and neglect.

She wasn't in any of the other upstairs chambers, either. His heart started pounding as he once again imagined her stuck somewhere, arms or legs broken, perhaps lying in the freezing snow or at the bottom of the oubliette. He should have toured her around the castle and offered to help her prepare dinner.

What had he been thinking?

He'd been thinking about getting away from her for a while, that was what. He'd been pretending she had no effect on his life, that he could set to work as usual, regardless of her presence. He'd been hoping that a few hours of separation would break the spell she seemed to have woven around him.

It had all been for naught—he was as spellbound as ever, and now she might be hurt. He cursed at himself. She was his responsibility, and at the very least he should have asked her to stay in the bedchamber with a book while he worked.

The bedchamber. He hadn't even looked there. Maybe she *was* in the bedchamber with a book. As he hurried down the stairs, he pictured her curled on the bed, lost in the world of literature or perhaps even napping—she'd been awake in the night, after all. He could hardly blame her for losing track of time.

He knocked softly on the door, half afraid he'd wake her up, half afraid she wouldn't be there at all.

No answer.

"Amy?" he called, his voice muffled by the thick oak. "Amy? Are you in there?"

He knocked louder. "Amy?"

On the faint hope she was inside, sound asleep, he eased open the door.

His jaw went slack at the sight that greeted him.

The room was strewn with glittering jewels. She knelt on the floor beside her trunk—that deuced heavy trunk that she'd insisted go with her everywhere. And no wonder. The thing was heaped with gold and gems and heaven knew what else.

"Why didn't you answer me?" he asked.

"I—I don't know. You surprised me."

"You were supposed to be preparing dinner, and I couldn't find you." He tore his gaze away from the treasure to look at her. Her face was inscrutable. "I was…worried," he finished lamely.

"I'm sorry. I forgot." She glanced out the window, but the sun was hidden behind snow clouds and gave no indication of the time. "Is it very late?"

"It doesn't signify," he murmured, frowning as his brain began catching up with his eyes. "Good heavens, I suggested you leave that trunk on carriages overnight! Why didn't you tell me what was in there?"

"I…was taught never to trust anyone." The guarded expression fell away, and now she looked troubled. "I'm sorry. I should have told you. You've given me no reason not to trust you."

Colin knelt beside her, instinctively wanting to soothe her distress. "It's all right," he said softly. "I understand."

When she smiled at him, he was surprised to see her eyes bright with unshed tears. She was still fragile emotionally, in a way that made him want to gather her into his arms and protect her from the world. He touched her instead, just lightly on the arm, and smiled back, a smile that widened as they seemed to reach a silent understanding and he saw her eyes clear.

He skimmed his fingers down her arm, and her cheeks flushed pink. She looked away quickly and began gathering the jewelry.

He grasped her hand, halting her efforts. "May I see some of your things?"

She glanced at him in surprise. "Of course." Her face lit with pleasure as she gave him the piece she was holding, a large diamond stomacher brooch.

"This is amazing." An enormous, rectangular step-cut diamond rested in the center, surrounded by round diamonds set into a spray of gold leaves. He turned his hand to admire how the gems caught the light.

"Papa bought the center stone from a dealer in Antwerp, then saved it for almost a decade before mounting it." She wasn't blushing now; she spoke with enthusiasm and confidence. She missed her craft, Colin realized. "He rarely showed this to anyone. I don't think he really wanted to part with it."

"It's a shame it's never been worn and enjoyed."

"I made some bodkins to go with it." She rummaged in the trunk for a few seconds and came out with a half-dozen long gold pins, each topped with a gold leaf set with a rose-cut diamond. She dropped them into his other palm. "They would have been so pretty in a lady's hair, with the matching brooch. I always thought that someday, someone very important would own them."

"Someone important owns them now," Colin said, half-teasing.

But her heart leapt into her eyes. He'd best be more careful.

Mindful not to stick her with the pins, he handed the jewelry back to her and watched her wrap it up in two of the many pieces of flannel that were scattered about.

She'd gone quiet again. He moved to sit on the bed, where a pile of trinkets glittered. "Is there anything here that you made?"

"Oh, many things." She jumped up to sit beside him, sifting through the jewels until she found an oval, coral-colored cameo and handed it to him shyly.

He smiled down at it. Set into a braided gold bezel, the intricate carving was a profile of a beautiful young woman. She wore a little necklace of twisted gold wire with a tiny diamond pendant attached.

Colin narrowed his eyes and looked more closely. "She looks like you," he suddenly realized, and she giggled.

"Papa said the same thing. I didn't hold with that at the time, but then Mama agreed, and others, and I finally decided she must be me after all. Although I swear I hadn't intended to carve a likeness of myself. See, her hair is loose, and I never used to wear my hair that way."

"Yet you've worn it loose since the fire. Why did you change it?"

"I never learned how to plait it myself." She thought a minute, frowning. "It seems to fit my life now; I feel like a different person." She shrugged. "I wore it plaited for practical reasons—I couldn't work with it billowing about, getting in the way. And I haven't made much jewelry the last few months, have I?"

"No, you surely haven't," he agreed with a wry smile. "I fancy it loose, anyway."

"Do you really?"

Colin cleared his throat. Now, why had he said that? "She truly looks like you now, at any rate," he rushed to say, hoping to gloss over the thoughtless remark. He held the cameo between a finger and thumb, glancing back and forth between Amy and her likeness. The resemblance was unmistakable. "May I have it?" he asked, surprising himself.

Amy beamed. "Oh, yes, I would love for you to have it! And anything else you want," she added, gesturing at the pile on the bed.

He laughed at that, pleased with her generosity, for he didn't know what he'd have said had she refused him.

He really wanted the cameo.

"No, this will do nicely. I thank you."

"My pleasure."

The underlying warmth in her voice enchanted him. She seemed genuinely happy to give him the trinket. He wondered if she had any idea how much it meant to him.

The cameo was but one piece from a virtual treasure trove of jewelry. Looking over the pile on the bed, mentally adding it to the amount littering the floor and left in the trunk, he came to the conclusion the trunk had been nearly full. Why, it was a cache any pirate wouldn't hesitate to kill for!

He shook his head, chiding himself for not realizing the contents of the trunk, and at the same time amazed at her deft concealment of it. The more he learned about her, the more he admired her. She had a streak of self-preservation that ran deep.

He set aside the cameo and sifted through the jewelry on the bed until something caught his eye—a brooch in the shape of a bow, encrusted with tiny rubies, sapphires, emeralds, and diamonds. "This is a pretty piece. Did you make it also?"

Amy nodded. "There are many similar pieces here. Galants, they're called, and very popular. I think we could all make them in our sleep." She smiled at the memory. "Shall I give it to Kendra, do you think? And we should choose something for Jason and Ford, too." Her face lit up at the idea. "Everyone was so kind to me—why didn't I think of this before?"

"Because you would have shocked us silly." When she laughed, Colin joined in. "Regardless, it's not necessary," he assured her. Chances were Amy would be living off this jewelry in the months and years to come; she shouldn't be giving things away.

"I want to do it." She dropped to the floor, already delving into the trunk for the perfect gifts.

"No." He put a hand on her arm.

She shook it off. "I insist." Gems flashed as she rummaged around, her attention wholly focused on the jewelry. "It was a terrible lack of manners on my part; I must thank them for their hospitality."

He gave up. She rivaled the Chases for stubbornness; he'd give her that.

After much searching and good-natured bickering, they settled on an aigrette for Ford. Of all the brothers, he liked to dandy-up a bit, and the fancy pin would make a smart statement on his hat.

Jason was another story. Amy insisted on giving him a large

pocket watch with an enamelled face and an open-work lid set with one enormous oval sapphire and eight smaller ones.

"It's too much," Colin protested. "Besides, he has a pocket watch."

"I've seen it. It's small and has no lid. The Marquess of Cainewood should pull out an impressive watch to check the time. Papa had someone just like Jason in mind when he made this."

"Here's a nice, large watch." Colin pointed out a likely specimen with a solid, simply engraved lid.

"No. I want him to have this one. He opened up his home to me, Colin—"

"I didn't leave him much of a choice," he interrupted wryly.

"That doesn't signify. He was perfectly wonderful to me, and this is the least I can do. Besides, Robert made that one. I want him to have one my father made."

"Robert?"

"Robert Stanley. Our apprentice."

"Your apprentice?" Twisting his ring, he had a sudden vision of an insolent blunt-featured young man leaning against the archway to Goldsmith & Son's back room. "You mean the red-haired fellow?"

She shot him an appraising glance. "You remember him?"

Distrustful pale blue eyes. He remembered, all right.

That settled it. Not only was Amy intractable, but Colin didn't want anyone in his family to own anything made by that apprentice. He felt uneasy just thinking about the man.

Amy was already wrapping up the remaining jewelry. He set the pocket watch with their other choices and began to help her. "Whatever happened to him? Do you know?"

"Who?"

"The apprentice. Robert." He disliked even saying his name.

Her hands stilled for a moment. "I have no idea. He went off to help fight the fire, and I never saw him again." She toyed with a flannel square. "I was supposed to marry him."

"Were you, now?" No wonder Robert had acted so hostile. An imagined scenario popped into Colin's mind, of Amy kissing the freckled, carrot-topped apprentice. It made him sick in his gut, and the question came out of his mouth before he could catch himself. "Do you love him?"

"No." Amy tensed visibly as she folded the flannel around a bracelet. "My father arranged the marriage when I was born. It had taken my parents many years to have a child, and he suspected they'd never have another. Lacking a son, he needed someone to run the shop, and he'd known the Stanleys forever." She moved to the trunk to set the bracelet inside, then returned to the bed. "My betrothal papers burned in the fire. It was the only good thing that came of it."

Colin released his breath, which he hadn't realized he'd been holding. Just because he couldn't have Amy didn't mean he wanted some dolt like Robert to get her.

Yet she had to marry...all girls had to marry. "Isn't he still expecting you to wed him?"

"That matters not." She slipped a topaz ring on her finger and pulled it off again. "I would never have wed him of my own free will."

"What of the church records?" he reminded her. "He may think to use those to hold you to the betrothal."

She shrugged, still gazing at the ring. "We were betrothed during the Commonwealth."

Colin nodded. The Puritans considered marriage solely a matter between the couple and the state, not a pledge before God. During Cromwell's rule, weddings had been performed by a Justice of the Peace, and betrothals had taken place without ceremony.

He lifted a torsade of pearls. "Still, you must wed, Amy. With these jewels you could buy a title—"

"And marry a nobleman?" The topaz ring fell from her hand to the bed, and her eyes burned into his. "No. I'd never be able to reestablish Goldsmith and Sons."

"No, of course you wouldn't." Absently, he fingered the heavy twisted ropes of pearls. "But you'll be in France, not London."

"I'll open a shop there. Not right away, but eventually."

"But you're a—"

"No buts, Colin." She smiled at her use of his words, then

turned serious. "Yes, I'm a girl. But I'm also a jeweler, and I promised my father I wouldn't let Goldsmith and Sons die with me. No, it was more than a promise—a vow. And our last real conversation."

Colin could see the subject was closed. Consumed by disturbing thoughts, he toyed with the necklace, admiring the way the creamy colors matched and the pearl sizes graduated along the strands. The little clicks of the pearls sounded loud in the silence.

"This must be worth a fortune," he said at last.

She nodded her head. "Pearls have doubled in price in my lifetime, and they're still rising. Would you like it? The clasp is beautiful, but I don't know who made it, so it has no particular value to me."

Colin glanced at the clasp, delicate filigree encrusted with sapphires and diamonds. He wanted nothing except the cameo. "I wouldn't dream of taking this from you. I know King Charles and his cronies drape themselves in such jewels, but no man in my family would be caught dead wearing ropes of pearls."

He couldn't give it to Priscilla—he'd never feel right giving her anything he'd taken from Amy.

"Besides, you'll need to sell it to open your shop. Such an undertaking will be quite expensive—"

She shrugged. "I have the gold."

"The gold?"

"In the bottom." She waved at the trunk. "My family has been accumulating coins forever. It was"—she hesitated—"a secret. There. Now you know." Her sudden disarming smile enchanted him. "It's why my father never worried when business fell off during the Commonwealth. There are a few gold bars as well—for fabrication, you understand. We never melted coins."

Surreptitiously, he hoped, Colin nudged aside some of the jewelry in the trunk, revealing a pile of gold coins, many of them old and pitted; he glimpsed one dated 1537. Gauging the thickness of the trunk's walls, he came to the conclusion there was a fortune in gold coins there. A vast, unbelievable fortune.

He was shocked speechless. Why, Amy was rich! Richer even

than Priscilla, or at the very least richer than Priscilla would be until the death of her very healthy father.

His gaze swept to Amy wrapping her jewelry, calmly making a pile of white-blanketed bundles, surrounded by gold, diamonds…riches beyond his comprehension. But what he felt for her had nothing to do with wealth or position, and everything to do with the way just looking at her made his whole body feel warm…

Stop. He clamped down on the thoughts, cast them aside. They were emotional. Dangerous.

He resumed helping her, full speed. The trunk should be locked and hidden. Although he'd been raised surrounded by beautiful, expensive things, because of the war his family had never had much in the way of coinage. This much gold, exposed, made him uncomfortable.

They placed the last pieces on top, and Amy retrieved the fitted tray and set it in place with a flourish. Then she reached for a small wooden casket that she'd apparently tossed halfway under the bed.

"The stones," she said, in answer to his unasked question. She flipped open the box's cover to reveal neat rows of paper packets. Pulling one out, she opened the precisely folded paper and placed the contents in his hand.

He marveled at the two loose, matched gems. "Diamonds?" he guessed.

"Yes. Waiting to be made into something wonderful. Earrings, perhaps." She took back the diamonds, her fingers flying as she refolded the paper in a complicated pattern. Even having seen her do it, Colin doubted he could make such a packet from a plain rectangle of paper.

Amy slipped the packet back and pulled out another, opening it to reveal hundreds of tiny diamonds. "Melee, they're called," she explained. "About five carats worth, averaging fifty stones to the carat." The pile of stones glimmered in their paper, and Colin leaned forward to look. Instead of handing them to him, though, she refolded the packet. "If they spilled, we'd never find them all in this carpet," she explained apologetically.

She replaced the packet and flipped through a dozen or

more. On the fronts, Colin glimpsed nonsensical numbers in tiny, precise handwriting. With a smile and a nod, she finally pulled out one and unfolded it, revealing an enormous blood-red ruby.

Spellbinding, it shone with a life of its own. Colin was no gem connoisseur, but he was certain he'd never beheld such perfection before. He reached for it.

"My father was working on a design for this when he"—she swallowed hard—"when he died. He meant to make it the centerpiece of a necklace. There are twenty carats of matched diamonds in here that he'd planned to set with it."

"It's beautiful," Colin responded gently. He examined the ruby, holding it up to the light before setting it back on the paper in her palm. "These gems must be worth an enormous amount." His vision clouded as he tried to imagine how one young woman could have so much in her possession.

"I'll warrant they're valuable," she admitted, "although I never think about it, really. You cannot easily use them to buy anything, like the gold." She folded the paper and returned it to the box. "They were always just there. Some of them have been in my family, waiting for the perfect mounting, for more than a hundred years."

Removing another packet, she spilled the contents into Colin's open hand.

He walked to the window, moving his palm so the twenty-odd diamonds shimmered in the light reflected off the snow outside. "They sparkle so..." he murmured. A myriad of subtly different colors, they ranged from a pure clear-white to a light but distinct yellow.

"About half a carat each. Not well-matched. They'd end up in different pieces."

He closed his fist around the glittering stones. "They're beautiful. I can hardly credit...Amy, there's so much here." He frowned in puzzlement. "Your family...you had so much. Yet you lived above your shop..."

She came closer, holding out the paper. He tipped the diamonds into it, a dazzling waterfall of costly gems.

"We weren't—I'm not—aristocratic. No one expected us to live lavishly. If people had known what we had, it would have been stolen." She folded the packet and returned it to the box, closing the lid.

"But—"

"We lived very nicely." She smiled at his confusion. "I had the best clothes, and we always had a maid and housekeeper. We ate well, and we never had to prepare meals or clean up after ourselves. Mama collected things—pretty, useless things—figurines and vases that made her smile. We had books, we went to the theater—the gold was security, so we never had to worry. It was collected over so many generations that I feel as though it's not mine, really...almost like I hold it in safekeeping for someone else." She walked to the trunk and set the box inside.

"But it *is* yours, Amy. It's all yours."

Silently she knelt by the trunk to close and lock it, then joined him again at the window. They both gazed at the snow drifting down. The storm was dwindling, and this would probably be the last night they'd ever be together.

"You're right," she said softly. "It is all mine. But in the last two years I've learned that what counts are the people you have around you. Money isn't important."

"It is if you don't have it," he returned bitterly, thinking about his struggles to get the estate into shape and restore his home, delaying his marriage plans.

"I'd trade it all—every bit of it," she whispered, "to have my parents again."

He felt a twisting sensation in his chest. She was right, of course. Turning to her, he took her face between his palms and tilted it to meet her eyes. "I know," he whispered back. "I know you would."

The chamber was quiet. The snow fell inaudibly outside the window; the crackling fire and their breathing were the only sounds. Her eyes deepened in color as he gazed into them, and he bent his head to meet her lips.

Amy felt her torn spirits mending in his embrace. His mouth was slow and gentle. His hands crept from her cheeks down the sides of her neck, to her shoulders and around to her back, where she felt their warm imprints pressing her securely against him.

A long, dreamy, melting time later they broke the kiss, and Amy laid her head on his chest. Beneath her ear, his heart beat strong and steady. He stroked her hair with unhurried movements and twisted it in his fingers.

Her gaze drifted to the jewelry that sparkled on the bed. The galant, the aigrette, the pocket watch…the cameo. The thought of him owning it made her skin tingle.

Would he treasure it? Years from now, would he look at it and remember the connection they'd shared? She hoped so. If he felt even a shred of the emotion she did, she suspected he'd remember it all his life, for she was certain she would.

"You said you wouldn't kiss me again," she reminded him, feeling a bit woozy.

"I know," he said, his voice laced with something—resignation? "But it's just a kiss, is it not?"

It *was* just a kiss. And though kisses were all she'd ever get from Colin Chase, she would take them, and gladly. How wrong could that be, after all? Once she got to France, who knew if she'd ever be kissed again?

"I owe you a dinner," she reminded him, pulling away with a grin. "Are you willing to try my very first stew?"

"With a side dish of pickled snails?" he asked, grinning back mischievously.

She groaned and headed out of the bedchamber.

THIRTY-FOUR

*W*ITH A HUM of satisfaction, Amy moved her bishop diagonally across the chessboard toward Colin's king.

"Check," she announced.

Colin was hard put to keep a smile off his face. After two complete games, it was clear Amy was the thoughtful tactician, while his style was fast and aggressive. But he'd put his mind to this match, planning his moves far in advance. He knew exactly what would happen from here on out.

He moved his king one space; then, the game well in hand, he turned his thoughts to something even more diverting: plotting the perfect prank.

Amy's gray marble knight made a decisive click against the black and white board. "Check."

As Colin's hand shot out to rescue his king, he decided he would offer to prepare supper. Alone in the pantry, he ought to be able to dream up a clever prank.

Ahh...yes.

She grinned, oozing confidence, and slid her bishop into place. "Check."

He managed to respond with no more than a speculative glance and a raise of one brow. Though he was relieved to find them much more evenly matched in chess than they'd been in piquet, there was no reason to rub his impending victory in her lovely face.

He tapped his king into place, threatening her knight.

Amy frowned at the board, then slowly withdrew the knight, relieving the pressure on his king.

Colin rubbed his hands together in glee. Now he controlled the events of the board, and he quickly moved one of his jade-green rooks across to threaten Amy's gray one.

She had no choice—either move her rook or lose it. Colin saw her freeze—she could see the inevitable. No matter which way she went, she'd be dead in two moves—checkmated by his bishop.

She looked up, a surprised, wry smile on her face, then her hand moved to her king and gently laid it down.

Colin reached across the table to offer the obligatory victor's handshake. "Good game."

"Shall we make it three out of five?"

He grinned. "I believe two out of three was the agreement." The slim margin of one game made victory all the sweeter. "Shall I collect supper?" Rising, he glanced at the clock on the mantel. "A midnight supper, as it turns out."

"I'll help," Amy offered.

"No, it's my turn." He shrugged into his cloak before she could offer again. "See if you can finish that book. You said you cannot bear to let me return it to Jason's library without seeing how it ends."

Reaching for the book, the tenth volume of Madeleine de Scudéry's *Clélie*, she smiled and settled back.

Apparently she wasn't suspicious.

He ducked out the door before she could change her mind.

THIRTY-FIVE

 *W*HEN COLIN came in whistling, Amy was jarred out of Clélie's adventures.

She'd never heard him whistle before. Although he did it quite well, he sounded a bit too cheerful, even for a fellow who'd just won a chess match.

"What might you be so happy about?"

"Oh, nothing." Still whistling, he moved the chess set off the table and laid out their light supper. "Sorry, but I've no bread," he said, apologizing for the unusual offering. Wine, oranges, smoked salmon, small dried biscuits, and another jar of those disgusting pickled snails.

Amy frowned at the stupid brown things. "Haven't you had enough of those?"

"Never," he said, and went back to whistling.

Amy's book lay open and ignored as he poured wine into two goblets. He was happy about something, she thought—probably that he'd finally be able to get rid of her tomorrow. The snow had stopped a couple of hours earlier.

Handing her a goblet, he leaned down to kiss the top of her head. She sipped, watching him through her eyelashes. He was hardly acting like someone who couldn't stand her presence—it was confusing, to say the least.

"Like it?" he asked.

"It's nice." Accepting a biscuit layered with fish, she popped it into her mouth, closed her book and set it on the table.

"It's Madeira." He took a swallow of his own wine, then raised the goblet in salute. "King Charles's favorite."

Chewing slowly, she watched him out of the corner of her eye. Underneath his light, meaningless conversation, she sensed a glee he could scarcely contain.

Something was up.

On the other hand, she reminded herself, she didn't know him very well.

Since he'd come charging into the bedroom half-naked last night, she knew him better than she had before, though, she thought, feeling her cheeks heat. Her gaze traveled his snug breeches and white shirt, which was loosely laced, revealing his tanned throat. And beneath that shirt, she remembered...

"Where did you get the scar?" she asked suddenly.

"The scar?"

"On your arm. The long, white—"

"Oh. That scar." He sat beside her and placed more salmon on a biscuit. "I seldom notice it anymore." As though the injury were of no consequence, he waved the hand with the biscuit airily. "It's an old fencing practice wound—I was fourteen or so."

"Didn't it hurt?"

"Oh, yes." He bit off half the biscuit and washed it down with a gulp of wine. "Someone poured brandy on it—that was the worst part—and then even more brandy down my throat. Then they stitched it up with a needle and thread."

"Marry come up! I cannot even imagine." Amy took a deliberate sip of her own wine, to fortify herself or wash away the image—she wasn't sure which. "And it was only a practice... didn't that make you angry?"

Colin stuck the rest of the biscuit in his mouth and chewed it slowly, considering. "No," he said finally, "it made me one of the best swordsmen in all of Europe. I made sure it would never happen again," he added with a grin.

Amy thought about that: How Colin seemed determined to turn every disadvantage life dealt him into a benefit. He'd done it with his disappointing childhood, resolving to do much better with his own family. He'd done it with his dilapidated estate, laboring tirelessly to turn it into something of value. He seemed to believe hard work and dedication—whether countless hours of swordplay or working the land with his own hands—were the best means to a happy ending. And he didn't expect the good things in life to be handed to him on a silver platter.

There was much to admire in such an attitude, she thought.

Colin, on the other hand, had ceased thinking about it at all. The jar of snails on the table had reclaimed one hundred percent of his attention. Those snails beckoned, practically begging to be opened and play their part in this evening's performance.

He considered himself a veritable model of patience as he waited until he'd polished off his fifth biscuit before reaching for the jar and removing the lid.

"Ready for one of these?" he asked innocently.

She held up a half-eaten biscuit. "Not yet," she said through a mouthful of fish.

With a shrug, Colin nonchalantly dipped his spoon into the jar, scooped a snail, and placed it in his mouth. Now came the difficult part.

Even the foreknowledge left him vastly unprepared for the taste of his concoction. Struggling to keep his face straight, he washed down the snail with a large gulp of wine as quickly as he could. If Amy succeeded in pretending she liked *these* snails, she'd be the best actress he'd ever seen.

She finished her biscuit and put together another, and then another. At last, when he doubted she could cram in another bite, she announced, "I'm ready."

"For what?" He fixed her with a puzzled, innocent look.

"For a snail, of course," she snapped.

"Oh, you want one?" Quelling a smile, he spooned out a snail and watched the liquid dribble back into the jar, his tinkering undetectable. He licked his lips.

"Here," he offered, moving his spoon toward her mouth with the mock generosity of a man reluctant to part with his favorite morsel of food.

When she opened her mouth, he delicately placed the snail inside. Though her face scrunched up in a look of dismay, she managed to swallow it. Then rushed to wash it down, draining her goblet of wine in the process.

Refilling the goblet with pretended indifference, Colin struggled to contain his mirth. "Is something wrong?" he asked, knitting his brows in feigned concern.

"It—it tasted a bit different. Do you suppose it might be a bad jar?"

Colin was enjoying himself immensely. "No, they all came from the same batch. Perhaps you simply don't care for pickled snails."

"No, no, I like them," Amy insisted. "But this one tasted different. Try one, you'll see."

"I already had one," he reminded her. "It was fine. Try another."

She put a hand on her stomach. "Please, I'd feel better if you have another one first."

There was nothing for it. He had to eat another snail or give up the game—and he was having too much fun to admit his trickery just yet.

He took a deep breath before popping one in his mouth, then swallowed it without chewing.

"It's fine," he declared. "Delicious, in fact. Perhaps there was one bad snail in the batch." He fished out a snail and handed Amy the spoon. "Here, try another."

While Amy moved at the speed of a snail herself, inching the spoon toward her lips, he took a long sip of wine and swished it around his mouth to remove the foul taste.

Relieved, he turned to her expectantly.

Her face was slowly turning red. When she gagged, he burst out laughing.

THIRTY-SIX

*A*MY GASPED as she finally realized what was happening. She spit the snail into her napkin. "Colin Chase," she demanded. "What have you done to these?"

Wiping tears from his eyes, Colin sputtered, "S-salt. And sugar."

A smile dawned as she reflected that she'd been well and truly duped. She deserved it, she decided, starting to giggle. "What else? What else was in there?"

"Nothing, I swear. You didn't care for them to begin with, remember?" His eyes glittered again, diabolically. "Oh, I forgot. You'd never admit to that."

"I admit it; I admit it," she choked out, laughing. "I hate pickled snails! I'll never eat another of those vile creatures so long as I live—with or without your special recipe."

She laughed again, partially because his prank *was* funny, and partially in relief, because she felt as though he'd just given her a test which she'd passed with flying colors.

One wasn't allowed to be close to Colin Chase if he or she couldn't take a joke.

And yet…he wasn't really trying to get closer to her, was he? She'd be leaving the country tomorrow, after all. His pleasure at her reaction, and the motive she'd credited him with, had to be figments of her imagination.

"Having coerced that admission from you," he declared now, "I proclaim my prank an unqualified success."

"Wait a minute, Lord Greystone. You were forced to eat two of those putrid snails, the same as I was. Surely a superior prank would not require its perpetrator to suffer the same consequences."

"You would dare to criticize the quality of my prank?" Though Colin's eyes went wide with pretended outrage, in truth he couldn't have been more pleased with Amy than he was at the moment.

He was pleased with her good-humored response to his prank. Pleased with her rediscovered ease in his presence. Pleased with her quick wit, pleased with her high color and those incredible sparkling amethyst eyes...all in all, he was very pleased.

"Mrs. Goldsmith, what qualifications do you have to recommend you as a prank judge?"

"My qualifications are beside the point entirely. The fact is, I saw the prank you played on Kendra a few days ago, and she told me about Benchley's fake murder and other tricks you've played over the years." She raised her chin. "The fact is, this prank was just not up to your usual standards."

Raising a brow, he brought his nose to within an inch of hers. "Is that so?"

Amy's heart beat a little faster at his nearness. "Absolutely. Without a doubt—" She broke off as his lips came down on hers, cutting off any further aspersions on his prank, not to mention her air supply.

Their good-natured argument was forgotten. This kiss was unhurried, his lips exploring her as though he were trying to commit her to memory. Time slowed until there was nothing else but the taste of him, the scent of him, the feel of him. She felt and heard his breathing become uneven, matching hers.

Colin heard a little sound escape her throat, driving him to distraction. He knew he was acting irrationally; he'd been irrational since the day he'd walked into her shop. But she would be gone tomorrow, and he could be rational for the rest of his life.

He'd be faithful to Priscilla for the rest of his life—just as soon as these incredible feelings faded away.

But he didn't want the feelings to fade away just yet, and so he kept kissing Amy. He eased her back onto the couch, still kissing her, then pulled away an inch to look at her. "Oh, my love," he found himself whispering.

Love? My love? What was he saying? And why? For heaven's sake, *why*?

He didn't know. All he knew was she was beautiful and sweet and intelligent and…

You're a fool, Colin Chase, said a little voice in his head, *a fool if you let her get away.*

But a louder voice was speaking, too, the voice that Colin considered his honor and his logic. It drowned out the other one, telling him he was committed to a lovely, aristocratic girl who fit his every need. Unbreakably committed.

He should be committed to Bedlam, he thought briefly. Then he silenced the voices by going back to kissing Amy.

But he couldn't keep kissing her forever.

When he finally lifted his head, her arms tightened around him.

"Are you all right?" he asked softly.

She nodded her head and squirmed closer still—and nearly made him fall off the couch.

He caught himself just in time. "We don't really fit here, you know," he teased. "And it's late. We'll be leaving early. We should both get a good night's sleep."

The intimate moment was shattered. Amy released him. "You're right."

Her flat tone took him by surprise. He felt a pang of hurt, or guilt, or he wasn't sure what. He struggled to keep his confusion hidden as he stood. "Let me get you settled," he said stiffly, and pulled her up beside him. "Shall we?" he asked, gesturing to the bedchamber next door.

Not wanting a repeat of last night's embarrassment, Amy kicked off her shoes but otherwise got into the bed fully dressed. She watched Colin stir up the fire and add a couple logs, thinking over the last couple of days she'd spent with him—eating, laughing, whiling away the hours. Kissing…

It had felt like someone else's life. A whole other Amy.

Amethyst. She pronounced the name in her head, drawn-out and elegant. *Amethyst, Lady Greystone.*

No, she decided, she was still Amy. "Lady Greystone" would never work with her hands and create jewelry, never own and run a shop. She wouldn't—couldn't—let herself contemplate the possibility of staying with Colin. Lucky circumstances had resulted in these stolen hours, and it was almost time to return to the real world.

But must she be wrenched from his side so soon? She knew full well she had to leave, but she wasn't quite ready to face her new life. She *needed* to steal a few more hours…a few more kisses. She cast around wildly for an idea, any idea—

"Good night," he said, turning to leave.

"Colin?"

He turned back toward her. "Yes?"

"I—I know we have to leave tomorrow, but…"

"But what?"

"Do you think you could take me to London?" she asked on a sudden burst of inspiration. "I have no clothes at all, not anything, you know, and—well, it would take me naught but a couple of days to purchase everything I need, and then—"

"I'd be happy to take you to London for a few days." Was it her imagination, or did he sound relieved? "We'll find you a chaperone there, and—"

"—I'd prefer not to arrive in France with nothing—"

"Amy." Colin walked closer and planted a warm kiss on her forehead. "I said I'd be happy to take you."

"Oh." It had worked. She could hardly believe it. A few more days with Colin. It seemed like a dream come true.

"We'll stay at the family town house," he said.

Amy's heart galloped with excitement. "Thank you," she breathed.

She was still smiling when he left the room.

THIRTY-SEVEN

*R*ETRIEVING HER book from the study, Amy dragged her trunk to the front door and sat on it to watch through the narrow window. She unfolded the note and read it again. *Amy*, it said in Colin's bold printing,

I have gone with Benchley to retrieve the carriage. Please ready yourself to leave. We will breakfast on the way to London.

Greystone

That was it. No "Dear Amy." No "Love, Colin." Amy told herself nothing was wrong—Colin simply wasn't demonstrative on paper—but she knew she was fooling herself. The Colin she thought she'd come to know here at Greystone had vanished.

She looked up from the note to see the carriage pass under the portcullis and onto the little circular drive in the courtyard. When Colin opened the door, she was standing by her trunk, book in hand, the note safely tucked away.

"Good morning, my lord," she said as cheerfully as she could manage.

Colin winced at the formal address. "Good morning," he muttered back, avoiding her gaze.

He lifted the trunk—more carefully than he had before he'd

known what it contained—and carried it to the carriage. Amy trailed slowly. Colin waved her inside and returned to lock the door, then climbed in opposite her, and they were off.

"Breakfast?" he asked, pulling Kendra's basket from under his seat and setting it on the floor between them. He reached in, selected an apple, and polished it on his shirt before taking a bite.

Amy dug out another apple. Any minute now, she expected him to smile and tease her or start pointing out the features of his estate, but as time crept by she realized it was less and less likely.

They drove a mile or so in awkward silence, the only sounds those of the wheels on the rutted, slushy road, the steady clip-clop of the horse's hooves, and the juicy crunch of apples being chewed and swallowed. Colin fetched a napkin from the basket and deposited his apple core in it, then held it out for Amy to do the same. Their eyes met, Amy's questioning, Colin's hooded and indecisive.

The core-filled napkin dropped from his hand to the basket. "Our time together changed nothing," he blurted out. "I'm still betrothed to Priscilla."

Amy stared at him sitting stone-faced across from her. Unbidden tears threatened to spill from her eyes.

He looked away first. "Don't cry, Amy," he said to the floor. "I don't think I could stand it."

She blinked back the tears. "I know you're betrothed. I haven't been thinking anything had changed. Have I said something to make you think I have?"

"Well, no…" He hesitated, then moved over to her side and took her hand. "No, you said nothing. But as much as I wish to spend time with you in London, there are those who would take note of it and make both our lives miserable."

"I know no one important in London."

"What about your former clientele?"

Amy bit her lip. He had a point. They may not have been her friends, but the fact remained she was acquainted with many of London's elite.

"I don't care," she declared. "I'll be in Paris the rest of my life, in all probability. What London thinks of me couldn't possibly matter."

"You don't know what course your life will take, Amy." He dropped her hand. "I'll set you up at the town house, but I won't be spending nights there myself. A carriage and driver will be at your disposal. I'll let you know where you can reach me so you can send word when you've purchased all the items you need."

"Where will you stay?"

"That depends upon who's in town. But I'll make sure everyone knows we're not sharing the town house." Distancing himself from her already, he moved back to the opposite bench.

The implication was obvious. He wouldn't risk anyone finding out they'd kissed, as a relationship with the likes of her could only be an embarrassment to him. It couldn't be that he was protecting *her* reputation—she was leaving the country, anyway.

Colin stretched his legs and crossed them, then retreated behind his book. Miserable, Amy withdrew into one protective corner of the carriage. There was no point in continuing the discussion. He had made his position clear, and he hadn't asked for her opinion.

He was so unfair!

She'd never asked to stay with him, or even hinted at it—she knew plain Amy Goldsmith didn't belong with the Earl of Greystone. She had her own life and obligations to fulfill. All she wanted was a few more days with him, a few more days of happiness, a few more days when she could pretend she wasn't alone in the world.

Even now, aloof as he was, she wanted nothing more than to reach out and touch him, to lose herself in his arms.

As hard as he was trying to be cold and demanding, he'd melted when her tears threatened. She should take solace from that, she told herself. The real Colin was in there somewhere, obviously just as confused as she was—if not more.

She opened her book and held it in front of her face, staring blindly at a page while she composed herself. If she had any hope of changing his mind, she wouldn't accomplish it by weeping and begging.

She took a deep breath and forced herself to focus on the words, until she was caught up in the exciting end of Clélie's long tale. Three hours of silence later, just as they crossed London Bridge, she finished and, with a sigh of satisfaction, laid the book on the seat beside her.

Gazing out the carriage window, she marveled at the changes the fire had wrought in her hometown. Street after street of naught but charred vacant lots. The odd chimney or blackened stone oven stood like gravestones among the debris. Except for the clip-clop of horses and the creaking and crunching of wheels passing through, the city was hauntingly quiet. As Amy moved closer to the window, a small sound of distress escaped her lips.

Colin looked up from his book. "It won't be like this forever," he said gently.

She listened carefully. Here and there came rare, banging sounds of construction. "Some are rebuilding," she observed.

"Yes, but it's forbidden until owners clear the rubble and establish their claims to the land. It will take time."

Driving along Fleet Street toward Chancery Lane, they passed into the unburned area at last. Amy breathed a deep sigh of relief as the familiar smells of London hit her. Odors of tar, smoke from incessant coal fires, and the stench of tanneries were overlaid with a pervasive reek from the open sewer that the Fleet River, commonly called the Ditch, had become over the centuries. Though rank and foul, the stench was a comforting memory of another life.

And the traffic! Carriages, hackney coaches, carts, mounted riders, sedan chairs, pedestrians, and animals jostled one another in the noisy, crowded streets. After months in the quiet country-side, Amy's ears seemed assaulted with the cacophony of hawkers peddling their wares in pushcarts, wheelbarrows, and simple baskets, crying out in singsong rhyme of the superiority of their goods.

One man called out, "Rats or mice to kill!" and Amy smiled.

"The rats," she mused. "How could I have forgotten the rats?"

Colin smiled in return.

Thieves, pickpockets, and beggars were everywhere, but so

were street singers ballading for pence. Amy caught sight of a familiar face and turned excitedly. "Oh, it's Richardson the fire-eater! May we stop and watch?"

Colin shrugged and knocked on the roof for Benchley to halt. Amy hung out the window, wide-eyed, as Richardson chewed and swallowed hot coals, then melted glass and, as a finale, put a hot coal on his tongue, heated it with bellows until it flamed, cooked an oyster on it, and swallowed the lot.

The audience burst into wild applause, and Colin dug in his pouch and handed Amy a coin to toss out the window before they moved on.

They finally reached Lincoln's Inn Fields, a fashionable neighborhood bordering a large, grassy square. It was a quieter area, but only in comparison to other parts of London: Lincoln's Inn Fields Theatre was here, known for spectacular moving scenery, and the square was often the scene of fights and robberies, as well as a place for public executions.

The carriage stopped in front of the Chases' town house, a four-story brick building on the west side of the square. Amy climbed out and gazed up at the distinguished facade. Giant Ionic columns held up a boldly projecting cornice and balcony. Triangular decorations crowned tall, rectangular windows.

Colin came out after her and stretched, yawning.

"It's Palladian," Amy breathed in an awed tone. "Was it designed by Inigo Jones?"

"Yes." He took off toward the front door.

Following him, Amy frowned, her exhilaration at being back in the City dampened by his attitude. Where were his usual chatty explanations? Colin loved showing his family's homes and recounting their histories.

Was he that unhappy with her, then?

The interior was every bit as impressive as the outside. The few aristocratic residences Amy had seen were paneled in dark, traditional Jacobean wood. Not this home; the comparison was like coal to diamonds. Her gaze swept up a wide, graceful curving staircase. Light, cheerfully painted walls were orna-mented with classical motifs and festooned with a riot of carv-ing: flowers, fruit, ribbons, palms, and masks.

She couldn't wait to get a tour of this magnificent house.

Colin prodded her forward, toward where the servants waited in a neat row.

"This is Mrs. Amethyst Goldsmith," he said, pleasantly enough. "She'll be staying here for a few days. Ida?"

A slight, blue-eyed girl stepped forward. She looked about Amy's age. "Yes, my lord?"

"Please see to Mrs. Goldsmith's comfort." The maid's blond curls bounced as she nodded, eagerly accepting the responsibility. Colin turned to Amy. "I'm going to take a nap. I suggest you do the same."

With that, he was off, his long legs climbing the stairs two at a time. Ida showed Amy to a chamber and pulled back the covers on the bed. Amy still wondered about the house, but she hadn't been anticipating a self-guided tour; she wanted Colin beside her, telling her all about it.

She lay down, and when she awakened from her fitful sleep, Colin was gone. On her way down to supper, Ida said something about him dining with Priscilla before making an appearance at some ball or other, but Amy listened with half an ear.

Although she'd had most of the day to get used to the idea, she still couldn't believe that Colin had left her alone.

THIRTY-EIGHT

*A*S THE DANCE prescribed, Priscilla performed a graceful bow and pointed one square-toed shoe, chattering over the slow music of the minuet. Growing more impatient by the minute, Colin wondered what on earth had possessed him to squire her to Lady Carsington's ball. He hated balls.

And why hadn't he ever noticed before what a gossip Priscilla was?

Her mouth was as mincing as the minuet. Perhaps if he backed her into that matron over there, who rather resembled the stuffed peacock on the buffet table, Priscilla might shut up.

"Excusez-moi!" The matron pinned him with accusing eyes.

"My apologies, madame." He wrinkled his nose against the cloying perfume that wafted from the woman's unwashed body. But his ploy had worked. Priscilla ceased babbling about Lady So-and-So and Lord Such-and-Such, and turned her attention to him instead.

"Really, Colin. You must be more careful."

"How clumsy of me," he said with an innocent smile, and quickly changed the subject. "You are looking quite well this evening." It was true. Priscilla was eighteen and a beauty. Her shoulder-length silver-blond hair gleamed in the candlelight from the blazing chandeliers. Her figure was tall and willowy rather than curvy, but she carried herself with a regal air, and her ivory satin gown accentuated her pale beauty. The complete opposite of Amy's coloring.

Criminy.

He deliberately pushed Amy out of his mind.

"Why, thank you." Priscilla smiled at the compliment, but no blush marred her complexion. Sedate and proper at all times, she never blushed. Unlike Amy, who—

"Colin, are you listening?"

"I was admiring your complexion. You're as flawless as a porcelain doll."

"Oh." She concentrated on the next dance step.

"And you dance so prettily," he added for good measure as they both balanced forward in three-quarter rhythm. When he reached to skim his knuckles along her cheek, she flinched and pulled back. He frowned, wondering if the gesture had been overfamiliar...but they had kissed before. More than once. Although it had been nothing like kissing Amy—

"Colin?" Priscilla waved a hand in front of his face. "As I was saying, Lady Beauchamp—"

"Do you think we might discuss something else?"

"I beg your pardon?" Her eyebrows lifted as her toe traced a half-circle. But her voice held no emotion, not even annoyance at the interruption. Without knowing what possessed him, Colin found himself edging her closer and closer to the peacock matron, until—

"Oh!"

"Well, I never!"

As the matron stalked off, Priscilla righted herself and smoothed her skirts. She would have fallen flat on her behind if Colin hadn't caught her at the last second.

He waited for a reaction. Anger. Indignation. Embarrassment. Anything.

There was nothing.

He frowned and mentally added to his list: She was as cold and passionless as a porcelain doll as well.

He would have to work on that.

"I'm so very sorry," he ventured, watching her untangle an

earring that had got caught in her hair. "I simply wasn't looking where I was going. You must be furious…"

"It's all right," she said mildly.

And it was.

And there was nothing for it but to resume dancing with her, though Colin suddenly felt unaccountably irritated.

"As I was saying, Lady Beauchamp—"

"I don't wish to discuss Lady Beauchamp," he said bluntly.

"What is it you wish to discuss?"

"Something…*relevant*. Our families. Our future. History. Art." He was steering her rather forcefully through the glittering, jeweled throng of dancers, though he was careful to avoid bumping into anyone. "What did you think of the play tonight?"

"Lady Scarsdale's gown was horrendous. The orange girls were better dressed. And did you see the earl's periwig? It had lice. I cannot believe we were forced to share a box with them."

The music ended, and Priscilla glanced around. "Lady Whitmore has arrived. I have something to tell her."

"By all means." With a great sigh of relief, he sent her sailing from the dance floor. He regretted his bad behavior, but he couldn't seem to help it. Why was he so out of sorts tonight? Was it just the prospect of spending every day of the rest of his life listening to Priscilla gossip?

Actually, the thought of that *was* rather depressing.

Could he find some way to discourage her habit before she drove him mad? Perhaps an instructive prank…

Ah…yes. He smiled as he caught the eye of a dear friend across the ballroom: Barbara Palmer, the Countess of Castlemaine and King Charles's mistress these past six years.

Barbara would be the perfect co-conspirator, for she enjoyed a prank as much as he. He made his way over to her.

Though she was five years older than Colin, Barbara's auburn hair and deep blue eyes made her the equal of any young woman at court. She was a rare beauty, which played no small part in her hold over Charles. Colin supposed he ought to be shocked and disapproving of Barbara's wicked ways, but he'd known her so long and so well—and the king's affairs were so universally accepted—that her behavior failed to diminish her in his eyes. She always remained the same old, marvelous Barbara.

"My Lady Castlemaine," With a little bow, he took her arm and drew her away from the group surrounding her. Barbara was always in the center of a crowd. Everyone was well aware she had the king's ear, and she wasn't a bit opposed to dabbling in politics.

For a price, of course.

"Greystone!" Barbara's eyes danced. "You have my thanks for rescuing me. Where have you been hiding these weeks past?"

"Some of us have to work, you know," Colin teased. Pulling her farther away from the masses, he dropped his voice. "I was wondering...might you be willing to help me play a little trick on Priscilla?"

"One of your pranks? On Lady Priscilla?" Barbara's musical laughter tinkled through the ballroom. "Count me in! What do you have in mind?"

"Well..." His ideas were half-baked. But suddenly inspiration hit. "Would you mind pretending you're with child?"

"How would that help?"

"I've discovered Priscilla is quite the gossip—"

"You're just finding out? For heaven's sake, I've known that for years."

"Well, I was thinking to tell her you're expecting again—Charles's babe, naturally—but not to tell anyone. She'll tell *everyone*, of course, and eventually someone will congratulate you. Then—here's the part you may not like—then you'll storm off, saying you are not with child but you'll certainly never be wearing this gown again! And Priscilla will be mortified that she started this rumor."

"I love it!" Barbara exclaimed. "It's *so* mean!"

Colin frowned. He didn't want to humiliate Priscilla; he just wanted to teach her a lesson. "Do you think so?" he asked.

"No, not really," Barbara recanted.

He looked at her sharply.

"Most any lady here would spread the rumor," she rushed to reassure him. "Lady Priscilla won't be thought of unkindly. Besides, no one will know where it started. One request, though. Afterwards, we must tell the poor soul I take to task—and Lady Priscilla, of course—that we started the rumor ourselves." She fluffed her skirts. "I quite adore this gown, you know."

Colin nodded. "You're stunning in it. And worry not—I'll make certain everyone learns the truth afterwards."

"Oh, that won't be necessary. It will do my reputation good for people to think Charles has come back to me again. He will, you know."

"Of course he will," Colin assured her. "He always has."

"He's made such a fool of himself over Frances Stewart."

Colin had heard this refrain before. A tall, beautifully proportioned girl some eight years younger than Barbara, Frances had arrived at court almost four years ago, and King Charles had been head over heels for her ever since. His love was unrequited, however, since Frances was that rarest of creatures: a chaste courtier.

"I cannot stand her," Barbara said. "She prances around in that man's dress made fashionable by the queen—as though I could wear such garb after bearing five of His Majesty's children!"

"Come now, such dress is ridiculous anyway. And no one could rival you in that gown."

"Thank you," she said as though such compliments were her due. "Charles wrote a poem about her, you know. 'Oh, then 'tis I think there's no Hell, Like loving too well,'" Barbara quoted in a sickly sweet voice. She rolled her eyes. "And still she wouldn't share his bed."

"There are those who think Frances must be simpleminded to persist in such virtue," Colin consoled her—carefully skirting his own opinion on the matter.

"Oh, she's a dunderhead, all right. Her favorite pastimes are playing blind-man's buff and building castles out of playing cards. Grammont said it's hardly possible for a woman to have less wit or more beauty."

"Then she's no true rival to you," Colin assured her. He spotted his intended making her way across the ballroom. "Priscilla is headed this way. You agree to my plan?"

"Yes, it shall be great fun. I shall dazzle you with my performance."

"Very well, then. I look forward to it." He walked toward Priscilla nonchalantly, hoping she hadn't noticed the long time he'd spent talking with Barbara.

After mingling a bit, he danced again with Priscilla, enjoying the jealous glances of the other men present. She was tall and graceful in his arms, and she wasn't gossiping, for once. At the end of the dance, he was pleased to realize he hadn't thought about Amy for quite a few minutes.

Coming off the dance floor, he said casually, "I've heard tonight that Barbara is expecting His Majesty's sixth child."

"She told you so?" Priscilla was more animated than usual, her interest piqued by the opportunity to be in on a juicy bit of gossip.

"No, it was someone else. You mustn't tell anyone, though, for she hasn't even told Charles yet."

"Oh, I wouldn't," Priscilla said much too quickly. "But who told you?"

"I've been sworn to secrecy. I chatted a bit with Barbara to see if she'd let it slip, but she didn't say a word."

"She doesn't look *enceinte*." Priscilla slanted a dubious glance to where Barbara was surrounded by a new group of hangers-on.

"She's only just had it confirmed, according to my source. She wouldn't be showing yet."

"Of course. I'm not well versed in such matters, since I haven't had children myself—yet."

Priscilla knew Colin wanted children; he'd made no secret of the importance he placed on family life. And she'd offered no arguments, he reminded himself now. She really was a good choice for him.

"Would you care for some spiced wine?" he asked, knowing it would be out of character for him to discuss such a gossipy subject too long.

"No, thank you," Priscilla declined prettily. "I'm not thirsty."

Colin saw right through her excuse: She couldn't wait to get back to her friends. However, he enjoyed his pranks tremendously, especially the anticipation, so he wasn't quite ready to let her get started.

"No, I insist." He drew her over to the refreshment table and handed her a cup of wine. Taking one himself, he grasped her firmly by the elbow. "Shall we enjoy the garden for a while?"

"It's freezing out there," Priscilla protested.

Colin smiled to himself. "Just for a minute. It's beastly hot in here."

She couldn't argue with that. Between the blazing fires on either end of the ballroom, the hundreds of candles burning in the chandeliers above, and the guests packed in elbow-to-elbow, it was difficult to breathe.

Priscilla reluctantly went with him, in no small part because he dragged her along physically, and he guided her through the crowd and outdoors.

"Ahh." He inhaled deeply of the fresh air. "It's pleasant out here, isn't it?"

Priscilla drained her cup and crossed her arms in a most unladylike fashion. It was quite foreign to her nature, and Colin was pleased; perhaps she was becoming more human. "I'm finished. May I go back inside now?"

"Not just yet." Colin drew her further into the formal garden, over to a low brick wall. He set down both their cups and leaned back against it, then wrapped his arms around Priscilla's waist and pulled her close. Ignoring the startled look in her eyes, he brought his lips down to hers—just a little bit down, he realized, momentarily surprised at the reminder of her height. But her mouth was warm in the cold night, and he was pleased to think this statuesque heiress was his, so it was a moment before he realized she wasn't kissing him back. Instead she was pushing away from him, her palms flat against his chest.

"Colin—not here."

"Why? No one's here to see."

"It's not proper. And there's no one to see because no one else is mad enough to come out in this weather."

"I'll keep you warm." Though taken aback by her reaction, he put on a smile and rubbed her arms encouragingly. She'd never seemed to mind kissing him before...

But Priscilla was ever well mannered and proper, and Colin realized with dismay that he'd never tried to steal a private moment with her before, that each of their kisses had had its customary time and place. But surely, with patience, he could teach her to enjoy a stolen kiss or two. Was there an instructive prank that might—

No! No. He quashed that idea immediately.

His arm lightly around her shoulders, he walked her back to the ball. In no time, she was gone. She'd spotted Lady Crowhurst across the room and said she just *had* to talk to her, and Colin let her go. He chuckled to himself when he saw her lips mouth the word "Barbara." And he laughed out loud to see Barbara herself flitting about with a hand laid discreetly over her middle.

Not five minutes later, Colin would swear there was a new buzz in the room as gossiping ladies rushed to be the ones to spread the delicious rumor. And in the end, it was Priscilla herself who couldn't resist approaching Barbara.

She waited politely until Barbara was free. "My Lady Castlemaine," she said, pulling her aside, "I hear congratulations are in order."

Colin sidled closer and concealed himself behind a post.

Barbara played her part to perfection. "Is that so?"

"I've heard in the strictest of confidence that you will be presenting His Majesty with another child soon."

Barbara's face tensed.

"Is something wrong, my lady?" At the sight of Priscilla's panic, Colin had to choke back laughter. "Am I mistaken?"

Barbara's cheeks blazed red—what an actress she was! "Do I appear pregnant, Lady Priscilla?" she said through gritted teeth.

Priscilla took an uncertain step back. "Oh, my lady, I didn't mean—that is, if I've caused you any offense—"

"On the contrary," Barbara hissed, her eyes flashing, "I'm all gratitude. How delightful it is when trim, younger women take the trouble to inform me that my figure is not what it used to be." With a dramatic huff, she turned on her heel and marched from the ballroom and up the wide staircase, fuming all the way.

Priscilla followed her into the hall and watched her flight.

She was still gazing up the sweeping stairs when Colin came up behind her.

"Is something wrong, Priscilla?"

She turned to him immediately, a frown creasing her beautiful forehead. "Oh, Colin, I've made the most dreadful error. I thought to congratulate my Lady Castlemaine, only to discover she isn't carrying after all. Now she's horribly angry, and everyone thinks she's with child. What am I to do?"

"Whyever would everyone think Barbara is with child?" he asked with a glint in his eye.

"I told them!" Priscilla wailed. "And they told one another."

"Priscilla! You promised you wouldn't tell anyone!" he exclaimed in pretended disbelief.

"You mean to say you really meant that?" Priscilla protested. "Why would you tell me if it were a secret?"

"You mean to say I shouldn't trust you? I shouldn't tell you anything unless I want everyone to know?"

"Yes! I mean, no! Oh, Colin, I shouldn't be such a terrible gossip, should I?"

Colin grinned—he simply couldn't help himself. The scene was playing out even better than he had hoped.

"Why are you smiling?" Priscilla demanded. "I've ruined everything! Barbara's never really liked me—she only invited us to her parties because of my father, and now she'll hate me. We won't be welcome anywhere."

"Now, Priscilla, you know that's not true. Barbara would never leave me off a guest list. We were in exile together—I'm one of her dearest friends. Besides, Charles is all but a big brother to me. He'd never allow her to snub us."

He was right, and Priscilla knew it. Colin's relationship with the king was her father's primary reason for agreeing to the match. Lord Hobbs had been a fence-sitter during the war, and consequently, though he hadn't lost his lands, he held no favor with Charles, either.

"I suppose you're right," Priscilla said with a sniff.

Just then, Barbara came back down the stairs, grinning from ear to ear, and Colin took one look at her and broke out laughing. Priscilla stared at Colin, then at Barbara, and back to Colin before bursting out, "What is going on here?"

Colin could do no better than sputter. "I—we—I—"

Barbara rescued him—sort of. "What Lord Greystone means to say, dear, is that we set you up."

"Set me up?" Priscilla's pretty brows furrowed in confusion. "You mean you aren't truly angry?"

"Colin started the rumor with my consent." Barbara chuckled. "He thought to demonstrate how gossip spreads."

Priscilla stared at her, openmouthed.

"It was a prank," Barbara finished weakly.

"You know I play pranks," Colin put in.

"A prank?" Priscilla repeated in disbelief. "On me?" She snapped him on the arm with her folded fan. "How dare you play a prank on me."

Colin rubbed his arm out of reflex, though it didn't really hurt. Priscilla had put as little enthusiasm into the blow as she gave to everything else. "I play pranks on everyone," he reminded her.

"You don't play them on me, Colin Chase. They're stupid and childish, and I won't stand for it."

"Don't you think it's funny?" The last of Colin's laughter died. "Don't you find it amusing that I know you well enough to devise a trap you would fall into perfectly?"

"No. I don't find it the least bit amusing." Priscilla turned on Barbara. "My lady, I find it difficult to imagine why you would play along with his trickery—now everyone thinks you're with child."

"It doesn't signify." Barbara waved a hand airily. "I probably *will* be with child by the time anyone could discover otherwise. I always am, it seems," she lamented.

Colin laughed. "You're a good sport, Barbara."

"There are those who would disagree," Barbara pointed out archly. More than one man had met his downfall at the hands of Barbara Palmer. Luckily, Colin and she had grown up together, so he knew her too well to make the sort of blunder that would turn her against him.

And he'd thought he knew his betrothed equally well, but all of a sudden he wasn't sure. He'd spent all eve trying to get under her skin, and now that he'd accomplished that goal with his prank, he rather wished he'd never played it. His relationship with Priscilla had never been complicated—why, now, did he feel so confused?

"Please call for the carriage," she requested calmly, breaking into his thoughts.

"What?" Colin blinked. Her face had regained its impassive expression. "The evening is still young."

"We will forget this ever happened. I trust it won't again. I wish to return home now."

"Lost your taste for gossip, Lady Priscilla?" Barbara asked sweetly.

The barb went right over Priscilla's head. "I merely find myself fatigued. Colin?" She took his arm and led him away.

Colin looked back at Barbara, shrugging his shoulders helplessly. She laughed and waved him on before gliding back into the ballroom.

THIRTY-NINE

"*I* HAVE A headache." Priscilla lifted her elegant chin and calmly shut her door in Colin's face.

Now what?

Distracted by his prank, he'd neglected to approach anyone at the ball to arrange lodging. At a loss, he wandered back to his carriage. He wasn't about to drop in on a friend unannounced. And no one would be in at this hour, regardless; it was much too early for any self-respecting man-about-town to make his way home.

As Benchley opened the carriage door, Colin sighed. "Take me to Whitehall Palace, please."

At Whitehall, the court stayed up until the wee hours gambling and playing billiards. Colin wasn't in the mood to enjoy himself, but he forced himself to play anyway. Fortunately, he didn't lose, but he wasn't as pleased as he'd normally have been to pocket the few coins he'd won.

And again he'd failed to ask any acquaintances for a bed, so when the sun was about to rise and the games were coming to an end, he made his way back to his carriage and gave Benchley instructions to return to the town house.

No one even knew Amy was there, he rationalized, shoving aside the concerns he'd voiced the day before.

Amy…now *there* was someone who appreciated his attempts

195

at humor. A vision popped into his head, of Amy laughing the loudest when the joke was on her. Her color high, her rosy lips—

Curse it! He shook his head to clear the image.

He'd suspected from the start that Amy's request to come to London had been naught but a ploy to stay near him longer. And he hadn't been ready to part with her, either. But he never should have agreed—he'd known it was a mistake the moment "I'd be happy to take you to London" came out of his mouth.

Now they'd be alone together in the town house. Alone, but surrounded by all of Charles's gossipy, meddlesome court. London was full of people like Priscilla, bored aristocrats who would gleefully shred an innocent young girl's reputation before breakfast.

This had been a spectacularly bad idea.

Well, done was done. And luckily, Amy would be sound asleep at this hour. He'd sneak in, get a few hours of rest, and be out again before she awakened.

Where he'd go, in the early hours before noon, when everyone he knew was sleeping off overindulgences of the prior evening, he wasn't sure. But surely he could find some way to amuse himself. Perhaps he'd call on Priscilla—she'd certainly turned in early enough to receive a morning visitor.

He entered the house quietly and ducked into the study to pour himself a brandy before stealing upstairs. No need to rouse the servants—even a hushed conversation might wake Amy, and he was perfectly capable of putting himself to bed.

Sneaking past her door, he nearly choked on a mouthful of brandy when he heard the unmistakable sound of weeping.

She was awake.

He paused, his fingers drumming on one thigh while he listened. Then he reached for the door latch—and jerked back, almost as though it had burned his fingers.

He knew all too well what could happen if he went in to comfort her. Would it not be kinder to leave her in peace and privacy? There was no sense prolonging the hurt, or giving her false hope. Hardening his heart, he slipped past her chamber and entered his.

But alas, he could still hear Amy through the adjoining wall.

Easing the door shut failed to block the sound. He cursed himself for allowing Ida to put her in the room adjacent to his, but he'd thought he wouldn't be staying here, so it hadn't occurred to him to interfere.

Sleep would be impossible now, he knew. Every sob was a fresh wrench of guilt, like a knife jabbing deeper into his chest. He unbuckled his sword belt and tossed it on the bed, started a fire as quietly as possible, then sat in the nearby chair and slowly sipped his brandy.

This was his fault. He was older and more experienced than Amy—if only by a few years—and so the duty had been his to put an end to things before they got out of hand. But he hadn't done that. Instead he'd given in to emotion, abandoned honor and compassion, and tread all over this poor girl's still-mending heart. And then he'd brought her here and abandoned *her*, too.

She was strong, and she would heal, and she'd probably forget him before long. She'd be better off without him. But thinking back on these last few days with Amy and the indescribable way she'd made him feel, he knew—sure as he knew the sun would rise in the east—that if he somehow could do it all over again, he would give in every time. He was a weak, despicable man, and that was the worst thing of all.

Though the brandy flowed a hot path down Colin's throat, it failed to melt the knot in his chest. Draining the glass, he set it on the small table by his chair and stared into the fire, twisting his ring.

Wondering how long she'd been crying, he tried to envision her: hair tangled, eyes red-rimmed and bloodshot, face puffy and swollen, creased from where she'd pressed it into the sheets to muffle those gut-wrenching sobs.

It was not a pretty mental picture.

Perhaps he *could* go to her—looking a fright, she might not be so difficult to resist. And she wasn't likely to be in a romantic mood herself. He stood up, shrugged out of his surcoat and removed his waistcoat, the better to offer a friendly, comforting shoulder to cry on—then stopped short.

Who was he fooling?

He silently finished undressing, slipped into a robe, and

padded softly out of his bedchamber, intending to head for the library. He needed a distraction.

But as he passed by her door, he heard a long moan. Soft and resonant, the sound ripped his wounded heart in two. He was into her chamber before he could form a coherent thought.

She was a long lump under the heavy quilt, her head buried beneath the covers.

He knelt by the bed. "Amy?"

"*Colin?*" She peeked out, then sat up. In the firelight, she looked beautiful—and not at all like he'd expected. Her face was pink and tear streaked, yes, but not even close to the puffy mess he'd imagined.

"What—what are you doing here?" She looked over the edge of the bed, taking in Colin's state of undress.

He stood up, belting his robe tighter.

Her gaze slid down to his bare feet, then slowly back up to his face. She sniffled, dashing the tears from her cheeks with an impatient motion. "How long have you been back?"

"Long enough."

"You've been...?"

"In the next room."

"*Marry come up.* You heard me, then."

She threw herself back to the mattress, pulling the covers over her rapidly reddening face. "Go away, please."

Her body rolled toward him as his weight dropped onto the edge of the bed.

"Go away!"

He didn't.

Amy lay rigid, apparently willing him to leave—or herself to magically vanish—until he folded the blanket away from her face. "I'm sorry," she squeaked out, her eyes filling again.

"*You're* sorry?" he asked, incredulous.

He couldn't credit it. *She* was sorry.

"I've been...wallowing in my misery, I guess you could call it. I...haven't been alone before tonight. Since the fire, I mean. Not all alone, where I was sure no one could hear me. Since my father died." She sniffed and let out a long breath. "I woke up and thought I was alone..."

Colin heaved a sigh of relief—though he felt a twinge of embarrassment. Here he'd been, certain he was all-important in her life, wracked with guilt for hurting her, and she hadn't been thinking of him at all. How vain could he be?

"It's nothing to be ashamed of." He gently wiped fresh tears away. "A good cry was probably just what you needed. I apologize for interrupting."

"I was just feeling sorry for myself," Amy said to her lap.

He believed her. But there was something in her voice…

And she wouldn't look at him.

He lifted her chin, forcing her gaze to meet his. "Is that all?"

She nodded. "Though I did wish you were here with me," she admitted softly.

Her eyes were wide and trusting, darkened in that compelling way that drew him in. Without thinking, he leaned over to kiss her, his mouth moving gently on hers in a silent apology.

It felt so…natural.

When he pulled away, her voice dropped to a whisper. "Why did you come back?"

"I couldn't stay away," he confessed, knowing it was true the moment the words left him. "I never made any other plans. I couldn't bear to think of you in my house and me somewhere else entirely." He pushed a hand through his hair. What was he saying? "Amy, I—"

"Shh." She pressed a finger to his lips. "Don't say it. I know you're promised, Colin, and I've a destiny of my own. But I'm not quite ready to meet that destiny, so for now I'm here. I know you have things you must do, but if you could save me an hour for cards or chess, or for showing me your house, or for…"

Or for kissing, he knew she was thinking. But she was mirroring his thoughts. It was impossible for him to stay away from her when she was so close by. Absolutely impossible.

He'd never been able to resist her pull. *Never.*

"All right," he agreed. "The shops are closed tomorrow, but I'll take you to order a few gowns on Monday, we'll have them delivered Tuesday, and the next morning we'll leave. Three more days you'll stay here—and so will I. No one need know you're here."

"Won't Lady Priscilla—"

"Shh," he admonished, borrowing her gesture and placing his finger on her lips. "I'll take care of it. Don't worry."

Three days.

In truth, he had no idea how he could keep her presence secret from Priscilla or anyone else, but he would find a way.

~

"*T*HREE DAYS," Amy agreed solemnly. Three days. Three days more than she had any right to hope for or deserve.

As though to seal their secret pact, Colin lifted her hand and kissed the back, then, his gaze locked on hers, he turned her hand over and kissed the palm, his lips warm and tender. Amy closed her eyes as shimmering tendrils of feeling swept up her arm.

Colin moved closer, pulling her up to sit and gathering her into his arms. For a fleeting moment she worried that she wore nothing but her chemise—again—but then all thoughts fled when his mouth met hers.

Amy felt like she floated on a puffy, comforting cloud. She tasted warmed, rich brandy. By degrees the kiss grew deeper, possessive, imprinting the memory of him so deep inside her that she knew she'd always carry a part of him with her, though they be parted by a sea and the impossible gulf of lives that had never been meant to cross.

Colin kissed her for a long time, then pressed her cheek to his shoulder. He sat motionless, enjoying her light rose fragrance and listening to her ragged breathing, matched by his own. In the stillness, he could feel her heart thudding, for him. And he was seized momentarily by a profound sense of sadness, for what was, and what couldn't be.

At last she lifted her head, raised a hand to shove the long, inky black strands from her face, and gazed at him wordlessly.

Her eyes were deep purple, brimming over with a complicated blend of affection and pain.

Incredible, incredible pain.

He pulled her closer, unwilling to look into those sorrowful eyes just now. "Hush, love," he whispered into her hair. "Don't think on it. We have three more days. It's a lifetime."

It's not, she thought. But it had to be. It was all she would ever have.

Colin brushed his lips over hers once more. "Don't think," he repeated, and then he proceeded to make sure she couldn't, with his lips and the incredible power he had at his disposal—the power of two souls that were made to be one.

FORTY

*H*EARING VOICES in the corridor a few minutes later, Colin pulled away from Amy. Weak morning sunlight streamed through the window. When had that happened?

Hang it, it must be later than he thought.

Or earlier.

Whichever, it was bad.

Now the staff was up and about, and he'd be hard put to leave Amy's chamber unnoticed, which was imperative if he wished to keep the gossips at bay. The servants' grapevine was well established in London; should he be caught in here with Amy, the news would be common knowledge before the day was out.

"What is it?" Amy asked.

"Hush." He sat still, listening, waiting for the best time to stand and make a run for it. Listening…

Wait, he thought with a silent groan. Those weren't servants' voices, chatting in passing as they went about their daily chores. The voices were louder and much more familiar. Jason's voice, and Ford's and Kendra's.

Of all the rotten luck.

He'd thought he could spend his evenings with Priscilla and

an hour or two in the daytime with Amy, playing a game and pleasantly passing the time. And, all right, kissing. He'd be kidding himself if he thought there would be no kissing.

But it would be harder now, perhaps even impossible, to keep Amy's presence a public secret.

Or maybe...ah, yes. His mind raced as he slowly released the breath he'd held since recognizing the voices. His family liked Amy. They didn't know he'd been kissing her. They could even act as his cover—*yes*, she'd stayed at Cainewood, after all, and they considered her their friend.

It would work—so long as he wasn't discovered in her bedroom. They'd never approve of that.

The voices faded. "I must leave now," Colin whispered. "You get some sleep." He brushed a last kiss across her lips, then rose, padded to the door, and pressed his ear against it.

All clear.

He opened the door a crack, pleased that it didn't creak. Poised to run next door to safety, he took a deep breath and flung it open—and was greeted by Kendra's startled face.

He backed up and slammed the door shut.

"Colin?" Kendra's muffled voice came through the wood. "Is that you?"

He cursed at himself. In one split second, he'd made a complete mess of everything. Why on earth hadn't he walked brazenly into the corridor as though nothing were amiss? He could have simply explained that Amy had been crying and he'd stopped in to make sure she was all right. Or claimed she'd had a nightmare, as had happened the other night.

Now he looked every bit as guilty as he was, no doubt about it.

Kendra hammered on the door. "Colin? What are you doing in there?"

A hand on the door latch, Colin stood rooted to the spot, his gaze riveted to Amy. She watched him, her eyes wide, her mouth gaping open.

The mouth he'd just kissed.

Footsteps approached. "What the dickens?"

He sagged against the door. Curse it, Jason was there now, too.

"Colin's inside." Hearing Kendra's smug tone, Colin could cheerfully wring her neck. "Hiding. With Amy."

There was nothing for it. With a last, lingering glance at Amy, Colin opened the door and slipped through. Closing it behind him, he leaned against it protectively. "Shh!"

"What were you doing in there?" Kendra hissed back.

He mustered his most convincing whisper. "Amy was having a nightmare. I was just checking on her."

"Is that so?" Kendra crossed her arms. "Then why did you shut the door when you saw me?"

He wrinkled his brow in what he hoped was a puzzled expression. "Were you there? Amy was calling out again, so I went back inside."

"Poppycock! You think I'd fall for such an old chestnut? I didn't hear a thing. This looks mighty suspicious."

"What business is it of yours?" Colin spat defensively. "I needn't answer to you, little sister!"

"Amy is my friend, and if you've taken advantage of her, it's my duty to see you do right by her, Colin Chase!"

Both of them had long since abandoned whispering. Jason stepped between them and faced Kendra. "If Colin says he was just checking on her, we'll have to take his word for it."

Ah! Some male loyalty. Colin smiled.

Until Jason swung around to confront him. "What is she doing here? I thought you were taking her to Dover."

"She wanted to buy some things before she left. She lost all her clothes in the fire."

"Is that all?"

"Of course it is! I spent last evening with Priscilla, at Lady Carsington's boring ball." Colin yanked the belt of his robe tighter. "This is ridiculous. I needn't explain myself to you two." He stalked toward his chamber and had his hand on the door latch when Kendra opened Amy's door.

Instinctively, he whirled around and hastened back to... protect Amy? He didn't know. But he saw Jason go red and prudently avert his eyes, and then Colin had to see what they were looking at. He leaned around the door frame.

Inside the bedchamber, Amy was still sitting up in the bed, her hair tangled, her lips rosy and swollen from kissing. She looked adorable.

Colin was horrified at the sight of her.

Kendra and Jason shared a long, meaningful look.

"I'm surprised to find you here," Kendra said brightly. "Colin said you needed some clothes?"

"Yes." Amy threw Colin an apologetic glance before looking back to his sister. "What are *you* doing here?"

"We came to London for Christmas shopping. We always do, in early November," Kendra explained, walking into the room. "May I come inside?" she asked, though she already was. "Let me help you dress, and we'll talk."

She shut the door behind her.

Intending to make a quick escape, Colin headed next door to his own chamber, but his older brother swung him around by the shoulder and leveled a stare at him. "Well?"

"Well, what?"

"Confound it!" Jason looked heavenward as if praying for patience. "You cannot fob me off that easily, Colin." His lips thinned beneath his mustache. "We all know what went on in that chamber. In that *bed*."

Now it was Colin's turn to go red. "Nothing happened in that bed! I know it looks bad, but…" He sighed, realizing it was time for the truth. He lowered his voice, in case any servants might be listening."We've done naught but kiss. Trust me, it's gone no further. Give me three days, and I'll have her delivered out of our lives forever. And don't tell her you know I've kissed her," he warned. "She'd die of embarrassment. She's no courtier —she's been sheltered all her life."

"I'm too much a gentleman to embarrass her," Jason assured him coolly. "Unlike you."

"What on earth is that supposed to mean?"

"Only that you should do right by the girl and marry her. In her world, a kiss—"

"We've been through this," Colin growled in warning.

"Things were different then. It was naught but a suggestion. Now I insist."

"A pox on you." Colin paused for a deep, calming breath. "I have other plans, as does she. The match is suitable for neither of us. I know that kissing her was a mistake, but I just..." He trailed off lamely.

Jason gave him an appraising look. "I take it you won't be continuing to make the same *mistake* now that we're here?" He asked stiffly.

Colin's fists clenched. "That's none of your concern."

"I'm afraid it is," Jason argued. "She's under my roof, under my protection. And she's no lightskirt. She's a lovely, gently raised girl who doesn't deserve to be treated like this."

"Treated like *what*?" Colin erupted. "Believe me, she hasn't complained!" He dropped his voice, afraid Amy might overhear. "Unlike you, she never expected me to marry her. In case you've forgotten, I'm betrothed. And Amy has family and a new life awaiting her on the Continent. I regret disappointing you, but my mind is made up." His jaw set, Colin turned to the door.

"But we all love her," Jason muttered under his breath.

Colin was seized with such an unreasoning fury, a hazy red mist seemed to explode across his vision. Swiveling back, he glared straight into his brother's eyes. "Well, I *don't*." His voice was low and dangerous. "Since you all love her so much, why don't you all take care of her? Just see that she gets to France this time, will you? I'd prefer not to deal with her again." He backed into the chamber. "Do me a favor, and let Priscilla know I returned to Greystone. I have work to do."

He slammed the door and kicked it, then hopped around clutching at his aching bare toes. What was happening to him? He'd never been such a hothead before, banging doors and kicking things. And though his family had always been loud and argumentative, of late his exchanges with them were less good natured and more acrimonious.

And now, in a moment of unthinking anger, he'd thrown away his last three days with Amy.

A pox on everything!

He had to leave or risk looking like even more of a fool than he was. And he couldn't so much as tell Amy goodbye. One look at her face and he knew his heart would break, as well as his resolve.

He threw on his clothes and left, cursing himself a hundred times for the hothead, fool, and coward he'd become.

FORTY-ONE

*K*ENDRA STOOD back, casting a discerning eye as Amy twirled around in the sapphire and cream gown. "It's gorgeous!"

Nothing like the day dresses Amy had planned to order, the shimmering satin gown's scooped neckline was set off with a wide vanilla lace collar, enriched with lustrous pearls. Matching lace spilled to her wrists from beneath tight three-quarter length sleeves. The full cream overskirt was split and gathered to the back to show off a pearl-embroidered sapphire petticoat.

"It makes me feel pretty," Amy admitted, "though I still cannot believe I let you talk me into it. I haven't a clue where I'll wear it."

"Colin will take you to a ball—"

"No, he won't." Though her initial reaction to Colin's disappearance had been hurt, in the past two weeks Amy had resigned herself to the facts. "Colin wants nothing to do with me; he's made that perfectly clear. And most certainly not in public."

"He'll come around. Trust me. I know my brother. He's stubborn, but he's not addlepated."

Amy's finger traced a row of embroidered pearls on her skirt. "Colin and I don't belong together, and we both know it, Kendra. I'm meant to be a jeweler in France. It's not only what I want, it's what I have to do." She smoothed the slick satin, then turned to the seamstress with a rustling swish. "Unlace me, please, Madame Beaumont."

Amy had been distraught to find Mrs. Cholmley's shop burned to the ground, and the seamstress herself nowhere to be found. Owing to the king's passion for everything French, French dressmakers were all the rage. Kendra had insisted Amy order her wardrobe from Madame Beaumont, London's most sought-after *modiste*.

The seamstress's deft fingers loosened the gown, and Amy wiggled out of it. "The hem is fine." She stepped into the butter-yellow gown she'd borrowed from Kendra and pulled it up. "Will it be ready Monday?

"*Certainement*. Along with everything else." Madame Beaumont turned her around to lace her up in back.

"Thank you." Amy looked pointedly at Kendra. "Do you know if Jason is free Tuesday to take me to Dover?"

"I haven't the faintest idea, but it doesn't matter anyway."

Amy peered into the looking glass, rearranging her long, untamed curls. "What's that supposed to mean?"

"You still have to buy stockings, gloves, and ribbons, not to mention shoes for all of these gowns," Kendra declared gaily. "Then I want help with my Christmas shopping. You won't be ready to leave for weeks yet—perhaps not until after Christmas."

"Oh, no." Amy shook her head, remembering Colin's original plan to secure her wardrobe within a day or two. Madame Beaumont had taken a full twelve days to create her gowns, and that was after considerable begging and extra payments.

"Oh, yes. You had nothing whatsoever to wear; it takes time to outfit yourself properly. Besides, I'm having too much fun to send you on your way. Why, it's almost like having a sister."

"Colin would be furious."

"A pox on Colin! If he weren't so obstinate—"

"Marry come up, Kendra! Let's not start that again."

"Only if you agree to stop talking about leaving so soon."

"Well…I did forget about stockings and shoes…maybe I'll stay an extra week." Amy stopped fussing with her hair and turned from the mirror to look Kendra in the eye. "But that's all. Colin and I will never happen. I mean it."

"Of course you do," Kendra agreed a little too pleasantly.

A tinkling bell on the door announced another customer. Amy and Kendra prepared to leave as Madame Beaumont rushed out to greet the newcomer. Her melodious voice drifted back to the fitting salon. "*Bonjour*, Lady Priscilla."

"No, it cannot be..." Kendra muttered under her breath.

"Your gown is ready for your final fitting." Madame's accented words grew louder as she made her way to the curtained salon. "I'll fetch it from the back room. The salon will be vacant in a moment." The curtain parted, and Madame slipped inside. "Mesdemoiselles? Is there aught else I can do for you?"

"We were just leaving," Amy assured her.

The dressmaker stuck her head back into the shop. "*Une minute*, Lady Priscilla, *s'il vous plaît*." She hurried through the salon and into the back, murmuring "*Merci*, mesdemoiselles" as she went.

"Please let it be another Priscilla," Kendra whispered, her hand on the curtain's opening.

"What are you talking about?" Amy whispered back.

Kendra froze and stared at her. "Lady Priscilla."

"Lady Priscilla?"

"*Colin's* Lady Priscilla."

"Oh..."

Amy wasn't at all sure she wanted to meet the illustrious Priscilla, but she hadn't much of a choice, as Kendra grabbed her by the arm and pulled her into the shop.

"Lady Priscilla." Amy had never heard Kendra sound so sickly sweet, nor seen such a false smile plastered on her face. "It's a pleasure to see you."

"Lady Kendra." Priscilla's voice was cultured and emotionless, as though she ran into acquaintances everywhere and nothing ever surprised her. She leaned over and pecked Kendra on the cheek; a casual kiss between ladies was *de rigueur* upon meeting. "I didn't know you were in town. Is Colin back as well?"

"Oh, no. You know how he feels about the City," Kendra said slyly.

"Yes, but he was here barely a day last month."

"He's very busy at Greystone. Perhaps you should visit him there." Kendra's suggestion sounded sincere, although she'd told Amy that Priscilla loathed Colin's rustic home. "I'm sure he'd be glad to see you."

"Goodness, not in the state that place is in. Although I'd consider an invitation to Cainewood." Priscilla's cool gray gaze moved to Amy. "Who do we have here?"

"Forgive me for failing to introduce you," Kendra said smoothly. "This is Mrs. Amethyst Goldsmith. Amy, meet Lady Priscilla Hobbs."

Amy watched Priscilla look her over and instantly dismiss her as untitled and insignificant. "I'm glad of your acquaintance," Priscilla said with a small bored bow.

Amy opened her mouth to respond, but no words came out. The very sight of Priscilla had rendered her speechless. Dear heavens, if Priscilla were Colin's idea of the perfect girl...

Titles aside, she was Amy's complete antithesis. Priscilla was tall where Amy was diminutive, fair where she was rosy, straight where she was curvy, and cool where she was emotional. Priscilla's hair was blond, short, and styled, while Amy's was dark, long, and unruly.

And those were just the obvious differences.

Amy hadn't known it was possible to hate a virtual stranger. She felt like a sorry example of a human being, but she couldn't seem to help herself. If witchcraft weren't a sin, she'd surely be casting a spell forthwith.

Kendra nudged her with a discreet elbow. "I-I'm glad of your acquaintance," Amy managed to return.

Priscilla's pretty arched brows drew together. "Mrs. Goldsmith is a friend of yours?" She looked directly at Kendra, as though Amy weren't there, which Amy wished were the case.

"She's been staying with us since the fire. She lost her family and their jewelry shop."

"Their shop?" Priscilla's expression showed just what she thought of the Chases befriending a merchant, but the look also radiated resigned indulgence—as though the Chases were known to be rather eccentric.

"We've known Amy for some time," Kendra stated defensively. As her fingers moved to the center of her neckline, where she'd pinned the bow-shaped jeweled galant that was her gift from Amy, a glint came into her eyes. "Our family has acquired much jewelry from hers. Colin especially."

"Colin?" Priscilla frowned. "Colin has never given me any jewelry."

Though Amy knew her friend was deliberately misleading Priscilla—Kendra must know Colin had bought only her locket and the ring for himself—she decided to play along. "I can assure you that Colin often purchased jewelry, since he always asked for my assistance."

"Well then, perhaps *Lord Greystone* is waiting until after we are wed to gift me with it," Priscilla said.

"Perhaps."

The single word was a challenge, but apparently Priscilla chose not to see it that way, since she looked straight past Amy to where the seamstress waited between the parted curtains. "Madame Beaumont, you are ready?"

"*Certainement*, my lady."

"It was a pleasure seeing you, Kendra," Priscilla said on her way into the fitting salon.

No such pleasantries were directed at Amy, who evidently was beneath common courtesy.

"It was a pleasure meeting you, Lady Priscilla," she called out pointedly, if insincerely. But the curtain closed before Priscilla could reply, assuming such was her intention.

Somehow, Amy thought not.

"What a rude girl," she whispered to Kendra. "*That* is your brother's intended?"

"In all her glory." Kendra took Amy's arm as they headed into the street.

"I suppose this has been a bad day for her," Amy suggested, searching for a possible excuse for Priscilla's behavior.

"I doubt it. I call her Priscilla Snobs, you know." They shared a companionable smile before Kendra continued, "It makes Colin furious."

"Whatever does he see in her, I wonder?"

"You're not the only one."

Seeing their approach, Jason's coachman rushed to open the door. "We'd like to visit the New Exchange now," Kendra informed him before climbing into her brother's wood and leather carriage.

The coachman took her by the elbow to help her in. "As you wish, my lady."

Amy followed slowly, still thinking about Priscilla. She hadn't known what to expect, but Priscilla had turned out to be so perfectly upper class that any lingering unrealistic dreams Amy had harbored were swept away. No mere attraction could entice Colin Chase to trade such an aristocratic paragon for plain Amy Goldsmith.

Even though she couldn't wed Colin whether he wanted her or not, it was a depressing thought. As she dwelt on it, she nearly missed the voice that called from down the street. The shocked, all-too-familiar voice.

"Amy? Amy! Can that be you?"

"I wish they'd hurry and rebuild the Royal Exchange," Kendra lamented from inside the carriage. "It was so much better than the New Exchange."

Amy hesitated but a moment before rushing inside to join her. She pulled the door shut before the startled coachman had a chance to close it.

"What's happening, Amy?"

"Shh! Don't say my name out loud." She tugged the curtains over the windows, cursing the heavy traffic that perpetually clogged London's streets. "Oh, why can't we get going?"

The carriage gave a small lurch as it started into the center of the busy street, but it was too late. *Bang! Bang!* A fist hit the door, and the driver reined in the horses.

"Amy! I know you're in there!"

"Hey!" The driver jumped to the street with an audible *thump.* "Keep your hands off Lord Cainewood's carriage!"

Through a slit in the curtains, Amy glimpsed carrot-colored hair, but she needed no confirmation. Having worked with him for five years, she would have recognized Robert Stanley's voice anywhere.

"I don't give a care whose carriage this is!" she heard him yell. "Amethyst Goldsmith is inside, and I must speak with her."

Amy bit her lip. The door opened and the driver asked, "Mrs. Goldsmith, do you know this gentleman?"

She decided to pretend she was surprised. "Robert!" She jumped out and wrapped her arms around the freckled man in a hug that was halfhearted at best, but she hoped would be convincing since she'd never been overly affectionate with him. "'I'm so glad to see you're well—I've been wondering about you," she gushed.

And it was true, in a way. Robert had been in her life a long time; she was relieved to see him whole and healthy.

"Your letter didn't say where you were," Robert said doubtfully, setting her away from himself. "Did you at least tell your Aunt Elizabeth? I wrote to her to find out, but I haven't heard back yet."

"Yes, I wrote to her," Amy said slowly. Dear heavens…it hadn't occurred to her that Robert would contact her aunt. He would have found her even in Paris. She hadn't credited him with such resourcefulness.

No, she corrected herself, she'd known all along that Robert was intelligent, though a bit unimaginative. The truth was, she'd done her best not to think of him and what he would do at all.

"I'm sorry," she said now, meaning it. "I should have found you to discuss matters. I wasn't thinking straight. I was…mourning. Devastated." She took a deep breath. "What have you been doing?"

Robert shuffled his feet on the slushy ground. "Looking for you. Helping my father a little. Drinking with my old chums at the King's Arms, mostly." Shaking his head, he grabbed her by the shoulders. "I vow and swear, I cannot believe I've found you. I thought I'd never see you again."

When Amy didn't respond, he paused, apparently considering.

"Were you *ever* going to try to find me?" he finally asked in a slow, suspicious tone.

Amy looked down at the street. She wished he'd let go of her, but he had her shoulders in an iron grip. A faint, stale smell of ale washed over her; she could taste it in her mouth. "Of course. I—I just got to the City," she hedged. "I've been staying with friends. Out in the countryside."

"Friends? Friends I don't know about?"

She lifted her head and shot him a bold look. "There's much you don't know of me, Robert."

"I'm coming to see that," he returned, dropping his arms to fold them across his chest. "Our wedding date passed, as you know. We shall have to reschedule."

Amy stared at him. "Did you not read my letter?"

"Wedding date?" Emerging from the shadowed corner of the carriage, Kendra stuck her head out. "Amy?"

Amy turned to her gratefully; this talk of weddings was making her ill. "Kendra, this is Robert Stanley. Robert, my friend Lady Kendra."

He aimed a curt nod at Kendra. "This is your friend?" he asked Amy bluntly. "The one you've been staying with?"

"Yes."

"Fancy carriage." He said it as though it were a crime to own one.

"It belongs to my brother," Kendra explained.

"Lord Something-or-other?"

"The Marquess of Cainewood."

Robert blinked and frowned, as though he were trying to remember something, then gave a quick shake of his head. He turned back to Amy. "So…when do you want to get married?"

"Never," she said quietly.

"You were promised to me." Robert's voice was low and deep and even more quiet than hers.

Too quiet.

Though Amy looked at him defiantly, she was shaking inside. She didn't want to hurt him, but she had to make him understand she had no intention of becoming his wife. "My father is dead. Everything has changed for me. And"—she lifted her chin—"and I don't have to marry you."

"Blast it, Amy, you're supposed to be mine. I waited and waited. The shop was supposed to be mine, too, but now it's gone. The inventory..." His eyes lit up. "Where is the inventory?"

Amy swallowed hard. "I don't *want* to marry you, Robert."

Robert's jaw was set. His pale blue eyes flashed with menace. *"Where is the inventory?"*

"I don't have it." Her voice wavered, but it wasn't quite a lie. She didn't have it here.

"I don't believe you. I went back to look, but found not a trace. No molten metal, no diamonds in the ashes. And diamonds don't turn to ash." He took a step closer. "Where is it, Amy?"

"I don't have it," she repeated shakily. "I—I have to go now." She turned to enter the carriage.

He grabbed her by the upper arm, swung her around, and dug his fingers in painfully. "The inventory is *mine*. I worked five years for it. Where is it?"

Amy winced and threw a worried glance at Kendra, spurring her friend into action. Kendra planted herself firmly in the doorway of the carriage. "Leave her alone!" she yelled at the top of her lungs. "She doesn't have it!"

Visibly shocked at this outburst, Robert turned on Kendra. "You stay out of this! It's not your concern!"

Kendra's eyes narrowed recklessly. She came down from the carriage in a flash, curling one hand into a fist, which she propelled expertly into Robert's face. "Leave her alone, I tell you!"

Robert's pale eyes bugged out, and he dropped Amy's arm to grasp his rapidly reddening jaw.

With a triumphant grin, Kendra grabbed Amy's freed hand. "I haven't three brothers for nothing!" she informed nobody in particular, then jumped into the carriage, pulling Amy after her.

Amy stuck her head out and pinned Robert with a disdainful look. "Five years? My family worked five *centuries* for that jewelry. You learned your craft and were paid a fair wage, as well as bed and board. I owe you no more, and you'll never have more, Robert Stanley!"

She slammed and latched the carriage door.

Robert beat on it with both fists. "You're mistaken, Amethyst

Goldsmith! I'll have the inventory yet, and you as well. You just wait!"

Inside the darkened carriage, Amy hunched over on the bench seat, covering her head with her hands so she wouldn't hear him. After what seemed an interminable wait, the vehicle jerked and began moving.

Amy straightened. "I'm sorry about that," she apologized, massaging her upper arm. She was certain to have marks from Robert's fingers.

"It's not every day I get to practice my boxing." Kendra's laugh was shaky. She rubbed her bruised fist ruefully. "Gad, was he ever surprised!" She pushed open the curtains, and sunlight flooded the cabin. "Are you all right?"

Amy nodded mournfully. "I cannot believe what a perfect beast he was! And to think I almost married him." She shuddered.

"You never told me you were betrothed."

"I wanted to forget it. I never wanted to wed him in the first place—it was all my father's doing."

"He's so...he doesn't fit with you." Kendra's face turned contemplative. "He looked as though he might have an engaging smile when he's not angry, but he's quite...short. Of character *and* of stature. I cannot imagine you with him. Now, you and—"

"He always scared me a little," Amy interrupted Kendra's musings. "He lived with us as our apprentice the past five years, but we'd been promised since we were children."

"Did you like him at all?"

"At first, until I got to know him. He had strong ideas of what he wanted in a wife, and they didn't mesh with mine. Still, I could have done worse, and my father was insistent." She shuddered again. "I'll *never* marry him, especially not after this," she declared vehemently. *"Never, never, never."*

Kendra frowned. "Your aunt won't expect you to wed him, will she?"

Amy thought a moment. Aunt Elizabeth was a warm, motherly type who wanted to see everyone around her happy. And she'd never been particularly fond of Robert. "No," she said at last. "No, I don't believe she will. Or my uncle, either."

"Then you've nothing to worry about. Robert doesn't know where to find you while you're staying with us—"

"And I'll be gone soon. Very soon." The sooner the better, she thought morosely.

Her time in England was really at an end.

Kendra leaned over to touch her hand, then suddenly grinned. "Five centuries?"

Amusement lightened Amy's mood. "Well...perhaps I exaggerated, just a little." When her eyes met Kendra's, they both burst out laughing.

FORTY-TWO

*R*OBERT'S ALCOHOL-laden brain was trying to tell him something. Surrounded by his chums at the King's Arms, he was drinking too much and eating too little. He felt sick. Still, something in the back of his head was working its way out.

Kendra. Kendra. He took another swig. Was there not…

Yes! That worm Greystone had a sister named Kendra.

They'd come into the shop only once, but the way the fellow had looked at Amy, and Amy's flushed reaction, still burned in Robert's memory. He hadn't paid the sister any attention, having no taste for red-headed girls, but this could easily be her.

He rubbed his aching jaw. This Kendra, with her iron fist, didn't look much like Greystone. His hair had been black, and his eyes were a darker green than hers, too. She was petite, and the worm was tall—so tall that Robert had felt intimidated, although Greystone had ignored him.

Well, the sister intimidated him, too. Now.

Yes, she must be his sister. He squinted his bloodshot eyes, trying to better picture them both. They shared the same facial bone structure, he was sure of it, and the same shape eyes. And they both had the same cocky self-assurance.

And they were both "friends" of Amy's.

Amy. Pretty, elusive Amy. She'd promised to marry him. For

five long years he'd sat at her father's bench, with the promise of Amy and her riches in time.

The time had come. She was in London. If she wouldn't wed him willingly, he would have to force her. There were places he'd heard about, "privileged" churches where a man could marry a woman without posting banns, without taking out a license.

Without her consent.

He turned to the man next to him, one of the many who spent their evenings in this popular middle-class tavern. "Hey," he said, surprised to hear the word wavering, "have you knowledge of a privileged church? Not too far?"

"St. Trinity, in the Minories," the man answered.

"St. James in Duke's Place is another," a man sitting across the table put in. "They're the only two, I think. Claim they're outside the jurisdiction of the Bishop of London and can therefore make their own rules. M'sister was wed at St. James."

"Against her will?"

"Nah. She was just in a hurry. Got a predated certificate, too, so the babe wasn't early."

Robert nodded, digesting the information. Both Duke's Place and the Minories were nearby, just outside the old Roman wall. "I won't need a license or anything?"

"Nah. Just two crowns for the curate and a couple of witnesses."

Not a problem, thought Robert, imagining the stash of coins, gold, and gems that awaited him upon his marriage.

His stomach roiled, protesting another swig of ale. He was sorry it had come to this, sorry she wasn't submitting to him of her own accord. But she was his due, and once the deed was done she'd get used to the idea. She'd come to his bed and bear his children. Eventually. She'd always been a cold one, anyway —he'd never expected to find her a warm and willing wife.

And when she was his, everything she owned would be, too.

He looked up at his two drinking companions. "Either of you heard of Lord Greystone?"

"Nay, never heard of him," the man next to him muttered.

"Nah." The man across from him shook his head.

"Hey," he called out, his voice slurred. "Anyone here know a Lord Greystone? Colin Something-or-other?"

"Chase," someone called out. "Colin Chase." The man wore a long, crimped periwig and was dressed a tad more stylishly than the average patron of the King's Arms; Robert believed he could be acquainted with Colin Chase, or at least know of him.

"He got a brother? The Marquess of something?"

"Cainewood. The Marquess of Cainewood. Jason Chase."

"Right." And Amy had been riding in Cainewood's carriage, with Cainewood's sister. It all fit together.

Pleased with his powers of deduction, Robert paused for another swallow and dragged his sleeve across his mouth. "Anyone know where Cainewood lives? I'll pay someone"—he burped loudly—"ten shillings to show me where he lives."

There was a scraping of benches as men rose, eager to collect ten shillings for such an easy job. Robert wasn't so sotted, however, that he didn't realize most of them probably didn't know Cainewood's house from the London Bridge.

"You," he said. He rose unsteadily and pointed at the man who had answered his questions. "You're the one. Come along."

Gesturing for the man to follow, he stumbled through the door and out into the street. His companion pressed himself up against the wall as Robert paused to throw up in the gutter, his vomit barely adding to the refuse and filth already there.

Robert stood up, swiped a sleeve across his mouth, and let loose a loud belch. "That's better. Let's go."

Shaking his head in disgust, the man led the way all the same.

Ten shillings was ten shillings.

FORTY-THREE

*A*MY JERKED awake, struggling against a hand over her mouth—a grimy hand, smelling of ale and sweat and vomit. She gagged.

"Hush," came a hiss in her ear. "Make a sound and I'll kill you, I swear it. I've got a knife."

She froze at the sound of Robert's voice, but didn't believe him for a second. Jeweler's tools were the closest thing to a weapon he ever touched. He wouldn't know what to do with a serious knife even if he truly had one.

She lashed out, scratching at his face and kicking her legs wildly. He fell awkwardly on top of her, pinning her legs beneath his heavier ones. Her arms came around, and she sank her fingernails into his fleshy back.

"Blast it, Amy, I didn't want it to be like this," Robert whispered fiercely. His body held her crushed to the bed as he groped with a hand in the darkened room. Something fell and rolled along the floor. "Blast it all!" he muttered, coming up on one elbow.

Her head exploded in pain. One second she was fighting for her life, and the next second the world went black.

~

*R*OBERT PULLED himself off her, panting from unaccustomed exertion. The heavy candlestick thudded to the floor as he dropped to his knees and scrabbled under the bed for the candle. When his fingers closed around it, he ran to the fireplace to light it and rushed back to examine Amy.

A thin trail of blood ran from her scalp down her forehead. For a minute Robert panicked, searching incompetently for a pulse. He pressed his ear to her chest, heard her heart beating, felt the rise and fall of her even breathing. *Thank the heavens.* Dead, she was useless to him.

He needed to marry her to get his hands on her fortune.

He ripped long strands of the sheet and tied one around her head as a crude bandage, used another as a gag, and a third to bind her hands together. Hoping she'd cooperate and walk when she awakened, he left her feet unbound.

He wrapped her awkwardly in one of the blankets, then grabbed her under the arms and tugged her limp form off the bed. He hadn't counted on the dead weight. Petite Amy felt heavy as a horse. Pausing twice to rewrap the blanket around her, he dragged her to the open window, where a ladder waited.

With a mighty effort, he hefted her inert body over one shoulder and ducked out, feeling for the ladder with an unsteady foot. Balancing her precariously, he lurched down a rung at a time, more than relieved when the hackney driver met him halfway and relieved him of his heavy burden.

The driver dumped Amy onto the bench seat, and Robert climbed inside. "You know where to go," he growled under his breath, sending the man up top with a wave of his hand.

Robert wedged himself next to Amy and fought to catch his breath as the cab squeaked through the quiet streets.

The sidelamp threw light into the interior, casting a yellowish glow onto Amy's slack face. Thankfully, her wound was superficial, the bandage stained but the bleeding stopped. He tucked the errant blanket tighter around her, then slumped against the side of the coach, relieved and exhausted.

A bellman called the hour of midnight, the words resonating

through the thick, clammy fog. Three-quarters of an hour later, the springless cab bumped through Aldgate and into Duke's Place, rattling to a stop in front of St. James.

The door was unlocked, it being a church, but no one was inside. Robert walked to the altar, his footsteps on the stone floor echoing in the deserted chamber. Votive candles were set about the sanctuary, flickering, contributing to the eerie atmosphere.

Robert had never been in an empty church before. Truth be told, he hadn't been in a church at all in recent memory. In his opinion, life was for living, and there would be ample time for regret and penance when he was older.

He shivered.

"Anyone here?" he called, half expecting the figure on the cross to look down and answer him. But it didn't, of course. The sanctuary was silent save for his own breathing, which sounded louder and louder as he became more agitated.

The place was giving him the creeps. Everyone knew that dead clergymen were buried under the floors of these churches, and suddenly Robert was certain one of their ghosts was about to pop up and grab him. He turned and ran down the aisle and out the door.

"No one's there," he yelled at the hackney driver, as though it were the man's fault.

The driver shrugged. "It's Saturday evening."

It was actually Sunday morning by now, but Robert didn't bother arguing. Besides, what if someone needed a priest on a Saturday night? They must be available somewhere. "Take me to St. Trinity, in the Minories," he ordered before jumping into the cab and kicking the half-door shut.

The driver shrugged again, then took a swig of the brandy he carried with him against the winter chill. He didn't care if the young fellow wasted his time. Robert had promised him a full evening's pay, and he'd quoted triple his usual night's take and demanded half in advance.

St. Trinity was a scant three streets away, much too close for Robert, who had yet to recover from the last stop. The deserted streets contributed to his unease. Londoners stayed inside at night, venturing outdoors only for necessary travel, and then generally with an escort of footmen and linkboys to light the way. The law required citizens to hang lamps outside their houses on dark nights, but no one complied; the unlit, foggy streets were spooky, and Robert felt nervous and shaky.

He forced himself to get out of the cab and slowly walked up to the massive church doors.

Inside, St. Trinity looked much like St. James. His feet made a shuffling sound as he crossed the threshold, and his heart hammered in his chest as he scanned the flickering, shadowed walls. When a door at the other end opened, he jumped, letting out a little shriek.

A florid, balding man stuck his head into the sanctuary and smiled. "Feel free to pray here, my son. Problems seem smaller when you share them with our Lord."

The curate stepped out into the sanctuary, and Robert saw that he was plump and healthy, evidently well fed and cared for, unlike most parish priests. Apparently the curate of a privileged church enjoyed a highly lucrative position. The man didn't look frightening in the least.

The whole chamber seemed to lighten, and Robert heaved a sigh of relief. "I've come to get married, Father."

The clergyman looked pleased. "Ah, I see. Have you need of a—shall we say 'special'—certificate?"

"Nay, the date matters not. But the lady is…reluctant."

"That's none of my concern. The price will be three crowns."

"I heard tell it was two."

"Two and a half, then. Special, for you."

"Done." In truth, Robert would have paid ten crowns or more, and gladly, for securing Amy and her riches.

He turned toward the door, intending to fetch Amy posthaste and get it over with. He hoped mightily that she had awakened, or that it wouldn't matter either way to the curate.

"I'll see you Monday morning, then," the curate called out.

"Monday?" He swung back. "I—can we not do it now?"

The clergyman smiled wider, showing large, uneven teeth. "The Sabbath approaches, my son. There will be no weddings until Monday."

"But…"

"Bring with you two witnesses and a pistol—the latter will make it go faster." He winked at Robert. "I have five other weddings Monday, so come early or expect to wait. Good evening." He disappeared, shutting the door behind him, leaving Robert standing openmouthed.

Where was he going to get a pistol? And, even more difficult, whatever would he do with Amy until Monday? He cursed himself, loudly, for acting without planning first, then clapped a hand over his mouth. Surely cursing in a house of the Lord was much worse than cursing elsewhere.

He bolted for the door.

His heart was pounding so hard that it took him a few moments to notice the hackney's door was wide open and he could hear someone running down the street.

Amy had escaped.

FORTY-FOUR

*A*MY RAN AS fast as she could, clutching the blanket in front where her hands were tied together. It flapped behind her, floating in the draft, not providing any warmth to speak of. But she held on to it for dear life, knowing it could save her from freezing to death later on, if she couldn't find shelter.

With every jarring step, pain burst in her throbbing head. Racing along the scum-lined street, she stumbled over rocks and debris. A sharp sliver sliced into one bare foot, but she scarcely noticed. As she turned onto Whitechapel she developed a stitch in her side, but she scarcely noticed that, either. She was too preoccupied with the pounding feet she heard approaching—feet that were bound to be Robert's, since she'd seen no other soul in the gray, foggy night.

She ducked into a narrow space between two buildings and hunched over there, trying with little success to maneuver the blanket around her shivering shoulders. The nightgown she'd borrowed from Kendra was all but useless against the winter cold.

Robert ran past, panting heavily, a dark shadow against the fog. She held her breath and flattened herself against one of the walls, trying to make herself invisible.

As his echoing footsteps faded away, Amy released her breath. The stench of rotting refuse made her want to gag. Still, she forced herself to stay motionless, pressed against the rough, cold stone wall for what seemed like hours, though she knew it was only minutes.

As the chill seeped into her body, penetrating to her very bones, she listened. She heard a baby crying, a couple's raised, angry voices, her own heart thudding in her chest.

The footsteps didn't return.

Minutes ticked by. She grew colder still; she would have to find shelter soon. Barefoot, clad in only a thin white nightgown and blanket, gagged and with her wrists bound, she imagined herself to be quite a sight. Regardless, someone would doubtless help her, take her in for the night, if only she could get to their front door. The arguing couple was her best bet—at least she knew they were home and awake.

Not an attractive alternative, but she was in no position to be choosy.

She waited a few more agonizing minutes, while her heart slowed to its normal rhythm, her breathing became more regular, and her shivering escalated to new heights. Finally convinced she had escaped successfully, she decided to venture forth.

Her deep, fortifying breath created a cloud in the frigid air. She peeled herself away from the wall and limped to the edge of the buildings. Her eyes now adjusted to the unlit London streets, she stuck her head out and looked both ways, seeing nothing that alarmed her, although she couldn't see far through the fog.

She thought the bickering couple lived across the narrow street, down Whitechapel to the right. The hazy yellow of a lit window in approximately the right place confirmed her guess.

Steeling herself to leave her cramped, freezing cold haven of safety, she counted. One, two, three...*now*.

She bolted across the street, angling toward the comforting light of the window. Suddenly, a rickety noise sliced through the blanket of fog as a coach came barreling around the corner. Releasing a whimper of fright that was muffled by the gag in her mouth, she dropped her blanket in the middle of the street and, reaching the other side, took a sharp left, running the opposite direction of the coach's travel.

It was no use. Before the hackney even screeched to a halt, Robert jumped off and gained on her immediately.

A fierce tug on the back of her nightgown brought her stumbling to her knees. She broke her fall with her elbows and bound fists. Numb with cold and shock, she scarcely registered the new scrapes. An instant later, Robert threw himself on top of her, forcing her facedown into the dirt and knocking the wind out of her lungs.

"Curses and furies!" he hollered. "Did you think you could actually escape me?"

Even had she not been gagged and breathless, she wouldn't have answered him.

Darkness had closed in again.

~

*O*RNING SUN fought to illuminate the room through a small dirt-streaked window. Blinking in the dimness, Amy struggled toward consciousness. Although she was alone and ungagged, her hands were still bound together. She was lying in a bed. Beneath a dirty, threadbare blanket, her feet were tied to the bedposts.

She lay still, taking stock of herself. Her head ached, her knees and elbows burned, her body felt stiff and sore, bruised all over. She needed a chamber pot, but that would have to wait.

Diminished but still whole, she was determined to fight Robert to her last breath.

Her scraped elbows were roughly crusted over with new scabs that cracked and opened when she moved. She licked her dry lips, tasting coppery blood in the corners where the gag had rubbed them raw. She tested the bonds on her wrists, twisting them experimentally. They chafed horribly, the skin red and abraded. But, with patience and her teeth, she was sure she could untie the cloth strips. This time, however, she'd have a plan before she did anything.

The room gave no clue to her location. The window was so obliterated with dirt that she had no view of the outside. Dark shadows against the panes told her it was barred, anyway. The plain chamber contained nothing more than her flea-ridden bed, a rough table, and two chairs on a filthy, bare wooden floor. A paltry fire gave off little warmth and a fair amount of smoke, laid as it was in a blackened fireplace that had long been in need of cleaning.

She had no memory of her arrival here. She thought she'd been in Whitechapel when she made the failed attempt at freedom, but she could be a day's ride from there for all she was aware of the lapse of time. She would have to wait for Robert's return before she could begin to plot her escape.

Closing her eyes, she prayed for the oblivion of sleep.

FORTY-FIVE

$\mathcal{C}$OLIN LEANED LOW over the saddle, his hands clenched on the reins, the paper crumpled in one fist. He couldn't read it while Ebony's pounding hooves ate up the miles of rutted road, but Ford's scribbled words were burned into his brain.

Amy is missing. Come immediately.

His heart had been hammering since he'd set eyes on the cryptic note. He'd wasted no time setting out for London, his fevered imagination conjuring up scenes featuring every possibility, from Amy deciding to leave England on her own, to Amy lying dead in a ditch, a pistol wound in her chest.

The wind whipped past as he barreled along, praying mightily. He made the most outlandish promises, bargaining with the Almighty for her safe return. He would dedicate himself to the rebuilding of St. Paul's Cathedral (though the great architect Wren hardly required his assistance). He would give all his riches to the needy (what riches?). He would marry Priscilla immediately, remain faithful and devoted to her the rest of his days, and never spare a single thought for Amethyst Goldsmith again.

This last promise was the most unlikely of all.

He'd been at war with himself for months now. It was a

losing battle. As he shot through the City gates, one spurred boot nicked a vegetable barrow. He turned in the saddle, watched lemons and artichokes plop to the muddy street, yelled an apology to the vendor...and finally admitted to himself that he couldn't let Amy go to France.

The thought of passing days, months, years of his life at Greystone without her—whether she was living with her aunt, married to someone else, or cold in her grave—made him sick in his gut. They belonged together.

It felt good to accept that inevitability. Now his course was clear. Now that he knew neither his pride nor his honor could stand between them, he certainly wouldn't let some rotten criminal keep them apart. He would find her, make her safe, and then somehow convince her to stay. She simply had to stay.

Because he was in love with her.

Criminy, when had that happened?

He didn't know; perhaps he'd fallen in love the very first day they met, or perhaps it had happened gradually. It wasn't something he could analyze or account for. He only knew she was meant to be his. He needed her.

And right now, she needed him.

Ebony was lathered long before Colin reached Lincoln's Inn Fields, but he merely tossed the reins to a groom instead of rubbing the horse down himself as he normally would after a hard ride. He threw open the front door of the town house and raced into the marble entry, heedless of the mud on his boots.

"Jason! Ford! Kendra!"

"Colin!" Kendra appeared from around the corner and threw herself at him. "Thank heavens you're here!"

"Jason isn't home." Ford called down the stairs. "He left early this morning, before we discovered—"

"Discovered what?" Colin pulled Kendra's arms from around his neck and set her away. "Tell me what you know, *now*," he demanded.

"I'll show you." Kendra seized him arm and dragged him toward the staircase. "Yesterday Amy and I visited Madame Beaumont. When we came out, Amy ran into a young man named Robert, and they had a huge row."

Colin held up a hand. "Robert Stanley?"

"I cannot remember his surname," Kendra said, "but he was her father's apprentice, and he was betrothed to Amy."

"Robert Stanley," Colin forced through clenched teeth. "Go on."

"When she told him she'd no wish to marry him," Kendra continued, "he lost control. He seized her and threatened her—"

"—and Kendra punched him in the jaw." Ford met them on the landing. "Can't you just picture it?"

Kendra's eyes flashed green fire. "This is *serious*, Ford! And it was clearly a half-witted move on my part. Look what's happened!"

Colin growled impatiently. "What *has* happened?"

"Come see." She beckoned him down the corridor. "After I struck him, he let go of Amy, and we jumped into the carriage and rode away."

"But not"—Ford stopped, his hand on the latch to Amy's door—"before he claimed he would have Amy's jewelry and Amy as well. It looks like he meant it." He pushed open the door.

Colin was struck by a blast of cold air.

Momentarily dazed, he walked to the open window and peered outside. Below, a ladder rested against the house. He swung back around. The fire had long since burned out, and judging by the frigid temperature of the chamber, the window had been open for some time. Bedclothes littered the floor, and the blanket was missing.

"We left it as we found it," Kendra whispered. "Look."

Colin followed her gesture to the bed. Spots of blood dotted the sheets.

He dropped to sit on the mattress. A rose scent—Amy's scent —wafted into the air. "You think he's made off with her?"

Kendra dropped down beside him. "It's the only explanation. Amy would never leave without telling us. And the blood...she might be dead. Oh, Colin!" She buried her face in his shoulder.

One hand absently patted her back while his other fingers traced the dark red spots on the sheet. Blood. Amy's blood. His stomach knotted, and he couldn't seem to think straight.

Ford paced the room. "As usual, Kendra, you're jumping to conclusions. There are but a few drops of blood here, and none trailing toward the window—I doubt she was seriously injured, let alone murdered. Why would this fellow want to kill her, anyway? You said he wanted to marry her."

"But she wasn't agreeable!" Kendra wailed. "I'm telling you, he was furious."

"Look here." Ford pointed to Amy's trunk in the corner of the room. "He hasn't taken the jewelry, has he?"

"No..."

"Perhaps he means only to persuade her to marry him."

"By wounding her? For heaven's sake, Ford, *think*. He's taken her. If she's not dead, he obviously intends to ransom her, for her own jewelry or our money."

With a violent shake of his head, Colin regained his senses. He rose and went to the window, shutting it with a resounding *bang*. "I doubt he intends to ransom her. He cannot be at all certain we'd pay—we're not even related." Colin's mind raced. In truth, he wasn't sure whether he was relieved or alarmed that Amy's abductor seemed to be her ex-betrothed, rather than some crazed criminal. "Are you sure he knows where the jewelry is?"

"No." Kendra stood up slowly. "No. She didn't actually admit to having it."

"I assumed as much." Ford shot a meaningful look at the trunk. "Otherwise, he wouldn't have left it here."

Kendra stamped her foot. "All right, we bow to your scientific logic. What do *you* think this is about, then?"

"My guess is he plans to force her to wed him. Then he'll own her fortune outright."

"He couldn't do that!"

"It happens."

"Ford is right." Colin's voice was a command.

The twins turned and stared at him.

Under the circumstances, his imagined scenarios of violent death seemed unlikely. On the other hand, Ford's conclusion seemed chillingly possible.

Colin took deep breaths to keep from retching at the thought.

His hands curled into fists at his sides as he strode to the door, then whirled to face his brother and sister. "Stay here, in case we're wrong and a ransom note arrives. I'll be back. With Amy."

FORTY-SIX

*T*HE SCREECH OF a key working a rusty lock brought Amy instantly alert.

Finally.

Robert slunk in and shut the door behind him, taking pains to lock it before he turned to face her. His pale blue eyes impaled her as he slowly slipped the key into the pocket of his loose breeches. If only she could reach that key, she'd be halfway out of here. But it was impossible at the moment.

Patience, she reminded herself, forcing herself to breathe in a slow, measured rhythm.

He looked much the worse for wear. His shirt was torn, his fawn-colored breeches wrinkled and filthy. His hair hung in lanky strings, and the freckles on his face were obscured by a thin coat of grime. Then again, she thought wryly, she was hardly in a position to pass judgment. Clad in nothing but a ripped nightgown, bruised and bloody, it wasn't likely she presented an appealing picture herself.

"How are you?" he finally asked.

Her answer was a scornful roll of her eyes. Regardless of her firm decision not to agitate him, she couldn't bring herself to engage in conversation as though her situation were ordinary.

"Very well, then. Are you ill?"

"No."

"Are you injured?"

"Not mortally."

"Good," he said, striding over to the fireplace. He tossed another log inside, then wiped his hands on his dirty breeches. "I've got some errands to run. I just wanted to see that you were all right before I left." He headed for the door.

She couldn't let him go so fast. She knew nothing that could help her make plans. "Where am I?" she blurted out.

He hesitated, then turned back. "At an inn," he answered slowly.

"But where?"

"It doesn't signify. You'll be here only until tomorrow."

"And then?"

"I'll let you know later. When I'm prepared."

For what? The words stuck in her throat; she knew it would be useless to ask. "Wait!" she called when he turned to leave again. "I have to…you know…use the chamber pot."

His lips puckered, but he strode to the bed and reached underneath, retrieving a dusty, chipped pot. When he lifted the edge of the blanket, Amy moved her bound wrists to press down on it.

"Robert, no!" She'd rather lie in a wet bed than have him assist her in this matter.

"Did you honestly think I would untie you?"

"Just my hands, please. I promise I won't try anything."

He stared at her, the sound of his heavy breathing filling her ears while she shifted on the bed. "Very well," he said at last. "But only your hands."

He newly abraded her wrists as he unbound them, but she gritted her teeth and held her tongue. He slipped the chamber pot under the blanket and stepped away, turned his back and waited expectantly.

Mortified, Amy gasped. "You have to leave."

He swung back around. "Oh, no…no, I don't."

"*Please*. You cannot do this to me, Robert." She thought quickly. "I'm sorry we quarreled yesterday," she lied. "I—I'm sure we can work something out. And—and we cannot really start this way if we're going to be happy together."

His eyes bore into hers. She met his gaze, willing him to believe her.

The fire crackled on the hearth.

"I'll wait outside, but for only two minutes," he said at last and unlocked the door. "Then I'm coming back in, whether you're ready or not."

When he pulled out a pocket watch, Amy recognized the ruby-encrusted case that he'd labored hours over, back in the days when life was normal. With a meaningful glance in her direction, he flipped open the lid and stepped out into the corridor, banging the door closed behind him.

Inspired by his threat, she finished in record time. Leaning halfway off the bed to set the chamber pot on the floor, she was contemplating whether she had enough time left to untie her ankles, when he barged in. She bolted upright.

"Finished?"

She nodded mutely. He retied her wrists, yanking the knot tight in a silent show of domination, then peeked beneath the blanket near her feet.

Her heart pounded at the thought that he might have discovered her duplicity.

When he reached the door, he turned back to face her. "You know, I'm not nearly the simpleton you think I am. But you'll learn that over time."

And he turned and left, locking the door behind him.

FORTY-SEVEN

*C*OLIN STRODE out the door of the town house, his stomach churning with anxiety and frustration. *Amy-Amy-Amy-Amy-Amy*, repeated over and over in his brain, accomplishing nothing but the beginnings of a massive headache.

He had to find her, but how? London was bursting at the seams with buildings and humanity, and Robert could have taken her anywhere.

Assuming it was Robert who had taken her. And assuming they were still in London. The sheer number of possibilities was overwhelming.

Leaning against the stable wall while his horse was resaddled, Colin forced his pulse to steady and his head to clear. He took slow, deep breaths, rubbing the white star on Ebony's forehead in a soothing rhythm.

Robert. How could he find Robert?

The man must have family somewhere. And that family would be jewelers, no doubt. Robert had been Hugh Goldsmith's apprentice, and if Colin understood how the guild system worked, apprenticeships were arranged between families well nigh at birth. He would lay odds that Robert's father was in the same business.

He just had to find the elder Mr. Stanley.

~

*R*OBERT RETURNED several hours later, his freckled face scrubbed clean, his damp orange hair slightly curling at the ends. He was dressed in an immaculate brown suit, the jacket's wide cuffs trimmed in icy blue, the loose breeches beribboned with poufs of blue loops. As he entered, he unfastened his knee-length cloak and folded it over the back of a chair, revealing a starched white, lace-bordered cravat tied neatly at his throat and secured with a diamond brooch. His wide-brimmed hat boasted a blue ostrich plume and a jeweled hatband. He swept it off his head and tossed it on the battered wooden table with a flourish.

"I'm ready," he announced.

Amy eyed him dubiously. Clearly he was decked out for an important occasion—he almost looked handsome in his finery. She lifted her head to inspect him more closely. "Ready for what?"

"Our wedding."

Nonplussed, she dropped her head back to the dirty pillow. A puff of dust whooshed out, clogging her nostrils and making her cough. How could he think she would agree to marry him now, after a forcible abduction? It was beyond her comprehension.

This was hardly her idea of courtship.

When she offered no comment, he continued, his cheerfulness unabated. "Of course, today's Sunday, so we'll have to wait until tomorrow. But I decided to ready myself now, since I don't plan to leave you again beforehand. It makes me nervous."

So now she was stuck with him. This turn of events was unlikely to facilitate her escape, which she was more determined than ever to achieve. In the course of the past twenty-four hours, she'd decided that besides harboring an unforetold capacity for violence, Robert was quite obviously insane.

A shadow of discomfort crossed his face. He flexed his shoulders restlessly before dropping onto a chair. "Aren't you going to say anything?"

"I'm not marrying you," she said bluntly.

In answer, he rose from the chair and reached behind his back, drew a pistol from the waistband of his breeches, and set it on the table. Softly, but she heard the metallic thud. "Yes, you are marrying me."

Amy was fairly certain he'd never use the gun on her—or anyone else, for that matter. She doubted he knew how to load it, let alone shoot it. But apparently she wasn't able to hide her apprehension, because Robert reseated himself with a self-satisfied smirk on his face.

"We've an appointment at St. Trinity tomorrow morning," he explained. "I have two witnesses meeting us here. We'll tie you up and cover you with my cloak. The proprietor here already believes you're ill; he'll think naught when we carry you out and over toward the church."

St. Trinity was in the Minories. If he planned on carrying her there, they must still be in the City, or at least somewhere in greater London. That was welcome news.

Robert would have to leave sometime, at least to order some food, and perhaps she could untie herself, knock him senseless upon his return, steal the key and escape, losing herself in the rabbit warren of streets that made up London. She'd take his cloak to cover her nightgown...

"...gown and slippers will be delivered for you within the hour," Robert was saying. So she'd have something to wear. Things were looking up. "I've arranged for food to be delivered." *Gad.* There went his reason for leaving. "Are you hungry?"

"It doesn't signify. I wouldn't sit at table with you in either case."

"You're right. You're staying in that bed."

They glared at each other. Robert looked away first.

Amy kept her gaze on him. "No banns have been posted."

"No matter. It's a privileged church. You've heard of them, I presume?"

She nodded curtly. "I won't say 'I will.'"

"Oh, you'll say it." He picked up the pistol and hefted it as emphasis to his words. "I doubt the curate cares what you say, anyway. So long as he gets his blunt."

He had an answer for every protest. Nonetheless, from somewhere deep inside, Amy was confident she'd find a way out.

The alternative was too ghastly to consider.

FORTY-EIGHT

"*I* DON'T KNOW where he is, my lord. I'm sorry."

"Think, Mr. Stanley. *Please*," Colin begged. "I must find her. I—I love her."

There. He'd said it. Out loud, to another human being.

Sadly, his confession, however difficult, didn't seem to make any profound impression on Robert's father. "I'm sure Robert loves her too, my lord," James Stanley said warily.

He was an older, much fatter version of Robert, exhibiting the likely result of an inactive life seated at a jeweler's bench. He looked affable enough, in much the same way Robert did. Still, the sheer resemblance of the two men led to Colin's instant resentment.

Was this jealousy? If so, it was a deucedly intolerable emotion.

"She's been promised to him since they were children," Mr. Stanley continued in a reasonable tone of voice. "They come from similar backgrounds. They can build a life together. What can you offer her?"

"That is none of your blasted business."

James Stanley's face shut down, the straight line of his mouth indicating his unwillingness to cooperate.

Colin sighed, dropping his head. He stared down through the glass of the empty jewelry case. The little shop was closed, it being Sunday, but Colin had pounded on the door until Mr. Stanley came downstairs.

Confident until now, Colin had been on his quest for half a day already. Cheapside was still in ashes; no one near the ruins of Goldsmith & Sons had known of Robert Stanley. But on the Strand, home to more than fifty jewelers for the past two centuries, he'd hit gold: the elder Stanley's name and location.

Weaving Ebony across town through London's afternoon traffic, Colin's spirits had remained high. He was counting on a potent combination of ingenuity and sheer determination to help him locate Amy in this city of over a quarter million inhabitants, and he'd convinced himself James Stanley would know his son's plans.

But apparently Mr. Stanley either didn't know or wouldn't tell. And now Colin had alienated him with that thoughtless, hotheaded remark. He silently cursed himself; he hardly recognized the person he'd become since he found Amy outside her blazing shop.

He stared down at his reflection in the case's glass, and narrowed green eyes stared back up at him. His jaw was tense, his mouth twisted into a threat. He blinked, shocked at his forbidding countenance. He wouldn't send such a man after his son, either, he supposed.

Determined to regain his self-control, he forced his lips to part in a stiff, toothy smile and looked back up at James Stanley. "I just want to make sure this is what Amy wants. I would never harm her, physically or otherwise."

"Robert would never harm her, either," the older man snapped.

Colin lifted his chin, meeting Stanley's icy blue gaze—so like Robert's—straight on. "There was blood on the sheets, Mr. Stanley." The words were calm, unemotional. Inside, Colin was seething, but this man was his best hope for information, so he couldn't afford to let him see it.

James Stanley blinked, and his sharp indrawn breath revealed his shock. "I honestly don't know where he is," he said after a few moments. "He doesn't confide in me. But he spends his free hours at the King's Arms, on Holborn."

FORTY-NINE

ROBERT PUSHED the spoon between Amy's lips, but it met clenched teeth. "Amy, you have to eat. I won't have you fainting in church tomorrow."

"Untie me, and I'll feed myself. Otherwise…" She shrugged.

Robert dropped the spoon in the bowl. Ragout of mushrooms, sweetbreads and oysters splashed up, brown bits landing on the coverlet. "Have it your way. You'll let me feed you when you get hungry enough."

Never, Amy thought. She'd never grant him the satisfaction.

He rose from the bed, wandered to the window, and rubbed a fist on the grimy pane in an effort to see out. Then, giving up, he threw himself onto one of the wooden chairs, his legs sprawled out in front of him in an awkward attempt to recline.

Amy's carefully veiled eyes followed his every move. He was growing bored, tired of waiting. Good. Perhaps he'd become restless enough to consider leaving for a while.

He yawned, loudly, not bothering to cover his mouth. She grimaced at the sight of his overlapping teeth, wondering how she'd ever had the stomach to let him kiss her.

He yawned again. This was encouraging. If he fell asleep, she'd have a chance to untie herself. She ground her teeth lightly, anticipating using them to loosen her bonds.

A knock at the door jerked Robert back to life.

"About time," he growled, rising to answer it.

A man pushed a large box into Robert's arms. Reaching into his pocket, Robert fished out a coin and slapped it into the man's palm, then turned and kicked the door shut behind him. He set the box on the table. "Want to see it?"

Without waiting for an answer, he threw aside the box's lid and pulled out an ice-blue gown. Shaking it out, he held it up. "See? It matches my suit," he pointed out with a foolish grin.

He was obviously pleased with himself, his good humor restored. And why not? Amy reflected. He'd planned everything down to the last detail, and it was all proceeding perfectly.

"We'll appear the proper bride and groom," Robert boasted.

Amy snorted. Matching his outfit was the last item on her list of priorities. She had to admit, though, he had good taste.

However had he managed to procure such a lovely gown on a few hours' notice on a Sunday? The satin was embroidered with silver flowers and leaves, and scattered clusters of pearls suggested bunches of grapes. He spread it across the foot of the bed and laid coordinating blue slippers on top; they looked as though they might fit.

Amy was heartened. In such a gown she could flag down a hackney without the driver suspecting she had no means to pay. Another problem was solved.

She allowed herself a smile—but just a tiny one, so he wouldn't suspect.

FIFTY

*T*HE SIGN ON the middle-class tavern swung gently in the light wind, the words "Kings Arms" spelled out in bright new paint. Colin stepped inside.

The clientele were seated in convivial bunches at long, clean-scrubbed wooden tables with matching benches. They were by and large a well-off group, although not of the aristocracy—merchants and solicitors, architects and publishers, gathered to share the news and some companionship at the end of a busy day. Many drank coffee, well known as a means of overcoming drowsiness and stimulating the wits, and the cheerful room was filled with the buzz of animated conversation and the faint scent of tobacco smoke. Colin could well imagine that a titled peer or two stopped by this warm, friendly establishment when they fancied slumming with the common people.

From behind a serving counter, the proprietor looked up then bustled over. Noting Colin's sword and spurs, and the fine fabric and cut of his surcoat, he immediately took him for exactly what he was.

"May I be of service, my lord…?"

"Greystone. I'm looking for a man said to frequent this establishment, a Robert Stanley."

The proprietor's dark, intelligent eyes scanned the room.

"Your information is correct. However, Mr. Stanley is not here now."

"Perhaps someone here may know of his whereabouts?"

"That's a possibility. He usually sits over there—men are creatures of habit, you know."

The man indicated a table in the center of the room, crowded with jovial young men with tankards of ale before them. Their conversation ceased as Colin approached.

He did his best to put a smile in his voice as well as on his face. "I'm looking for Robert Stanley."

Silence reigned for a moment, the faces around the table cautious and suspicious. "Is he in some sort of trouble?" one man asked slowly. "Lately, he's been—"

His words were cut off when the man beside him dealt him a sharp elbow in the ribs.

The smile left Colin's face. He surveyed the table, focusing on each of Robert's friends in turn. "This is a matter of some urgency. It seems Mr. Stanley has abducted a lady of our mutual acquaintance. I'll pay for information."

Friendship apparently went only so far. Whether it was the severity of the charge or the offer of money, Colin didn't know, but the men suddenly came alive.

"He's been searching for his betrothed for weeks. Is it her? She may have gone willingly."

"He paid someone to show him the Marquess of Cainewood's house."

"Yesterday, he asked where to find a privileged church. I told him St. Trinity, in the Minories."

"I told him m'sister was wed at St. James."

A privileged church. Colin wanted to kick himself for not thinking of the necessity—where else could a forced marriage take place? He could have saved hours by simply enquiring as to where such churches were located and riding straight there.

Well, at least Ford's hunch had been confirmed.

He was on the right track.

"Might anyone know where Mr. Stanley is now?"

The men shook their heads. "He hasn't been here since yesterday," one of them volunteered.

"Where is St. James?"

"In Duke's Place."

"Thank you, gentlemen." Colin dug in his pouch and threw a handful of silver coins on the table. He left without another word, at a run.

The two churches in question were just outside the City walls, and Amy had been taken last night. If Robert Stanley had timed it early enough, she might be a wife already.

FIFTY-ONE

*R*OBERT LEANED back, balancing precariously on the hind legs of the rickety wooden chair, picking at his teeth with a fingernail. "So…are you ready to talk?"

Watching him, Amy shuddered. She hoped he'd fall over and crack his head open. "You mean, discuss something? As though you still lived in my father's house and we cared about each other?"

"I care about you, Amy."

"You actually sound sincere." She lifted her tied wrists, the skin red and raw. "You have an unusual way of showing it."

He leaned forward, and the front chair legs met the floor with a loud *bang*. "That's for your own good. We were meant to be together, and you refused to cooperate. After we're wed—after you have my babe—you'll agree."

Dear heavens, could she even love a baby fathered by Robert? She prayed she'd never have need to find out.

"Where's the jewelry?" he asked suddenly.

She stared at him, unblinking. "I don't have it."

"That is quite obvious. And unfortunate, as I'm sure you'd like to choose a few pieces to complement your wedding gown tomorrow." He flashed a facetious grin, but it faded swiftly. "No matter. It will all turn up once the deed is done, won't it?" He rose from the chair, walked to the bed, and leaned over her. *"Won't it?"*

She spat in his face.

He hovered above her for a moment, disbelief marking his features. Then his hand shot out and slapped her across the face, snapping her head to one side.

Tears sprang to her eyes, but she wouldn't cry. She wouldn't allow him the gratification of seeing her reduced to a quivering bundle of emotion.

"That was a mistake," Robert ground out through clenched teeth. "Care to try it again?"

She shook her head infinitesimally.

"Very well, then." He turned and slunk back to the chair, stretching out his legs and crossing them at the ankles. "Now, you said earlier you were sorry we quarreled, and you were willing to work something out. Were you lying?"

She didn't answer.

"Were you lying?"

"I won't marry you," she whispered to the wall.

"What? What did you say?"

"I won't marry you, Robert Stanley!" she fairly yelled. "Not now, not tomorrow, *not ever!"*

She knew it was the wrong thing to do; she should act as though she were willing and wait for her chance to escape. But she couldn't help herself.

He leapt up to stand over her again. "Oh, yes, you will marry me. I'm a second son. There are no jeweler's heiresses lining up to wed me. If I don't have you, I have nothing. That pistol"—he gestured toward the table—"will guarantee you'll marry me."

At that moment, he looked angry enough to use it.

"You'd never—" she started.

"And as insurance," he continued, his pale eyes flashing and wild, "I've a mind to take your maidenhead tonight." He paused, seeming to consider the idea. "A consummated betrothal is as good as a marriage, isn't it?"

Amy struggled up on her elbows. "Our betrothal papers burned in the fire. It would be your word against mine. My Aunt

Elizabeth would swear her brother never betrothed me to the likes of you."

His face went slack, but only for an instant. "You'd still be ruined. You'd have no choice but to marry me then."

"You'd better think twice, Robert Stanley," Amy shot back without thinking. "I have friends who would make you sorry."

He pounced on the bed, crouching over her with his hands on either side of her head. "Who would make me sorry?" He pushed his hands down at each word, for emphasis. *"Who?* Whoever they are, I'll kill them if they come after me. I swear it!"

Amy would have been terrified by this evidence of his obvious madness, had she not been distracted by the bouncing mattress escalating her diminished headache into a virulent pain.

His pale eyes narrowed as he growled deep in his throat. "It's Greystone, isn't it? And his blasted family."

She froze.

Evidently the look on her face was all the confirmation he needed. He raised a fist and slammed it toward her, but she was ready and jerked her head to the side in time.

"Robert!" she screamed. "What have you turned into? Look at yourself!"

And miraculously, he did. He picked up his fist from where it was buried in the mattress and stared at it as though it were a foreign body. Then he slowly climbed off the bed and wandered over to the table.

He sat down, dropped his head to the surface with an audible *bump,* and stayed there, perfectly still.

Amy released her breath. She was shaking from head to toe.

She had to get out of here before he stole her innocence. She choked back a sob at the mere thought, the possibility of him violating her physically. She didn't think she could bear the disgust and humiliation.

Robert lifted his head from the table. His steely blue gaze locked on hers. His breath came in loud, ragged gasps.

Silent moments ticked by.

His expression grew hard and resentful. "You'll be mine," he stated in an ominous, deep whisper.

A chill slithered down her spine.

"Cold, proper Amethyst Goldsmith will be mine for the rest of my life."

FIFTY-TWO

*C*OLIN REACHED St. James, the first church outside Aldgate, just as the evening service was concluding.

The congregation was sparse. Religion had lost favor when Charles and his loose-moraled court took over London, and most people attended church only for baptisms, weddings, and funerals. Colin shifted impatiently, twisting his ring back and forth as the curate completed his sermon.

The minute the parishioners began shuffling out, Colin strode toward the pulpit, jostling shoulders in his haste.

"Excuse me, Father," he called when he was but halfway down the aisle. "Did you marry a couple yesterday—he red-haired, and she small with black hair and—"

"Would you care to examine the marriage register, my son?"

Colin winced at the humor in the curate's voice; clearly the man was no stranger to lovesick swains having their intended brides stolen out from under them.

The register was duly produced, and there were nine recorded weddings dated the previous day—none of them Robert's or Amy's.

"Did you see them?" Colin persisted. "Perhaps you know where—"

"No one came to be wed yesterday who wasn't accommodated. Perhaps they went to St. Trinity?"

Colin was already out the door.

The marriage register at St. Trinity had logged eleven ceremonies, and Colin's heart seemed to grow larger in his chest as he scrutinized the long list. When he reached the end without seeing either name, he stumbled to a front-row pew and plopped down.

"Did you find what you were looking for?" the plump curate asked kindly.

"No, which is a relief. They didn't wed here, and they didn't wed at St. James." Amy was yet unmarried. Colin slumped on the bench, his pulse returning to normal.

Until another thought occurred to him.

He jumped up. "Is there another place in London where one can be wed—ah—in a hurry, without a license?"

Robert's friends had recommended only the two, but—

"Nay." The curate grinned, clearly pleased that he shared his lucrative business with but one other clergyman. "Not in London. In the countryside, near Oxford…"

Colin exhaled a long breath. "Too far to signify. They got a late start last night."

The curate ran his tongue over his uneven teeth, thinking. "This couple, from late last night. He wouldn't have had red hair, would he?"

Colin's heart skipped. "Yes! And she's small, dark-haired—"

"I never saw her. He said she was waiting outside, and she was likely to be…reluctant, I believe he termed it."

Thank heavens. Having left Amy at the town house without so much as saying goodbye, a tiny, insecure part of Colin had been wondering if the blood could have been an honest accident, if Amy might marry Robert willingly, given the circumstances.

"I expect them back here in the morning."

"I must find them tonight. She could be injured…"

The clergyman frowned. "They're likely close at hand, as he's planning an early return. Perhaps at a nearby inn. You might try Fenchurch Street."

"Thank you, Father." Colin was so relieved he felt like kissing the fat, bald man, but he thought that would be improper with a man of God. Instead, he dropped a coin into the collection box on his way out.

The curate hurried to retrieve it when the door shut. Silver. It wouldn't quite cover the loss of the red-haired lad's wedding fee, but it was something. His sudden—and unexpected—surge of sympathy for the young woman may have cost him a few shillings, but no matter. Over fifteen hundred paying couples a year found their way to his altar.

~

*N*O RANSOM NOTE arrived.

A crackling fire warmed the drawing room, but the cold knot inside Kendra refused to thaw. Ford sat next to her and held her hand, which may have provided a small comfort if Jason's constant pacing weren't driving her to distraction.

She bit the inside of her cheek, worrying the soft flesh with her teeth. She couldn't shake the feeling that she was partially at fault. She should have checked on Amy much earlier. She should have taken Robert's threat more seriously. Over and over, she replayed yesterday's scene in her mind, looking for a clue to his plans.

Suddenly, the blood drained from her face, and she sat up straighter. "I just remembered something," she breathed.

Jason stopped in mid-track. "What?"

"He said he spent his time drinking at the King's Arms. Maybe someone there—"

"Oh, *that* is useful information," Ford scoffed. "The King's Arms." He rolled his eyes. "There must be two dozen of them in town, at least. Not to mention the King's Head and other assorted royal body parts—why, half the taverns and inns have been renamed since the Restoration."

Kendra stood. Planting her feet in a wide stance, she placed her hands on her hips. "I cannot just sit here, waiting, any longer," she declared.

Ford's gaze swung to Jason's, inquiring, and Jason shrugged. "I suppose it wouldn't hurt to ask around," he said with a sigh.

And Kendra was out the door, leaving her brothers to follow in her wake.

FIFTY-THREE

*A*S THE SUN disappeared, the grimy window darkened to black. Amy struggled to stay awake. Her life depended on it. If she nodded off and slept until morning, her chance for freedom would be lost.

And life as the forced bride of Robert Stanley was too hideous to contemplate.

Her only hope lay in his falling asleep, deeply enough for her to escape her bonds and retrieve the key from his pocket. He had dozed a couple of times, but his body would jerk awake, his cold, suspicious eyes searching her out.

He hadn't said a word since he threatened her maidenhead.

While she waited long hours for him to nod off, her emotions swung wildly. Deep inside, she seethed with mounting rage at his ability to control her just because he was bigger and stronger. Other young men took fencing lessons, trained with knives and pistols, spent hours in boxing parlors perfecting their skills. Not Robert. He spent his off-hours drinking and gambling, and he had the soft physique to prove it. Yet that unhardened body was twice her weight, coupled with a deranged force that rendered her well-nigh helpless.

She lay still, as unobtrusive as humanly possible in an effort to avoid his wrath, feeling alternately angry, defiant, despairing, determined, and frustrated. In between, she made paltry attempts to calm her irregular pulse, telling herself to think of better times in the past and those to come, when she somehow extricated herself from this impossible situation.

Mostly, she thought about Colin.

To distract herself, she relived every one of their kisses in her head. She caught herself smiling before she remembered her predicament and looked across the chamber to Robert. He was sleeping, his head lolling to one side, his mouth open and slack. His breathing was deep and measured.

Thank heavens.

Her heart galloping with excitement, she brought her wrists to her mouth and tested the knot. Her teeth slipped off the hard knob and clicked together with a sound that seemed loud in the still room, but Robert didn't stir, and she continued working at the knot, loosening it bit by bit.

Half an hour later her arms ached from holding them up, and her lips were chapped and sore from rubbing against saliva-drenched fabric, but her hands were free.

She made short work of the bonds on her ankles and stood on shaky legs. After twenty-odd hours flat on her back, her knees threatened to buckle under her, but she refused to give in to her weakness. Sternly forcing her body to comply, she drew the ice-blue dress off the foot of the bed and dropped it over her head, holding her breath when the satin rustled as it settled into place. She shoved the nightgown's sleeves up under those of the gown, jerked the lacings closed, and attached the stomacher haphazardly. She could finish dressing properly when she was safely outside.

She slipped her feet into the matching slippers, which were a little large but would have to do, and tiptoed over to Robert. Her heart was pounding so loudly she was half-convinced it would wake him.

Silently blessing the powers that be for decreeing loose breeches with deep pockets were fashionable, she crouched behind him and eased her hand into one pocket. Her first try found a small gunpowder flask and a few balls and cloth patches, but no key.

She paused, taken aback by the evidence that he was

prepared to fire the pistol. As she pulled out her hand, Robert took a deep, ragged breath, inhaling with a resounding snore, and Amy froze for a good two minutes before daring to try the other pocket.

When her fingers closed around the cold, heavy key, she could barely contain her glee. She was mere steps from freedom.

Reminding herself to be light-footed regardless of her haste, she slowly rose. Her gaze lit on the gun on the table. It gleamed in the weak firelight, the stock profusely inlaid with silver wire in a display of workmanship akin to the finest jeweler's. She briefly considered taking it, but the gown had no pockets, and she hadn't the faintest idea how to shoot it, in any case. Forcing her eyes away, she tiptoed to the door.

The key in the lock made a hideous grating noise, but she didn't look back.

She bolted into a dim, dusty corridor.

One of the too-loose slippers threatened to come off, making her trip and stumble. Suddenly she heard scuffling behind her, then a horrible ripping sound as, for the second time in as many days, she found herself tugged to her knees. Robert's considerable weight landed on her back, and she plunged forward.

"Curses," he hissed into her ear. "I'd have thought you'd've learned your lesson by now." He jerked her up, one hand coming around to cover her mouth and muffle her impending scream. She glanced frantically around the dingy corridor, but there was no one to help her.

The cold steel of the pistol's barrel pressed into the side of her neck. She should have taken it.

FIFTY-FOUR

*C*OLIN HAD checked the eight inns closest to St. Trinity, but there was no sign of Amy.

His disappointment was a physical pain, a heaviness in his chest that was weighted with a creeping sense of foreboding. To have come all this way, crisscrossing the City, one clue to another, and then...

Nothing.

And somewhere out there, Amy was...what? Sleeping, suffering, frightened, abused? Well, it was still Sunday, so even if she'd left London, he was fairly certain she wasn't married.

Yet.

Perhaps he was on the wrong track. Perhaps he should go back to Robert's father, or the King's Arms, and ask if anyone had heard from Robert in the past few hours.

Intending to make the depressing rounds again, he'd no sooner untied Ebony when a yellow glow caught his eye, penetrating the fog from down the street. At this hour, in this neighborhood, where citizens couldn't afford the luxury of candles at midnight, where decent folk went to bed with the dusk and rose with the dawn, that light could mean only one thing: a tavern.

He leaped onto Ebony and clip-clopped down the dark, empty street toward the glow. Bereft and desolate, Colin could only muster a faint hope that he might have reached the end of his search. As he drew nearer, the light from the grimy window illuminated a cracked wooden sign proclaiming it the Cat & Canary, and a swift glance up at the overhanging story assured him that it did, indeed, boast a few rooms for rent.

Colin tethered Ebony in a rough shed across the street, then took the time to thank him for his service and companionship with a bucketful of brackish water and a forkful of hay. After all, of all the multitudes of places in London, he had no real reason to think Amy was here.

~

*R*OBERT SHOVED Amy back into the room and threw her on the bed. He pointed the pistol in her direction with one shaking hand while he attempted to lock the door with the other.

"Please, Robert—"

"*Shut up.* I don't want to hear one word from you." He frantically worked the lock, his hand fumbling. "You'll pay for this, Amy. Mark my words."

At last the lock clicked into place, and he whirled around, wild-eyed, searching the room. A sinister laugh echoed forth as, with a flick of his wrist, the key landed in the flames of the fireplace.

"There," he said. "I'll take it back in the morning, when the ashes grow cold. Until then, we won't be needing it, will we?"

Cringing, Amy scooted back until her spine pressed against the dirty headboard. She pulled her knees up and hugged them tight.

Robert raised his arm and aimed the pistol at her again. "Lie down!" he barked, waving the gun wildly.

She dropped to the mattress, curled up in a ball, and let out a whimper as panic welled up in her throat. She whimpered again as she watched Robert switch the pistol to his left hand so he could work the buckle on his belt with his right.

She shut her eyes tight, as though by doing so she could banish Robert and his pistol and his belt from the earth. Any second now, she expected to feel the belt on her, the leather striping her flesh in Robert's fury.

Instead, she felt Robert throw himself on top of her, flattening her to the mattress. The gun fell to the wooden floor with a meaty thud, and she twisted under him, intending to lunge for it. But Robert pressed her shoulders against the bed with his two fleshy hands, and his head descended on hers, blocking her vision and her access to the weapon.

He ground his lips against hers in a cruel approximation of a kiss, until she tasted coppery-tinged blood. She gagged. Her hands came up and pushed at his head, but to no avail: he was quite simply stronger and heavier than she.

She wished he had lashed her instead.

A lifetime later, after pinning Amy beneath the weight of his body, Robert came up on his elbows. Her mouth finally free, she screamed.

Robert laughed wildly. "No one will come," he taunted. "They all think you're delirious. And they've been well paid. You'll be *mine* after tonight," he growled. "No other man will want to touch you for the rest of your life."

FIFTY-FIVE

*C*OLIN PUSHED on the Cat & Canary's door, and it swung open with a prolonged creak, revealing a plain wooden interior encrusted with years of accumulated dirt. He stepped inside and glanced around the tavern. It was a shame the blaze had missed this street, he thought with a grimace. This was the kind of firetrap London needed to rid itself of.

A nauseating reek of rancid food choked the air. A few scruffy men sat conversing morosely at one table. No proprietor was in sight. All was quiet.

Colin couldn't imagine Amy in a place like this, even as Robert's hostage. He turned to leave, but caught himself glancing uneasily over his shoulder. After a pause, he addressed the motley group at the table. "Pardon me, but is anyone staying above?"

The answer was a mix of shrugs and grunts that he took to be a negative. One man looked up at him, his bloated face showing surprise at finding someone of Colin's class in this tavern.

Colin focused on him. "I'm looking for someone…"

"Anyone *you'd* be lookin' fer'd be on Leadenhall Street," the man offered, inclining his head toward a street across the way, behind the shed where Colin had stashed Ebony. "Try the Rose 'n' Crown."

"Thank you kindly," Colin replied, moving to the entry. He

couldn't wait to get out of this depressing establishment.

Halfway through the door, he heard a thud from above. His blood chilled. He swung back around. "Are you certain no one's up there?"

He would swear he heard a muffled yell. The men didn't react. One of them slowly rose, the legs of his chair scraping back on the wooden floor.

"No one's up there," he stated, running a dirty hand through shaggy hair that might have been yellow if it weren't so greasy.

A scream. Hysterical. Unrelenting. Anxiety sent Colin's pulse racing, and he felt as though his chest might burst. Noting a rough staircase in the back, he started toward it.

The yellow-haired man moved swiftly to round the table and block him. He wrenched a long, rusty knife from his belt and brandished it in Colin's face. "You cannot go up there."

Another scream sounded above. Colin's hand went to the hilt of his sword...and then to his pouch. He pulled out a gold guinea and flung it on the table, his eyes boring into the other man's.

"Room six," the man muttered, turning to scoop up the coin and test it between his teeth. "Third floor."

Colin bolted up the rickety staircase.

~

*R*OBERT RIPPED off one side of Amy's stomacher. His pale eyes gleamed recklessly.

He tugged at her laces, heedless of her screaming. Neither did he stop when she tore at his neckcloth and pulled on his hair. His breath was heavy and labored; the stench of stale ale and old vomit suffused the air around them.

She clawed long, bloody scratches along his cheeks. But instead of relenting, he growled low in his throat and tugged up on the voluminous skirts of the wedding gown.

Though she'd thought she could feel no more panicked, the cool air on her legs fueled her useless howling to new heights. When Robert shoved his knee between hers, her anguish was so acute that it overwhelmed any physical pain.

FIFTY-SIX

*T*HE NUMBERS on the doors were too faded to read in the dark corridor. But there was only one room Colin sought, and Amy's unmistakable sobs led him straight to it.

"Stanley!" He pounded with both fists on the rotting wood that separated him from the girl he loved and her abductor. "Open up! *Now!*"

He ripped off his surcoat and threw it to the floor. Backing up a few feet, he made a run at the door and rammed it with a shoulder— the old lock gave with a satisfying snap, and the door flung into the room and slammed against the wall, barely staying on its hinges.

Startled, Robert rolled off Amy and slid over the edge of the bed, scrabbling to find the pistol on the floor.

Amy struggled up on her elbows, her gaze riveted to Colin in the doorway. He took a step forward as Robert rose, one hand holding up the waistband of his unlaced breeches, the other clenching the gun. A feral look hardened his bloodied features.

Colin took another step.

"Stay back, Greystone, you vile beast." The pistol wavered as Robert growled. "She's *mine*." The flintlock had been half-cocked, primed and ready, and now he pulled back the lock.

The room reverberated with an ominous click.

A scalding fury burning in his chest, Colin advanced.

Robert's face registered sheer, unreasoning panic. His arm swung wildly as he squeezed the trigger. The pistol went off with a thunderous report.

Amy let out a shriek of terror, but Colin didn't flinch; his advance continued unchecked. The bullet was lodged somewhere in the wall of the corridor. Robert was left with a smoking gun in his shaking hands, the pungent scent of exploded gunpowder swirling around him.

There was insufficient time for an expert to reload, and Robert had already proven he was no expert. He flung the heavy pistol at Colin's head.

Colin ducked, and as his head came back up, he pulled his rapier out of his belt with smooth, practiced ease.

Without the false sense of security the pistol had provided, Robert seemed to shrink into himself. He backed up against the wall, his pale eyes glassy with terror, fastened on the gleaming silver length of Colin's blade.

Flinging the sword away, Colin rounded on Robert with his fists clenched. He grabbed the shorter man's shoulders and yanked him away from the wall, then rammed him back into it with a raging force. There was an audible *crack!* as Robert's head met the rigid wood, and when Colin let go, Robert slid to the floor in an ungraceful heap.

The fight was over before it began.

Clutching her torn dress closed in the front, Amy watched, silent, as Colin bent down to reclaim his rapier. "Do you want me to kill him?" he grated out, his breath coming in large gulps as he fought to control his fury.

She shook her head violently, still mute. Colin stood motionless for a moment, registering the shock in her disbelieving eyes. Then he slid the sword into his belt and moved to the bed, reaching down toward her.

"You're...you've been *shot*," she whispered, beginning to shake.

He straightened and looked down to where her gaze was riveted, surprised. His shirt was plastered to his ribs by a dark, sticky patch of blood, but it wasn't spreading. "It's but a scratch," he said. He still couldn't feel it—the white-hot maelstrom of his emotions overrode any pain.

Still, he had enough presence of mind to retrieve his surcoat from the corridor and shrug back into it, wrapping it tightly around himself to cover the blood before he scooped her up in his arms.

She trembled in his embrace. With a lingering, murderous look at Robert's still form, he carried her down the stairs and out into the street.

FIFTY-SEVEN

*O*NLY A STREET from the ramshackle Cat & Canary, the luxurious Rose & Crown seemed a world away.

Amy seemed a world away, too.

"I'm cold, Colin," she whispered as he gently laid her on the bed.

After starting a roaring blaze in the fireplace, he went downstairs to ask for a bath to be prepared. He returned to find Amy huddled in a chair, staring into the flames.

Concerned, he glanced back at the bed.

"I've been tied to a bed..." she murmured in answer to his unasked question.

He unbuckled his sword and set it on a low table, then lifted her up, took her place in the chair and settled her on his lap. Silent, they watched the fire together, Colin holding her close, her head against his chest.

He buried his lips in her tangled curls, and they stayed that way for a very long time, motionless except when Colin's mouth moved against her hair. His kisses were gentle, slow and warm. Possessive, healing. Cherishing. His heart seemed to burst at the miracle of her back in his arms.

Servants dragged a tub into the chamber and filled it with bucket after bucket of steaming water, scented with oil of roses. Hard-milled perfumed soap was left, along with a comb and a brush and large linen towels. They set up the screen Colin had requested to shield everything.

Alone again, Colin rose and stood Amy on her feet. "I should have killed him," he whispered, looking at her. Her wrists and ankles were raw and abraded. He could only imagine what damage lay hidden. Purple marks marred one side of her face; dried blood crusted her forehead. Her lips were bruised and swollen, her hair a tangled mess tumbling down her back.

He had thought he would never see her again.

She looked beautiful.

Taking her hand, he led her to the tub. "Do you need help?"

"No, thank you," she said quietly, her eyes on his blood-stained shirt.

"It's naught but a scratch," he reminded her, his voice low and steady. "I'll clean it up while you bathe." With a sigh, he left her behind the screen.

He winced when he pulled the fabric from the wound and slipped the shirt off over his head. But it *was* just a scratch, the barest graze, and wouldn't even require stitches. It stung, but not so much that he couldn't ignore it.

Had it hit a quarter of an inch to the right—the thought made Colin suck in a breath. A broken rib, perhaps bone fragments puncturing his lung. It would have wreaked havoc, would certainly have impaired his swift action, if not killed him outright. Well, it hadn't happened. He'd been lucky—very, very lucky—and he would never reveal to Amy just how narrow their escape had been.

At the washstand, he poured water from the ewer and dabbed at the shallow laceration until it was clean. Then he shrugged back into his surcoat.

He heard the water swishing behind the screen and imagined Amy washing away the blood, the dirt, and—he hoped—the memories. He knew her wounds were merely surface deep, nothing that wouldn't heal in a few days at most. But he was furious nonetheless, feeling somehow responsible for her suffering, for the damage to her perfect young body.

He should never have left her.

He would never leave her again, he promised himself as she stepped from behind the screen. The nightgown was ruined and the blue dress ripped in the back, so she had wrapped herself securely in one of the inn's large, luxurious towels. She was blushing furiously, one hand holding on to the towel for dear life, the other resting across her shoulder as if to cover its nakedness.

"Look, Amy," Meaning to distract her, he opened his surcoat to show her his cleaned wound—but that only made her blush even harder. "See the scrape? It's nothing."

She stood still for a long moment, seeming to have some kind of struggle with herself. Finally she reached out tentative fingers, touching him lightly, and when he didn't flinch, she nodded her satisfaction.

He dragged the chair closer to the fire and drew her long hair out as she sat down, draping it over the seat back. Then he sat behind her to brush it dry. He had never brushed a girl's hair before. It was oddly intimate. He hummed as he worked, a soft lullaby his mother used to sing to him, and watched the firelight play off the glistening mass of black silk.

"It's so beautiful..." Had he said that out loud? She froze as though she were surprised, and he would swear she even stopped breathing for a few seconds. But she didn't say a word, and he went on with his task.

When her hair was dry and gleaming, he rose and she came up with him. She turned to him with a shy smile. "Thank you," she whispered. "I feel much better now."

"I'm glad." She stood so close he could feel the heat from her body. He swallowed hard. "Can you face the bed now?"

She nodded, her smile wobbly but determined. "It's a different bed."

"Yes, it is." He led her to it and lifted a corner of the covers; she slipped between the sheets.

Her gaze followed him as he poured more water from the ewer to rinse the bloodstain from his shirt, then moved to the hearth to lay it out to dry. His insides warmed at her peaceful, sleepy expression. When his boots hit the floor with two dull thuds, she closed her eyes.

"Will you sleep by me?" she whispered. "I don't want to be alone."

It was that or the floor, so he nodded, even though she wasn't watching him. He blew out the candles, then slid into bed beside her, leaving as much space as he could between them.

"Amy?" he called softly through the dark.

"Hmm?"

He had to know. "Did he? ...I mean..."

She rolled to face him, opening her eyes to search his in the firelight. "No." she whispered. "You arrived just in time. Like magic."

His body sagged into the bed with the release of tension he hadn't known he'd been holding.

Moving closer, she touched his face with feather-light fingertips. "I still cannot believe you're here." Her eyes turned luminous as her fingertips stroked his jaw. "It was dark in that corridor—so dark that once you battered down the door, I could see only your outline framed in the opening. But I knew it was you. I knew it, but I couldn't believe it. I'd prayed my screaming would draw someone to help, but I never imagined the help would be you." Her fingers stilled on his face. "Am I dreaming?"

He brought his hand up and laced it together with hers. "No," he managed to say. "You're not dreaming."

"You were far away—at Greystone—then suddenly you were there. Exactly when I needed you. Just like during the fire."

The wonder in her voice, the total trust her words implied, made Colin's heart skip a beat. If he hadn't known it before, in that moment he knew for certain they were destined for each other. It seemed the harder he tried to ignore the truth, the more it persisted.

He swallowed past the lump in his throat. "I'll always be here when you need me," he said simply. "Always."

He squeezed her hand tight, then drew her closer and rested her head on his shoulder. She closed her eyes and settled her small, soft body against him. He felt her respiration slow into an even pattern, her body relax in the solace of long-denied sleep.

The weight of her head on his shoulder, the warmth of her

breath on his neck, the silky feel of her nestled against him—*she was a dream.*

Yet he felt as though he were in a nightmare.

Though he knew it deep in his bones, it seemed impossible to accept that the very essence of Amy—her inherent goodness, her intelligence, her resilience, her passion for life—more than compensated for her incompatible background. She would make a tremendous mother someday; her strength and compassion would create a haven of security no title could provide; he saw that now. The bond he felt between them—as though she existed for him alone—would extend to the children of their bodies as naturally as Amy's affection had spread to his siblings.

And yet, he remembered another strong bond: that of a little boy for his parents. And he remembered the soul-rending pain of abandonment. The pain he was determined never to face again.

How had this happened to him? He'd been in control. He'd had a plan.

He hadn't wanted to love anyone.

FIFTY-EIGHT

*T*HERE WAS A King's Arms not three streets from the Chases' town house. The few patrons still there had never heard of Robert Stanley, but the innkeeper directed Kendra and her brothers to another King's Arms, which directed them to a third.

The place was deserted, but a weary serving maid was still in the back, sweeping up, and she was able to confirm that they had indeed found Robert Stanley's haunt. Perking up at the sound of his name, she informed them that rumor had it he'd taken off with his love, bound for either St. James or St. Trinity.

"There would be no marriages on Sunday." Kendra's eyes sparkled with excitement. "Perhaps we're not too late. We'll go and warn—"

"Oh, no, we won't," Jason interrupted in a tense, clipped voice that forbade any argument. "There's no sense in chasing out there tonight. The morning will do fine."

"But—"

"Listen, Kendra," he said more gently. "We're as concerned about Amy as you are. But I know that neighborhood—it's no place to visit late on a foggy night. The clergy will have been long since abed, anyway. We'll go first thing in the morning."

Crestfallen, Kendra felt her enthusiasm evaporate. It had felt so good to be in active pursuit. Still, she knew there was nothing to discuss—Jason made perfect sense. "I want to get there early," she proclaimed. "Before anyone can possibly be married."

"We will. We'll be there when the sun rises."

"Promise?"

"Promise."

With a heavy sigh, Kendra resigned herself to a sleepless night of waiting.

⁓

*C*OLIN WAS awakened by a warm kiss brushed across his mouth. He opened his eyes lazily, gazing up through half-closed lids. In the hazy light of dawn, he saw Amy's face just inches from his.

"Colin, kiss me. Make me forget," she whispered.

He brushed the hair off her forehead. His eyes searched hers for confirmation, but what shone from their amethyst depths was such a deep, abiding love that he was momentarily taken aback. His breath caught in his chest, and he blinked, but when he opened his eyes the look was still there.

Unconditional and unfaltering.

His arms went around her, and she lowered herself, slowly but deliberately, until her lips touched his.

He held back at first, mindful of her bruises both physical and emotional. But soon his prudence melted away, and he kissed her until both of them were breathless.

When he broke away, he could feel her heart beating against his in the still room. In that moment, he knew with a stunning clarity that they'd never be parted again. He would never give her up. He had tried to protect his heart—tried and failed. Now it was bursting with love, and he couldn't deny it a moment longer.

His lips drifted over her eyelids, her forehead, the smooth skin of her temple. In her ear he whispered, "I love you."

Amy drew away, still clutching the towel around herself like a shield. "Wh-what?"

He kissed one downy cheek and the tip of her nose. "I love you," he murmured, the words coming out husky and unsteady.

275

"No! You cannot. *We* cannot."

His head snapped up. Did she not...? "But I saw it in your eyes. Just now. I thought—"

"I love you, too," she whispered fiercely, her arm snaking around him. "I do. It's just—"

"Hush." Colin touched his fingers to her lips. They could work out the complications later. "I've never told a girl that, you know," he admitted with rueful candor. "You've disrupted my entire life, Amethyst Goldsmith."

In contrast to his words, he felt immensely pleased with his new life. He kissed her with all the tenderness he felt in his heart, completely at peace for the first time in months.

"Tell me again." There was a smile in her voice.

"I love you," he said simply, and it was easier than he'd ever thought possible.

FIFTY-NINE

*I*T WAS STILL dark and foggy when Kendra and Ford left Jason and a footman at the deserted St. James. She was relieved to confirm they were not too late—at least not at this church.

The bleary-eyed twins traveled on to St. Trinity and were elated to find it empty as well.

They slipped into a back pew to wait, resting their exhausted bodies and chatting quietly. A couple arrived with two witnesses in tow, and then another couple, the woman visibly pregnant. The two groups stood in separate clusters in the back of the sanctuary, shifting nervously on their feet as they waited for their respective ceremonies to commence.

The light grew steadily brighter, passing through the ancient leaded windows and projecting brilliant colored patches on the walls and floor of the church. At last, a door opened at the far end, and a plump curate entered. He bustled about, lighting a few tapers before turning to address the small crowd.

A satisfied smile spread on his face as he viewed the assemblage. "Now, who was here first?"

"We were, Father." Kendra rose, tugging on Ford's hand to pull him up after her and down the narrow aisle.

"Where are your witnesses?" the curate asked as the twins came up before him.

"But—" Ford sputtered, "but she's my sister!"

The man's crooked teeth disappeared as his smile reversed to a stern frown. "Young man, I realize we're known for being, ah, *tolerant* here at St. Trinity, but the church expressly forbids—"

"Od's fish!" Kendra's laughter rang through the sanctuary. "We're not here to be wed, Father—we're here to find out if someone else was wed on Saturday. We hope to prevent the marriage if it hasn't already taken place."

"Well, why didn't you just say so?" the clergyman asked peevishly. "Whom are you inquiring about?"

"Amy—Amethyst—Goldsmith and Robert Stanley."

The curate's eyes opened wider. "I declare, I cannot recall the last time there was so much interest in one wedding. Why—"

"Then they're already married?" Kendra's heart seemed to drop to her stomach.

"No. Not to my knowledge." When she sagged in relief, the clergyman smiled. "I believe they were here Saturday evening, however, and yesterday a tall gentleman with dark hair—"

"Our brother," the twins said in unison.

The stout man looked them both over thoughtfully. "Yes, he could have been. In any case, the groom in question planned to return this morning, and your brother went off to search the inns on Fenchurch Street last night."

"Thank you *so* much." Kendra handed the man a coin.

Her wide smile must have been contagious, because the curate's uneven teeth reappeared, although his gaze was already shifting to the other couples. "Now, who was next?"

Kendra and Ford retreated to the front steps of the church, where they quickly decided Ford would wait inside in case Robert and Amy appeared, while Kendra took the carriage to fetch Jason.

She arrived at St. James to find Jason pacing outside. He strode to the carriage. "What's news?"

"They're not wed." Kendra grinned. "But he plans to wed her today, at St. Trinity. Jason..."

"What?" He climbed inside and pulled the door shut.

"I'm hoping you won't mind, but I asked Carrington to head for Fenchurch Street. The curate said Colin was searching the inns there last night. I'm thinking perhaps he grew tired and slept at one of them." Jason began to protest, but Kendra held up a hand, rushing to finish. "Won't you check a few of the inns, *please*? I cannot just sit and wait."

"But you said Robert and Amy are due back at the church."

"It's still early. Besides, Ford will see to matters should they arrive."

"There's no arguing with you once your mind is set, is there?" Jason muttered.

For the next half hour, he obligingly walked along Fenchurch, checking a few likely places while the carriage followed at a crawl.

Kendra regretted the detour almost immediately. Waiting in the carriage, she grew more and more impatient as she watched Jason go in and out. When the carriage lurched to a halt at the seventh inn, she noticed a sign in the window of Mr. Farr's Tobacco Shop, proclaiming it had "The Best Tobacco by Farr." A few shops down there was another sign, that of his rival, "Far Better Tobacco than the Best Tobacco by Farr." She smiled, but mostly she was bored and restless, wondering what was happening back at the church.

Coming out of the seventh inn, Jason stalked to the carriage, his face set in purposeful lines. The door was flung open just as he arrived.

"Kendra, this is—"

"—a waste of time. They may have turned up at St. Trinity by now. And much as I trust Ford to intervene, I'd hate to miss the resulting scene. It ought to be better than Shakespeare."

Worn out as he was, Jason couldn't help but smile. "You're something else, you know that?"

"I'm *your* sister." She punched him lightly on the shoulder. "Come along."

Before climbing inside, Jason instructed his coachman to turn around at Mark Lane and head back to St. Trinity. But they'd driven less than two minutes when Kendra began banging on the roof of the carriage. *"Stop! Stop!"*

"What on earth—"

"That's Ebony! There, in that shed. Colin's here!"

She was down from the carriage before the wheels stopped turning. Jason groaned as he followed her out. "Now, Kendra, not every horse with a white star on his forehead is Ebony."

But it was. Whickering softly as they approached, Ebony bent his big head to search Jason's pockets for a treat.

"Colin must be in there." Kendra indicated a dubious establishment called the Cat & Canary.

"I think not." Jason shook his head. "Colin wouldn't stay in a place like that, no matter how tired he was."

"Then where?"

He pointed to the back wall of the shed. "Behind there is Leadenhall Street. And a very nice inn, if I'm not mistaken."

SIXTY

MINUTES LATER, Kendra and Jason were knocking on the door to Number Three at the Rose & Crown. A sleepy, barefoot Colin came to answer, no shirt beneath his rumpled surcoat, his hair in disarray, and a stupid, sunny smile plastered on his face.

Needing no other evidence to conclude she'd find Amy in his bed, Kendra pushed past him. She wasn't sure whether she was thrilled to see Amy sitting up against the pillows—alive and well —or horrified to see her wearing nothing but a large towel.

"She's in here, Jason," Kendra shouted.

"Is she decent?" came his voice from the hall.

"Enough," she answered doubtfully.

Amy pulled the quilt over her bare shoulders as Jason shoved Colin back and followed him into the room, shutting the door with a little more force than was necessary. "Now you've done it."

Colin's smile was infectious. "I know. I found her. I can scarcely believe it myself." Kendra averted her eyes as he peeled his surcoat off and grabbed his shirt from the hearth. "A fine bit of sleuthing, wasn't it?" He dropped the shirt over his head. "Hey—how did you find us, anyway?"

"That's not what I meant," Jason growled. "Once again, you—"

Shouldering Jason out of the way, Kendra took his place before her obstinate brother. "What he meant is, you'll have to marry her now, you—"

"I fully intend to," Colin said as he tucked in the shirt.

His words were quiet and matter-of-fact—so much so that Kendra failed to register them.

But Amy did. She let out a small gasp of surprise. *Marriage!* Colin had said he loved her, but he hadn't mentioned...

No, it would never work. Her stomach felt leaden and her eyes grew misty, but the siblings were too busy with one another to notice.

"Why are you grinning, you idiot?" Kendra railed. "You couldn't just bring her to the town house, could you? Now we have proof you've ruined—"

Jason shoved Kendra over with his hip and stood beside her, the two of them effectively making a solid wall that obscured Colin from Amy's view. "You've really made a mess of things now, Colin." Usually the calm one, Jason's voice seethed with uncharacteristic rage. "You couldn't leave well enough—"

"Jason. Kendra. I said I'm going to marry her. Even though I have *not* ruined her."

Though Amy couldn't see Colin, she could hear the smile in his voice. He was enjoying this little scene. And she hadn't heard wrong the first time—he really *did* intend to make her his wife.

A prolonged silence settled as Kendra and Jason were apparently shocked speechless. Then Kendra whirled to face Amy. "Is this true?"

Was it? Amy bit her lip. Marry come up, she couldn't marry him. Her father would never forgive her.

"I—no. No." She shook her head slowly, then faster as tears sprang to her eyes. "No."

"What?" Colin strode to the bed and stood staring down at her. "I told you last night—"

"—that you love me." It hurt to look at him. She dropped her gaze, yanking the blanket right up under her chin. "I love you too, but I cannot marry you, Colin. I cannot. I have to reestablish the shop—I told you that. I vowed I would see it carried on. And when we were at Greystone, you said a peer's wife cannot run a business. You said if I married into the aristocracy, I'd never be able to reopen Goldsmith and Sons." She swallowed hard and looked up. "You said it, Colin—I heard you."

"Of course I said it!" He opened his mouth as though to say more, but then just stood there, red-faced and tongue-tied.

"You would choose a shop over my brother?" Appearing completely baffled, Kendra shifted on her feet. "Over becoming a countess?"

"It's not a matter of choice!" Amy brushed angrily at her tears. Why couldn't these people understand? "I was born to a craft. And I hold in trust a fortune. I cannot just hand the Goldsmith inheritance to a husband—it belongs to future generations of Goldsmith and Sons."

"I won't take it, Amy. You have my word on that."

"What?" It was Jason's turn to look astonished. His lips thinned beneath his slim black mustache. "You spoke truth when you said they belong together, Kendra. They're both totally, utterly insane."

Colin took a deep breath. The red faded from his features. "You have to marry me," he said calmly.

"Is something wrong with your hearing?" How many times could she refuse him without giving in? Every denial cost her a piece of her heart. "I said I cannot marry you. I cannot."

"You must."

"I said—"

"Robert is still out there. I knew I should have killed him." He looked thoroughly disgusted with himself. "He'll find you, Amy. Even in Paris. He'll find you, and then he'll try again to force you to the altar. Maybe he'll succeed next time, or maybe he'll just murder you instead. Then he can petition for your wealth on the basis of the betrothal…"

Amy felt the blood drain out of her face. She put her hands to her cheeks.

Dear heavens, Colin was right.

"…if you marry me, it would do him no good to come after you."

"Because my fortune would belong to you, then."

"Only legally."

She found herself caught in his emerald gaze. "It's meant for the business," she whispered.

"It's meant for your descendants. As security, no?"

She nodded.

"They'll have it."

"Colin," Jason interrupted. "How will you restore Greystone?"

"Slowly," Colin snapped without sparing his brother a glance. "My new bride doesn't require living in luxury."

"But—"

"Hold your tongue." Waving him off, Colin knelt by the bed and took Amy's hands in his. "Your descendants will have your inheritance," he repeated. "Now...will you marry me?"

She gazed at him, his beloved features wavering through her tears. To marry Colin Chase—her heart's most selfish desire—so selfish she hadn't even dared to let herself consider it. But he was right—she had little choice. She could either wed him or Robert, or forfeit her life.

Forgive me, Papa, she intoned in her head, then nodded at Colin. His hands tightened around hers, almost painfully, and he raised himself to brush a kiss across her lips. An unfamiliar and unexpected warmth surged through her—a feeling of belonging that she hadn't experienced in a long time.

Her senses were already reeling when Kendra let out a whoop of joy and threw herself on the bed, nearly dislodging the carefully tucked quilt. She pulled Amy to her in a tight embrace that reminded Amy just how bruised and battered she was, but Amy didn't care. It felt so good to know she was about to be part of a family again. And when Kendra gushed, "Oh, Amy, you'll really, truly be my sister now," Amy was so happy she thought her heart might burst.

"Good job, Colin." Jason slapped his brother on the back, beaming. "You finally came to your senses. Well, partially, anyway," he added under his breath.

Kendra disentangled herself from Amy. "You were such a blockhead," she told Colin, "I was ready to strangle you."

Colin just stood there grinning like an imbecile. Jason walked to the bed and, coloring only slightly, leaned to kiss Amy on both cheeks. "Welcome to the family," he said, and Amy would have thrown her arms around him if she hadn't been in such an embarrassing state of undress. As it was, more tears welled in her eyes. She blinked them back, and Jason straightened and cleared his throat.

"We'll have it at Cainewood," he said to Colin.

Colin had just sat to put on his stockings and boots. "Have what?" he asked blankly.

Kendra made a rude noise. "The wedding, of course." She looked to Jason. "He's still not himself, is he? A spring wedding... We'll have to start planning immediately."

"Oh, no." Colin's words were uttered in a voice that brooked no nonsense. "No spring wedding. We'll be married *today*."

"You cannot," Kendra said. "No banns have been posted. And you don't have a license."

"Nor did Robert Stanley—and yet, Amy was to have wed him this morning at St. Trinity. She can wed me there instead."

An indignant squeak escaped Amy's throat.

"St. James, then." Colin gave a nod of acknowledgment. "We will wed today at St. James. There's a madman loose. And even were that not so, I wouldn't wait a minute longer than necessary to make Amy my wife."

When Colin's gaze locked on hers, any objections she might have had to being married in a privileged church were swept away in an instant.

Colin loved her, and that was all that mattered.

"But..." Not one to be dissuaded easily, Kendra turned to Amy. "You want a real wedding, don't you? With guests and a wedding gown and dancing for hours afterwards?"

Amy slowly shook her head. She'd planned a big wedding once, with an abundance of guests and a dress covered in love-knots, and she'd been altogether miserable. A simple wedding today, even at St. James, sounded perfect.

And she'd be Colin's wife by tonight.

It still didn't seem real. It was too good to be true. *You cannot have everything,* she could hear her father saying—and he'd been right. But she had no real choice. Joy bubbled up inside her, and she hugged herself in blissful disbelief.

Now that was settled, Colin became all business. He strode behind the screen and fetched the ice-blue gown from where Amy had left it in a crumpled heap on the floor. It rustled as he shook it out, saying, "It's ripped in the back. Curse it."

Amy froze.

"Let me see." Kendra reached for the gown. No one noticed the color draining from Amy's face. "It's just a seam. I'm sure someone belowstairs can stitch it up in no time."

"*No.*" The word was nearly a whimper. Three sets of concerned green eyes fastened on Amy huddled on the bed. "I was supposed to marry *him* in that gown. I won't wear it."

Colin spread his hands and glanced around the room as though he expected a wedding gown to materialize out of thin air.

"*I won't wear it,*" Amy repeated through clenched teeth.

Colin's hands dropped; his fingers drummed against one thigh as he stared at the gown in Kendra's arms, its icy blue contrasting with her own vivid green dress. Then his fingers stilled, and he brightened. "Kendra, why don't you simply—"

Before the words were out of his mouth, Kendra wadded up the offending garment and thrust it into the fireplace.

It ignited with a great *whoosh*, sending sparks flying into the room. Colin blinked, dumbfounded. "What did you do that for? I was going to suggest—"

"A typical logical male solution—my swapping gowns with Amy. You poor fool. I can assure you she doesn't want that dress in the same city, let alone standing beside her as witness to her marriage." Shaking her head in mock exasperation, Kendra turned to Amy. "Men can be so stupid sometimes. Are you sure you want to marry this one?"

Amy's answering giggle brought a grin to Colin's face. He bowed in Kendra's direction. "Your servant, my lady. Since you're so intelligent, I'm awaiting your instructions on how to deal with this problem." He ducked back behind the screen to fetch the filthy shredded nightgown, dangling it at arm's length from two fingers. "Shall she wear this, do you suppose?"

Another giggle from Amy was drowned by a loud guffaw

from Jason. Kendra rolled her eyes. "No, I don't suppose. But I do have a plan."

"By all means, inform us. We're all dying of curiosity."

Kendra took a deep breath. "You, Colin Chase, are going to have to wait a few hours for your wedding. Do you think you can handle that?"

He raised one eyebrow, apparently reserving judgment.

His sister continued in authoritative tones. "Being Monday, Amy's gowns are now ready at Madame Beaumont's. I shall fetch one and bring it here. *You* will go home, clean up, and return in appropriate wedding attire. Look at you—your shirt is ripped."

"A bullet will do that," Colin said wryly.

"A *bullet*?"

He waved off her concern. "It's nothing, just a graze."

"Colin—" Jason started.

"It's *nothing*. Amy?"

"It's nothing," Amy said with a small smile.

She loved this bickering family.

Colin turned back to Kendra. "Continue."

"Well, then, you haven't shaved in two days!"

"I apologize for offending you," Colin drawled, rubbing his scratchy chin. "I've been a mite busy."

"Well, I'll admit we do have evidence you were occupied," Kendra returned, looking pointedly to Amy.

Amy had been so busy enjoying their argument and basking in the warmth of their acceptance, she'd almost forgotten her unseemly predicament. Now the center of their attention, she wanted to pull the quilt all the way up over her head.

"I *told* you," Colin gritted out, "We didn't—I didn't—"

"Now that you've thoroughly embarrassed Colin's bride," Jason interrupted, facing Kendra, "are you quite finished?"

"Yes," Kendra muttered. "Sorry, Amy."

"Colin, you seem to have forgotten one large obstacle to this hasty wedding." The good-natured bantering tone had disappeared from Jason's voice, and he looked toward Colin with all seriousness.

"What could that be?" Colin held up a hand and ticked off

imaginary impediments on his fingers. "Apparently there's a gown waiting for Amy, and we've established my need to shave and change my shirt...what? What is it?"

"The simple matter that you're betrothed to someone else?"

"Oh. There is that."

Amy's heart skipped in her chest.

"Yes, there is," Jason said.

"You don't suppose I could just write her a letter afterwards?"

"No, I don't think that would quite satisfy my sense of propriety."

"I didn't think so." Colin paused, staring at his boots for a moment, while Amy held her breath. "Well, there's nothing for it," he said at last. "I shall ride to Priscilla's house straightaway and explain myself. I don't expect they can force me to the altar."

"Let us hope Lord Hobbs agrees. There's the matter of the dowr—"

"Shh." With a furtive glance at Amy, Colin held up a hand. "He has no choice. He's a cold, calculating buzzard, but he won't get the best of me." Amy began breathing again when Colin suddenly smiled. "Can you imagine anyone voluntarily becoming his son-in-law?" he asked playfully. "Or, even more unbelievable, taking his daughter to wife, when she's such a—"

"Snob?" Kendra supplied helpfully.

"Exactly."

Jason clapped Colin on the shoulder. "Are you still determined to accomplish all of this today?"

Colin ignored his brother, smiling at Amy instead. "Absolutely."

Meeting his gaze, she melted a little inside.

"Shall I come along with you?" Jason offered.

"No." Colin's smile widened, his eyes crinkled at the corners, and she melted a little bit more. "I do believe I'm actually looking forward to clipping this buzzard's wings."

"Very well, then. Kendra and I will fetch Amy's clothes and meet you at the town house. We'll all return together."

Frowning, Colin tore his gaze from Amy's. "Wait a minute—we cannot leave Amy alone. That scoundrel Stanley is still walking the earth—an error I'm regretting more with each passing moment."

"I'll send up one of the footmen to guard the door."

"Make that two," Colin said. "And Amy will need breakfast sent up as well."

Jason nodded. "Done." He swiped Colin's swordbelt off the table and tossed it to him. "I'll have to cancel a couple of appointments, but I suppose this takes precedence."

Colin caught the sword and buckled it on, grinning mischievously. "Are you sure, now? I wouldn't want my *wedding day* to upset your schedule."

"I'm sure." The brothers' eyes met, sparkling leaf-green to glittering emerald. Jason moved to embrace Colin, slapping him on the back. "I thought this day would never come. A Chase, married."

"It was bound to happen sooner or later," Colin said, his voice a bit choked. "Shall we?"

He accepted the surcoat that Kendra held out, flinging it over one shoulder, then went to Amy and leaned to brush a kiss across her forehead. Her heart pounding at his nearness and the realization that he would be hers—all hers—from now on, she risked releasing her blanket to reach up her arms and wind them around his neck, pulling his mouth down to hers.

Their lips met and clung for a long, sweet moment, until Jason cleared his throat.

"Get some rest, love." Colin pulled away reluctantly.

Amy snuggled down in the bed, listening to all of their hurried footsteps as they left to prepare for the wedding. Her family—almost. And her husband.

Her *husband*.

And tonight they would...she felt a shiver run down her spine, of nerves or anticipation, she didn't know which.

Likely both.

Though the door had closed behind them, she heard Kendra's exclamation through the walls. "Od's fish—we forgot Ford!"

SIXTY-ONE

$\mathcal{C}$OLIN LEANED against the mantel in the Hobbs's massive drawing room, twisting his ring and steeling himself to face Priscilla.

Breaking the betrothal had seemed such a simple matter at the Rose & Crown. But now that he was here, he suspected it might be harder than he'd thought.

Priscilla would be unhappy, though mostly out of humiliation, if he didn't miss his guess. He was well aware she harbored little genuine affection for him.

Her father would be furious. Lord Hobbs had searched high and low for a son-in-law with Colin's connections, thrusting his daughter at every likely candidate. He wouldn't take lightly to having his careful plans thwarted.

Hearing heavy footsteps on the parquet floor outside the room, Colin stood up straight and tugged his surcoat tighter around his middle, hoping to conceal the rip in his shirt. His jaw tensed when Lord Hobbs entered alone. A tall, pale man, he was most definitely his daughter's father, though he did have a more animated personality—one that had always rubbed Colin the wrong way.

"Lord Hobbs. I had asked to speak with Priscilla."

"My daughter isn't home at the moment. I was thinking we might share a drink while you waited. King Charles—" Hobbs broke off and looked critically at Colin, sizing up his rumpled form. "Egad, Greystone, you look positively disreputable. Have you fought a duel, or what?"

"Something like that," Colin muttered, rubbing his stubbled jaw. "When will Priscilla be returning?"

"Lord knows. She's off shopping with a few friends—spending my money like there's no tomorrow, no doubt." He poured Madeira into two goblets and handed one to Colin with a jovial slap on the back. "Glad that will be *your* problem soon."

Colin couldn't dally until Priscilla returned. Amy was waiting. "That's what I wanted to discuss, sir. I'm sorry Priscilla isn't here, but perhaps it's best I talk to you, in any case."

"About Priscilla's spending habits? I suppose you can put her on an allowance, but she won't take kindly—"

"No, sir. About our marriage." Colin took a mouthful of wine and swallowed it deliberately. "I want to call off our betrothal."

"You *what*?"

Colin hadn't eaten in two days. The Madeira burned a path down his throat and into his stomach, and courage flowed in after it. "I want to call off our betrothal," he repeated firmly. "Your daughter and I—we aren't suited. It's not a good match."

"Not a good match? You need her fortune, and I need the king's ear in order to obtain a license to develop my land on the outskirts of London. It's a perfect match."

"I don't love your daughter, sir."

"Pshaw! What does that matter? Take a mistress. I won't think the less of you for it." Hobbs put an arm around Colin and tugged him close to his side. "A warm, willing wench in the City and a beautiful heiress in the country—what more could a man want, eh?"

Hobbs's hot, alcoholic breath washed over Colin's face, making him pull away before he retched in response. The man was making him physically sick. Colin felt sorry for Priscilla—it wasn't her fault he couldn't love her—and angry with Hobbs for treating his own daughter so callously.

The despicable buzzard.

He took a deep breath and sidled away from the man. "I'm marrying someone else this afternoon," he said quietly.

Hobbs's jaw set, and his breath became labored. "You would leave Priscilla for another woman? *My* Priscilla? After a formal betrothal? After you—you *ruined* her?"

Despite the gravity of the situation, Colin felt an absurd urge to laugh. "Ruined her?" he said, incredulous. "I've only kissed her."

Hobbs's gray eyes darkened in anger. "Not everyone shares our good king's lack of morals, young man. Priscilla was raised properly, and—"

"Do you honestly believe I'm the first man your daughter kissed?" The outraged father role did not fit Hobbs well; Colin could see the truth in the man's eyes, and he'd had it with his pomposity. "After you tried to pawn her off on half the Royalists in England?"

"You...you..."

"There's not a name you could call me that would change my mind." With an outward calm he didn't feel, Colin set his goblet on the table, spread his feet and crossed his arms. "What will it take to satisfy you, Lord Hobbs?" His hand moved to his sword. "You may draw my blood if it will appease your sense of honor, but I warn you: I do not intend to lay down my life in order to be released from this betrothal."

The older man's eyes flickered toward Colin's rapier and back up, then narrowed connivingly. "I'm certain we can find a civilized way to settle this, Greystone."

"What do you want?"

"A private audience with His Majesty."

It was naught but an audience—it would cost Charles nothing but a few minutes of his time. He'd do it if Colin asked.

But it made Colin furious that he'd *have* to ask.

"I'll get you your audience. I'll get you ten audiences. You can have a standing appointment—"

"Just one audience. As long as you can guarantee my license will be forthcoming."

Colin paused. It was a tall order. Though Hobbs had professed neutrality throughout the war, he was rumored to be a closet Parliamentarian. The king did not look kindly on those responsible for beheading his father; Charles didn't merely disregard Hobbs, he actively disliked the man. More than a simple request, this would mean asking a special favor of Charles.

But Charles owed the Chases favors. And a license wouldn't cost Charles, either—to the contrary, he would probably milk Hobbs for an exorbitant fee. It grated on Colin, a scheming buzzard like Lord Hobbs getting his way, but it wouldn't be a problem.

He nodded once. "Consider it done."

Hobbs didn't smile. He seated himself at the drawing room's marquetry writing table and waved Colin into a chair opposite. "I'll expect my funds returned within the week, of course."

Colin's stomach knotted; this was the part he'd been dreading. "I cannot do that, sir. I don't have the funds. They were used for renovations—"

"Then the deal is off. You were legally betrothed, and you accepted part of the dowry. Surely you don't expect—'

"I'll pay it back. Just"—Colin sucked in a breath—"give me some time."

Hobbs fixed him with an icy stare. "You will sign a note. Eight percent interest, with the balance due before we see 1668."

A year. One year. If the renovations were halted, the fields produced bumper crops, the quarry was extra-productive, the sheep thrived...

It was a terrible gamble.

Colin pictured Amy waiting for him at the inn, and his vision blurred. They would have her inheritance. But he'd promised her he wouldn't take it.

"I'm waiting for your answer," Hobbs pressed. "Unless you'd prefer to pretend you never walked in here today."

Colin blinked. "I'll sign it."

Hobbs wasted no time producing paper, quill, and ink. He scribbled a hasty contract, which Colin signed, a weight in his gut, the scratch of the quill sounding like nothing so much as a death knell. Hobbs dripped wax by the signature. and Colin used his ring to set his seal, remembering the day he ordered it from Amy. How he'd walked away that day, expecting never to see her again.

Hobbs sprinkled sand on the ink, then dusted off and rolled

up the contract. "If you fail to pay up, I'll have you slapped into Newgate Prison so fast your head will spin. You'll see the devil in heaven the day I show you mercy."

Although it would never come to that—Hobbs would end up with Greystone instead—the thought of squalid, vermin-infested Newgate made bile rise in Colin's throat.

He pushed away the image. He'd find some way to pay back the money. Whatever sacrifices were necessary would be worth it in the end.

Hobbs tucked the scroll in a drawer, poured himself another goblet of wine, and downed it in one long gulp. "I won, you know." He swiped a hand across his mouth. "I'll have my license, and I still have my daughter."

"To sell to the highest bidder? The man with the next item on your agenda?"

"That's what daughters are for. You'll learn it when you have your own."

Colin ignored that, setting aside his own goblet of Madeira in disgust.

"Who is she?" Hobbs asked suddenly.

"It doesn't signify. She has nothing to do with my lack of love for your daughter."

"Love, hah! You're a weak man, Greystone—my daughter is well rid of you."

Hobbs's stare dared Colin to respond to the insult, but Colin forced himself to ignore him once again. "Please give Priscilla my regards, and my sincere apologies."

"She'll be fine. She'll suffer some loss of face, but she'll survive. I'll remind her how little she liked you—and your *countrified* family, as I believe she called them."

That should have hurt Colin, but it didn't. He felt nothing but relief and an overwhelming compulsion to escape.

He stood. "I'll take my leave, then."

To Colin's vast surprise, Hobbs held out a hand. "A pleasure doing business with you, Greystone."

Colin blinked. "There are no hard feelings, then?"

Hobbs shrugged. "It was all for the better."

"That it was," Colin muttered, proffering a halfhearted handshake. He shuddered to think how narrowly he'd escaped becoming this man's son-in-law. Claiming a favor from Charles and acquiring a monstrous debt were small penalties, indeed, for avoiding the biggest mistake of his life.

Still and all, if he never saw the buzzard's face again, it would suit him just fine.

SIXTY-TWO

*W*ITH KENDRA in tow, Madame Beaumont bustled into room Number Three and made her way to the window, throwing open the shutters. "Get up, mademoiselle. We must make you ready for the *mariage!*"

Amy sat up, blinking the sleep from her eyes. She winced as Madame clutched her chin, turning her poor bruised face this way and that to examine it in the early afternoon light.

"Mon Dieu!" Madame exclaimed, shaking her head. "We have a lot of work to do!" She clapped her hands. "Come in!"

Two footmen entered, toting a large wooden box between them. Madame indicated a spot on the floor where she wanted it placed, then shooed them out with an impatient wave of her hand.

Kendra rummaged in the big box. She pulled out a robe made of peach-colored fabric with a lavish lace edging, then helped Amy out of bed and into the garment, tying it at her waist as one would for a small child.

While Kendra sat Amy at the dressing table, Madame took a wooden case from the box. Carrying it by its ornate brass handle, she brought it over and opened its hinged lid with a flourish. The contents were a jumble of brushes and pencils, jars, bottles, pots and boxes filled with mysterious colored powders and pomades, all of which Madame set about the tabletop.

"Now…" she said, lifting a sinister metal tool.

In her jewelry shop, Amy had used something similar to pick up loose gemstones. She flinched as Madame tilted her chin up and leaned over her, the device hovering in the region of her forehead.

"Oooh, *charmant*," Madame gushed suddenly. "Perfectly arched. Just look." As though Amy were nothing more than a doll, Madame swung her head around toward Kendra, then dropped the implement on the table. "No plucking," she declared.

Amy gaped at Kendra. Plucking, indeed!

Madame set to work, conferring with Kendra from time to time, and Amy relaxed, as no other instruments of torture seemed to be forthcoming. They chatted excitedly about the upcoming wedding and Colin waiting below in the taproom with his brothers, "probably nursing a good stiff drink," according to Kendra.

Amy bit her lip. "I've never worn cosmetics."

"No?" Using a hare's foot, Madame powdered Amy's face.

"No. My father…I mean, he thought…it's not considered acceptable…"

At their vague smiles, her voice trailed off. Could she ever fit in their world?

She sneaked a wary glance in the mirror, then gasped. "Marry come up! The bruises are gone!" She touched her fingers to her face in wonder. "And the dark circles under my eyes."

"It's the Princesses Powder." Madame brushed away her fingers and applied more to repair the damage.

"Princesses Powder?" Amy clenched her hands in her lap to keep them from shaking. Merchants' daughters didn't wear powder made for princesses.

And they didn't wed earls, either…

"It's so called because four princesses, whose great *beauté* is known throughout Europe, have used it with such success that they've preserved an air of youth till seventy years of *âge*."

"Seventy years?" Kendra touched nonexistent crow's feet at the corners of her sixteen-year-old eyes. "I *must* have some."

Madame turned away to swipe powder on Kendra's cheeks.

"You can procure a supply from Madame Elizabeth Jackson, near Maypole in the Strand, for a price of sixpence per authentic packet."

Only half-listening, Amy stared at her reflection. Would her father be disappointed if he were here? She was breaking her promises, but he'd loved her ...would he really deny her love for Colin?

"A bargain at twice the price." Kendra's face appeared behind Amy's in the mirror. She frowned at her newly powdered complexion, then smiled. "I shall visit Elizabeth Jackson tomorrow. Will you come, Amy?"

Amy shook her head slowly, pressing her lips together to hide the telltale quiver.

"Of course not; how silly of me." Kendra's grin grew wider. "You'll want to be with Colin, won't you?" She handed Madame a kohl pencil.

With Colin. What a wonderful, magical thought. "Yes, I will," Amy said, surprised at how clear and sure her voice rang through the room.

Turning Amy from the mirror, Madame rimmed her eyes with kohl and darkened her lashes and brows with the end of a burnt cork. "Oh, did I get some in your eyes?" Concerned, she leaned closer, peering at Amy. "*Je regrette.* I'm so sorry."

"It's all right." Amy blinked back the tears, embarrassed that she couldn't seem to control herself. She sneaked another glance in the looking glass. "My eyes look huge," she worried. "Maybe Colin won't like me with a painted face."

"Don't be a goose," Kendra said. "I expect I'll have to wipe the drool off his chin."

Madame tore a sheet of red Spanish paper out of a tiny booklet and rubbed it lightly on Amy's cheeks.

"Did Colin talk to Priscilla?" Amy hesitantly asked Kendra.

"No, he talked to her father."

"And?" Amy watched as Madame took up a small pot. "What happened?"

"Shh," Madame interjected, applying pomade to Amy's lips.

Kendra shrugged. "I don't know exactly, but all is well. Don't ask him about it. He's rather furious. Still muttering about the buzzard or some such."

Amy was about to ask another question, but Madame took her by the shoulders and swung her around to fully face the mirror.

She stared, her eyes sparkling. "I-I'm beautiful," she breathed, watching in wonder as the words came from between her glossy lips.

"No," Kendra corrected. "You're magnificent. You've always been beautiful." She bent to wrap Amy in a hug. "My lovely sister—can you credit it?" Sniffing, she wiped her eyes, and Amy wiped her own, too. "Oh, we're both going to ruin our faces! Let's get you dressed."

As Madame fetched her clothing from the box, Amy stood in a daze, trembling from head to toe, plagued by second thoughts, yet excited at the unbelievable miracle of wedding Colin. Madame and Kendra didn't seem to notice as they slid off the robe and pulled a new chemise over her head, taking care not to disturb her carefully applied face. Next came the sapphire and cream gown that Amy had despaired of ever having the occasion to wear.

The moment they smoothed the satin skirts over her hips, her doubts scattered. It was going to happen. Dear heavens, she would be a countess before the day was out.

"Mine. I hope they fit." Interrupting her thoughts, Kendra held out stockings and a pair of fashionable Louis-heeled shoes.

With a distracted smile, Amy drew on the stockings and stepped into the shoes, teetering on the high heels while Madame twisted a sleeve here and tweaked the waistline there until she was satisfied. She led Amy back to the dressing table and tucked a kerchief into the top of her gown, to protect the exquisite pearl-studded lace while she powdered Amy's throat to match her face.

A curling iron was set to heat at the edge of the fire, and Madame set to work on Amy's hair. "You really should cut this if you wish to be *à la mode*." With the edge of her hand against Amy's neck, the seamstress indicated the preferred length, just below ear level.

Remembering the feel of Colin brushing her hair dry, Amy blanched and gathered her long tresses into both fists.

Madame chuckled. "Perhaps not today."

"Colin wouldn't like it," Amy stated flatly, and that was that. Madame's deft hands twisted, plaited, and curled, and before long Amy's hair was arranged in a semblance of fashionable style: long ringlets at the sides and a bun plaited together with sapphire ribbons in the back.

"No wires." Madame patted Amy's thick mass of curls.

"No fair." Kendra pouted. "I need wires and false ringlets besides."

"Now *you're* being the goose," Amy said. "What I wouldn't give for that rich red color. And have you any idea how long it takes to dry this?"

"*Mon Dieu*, mesdemoiselles," Madame clucked. "We all have to work with what God gives us, and you're both lovely." She rummaged with a fingertip through a tiny box of black beauty patches. "Hearts, stars, flowers…which do you think?"

"Hearts," Kendra decided. "It's for a wedding, after all."

"No patches. I'm painted enough as it is. Colin will scarcely recognize me."

Kendra snorted. "It's not as though you're painted like an actress. One patch?"

"This is not a negotiation." Amy laughed. "No patches."

"Madame?"

Madame took Amy by one elbow, stood her up, and guided her to the center of the chamber. Amy stood stiff as a poker while Madame walked all the way around her, looking her up and down. The seamstress backed across the room, her eyes narrowing as she contemplated her creation.

"Her complexion is flawless," she said to Kendra.

"What difference does that make?" Kendra wondered. "Patches are all the rage; they're not just to hide pimples and smallpox scars anymore."

"She's a perfect bride, *n'est-ce pas*?" Madame led Amy to the pier glass. "Look."

Amy gazed in the mirror, transfixed. All evidence of her mistreatment was hidden. Veiled by the cosmetics, her face and neck appeared creamy and unblemished. Vanilla lace spilled from her sleeves and over her wrists, concealing the unsightly abrasions.

The glossy sapphire satin shimmered; the pearls on her collar and underskirt gleamed. Fat, springy corkscrew curls spilled artistically over her shoulders, and suddenly the ebony color seemed to suit her perfectly. To her vast relief, she didn't look overpainted—to the contrary, owing to Madame's skill, she looked very much like herself, only enhanced.

Her eyes met Kendra's in the glass, and they shared a smile.

Amy had never felt so beautiful.

She would have stared at herself forever, but Madame gave them both a little push. "The groom is waiting. *Allez-y!*" With a graceful wave of her hand, she dismissed them.

SIXTY-THREE

$\mathcal{T}$HE CHASE brothers' conversation had long since turned to discussing the interminable length of time girls always took to get ready.

Colin popped the cork on another bottle of sack. "I vow, they must have food in there."

"Food?"

"Food. They never eat much in front of us, yet they always complain about how full they are after a few bites. My theory is they sneak food into their dressing chambers." Colin paused for a swallow of wine from the green bottle. "While we're out here, waiting and starving, they're dining and laughing at us."

Ford chuckled. "Just how long do you hypothesize this has been going on?"

"Since the dawn of time, at the very least."

Jason smoothed his mustache. "And they've kept this a secret over the centuries?"

"It's a vast conspiracy—every female is sworn to secrecy from birth." Colin spoke solemnly, but the glitter in his eyes betrayed his amusement. He lowered his voice and leaned into the center of the table. "We've always teased Kendra because she eats her dessert first. Well, that's because she already—"

An apparition coming down the stairs claimed Colin's attention, effectively cutting off his words. A vision in sapphire and cream, Amy glided toward him. His breath caught as he wondered how he'd ever considered letting her go.

Dressed in satin and lace, ribbons and pearls, she lacked only some of her exquisite jewelry to look every inch the countess she was about to become.

Not that it mattered, of course.

She could be wearing a burlap sack, and he would marry her.

⚬

A S SHE CAME down the inn's staircase with Kendra, Amy saw Jason jiggle Colin's elbow. Colin slowly rose to his feet.

"Oh my goodness," she whispered to no one in particular. He was quite simply the most magnificent male she'd ever seen. Once, months ago in her shop, she'd been overwhelmed by his good looks, but that initial impression had long since been replaced by a sense of the complex mix of heart and intellect that, to her, was Colin.

Now, seeing him dressed for his wedding—*their* wedding— the awe came rushing back.

The handsome planes of his face were clean shaven, and his freshly washed hair hung in dark waves to his shoulders. But it was his formal clothing that transformed him in Amy's eyes—a black velvet suit that reminded her of the one she'd found in the chest at the foot of his bed at Greystone.

Given Colin's simple tastes, the suit was a passable nod to fashion, the breeches fuller than he preferred, though not the divided skirts called "petticoat breeches" that were in vogue. Where a dandy's apparel would be dripping in looped ribbons— cuffs, waist, and epaulettes—Colin's was finished with gold braid. His full, snow-white shirt was trimmed with lace at the gathered cuffs. Matching lace adorned the cravat that flowed over the collar of his short doublet, Amy's gold-edged cameo pinning it in place. The signet ring she'd made for him was his only other jewelry.

Though Jason and Ford were decked out in similar finery, she had eyes only for Colin. When he started toward her, she saw he was wearing shoes—*shoes*, not boots!—heeled, with high tongues and stiff narrow ribbon bows.

Amy could scarcely believe this model of masculine perfection was about to be hers. She felt breathless, lightheaded, and nearly tripped at the bottom of the stairs, but Colin was there and caught her in his arms.

"No fainting, now," he quipped. "I may look like a peacock, but I assure you I'm the same man you consented to marry."

Clad head to toe in black and white, he hardly looked like a peacock. "No...you look..."

"Like a featherbrained fop, no doubt. These are my court clothes." Setting Amy down, Colin threw a peevish glance up the staircase. "*She* made me wear them."

Kendra's laughter floated down. "No one makes you do anything, Colin Chase. Though heaven knows we've tried."

"Besides," Amy declared, "I was about to say you look incredibly handsome."

Colin's face flushed pink beneath his tan. He clutched the sides of his full breeches in a show of annoyance. "Just don't expect me to dress like this often. A fellow cannot move properly with all this extra fabric hung about his person."

General laughter greeted his comment.

Moving closer, Colin linked his arms around her waist and sought her gaze with his. "You look unbelievably splendid in that gown," he murmured, his voice low so only she could hear. Then he smiled mischievously. "Though I look forward to helping you out of it."

Amy's cheeks burned hot as she remembered tonight would be her wedding night.

Someone cleared his throat, and she broke free of Colin's embrace. Jason nodded toward her. "In the absence of your father, Amy, may I have the honor of giving you to my brother?"

For the countless time since this incredible day had begun, Amy's throat closed with emotion, and her eyes filled with tears. Although saddened by the absence of her parents, she was oh so gladdened by her acceptance into this marvelous family.

She nodded mutely.

"Well, then, what are we waiting for?" Jason's smile was warm and understanding as he offered Amy his arm. With a return smile and a swish of her satin skirts, she sailed past Colin and linked arms with her almost brother-in-law.

SIXTY-FOUR

*A*MY COULDN'T really remember her wedding. From the moment they entered St. James until she was handed a rolled parchment declaring her officially Amethyst, Countess of Greystone, the time swept by in an incoherent blur of unreality.

Oh, she remembered saying "I will" and hearing Colin's "I will" boom confidently through the sanctuary. She remembered him slipping a cool circlet of metal onto her ring finger, and she remembered his long kiss, sealing her to him forever, the taste of him tinged with the sack he'd sipped while waiting. Jason had finally tapped Colin on the shoulder, and he'd reluctantly released her, and she remembered that, too. But the curate's words—the continual drone that tied these events together—had been muffled by a distracted fog.

The ceremony was followed by a hastily prepared wedding feast at the Chases' town house. Their formal dining room was filled with laughter from the inlaid wooden floor to the ornate painted ceiling.

Portraits of ancestors watched the proceedings from the walls overlooking the laden table. Silver platters bearing suckling pig, a roast round of beef, and duck stuffed with oysters and onions were brought steaming to the table, surrounded by bowls of peas, cauliflower, lettuce, corn, potatoes, and rice spiced with saffron and chopped nuts.

The scent of fresh, hot bread and sweet butter tickled Amy's nose. Her cup was filled with claret wine punch spiked with brandy, nutmeg, sugar, and the juice of a lemon. As she drained it for toast after toast, she grew giddy with laughter and companionship, not to mention the unprecedented amount of drink she consumed.

In the center of the table sat a white-iced wedding cake decorated with candied violets and roses (in the middle of winter!), which Kendra insisted they cut and serve immediately in celebration of their marriage. Amy and Kendra ate their portions, but the men pushed theirs aside to have later.

Colin raised a brow, his gaze searching out each of his brothers in turn. "See?" he asked them, his tone deep with hidden meaning. "It's just as I said…"

Ford and Jason laughed, while Kendra and Amy exchanged a look of confusion. But then dishes were passed back and forth across the table, plates were filled, more toasts were drunk, and the odd comment was forgotten.

Amy could eat no more than a few bites of the impressive feast. Her stomach churned with a combination of excitement, exhaustion, and a tinge of inebriation. Besides, the press of Colin's thigh against hers, under the cover of the table, kept her thoughts elsewhere.

Conversation whirled about her. She paid scant attention to most of it, but she did take notice of Kendra's reaction when Colin announced they were leaving. Kendra wasn't at all pleased to be having her brand-new sister snatched away so soon.

"You cannot!"

"The dickens we cannot. If you think I'm spending my wedding night with my little sister hanging outside the door…"

"But you have only Ebony. Surely—"

"You can borrow my carriage," Jason offered pleasantly.

"Thank you, but I sent for my own carriage this morning."

"But—but—"

Colin smiled when his sister sputtered.

"Amy has no clothes!"

"She has a trunk full of clothes you picked up from Madame Beaumont only this morning."

"She has no shoes, no stockings, and no nightclothes," Kendra returned smugly.

"Surely you can lend her a pair of shoes and some stockings." Colin grinned. "And she has no need of nightclothes."

At this announcement, everyone fell into embarrassed silence —even Colin, who looked down and gulped from his goblet of claret. But Kendra quickly changed the subject, and thankfully *that* odd comment was forgotten, too.

Amy hazily remembered being bundled into Colin's carriage and settling her head against his shoulder. The next thing she knew, she was back at Greystone, in his—*their!*—bed, wearing naught but her chemise. But she wasn't cold. A blaze roared in the fireplace, and Colin's breath was warm on her neck where he'd nuzzled her awake. And though the thin fabric of the fine chemise left little to the imagination, she didn't feel nervous or embarrassed under his emerald-green gaze. She only felt happy.

"Have you slept enough yet?" he'd whispered. And at her answering smile, he'd proceeded to keep her awake until dawn illuminated the sky.

Not that she was complaining. Not one bit.

Judging by the bright sun through the window, it was after-noon now. Amy stretched beneath the sheets, content. She ran her hand over the shallow hollow where Colin had lain, breathing in his distinctive scent and imagining she could still feel his warmth. She had no cause to be concerned about his disappearance—he was her husband now.

The thought brought a smile and a vision of herself standing beside him in the old church. Sapphire and cream, black and white. They hadn't matched. It had been perfect.

No...

No, it *hadn't* been perfect. A disturbing emptiness seemed to open in Amy's middle.

What had she done?

She'd taken one vow and broken another. She'd never be able to reestablish Goldsmith & Sons now. Dear heavens, would her father ever forgive her? Would she ever forgive herself? Generations of craftsmanship, all ending with her, ending with her self-ishness.

She should have married Robert willingly—then none of this would have happened. No matter that the mere idea twisted her insides; she would have had the solace of Goldsmith & Sons, of her craft, of knowing she'd done the right thing.

And she'd done Colin no favor, either. What had he said? *I knew I should have killed him.* Instead, he'd married her to save her from Robert. And now he was stuck with a commoner for a wife, when she knew he'd wanted a titled lady.

Did he really even love her? She curled into a ball and squeezed her eyes shut tight. Strange patterns danced behind her lids, making her dizzy. The claret punch from last night wasn't sitting well in her stomach.

She lay there for long minutes, hugging her knees, blanking her mind, forcing her breathing to slow and her heart to gradually calm.

At long last, she felt able to think more clearly.

What was done, was done. She would have to bury the guilty feelings deep. Her love was so overwhelming, surely everything would work out. She'd had no choice.

No other choice she could have lived with.

Opening her eyes, she straightened and rolled onto her back, gazing up at the cream-colored canopy. A warm fire crackled on the gray stone hearth. Yellow sunshine streamed through the window. A brilliant flash of purple arced from where her hand lay on the blanket.

She sat up, drawing a quick breath. In all the excitement, she hadn't found time to inspect it last night, but the ring was magnificent: a large heart-shaped amethyst surrounded by tiny seed pearls and table-cut diamonds, set in a framework of delicate filigree reminiscent of the finest sixteenth-century artistry.

Where had Colin come by such a masterpiece on such short notice? She waved her fingers, watching the play of light on the deep purple amethyst and old diamonds. The ring was eighteen karat gold, the shank worn thin with age and use, but still a rich yellow. Lovely, yet strange somehow...foreign...she'd never worn jewelry not made by a member of her family.

She pulled off the ring.

At her burst of laughter, Colin appeared in the doorway, sporting a wide grin.

"Good afternoon, sleepyhead. What's so funny?"

Sunlight flashed off the amethyst in the palm of her hand. "This," she choked out between giggles. "This ring."

His smile disappeared, replaced by a frown of hurt. "It was my grandmother's," he mumbled grimly. "I thought..."

Her laughter died as she realized he thought she was disparaging the beautiful piece of jewelry. Clutching the quilt around herself, she jumped off the bed and rushed to his side. "No, it's lovely," she cried. "But look—just look inside."

Colin took the ring. "Inside?" he asked blankly.

"Yes! Look there—do you see it?"

He frowned, squinting at the tiny marks. "An eagle?"

"A falcon! And the letters GSJ."

"So..."

"Goldsmith and Sons, Jewellers. Don't you remember the falcon on our sign? Colin, someone in my family made this ring!"

He glanced up quickly, then back down, staring at the ring in disbelief. "Are you sure? There's also an animal head of some sort stamped in here."

"A leopard's head. That means the gold was assayed at Goldsmith's Hall in London. It's why we call it hallmarking. And the leopard head is in a circle—an old mark used before 1519. Colin, this ring must be more than a hundred and fifty years old."

"I knew it was old, but—"

"It's *very* old. And very wonderful. Look at the filigree." Before Colin could look at the filigree or anything else, she snatched the ring from him and slipped it onto her finger. Extending her arm, she gazed at it possessively. "However did it survive this long? Most of our business was designing new mountings for old stones; fashionable people have their jewels reset every two or three years."

"Grandmother was never fashionable. She gave the ring to Jason—otherwise it would have been sold years ago to help fight Cromwell. Is it valuable?"

"Quite. Fine large amethysts are rare—they call amethyst the Jewel of Royalty. But it's the workmanship I treasure…I wonder who made it? My great-great-grandfather?" Happiness spurted through her as she looked from the ring to her husband. "Oh, Colin, this is the best wedding ring ever!"

Colin's eyes glittered in response. He moved to her, slipping his arms beneath the blanket to encircle her waist. "I'm glad you like it, love," he murmured before his mouth descended on hers. "And I second your opinion concerning the rarity and value of Amethyst…"

His large hands were warm on her bare back, and he kissed her long and deep, breaking off only when the quilt slid from her shoulders and she pulled away and stooped hurriedly to retrieve it.

Colin wrapped it back around her. "Benchley has our dinner waiting. How quickly can you dress? Unless you'd rather have, uh, dessert first?"

"Kendra is the one who has dessert first."

Colin chuckled deep in his throat. "That wasn't what I meant." He leaned down and kissed her again, sending a tremor through her body. When he pulled back, his eyes bore into hers suggestively.

Two hot spots burned on Amy's cheeks, but nonetheless she murmured, "Oh. Dessert would be nice."

This time, when the blanket fell, she didn't reach for it.

And as he carried her to the bed, she told herself it was impossible for something this perfect to be wrong.

She wouldn't let it be.

SIXTY-FIVE

Six weeks later
December 24, 1666

COLIN ENTERED the bedroom, careful to keep his expression neutral. "Will you come upstairs with me, love?"

Amy's reflection looked puzzled in the dressing table mirror. "Upstairs?" She folded the letter she'd just written to Aunt Elizabeth with news of her life since the wedding. "You keep telling me it's dangerous up there. Besides, don't we need to leave for Cainewood?"

"Christmas Eve can wait a few minutes yet." Struggling to keep a smile off his face, he took her by the hand and led her down the corridor to the staircase.

She followed him up the steps. "When will the upper level be renovated?"

"I'm not sure. I've put all the renovations on hold. The farmstead is nearly self-supporting, and then—"

He turned when he felt her stop. Her words came forced and quiet. "Colin, I have a trunk full of gold."

"So you do." He backed down a step, twisting his ring. "I promised you I wouldn't touch it."

"But—it's yours. Legally, it's yours." Her fingers trailed back and forth along the oak rail. "You...you'd have taken Priscilla's dowry, wouldn't you?"

Colin noticed the catch in her voice. It would kill her if he spent her gold. It would kill their marriage. Kill her love for him.

"Priscilla was different," he said carefully. "That was a business arrangement." He moved down another step to encircle her in his arms. "I love you," he said low. "We'll wait, see what happens. If you don't mind living like this for now—"

"I could live like this forever," she said quickly.

Very quickly, Colin thought. Much too quickly.

As he took her lips in a gentle kiss, a disturbing image of Lord Hobbs flashed in his head.

He didn't have forever.

~

*A*MY FOLLOWED Colin down the corridor, feeling troubled by his sudden change of temperament. What she'd seen in his eyes had worried her. He'd seemed so light-hearted when they'd started upstairs—what had happened to lower his spirits?

It was odd and disturbing to find that his state of mind affected hers. It seemed that if he wasn't happy, then she couldn't be, either.

Love was more complicated than she'd ever imagined.

His step lightened as he reached the end of the corridor. Despite his earlier warnings, she'd seen no rotting wood along the way, no holes in the floor. He stopped in front of a stout, arched oak door and slipped a key into the lock.

After it clicked open with a rusty screech, he took her hand and placed the key in her palm. The metal was warm, retaining his body heat. She closed her fingers around it and looked up at him.

"Go ahead. It's yours," he urged, indicating the door and whatever lay beyond.

The door squeaked a protest of disuse as she pushed it open. The smallish chamber had a carved marble fireplace. A long upholstered couch sat in the center, and there was a heavy, dark wooden desk that belonged to the previous century. But best of all were the books, multitudes of them, lining the walls from floor to ceiling.

"A library…"

Her mood suddenly lifted, her uneasiness flitting away as it tended to do in the bliss of being wed to Colin. If they really loved each other, it should be enough.

It *would* be enough.

"It's yours," Colin repeated. "Your own place, like the study is mine. Though I'm hoping you'll let me in now and then. To borrow a book, you know."

He winked at Amy, but she only smiled faintly at his humor. She moved to the windows and gazed down into Hidden Court. The plants were mostly dead from the cold and last month's brief snow, but it would be lovely come spring. And the little library was perfect; she could already imagine herself curled up before the fire with a stack of books by her side.

"Do you like it?" From behind her, Colin's voice sounded warm and pleased, as though he knew her answer. It flowed over and around her, making her body hum with contentment.

She turned to face him. "It's the most wonderful thing anyone's ever given me. Well, maybe except for my ring."

"We'll furnish it however you like. Benchley cleaned it for me. I don't know about the books—they probably haven't been disturbed in decades."

She wandered to the bookcases and ran a finger down the dark green leather spine of one volume. Her fingertip came away smudged, leaving the green stripe noticeably brighter than the rest of the cover. But it didn't matter; cleaning and organizing the books would be a joyful endeavor.

She'd felt rather useless as a countess these past six weeks.

"It's amazing," she said, looking back to Colin. Winter sun streamed through the windows and seemed to create a halo around him, swimming with brilliant dust motes from the recently swept room.

His lips curved in a wry smile, and he gave an elegant shrug. "I had nothing else to give you for Christmas."

Amy's heart plunged. "Oh, Colin, I have nothing for *you*. And this—this"—she gestured helplessly—"it's so *much*."

Colin moved to enclose her in his warm, strong arms. His face mere inches away, she lost herself in his emerald gaze. "I need no gift from you, love," he said, his voice low and slightly rough. "You're my Christmas present. You're all I want and more than I deserve. Besides, how could you get me anything? I haven't left you alone for a heartbeat."

He grinned, and it had a devastating effect on Amy's insides. Suddenly, she realized she did have a gift for him. She smiled to herself. An idea flickered in her brain. A clever Christmas prank.

She'd need Kendra's help...

He kissed her then, and her fledgling plans drifted away, replaced, as always, by the overwhelming feelings Colin engendered with his slightest touch.

His touch now was by no means slight. They made love on the couch—"christening" the room, as Colin put it, though Amy protested this was quite unlike any christening she'd ever attended. Evidently they disturbed years of accumulated dust in the process, because afterward, Colin ran a fingertip down the bridge of her nose, just as she'd done to the book.

Laughing, he called for a bath, and they moved downstairs to wash each other in their enormous tub. Benchley had the horses hitched and had been waiting a good half-hour by the time they emerged and climbed into the carriage to make their way to Cainewood.

The road was hard and dry today, and their carriage barreled toward Cainewood in record time. Besides clothing for a short stay, their trunks had small packages tucked inside—Christmas gifts of jewelry they'd chosen the night before. Amy's heart galloped with excitement at the thought of everyone's pleasure in their gifts, especially the surprise she was planning for Colin.

Before she knew it they were in the village, knocking on the door to Clarice Bradford's whitewashed cottage. Little Mary came to answer, Clarice at her heels. The child looked well fed and pink cheeked, and with a whoop of joy she threw herself into Amy's arms.

"Oh, my lady—I mean, Amy! I didn't know if I'd ever see you again!"

Amy knelt to return the embrace, then pulled back. The girl's big blue eyes sparkled with happiness, and not just at seeing her old friend. She was content here with Clarice—the two had needed each other.

Just as Amy and Colin had been meant to be together.

"I *am* a lady now, Mary. Can you believe it? I've married Lord Cainewood's brother. Do you remember him?" She rose and put her arm around Colin's waist.

"'Course I 'member him." Mary tilted her head back to look up at him. "You saved me so I could be Mama's little girl."

Amy had to jump to the side when the child launched herself at him, leaping high, wrapping her arms around his neck and her legs around his waist. "Oh, my lord, thank you!"

"I cannot find the words to tell you how grateful I am." Clarice bowed her head and bobbed a curtsy. She reached for her daughter, but Colin shifted Mary to his hip, supporting her with one arm while he gave Clarice's hand a quick squeeze.

"It was my pleasure." He smiled at Mary and brushed blond ringlets from her face. "I'm delighted to see Mary so happy."

"No more delighted than I am to have her." Clarice reached again, and this time Colin handed Mary over. "Thank you, my lord." She cradled her daughter tight, tears brightening her gray eyes.

"I brought you something, Mary." Amy held out a tiny package wrapped in bright cloth and tied with a pink ribbon. "For Christmas."

"For me?" Mary's mouth dropped open in a little O. "What is it?"

"Open it and see."

Clarice set her down, and she fumbled with the ribbon until Colin took it and untied it for her. The cloth fell open in his hand, and Mary gasped.

"Is it really for me?" Without waiting for an answer, she reached for the sterling silver locket and brought it to her lips. "Oh, my lady, thank you!"

Amy had strung it on a narrow black ribbon. Clarice eased

Mary's hand from her mouth and turned her to tie it around her neck. "A heart." She smiled at Amy. "Mary loves hearts. And it's engraved so prettily. It's lovely, my lady."

"I made it a long time ago." Amy took the pink ribbon from Colin and tied it in Mary's curls. "When I was yet a girl in London."

"I have something to give you, too." Mary dashed into the cottage.

Clarice spread her hands in question, but Mary was back in a moment, holding forth a scrap of paper. "For you," she said, handing it to Amy.

Tears pricked the back of Amy's lids as she gazed at the picture Mary had drawn. The cottage. A smiling sun. And two stick figures with a crooked heart between them. "Surely your mama would like to keep this."

"You keep it," Clarice said simply.

Amy bent to gave Mary a heartfelt hug. "I'll treasure it always."

Thank you, Clarice mouthed with a smile. "Will you come in and share some Christmas cake?"

"I could use some sustenance," Colin declared, and they all laughed.

SIXTY-SIX

*B*ACK IN THEIR carriage on the way to the castle, Amy leaned across to take Colin's hands. "Wasn't that wonderful?"

"Yes, it was delicious. I was famished."

"You and your stomach." Giggling, she tried to pull her hands back, but he held them tight. "I meant Mary, and how happy she is."

"Oh," he said with an innocent grin. He squeezed her fingers and arched one dark brow. "I'm hoping we'll have a little girl just like Mary someday."

She looked pointedly at his dark head, then freed one of her hands to lift a hank of her own ebony hair. "I think not, no matter how hard we tried."

Colin laughed. "I didn't mean blond; I meant sweet. Surely we can make a sweet daughter? We'll have to work on it more often."

"Haven't we been?" Amy mused with a secretive smile.

As they pulled through the gatehouse and onto Cainewood's private road, he grumbled under his breath, "So much for working on it."

"Pardon me?"

He reached to take Amy's hand and pull her onto his lap. "Our days of solitude are over—not to mention our nights."

Amy laughed. "It's not so bad as all that! Surely we'll have time alone together. And the family..."

Amy was very much looking forward to spending time with her new family.

"The family. The loud, boisterous, meddlesome, teasing..." He swept the hair off the nape of her neck and bent his head to kiss her there with each word. "Argumentative, childish, outspoken, pigheaded—"

Amy turned on his lap. She touched her mouth to his, just barely, so he could feel her lips move. "Affectionate, generous, enthusiastic." She kissed him lightly. "Playful, thoughtful, *alive*." Another kiss, more forceful. "Intelligent, lovable—"

Colin pulled back in mock surprise. "Good heavens, are we as wonderful as all that?"

"Well, *they* are. I'm not so sure about you." The carriage wheels clattered over the drawbridge, and Amy leaned back to part the curtains as they passed through the barbican and into the quadrangle. "Oh, Colin, *look*."

All around the quadrangle, garlands of ivy graced the ancient walls. A large red bow hung over each door and window, the swagged ends wound with holly and laurel.

"It's beautiful!"

"Wait till you see inside," Colin promised drolly. "Kendra quite outdoes herself this time of year." But he was smiling, clearly caught up in the Christmas spirit despite himself.

Indoors, the monotone, cream-hued stone hall was asplash with red and green. Winter foliage and red ribbon twisted around the gray handrail, marching up the stairs and across the balcony at the top. Hundreds of beeswax candles sat at intervals, waiting to be lit when darkness fell. Cloth of gold swagged lavishly between the columns, held in place with enormous red bows.

Amy paused on the threshold, aghast at the splendor, and Colin seized the opportunity to kiss her, reaching overhead to pull a berry off the mistletoe afterward.

"Ah, our bride and groom," Kendra called, coming down the stairs. "Thank heavens you've arrived. Our mistletoe's been sadly neglected this season."

"We can remedy that situation." Colin gave Amy another light kiss and removed another berry.

Moments later, the brothers appeared. They both had resounding kisses for Amy, and the mistletoe was relieved of two more berries. Then Kendra claimed a kiss from Colin, albeit a mite more sisterly, and another berry was plucked.

"That's more like it." Kendra grinned, looking up. "At this rate, it'll be bare before evening!"

SIXTY-SEVEN

"*H*EY, DOWN here!"

Amy looked down from the wall walk to see Kendra waving frantically and Jason and Ford toting a large saw between them. Colin laughed at the question in her eyes. "Come, love, we're going to cut the Yule Log," he said as he beckoned her to follow him down.

Spirits high, the five of them trudged outside the castle walls and into the bordering forest. Much good-natured arguing followed, as each claimed to have discovered the largest tree trunk. Teasing laughter pealed through the fragrant woods until Jason, as usual the peacemaker, swept off his cloak and shivered stoically while they used it as a crude measuring device.

Amy's tree was the winner. Her cheeks bright with the flush of victory, she watched the Chase brothers struggle manfully to cut it down. At last it fell, with a resounding crash and a great cheer from all. They cut a long chunk from the thickest part, which Amy eyed incredulously, considering they'd brought no cart or horse.

"How will we get it back to Cainewood?" she asked Jason.

"We'll manage." Beneath their cloaks, Jason and Ford both had lengths of rope coiled about their waists, which they unwound and tied around the colossal log, creating six long looped handles to pull it by. "Can you and Kendra handle the saw?"

"Of course, but must the log be so big?"

"Tradition says it will be a good year if we can keep it smoldering through Twelfth Night." Ford made a small grunt as he tugged a knot tight. "The bigger, the better."

"But that couldn't possibly fit in the fireplace."

Colin's laughter rang through the trees. "Don't be such a worrywart, love. We've done this a time or two."

"Hmmph." Tilting her nose in the air, she moved to help Kendra with the heavy saw. "You're the one who has to carry it, not me."

Kendra hurried Amy ahead while the boys struggled behind. "Everything is all set," she whispered. "When it's time, a maid will come to your room and escort you to a chamber downstairs, where several footmen will be on hand to help."

"I cannot wait," Amy said with a conspiratorial smile. "Thank you so much."

"I cannot wait, either!"

Despite the frosty air, the boys were covered with a thin sheen of sweat by the time they managed to haul the log to the front door. They needed the help of three additional men to lift it over the threshold and carry it into the great hall.

"Careful, the floor!" Kendra warned. "It's just been polished."

In fact, the servants were not quite finished: at the far end they were still spreading the milk that would dry to a high sheen. Amy gawked at the buzz of activity. From the planked floor to the intricate oak hammerbeam ceiling, the immense great hall swarmed with people. Paintings were dusted, tapestries cleaned and rehung on the stone walls. Servants chattered excitedly as they brought in heavy, ancient trestle tables and set them with row after row of trenchers and cutlery.

"What's happening?" Amy asked, one eye on the men struggling to get the log into the enormous fireplace.

Kendra crossed her arms and tapped a foot disapprovingly. "Didn't Colin tell you about Christmas at Cainewood?"

Amy shook her head. "Is there to be an entertainment tonight?"

"Tomorrow. All the castle retainers, tenants, and villagers will come for Christmas dinner, complete with gifts for everyone." Kendra waved a hand expansively. "Isn't it glorious? I love Christmas!"

Amy laughed. "I love Christmas, too. I was too young to remember it before the Commonwealth."

"As was I. That wretched Cromwell..." Kendra wiped her tongue and spit. "That I should even say such an evil name. Eleven years with no Christmas—look, Amy, it fits!" She clapped her hands.

The log snugged in the fireplace with room to spare. The brothers were remarkably well behaved, throwing nothing more than a few gloating glances in Amy's direction.

"You told me so!" she said for them with a giggle, and their answering laughter echoed in the cavernous hall.

"Food." Colin wiped his palms on his breeches. "After all that work, a man needs food."

"Christmas Eve supper awaits," Kendra announced.

In contrast to the great hall, the private family dining room seemed small and intimate, the air suffused with savory scents that made Amy's mouth water. Colin loaded her plate with clove-studded turkey, Yorkshire Christmas pie, artichoke bottoms and potatoes in pastry, spinach tart, and one of the new French rolls. Kendra started with a slice of almond cheesecake, a wedge of pumpkin pie, and an apple taffety tart.

"Kendra, Kendra." Jason heaved a good-natured sigh. "Pumpkin pie when there's Yorkshire pie on the table?" He spooned up a bite, the hearty crust filled with a mixture of turkey, goose, partridge, pigeon, hare, and woodcock, all swimming in butter. "When will you grow up?"

"Buttered ale?" Kendra said sweetly, ignoring him as she poured a dipperful from the huge, ivy-garlanded wassail bowl that dominated the table. She floated a square of brown toast on top and handed the cup to Amy.

"Thank you." Amy sniffed deep of the hot ale, mulled with beaten eggs, sugar, spices and the pulp of roasted apples. When she took a sip, it warmed her to her very bones. "It's so lovely here," she said, thinking of Christmases past in the single room her family had used for cooking, eating, and socializing. "A different world. Look at the firelight dancing on the beveled windows."

"It doesn't hold a candle to the sparkle in your eyes." Everyone groaned as Colin took a big gulp of buttered ale. "Or the blush on your cheeks," he added with a laugh.

Ford lobbed a bit of toast at him.

When everyone had crammed in the last possible bite, they all walked to the great hall with many competing moans of regretted gluttony. There they lit the Yule Log and sang the traditional Christmas carols, with Kendra accompanying on the harpsichord, which had been moved into the hall for the occasion.

The five of them were dwarfed by the enormous chamber, but warm and merry, clustered at one end with the fire burning cheerfully. When they ran out of songs, they opened their gifts.

Jason's serious face split into a smile when he saw his pearl cravat pin, and he put it on immediately. Kendra slipped the emerald ring on her finger and declared it her favorite piece of jewelry. Ford disappeared upstairs after opening his gift, returning with his new jeweled hatband adorning a fashionable wide-brimmed hat, which he wore the rest of the evening.

Amy couldn't have been more pleased.

Kendra's gift to Amy was a large selection of shoes, stockings, ribbons, and nightgowns in an assortment of colors—the latter made of a sumptuous, filmy material that whispered over Amy's skin.

Jason had wrapped up the history books Amy had left piled on the mosaic table in his library, and she clutched them to her chest in delight.

Looking pleased with himself, Ford presented her with a selection of hard-milled scented soaps, floral bath oils, and French perfumes that had Colin wondering aloud at why such a gift would come from his *little brother*—until Amy playfully punched him in the stomach. He doubled over, in laughter, not pain, and Amy couldn't remember when she'd had as much fun.

After everyone's gifts had been opened—a long proceeding,

as each individual present was passed around and properly admired—Jason called for the plum porridge.

Amy groaned. "I cannot eat another bite."

"Oh, but you must have a serving." Kendra scooped a healthy dollop and plopped it in Amy's bowl. "Hidden within it are tokens that foretell of the year to come."

Colin's bowl held the first prize, a silver penny, predicting a fortune in the offing. "I've fortune enough for a lifetime already," he declared in a chivalrous tone, his gaze fastened on Amy.

This earned him another chorus of groans and several balled-up wrappings aimed at his head—from everyone but Amy, who found herself entranced by the heat of Colin's expression. The room suddenly felt overwarm.

"Oh, no." Jason pulled a ring from his mouth, rolling his eyes as he licked it clean. "This should be Kendra's, surely."

They all laughed again.

"What does it mean?" Amy asked.

"It's a sign of marriage," Kendra explained. "Ah, the thimble!" She placed it on a fingertip, flashing an angelic smile. "A life of blessedness."

"When are you joining the convent?" Ford chortled.

He had to duck to avoid the flying thimble.

Colin snorted. "Well, so much for the tokens."

"Thank heavens." Amy set down her bowl.

Kendra glanced up. "Aren't you going to finish it?"

Amy shook her head. "I've had enough," she said quietly. "I'm really not feeling too well." She threw Kendra a surreptitious wink, then turned to Colin. "I think I should go to bed."

He shot up at once and placed a hand on her forehead. "You're not feverish," he reported, visibly relieved. "But if you feel ill, then of course we must go to bed."

"But the games…" Ford protested.

"What games?" Amy asked innocently, finishing with a weak cough for effect.

"We always play games on Christmas Eve, charades and the like, until the wee hours." Grasping her hand, Colin pulled her up and put a protective arm around her. "But that was before one of us was married. Besides, your health is more important."

He started moving her toward the door.

"You must stay and play, Colin. It's only fatigue, I'm certain, and overeating and a bit too much buttered ale—though it was all delicious." Amy sighed prettily and placed a delicate hand on her abdomen.

Unfortunately, Colin proved to be overly solicitous. The best they could do was convince him to see her to bed and then return for the games.

He undressed her himself, pulled one of her new nightgowns over her head, then stood back to judge the effect.

He gave a low whistle. "Are you certain you're ill, love?"

"Quite certain." She forced another cough and clutched at her stomach. "Leave now, please, before I embarrass myself in front of you." She climbed into the bed, moaning softly to demonstrate her illness. "Could you put the chamber pot beside me before you go?"

"Sickness is nothing to be embarrassed about," he assured her. With a small thud, he deposited the chamber pot on the bedside table. "Are you sure you don't want me to stay?"

"I'm positively sure. Go enjoy the games." When he hesitated as though not quite convinced, she added, "If you'll but let me rest, Colin, *alone*, when you return in a few hours I'm certain to be feeling better."

"Well…"

"*Much* better," she repeated meaningfully.

She watched his eyes light up before she rolled away with a groan and pulled the covers over her head.

SIXTY-EIGHT

*H*ALF AN HOUR after the charades game began, Colin and his siblings were interrupted by the head butler announcing the unexpected delivery of a crate. They all hurried to the stone hall to see what it might be.

The crate was enormous, standing taller than Colin himself, and his name was scrawled across the front. There was no indication of where or whom it had come from.

"Do you suppose it's a wedding gift?" he asked, coming up to stand beside it.

"Open it and see," Jason suggested.

The buoyancy in his voice had Colin turning to him sharply. "It's from you, then?"

"I didn't say that. Just open it."

"It must be furniture. A nice thought, Jason, but much too generous—and besides, I have no place to put anything yet."

Jason laughed. "Look, it's not from me. Just open it."

Colin considered. "Very well, but Amy should be here. Perhaps she's feeling better now. I'll just go and check."

"Let her sleep," Kendra said. "She felt beastly. Checking might wake her, and you mustn't do that."

"I'm not sure what to do, then." Colin twisted his signet ring on his finger. "I expect this can wait until morning."

"It's addressed to you, not Amy," Kendra said. "She can see it in the morning. Open it, please—or I'll do it for you. I want to see what's inside."

"Well…"

"I'll fetch some tools," Ford offered, rushing off before Colin could protest.

Not that he really wanted to—he was at least as curious as Kendra.

A minute later, Ford was back, and together they pried off the front of the crate—only to find another box enclosed inside. They pulled the remaining three sides of the crate apart, but there was still no clue to the contents. The new box was unmarked.

"It must be fragile," Colin remarked uncertainly. "Let's be more careful opening this one."

The second box revealed nothing more than a slightly smaller version of itself hidden inside.

He threw his siblings a sidelong glance and silently set to opening it. When a fourth featureless box was revealed, he grinned at the profusion of wood littering the hall. "What on earth is going on here?"

"I'm sure we don't know," Kendra protested.

"We were just minding our own business, playing charades," Ford offered.

"Just open it," Jason said.

Colin shrugged, trying to hide a smile. He loved a prank played on himself almost as much as being the perpetrator of one. "I think I'll wait until morning, after all," he said blandly, turning to leave.

Kendra lunged at him, tugging on his shirt. "Colin Chase, you open that box right now. I'm—I'm *dying* of curiosity."

He turned back and fixed her with an innocent look. "Well, then, I suppose I must. I wouldn't want you to *die* on account of me."

They laughed as he pulled the box apart, and he was not at all surprised to find a fifth box inside. This one had a sign on it, though, spelling out the words CONTAINS THE EARL OF GREYSTONE in neat block letters.

"It should say '*Contents for* the Earl of Greystone,'" he pointed out. "Somebody doesn't know how to spell."

His siblings shrugged.

"It cannot contain the Earl of Greystone," he insisted, staring at their blank faces. "*I'm* the Earl of Greystone, and I'm quite obviously not in that box. I'm not certain I would even fit," he added as an afterthought.

A cough came from within the box.

Colin swung around. "What the deuce..."

The top was hinged. He threw it open. Amy slowly rose, completely captivating in a soft peach gown, a dazzling smile on her lips and in her eyes.

"*You!* Uh—aren't you ill?" Colin sputtered.

"Do I look ill?"

"No. And you don't look like the Earl of Greystone, either."

Laughter came from behind him, and he turned, confused. Kendra tilted her head. "Don't you like your Christmas present, Colin?"

A grin of amusement twitched on his lips as he turned back to Amy. "You're lovely, but you're not a present, love. I have you already." He grasped her under her arms, effortlessly lifting her out of the box. "It was a good trick, though," he conceded as he set her on her feet. "Even if the sign was spelled wrong."

"No, it was spelled correctly," Amy said.

He remained silent, his brows drawn together in puzzlement.

"The box contains the *next* Earl of Greystone."

Colin could sense all their eyes on him, but his brain refused to work. His head felt completely blank. He leaned over a little, gazing into the empty box.

"It *contained* the next Earl of Greystone, I mean," Amy clarified. "He's not inside the box anymore."

Colin blinked stupidly.

"You'll have to wait to see him, though—about seven and a half months, I suspect."

His heart faltered in his chest.

"He's inside *me*, Colin," she finished softly.

His mouth opened, closed, then he let forth a whoop of joy as he swept her up and swung her around and around in a wide circle. Jason and Ford both laughed, while tears brightened Kendra's eyes.

Suddenly, Colin stopped and set Amy down with exquisite care. "Have I hurt you?" he asked earnestly. "Either of you?"

"No, we're not that fragile. Though it's a good thing I don't seem prone to morning sickness."

Ford snorted. "You'd have got it straight in your face, I expect."

"Ford!" Jason and Kendra shouted together.

"Forgive him," Jason continued to Amy. "He's hopelessly uncivilized."

"*I* think he's funny," Amy declared between giggles. "And quite handsome, besides."

Ford's neck turned red.

"Well, Colin, I reckon the honeymoon is over." Jason's smile belied the seriousness of his tone.

"Come again?"

"She played a prank on you. She's challenging your virtuosity as a prankster already."

Colin looked at his bride, his heart swelling with emotion. "*Au contraire,*" he said slowly. "The honeymoon is only beginning." He swept her up, bearing her slight weight as one would a sleeping child, his arms beneath her shoulders and knees. Cradling her against his upper body, he strode toward the staircase

"Wait!" Kendra shouted. "The games!"

"Go ahead, children," Colin called over his shoulder. "We have our own games to play."

"Colin!" Amy chided, shocked at his indelicacy. But she kept laughing all the way up the stairs.

SIXTY-NINE

*C*OLIN KICKED the door closed behind them and gently deposited Amy on the bed. The sudden apprehension in her eyes made his gut clench.

"Are you truly pleased?" she asked in a small voice. "I mean, it's so soon...and maybe I should have told you first, privately..."

She looked away, staring up at the underside of the canopy.

"Oh, love, how could you doubt me so?" He lowered himself to the bed and turned her face toward him with a fingertip. "A babe...a family..."

Amy's breath rushed out, and she offered him a shaky smile. "A son," she said. "I don't know why, but I'm sure of it, Colin."

He didn't care whether she carried a son or a daughter. Either way, his throat tightened as he thought of their child growing within her. "A son," he echoed, suppressing a chuckle. "How long have you known?"

Her fingers toyed with a lock of her hair. "I think it must have happened the very first time, on our wedding night."

"But you said nothing until now."

"It's been too soon to tell till now, only six weeks," she defended herself. "Besides, I wasn't sure you'd be happy. Our wedding happened so quickly, and now this..."

Colin suspected she was thinking they hadn't been meant to

wed. He'd manipulated her by bringing Robert's threat into the equation. And look where it had landed him: He was happy beyond belief, but those days were numbered. A year—one precious year—until that buzzard's debt was due.

He laced his fingers with hers. He'd been right all along: marrying for love was irrational. A mistake. But one he couldn't bring himself to be sorry for—yet.

"Go on," he said, squeezing her hand.

She took a deep breath. "When I became convinced—and don't ask me how, I just *know*—I didn't know how to tell you. I wasn't sure whether you'd be pleased." She bit her lip. "But I wanted to give you a Christmas present, and this was all I had." Her mouth curved in a tiny smile. "Since you won't take my diamonds and gold."

"My Amethyst is the most precious gem of all," Colin teased. "Why would I want any others when they all pale in comparison?" He brushed a gentle kiss across her lips.

"Then you're really, truly pleased? You're not vexed we conceived so soon? Because, heaven forgive me, I cannot find it in me to be sorry. I want your son more than anything in the world," she finished on a sigh.

What had he done to deserve her? And how—heavens, *how*—could he manage to keep his promise and save Greystone, too?

And her amethyst eyes still radiated worry. "I'm more than pleased," he assured her. "I'm overjoyed...delighted... enchanted...elated..." A kiss punctuated each word, and his voice grew rough. "Ecstatic...intoxicated..."

"That's the buttered ale, I think." She giggled.

"No, it's you," he protested.

She blushed and cleared her throat. "Well, now that you've relieved my fears, we may as well go join in the games."

Colin laughed, the sound bubbling up from deep in his chest. "Not yet," he said flatly, one arm coming around to hold her hostage.

"But I've never before had a large family to play games with."

He nuzzled her neck, smiling when he felt her pulse speed up.

"I-I was so looking forward to it," she stammered out.

He kissed a trail to her ear. "First, I would meet my child."

"Your son. But he won't be arriving for many months."

"That doesn't signify. I shall meet him anyway."

His heart soared with anticipation. Though he hoped he'd never be forced to spend her inheritance, now, thanks to this miracle, he'd have something to bind her to his side. Their baby...surely she'd stay with him always for the sake of their child, even if he lost Greystone or depleted her gold in saving it.

He was so lucky to have her. He leaned over her, running his fingers through her dark tresses and arranging them artistically on the pillows. Criminy, she was beautiful. He smiled down at his handiwork. "Ahh," he said with a long, drawn-out sigh of contentment, running his hands down her sides to span her waist. "I haven't been able to touch you properly since morning."

"Improperly, you mean." Amy giggled, feeling light-hearted for the first time since she'd realized she was pregnant.

He smiled, that mischievous grin that made her heart flip-flop. "It's deucedly inconvenient having the family around." His stern voice didn't fool her. "I warned you."

She lifted her head for a kiss, but he seemed to have other plans. His hands were skimming over her hips now. "It has its compensations," she said, watching the firelight play over his perfect features.

"Such as?"

"Such as..." She felt him inching her skirts up, making concentration difficult. "They're quite helpful with prank arrangements."

"I see."

He inched them up more. "They...make interesting supper conversation," she managed to say.

"Is that so?"

"Mmm-hmm."

With sudden impatience, he hurried her out of her dress, and their inane discussion came to an abrupt end.

When his lips finally met hers, her heart swelled with

emotion. But not as much as when he glided down, until his scratchy chin and cheek grazed against her smooth belly.

"Are you in there, little one?" His voice vibrated into her body. "It's your father." His lips moved against her stomach, his breath warm.

Her hands reached down to tug insistently at his shoulders.

"Your mother wants me now," Colin gloated, throwing Amy a roguish look. "But first I want to say…we love you."

"Colin…"

"Goodbye for now," Colin murmured, pressing a final kiss to her stomach. "We'll talk again soon."

He lifted his head, and she knew right then that they wouldn't be joining his family for games that night. The eyes that blazed into hers were a deep, fathomless green, overflowing with more love than words could ever convey. Everything between Colin and herself seemed incredibly perfect, as though they belonged together, each and every minute particle of their bodies and souls.

No matter that her head sometimes told her otherwise, her heart had always known they were meant to be.

SEVENTY

Six months later
June 1667

*C*OLIN SLID his knife under the red seal and scanned the brief missive.

A pox on him.

Rubbing his temples, he dropped the vellum letter atop the ledgers and journals that covered the scarred wooden surface of his desk—ledgers and journals he'd be forced to abandon for the next few days. Beyond the castle walls, he imagined the rolling land, freshly green with the first new shoots from spring planting. Although it was all too far away to hear, he'd swear he could make out the bleat of distant sheep, the dull thud of a log being felled, the vague bangs and scrapes of quarrying—all work he was loath to let continue without his supervision.

The estate needed his attention too, curse it.

The year was halfway over, and he'd saved nowhere near half of his debt to Hobbs.

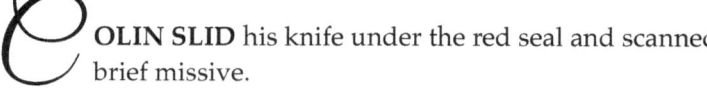

$\mathcal{T}$HE DOOR cracked open. "Are you napping, my lady?"

"Hah." Amy looked up from her book as her buxom blond maid stepped inside. "I wish. I'm so big and itchy, I cannot find a good position no matter how many I try."

As though he'd heard her complaint, her son swished in her womb, poking out fists, knees, elbows, and feet all at once, it seemed.

Lydia's kittenish blue eyes narrowed as she contemplated the rolling lumps on her mistress's abdomen. "Lud, that looks uncomfortable."

Amy laughed and set the book aside. "Sometimes I'm convinced I'm carrying a human octopus, or at the very least an accomplished acrobat." She pushed herself to stand. "Did you need me for something?"

"The lord said he has a matter to discuss. He waits in the study." Frowning, Lydia flipped through the gowns in Amy's wardrobe. "Cuds bobs, milady, you've got nothing decent to wear that will fit over your belly."

"I needn't dress up to visit with my husband!" Giggling, Amy went next door to see him in the study.

She quieted as she drew near. The door was ajar, and she could hear Benchley's voice. "Fernew was asking when the new thresher will arrive."

"I canceled delivery."

At Colin's grim words, Amy froze, her hand on the latch.

"You—"

"Canceled it. Fernew will have to get along without it. Tell him it's only till next year."

The defeat in his voice gnawed at Amy's insides.

"And the mill?"

She grimaced at Colin's heavy sigh. "That will have to be repaired; there's no way around it. Have Jenner order the parts; I should be back to help well before their delivery. No sense paying for more labor when it isn't necessary. Anything else, Benchley?"

"No. No, my lord."

Amy jumped back when Benchley opened the door. He nodded to her and headed toward the entrance hall.

As his footsteps receded down the corridor, she stepped into the room. Colin was bent over a sheet of vellum, shaking his head. She bit her lip.

Another financial problem he couldn't solve, thanks to wedding her?

"Amy." He glanced up with a distracted smile. "Come here, love."

She went to him, smiling in return when he ran a hand over the swell of their child, feeling for signs of movement.

"Charles wants to see us," he said, looking up from her middle with thinly veiled disgust. "Tomorrow night."

"Charles?" Amy eyed the paper in his other hand. A large red seal was attached, broken but impressive nonetheless. "Charles who?"

"Charles. The king."

Her heart paused before continuing at an unsteady gallop. Of course she'd known that Colin was intimate with the king, that she was now a countess and expected to move in court circles. But here at Greystone, in their own little crumbling castle, she'd felt very removed from the possibility. "But...why?"

"Who knows? Perhaps he's miffed that I didn't ask his permission to marry you."

She leaned weakly against the desk. "His permission?"

Colin sighed, tossing the summons onto the surface with a flick of his wrist. "As a peer of the realm, ancient law says I'm obligated to obtain the king's approval. But no one actually asks —not even his own brother James before his secret marriage to Anne Hyde." With the heels of both hands, he rubbed his forehead, as though a massive headache had just arisen. "It's archaic; I'm certain no one has asked for a century. Still, Charles has always been like a big brother to me." He squinted, and his eyes turned a glazey dull color. "I don't know."

"Can't you just send him a note? Tell him you're busy and I'm with child?"

Colin's laughter was immediate; his eyes cleared and turned to her, a glittering emerald green. "No, we cannot just send a note, love." He caught her hand and pulled her onto his lap. "When the king calls, one answers. It's off to Whitehall for us, I'm afraid." He was silent a minute, his fingers absently twirling one of her long ebony ringlets. "We'll leave first thing in the morning, to arrive at the town house by noon. You can nap before the evening festivities."

"I'm sure I won't sleep a wink tonight." She groaned softly and moved her hand to cover where their child registered his own protest, in the form of a particularly violent kick.

"It's nothing to be worried about. Charles is an affable sort."

"But there will be all those people…" She imagined hordes of svelte ladies, all dressed in the latest fashions. And haughty lords, beribboned and bejeweled, looking down their aristocratic noses at her bloated form.

"You already know some of them," he reminded her patiently, "from your shop."

"As *customers*. Oh, Colin, look at me! You're going to be sorry you married me, I just know it."

His fingers stilled in her hair, and he said very quietly, "I will never, ever be sorry I married you, Lady Greystone. You're the best thing that ever happened to me."

When his hand moved to the back of her neck, and he pulled her toward him and kissed her lightly, she almost believed him. "And you're beautiful, as beautiful as ever. I swear it." He kissed her again, this time long and deep, his mouth warm and possessive, and she *did* believe him.

For two seconds, at least.

SEVENTY-ONE

"*A*ND WHEN Harry kisses me..." Lydia shuddered expressively. "Oh, I cannot think how to put it."

"Ooh la la?" Madame Beaumont suggested, putting the finishing touches on Amy's face.

Lydia laughed. "Ooh la la exactly!"

"Ooh la la?" Amy echoed distractedly.

Madame Beaumont helped her to stand. "You're a million miles away, my lady."

"What? Oh...yes, I'm afraid you're right." Sighing, Amy set down the amethyst necklace she'd brought from Greystone. The deep violet pear-shaped gems glistened on the dark wood of the dressing table, beckoning her to hold them again. She flexed her hands and forced a smile. "I was daydreaming about wax and knives."

"*Pourquoi?*"

"Lady Greystone used to be a jeweler," Lydia explained, hiding a smile of her own.

"Oh, I see."

Madame looked as though she didn't see at all, but she didn't seem shocked or disapproving, either. Amy gave the older woman's hand a quick squeeze. "I cannot thank you enough for coming." Having received her frantic messengered note yesterday, Madame had been waiting at the London town house this morning, gown in hand. "You saved my life."

"Surely you exaggerate." Amusement twitched on the seamstress's lips as she drew off Amy's robe and laid a gentle palm on her abdomen.

Amy jumped a bit, then relaxed. Of late, she'd noticed everyone thought they had a right to touch her, as though her body had become public property since she'd swelled with the child.

Madame slipped a lacy new chemise over Amy's head, and Lydia held out the gown. "*I* never exaggerate." The blond maid giggled. "Lud, my Harry is so...so *virile*."

"Pray tell, Lydia, where did you find this *amour*?" Madame set the curling iron to heat in the glowing embers of the fire. "This paragon of masculinity?"

Amy grinned. "In our stables. Colin recently hired him to relieve Benchley of some duties. Your dream man, is he, Lydia?"

"Hmm," Lydia murmured noncommittally. Hiding her face, she made herself busy adjusting the gown over the bulge of Amy's stomach. "When he kisses me, yes, but...all is not perfect with Harry."

The seamstress eased Amy onto a chair and set to work on her hair. "Have you talked to your *amour* about your problems?"

Lydia puttered around the room, sighing as she folded Amy's robe. "I've tried. I suppose I should try again."

"I wish you luck." Amy frowned into the dressing table mirror. "Men don't care to discuss our problems. They always think they know what's best."

As Madame's eyes met Amy's reflection, her hands plaited faster.

"It's true," Amy muttered defensively. "When I talked to Papa about how I didn't want to marry our apprentice, he disregarded my feelings entirely."

"Not all men are like that." Madame's fingers caught and pulled at her hair. "Not my François."

"Surely not the earl?" Lydia's face appeared beside Madame's in the mirror, puzzled. "You confide in him, don't you? He loves you so."

Did he really? Amy bit her lip. It was pointless to confide in Colin, anyway; he'd made it clear before they wed that a countess would never run a shop. And he'd become more and more closed and distracted over the months.

Lydia and Madame were still staring at her. "Oh, I suppose you're right," she said. "It's just one of my silly notions."

"She's breeding," Madame said knowingly.

"That doesn't make me a nimwit," Amy said with a huff.

Lydia nodded, ignoring her outburst. "I've seen five different ladies through five different pregnancies. They're all this way."

"Hmmph." Looking down to her crossed arms, Amy glimpsed her cleavage exposed in the purple dress's low neckline. "Dear heavens," she whispered, her hands fluttering up to cover the bareness.

Madame's laugh tinkled through the room. "You'll be the most modest lady at court, just you wait and see."

With luck, the brazen display would draw attention away from her unfashionable high waistline. But Amy felt daring and embarrassed at the same time. She hoped Madame was right.

"*Voilà.*" Madame tied the last ribbon in Amy's hair.

While Amy watched in the dressing table's looking glass, Lydia clasped the amethyst necklace around her throat. Aching to make something like it again, Amy's fingers moved to touch the twenty-carat gem that dangled at the bottom. She gazed at its flashing brilliance in the mirror.

"Milady?" Lydia held out the matching earrings. "Shall I put these on for you?"

"Heavens, no." Amy took a deep breath and blew it out, then fastened the earrings on her lobes. Shaking her head to set them swinging from their clustered diamond tops, she smiled.

"That's more like it." Lydia slipped a simple amethyst and diamond bracelet onto Amy's left wrist, where it would complement her heart-shaped amethyst wedding ring. The maid stood back and grinned. "Cuds bobs, if you don't look the perfect lady. I'll just go tell the lord you're ready to leave."

"Come, see if your Lydia wasn't telling the bare truth." Taking her hand, Madame helped Amy rise from the chair and led her to the pier glass.

The rich purple silk gown shimmered as Amy approached the mirror, beaming at her reflection. The seamstress had worked her magic yet again. A gold tissue overskirt looped up, held on each side with golden bows, while matching gold bows marched down her full sleeves. The purple underskirt sparkled with hundreds of golden stars.

A low whistle of appreciation came from behind her. She turned to see Colin leaning against the doorjamb, his gaze fastened to her scooped neckline. She melted a little at the sight of him, even after nearly eight months of marriage.

He was devastating. Would she ever get used to it? She thought not. Not in eight months, or eight years, or eighty years, even.

"You'll be the most beautiful lady at Whitehall," he said softly.

"And you, the most beautiful gentleman."

Colin laughed. He was dressed, predictably, in the same black velvet suit he'd worn for their wedding, identical down to her cameo pinned in the lavish lace of his cravat. His crisp, dark hair was loose and fell in waves to his shoulders.

Amy felt a lump of emotion swell in her throat. She was so lucky to have him. Their marriage was beyond wonderful, and she had no cause to dwell on melancholy thoughts, especially on a day like today.

She moved to him and looped her arms around his neck, threading her fingers in the hair at his nape. She heard Madame bustling about, putting away cosmetics, but the sounds seemed to fade as Colin brought his lips to hers.

He kissed her gently, and she tried to pull him closer, but he tugged away and grinned.

"Later, love. We wouldn't want to spoil Madame Beaumont's accomplished artwork."

Amy's face flamed, and she stole a glance at Madame. But the seamstress was studiously looking elsewhere.

"Shall we?" Colin curled an arm around Amy's waist and drew her from the room.

Was she really on her way to Whitehall Palace, to be

presented to England's king and queen? She, Amy Goldsmith, merchant's daughter?

It didn't seem possible.

"Why so quiet, love?" Colin interrupted her thoughts. "You're not worried about tonight, are you?"

"A little, maybe. But…"

Her chest ached with the need to tell someone, and she shot him an appraising glance. But then she heard the old words again, *You cannot have everything*, and heaven help her, she couldn't tell if it were her father's voice or Colin's.

"It's nothing."

"But what?" The fingers of one hand drummed against his thigh.

"My goodness, Colin." Forcing a smile, she pulled him toward the front door before he could question her further. "You know how moody breeding ladies are!"

SEVENTY-TWO

*A*MY TREMBLED as she stood in line outside the Presence Chamber, a mixture of anticipation and sheer terror shuddering through her. Colin clasped her hand tighter and looked down at her sympathetically. "They're only people, love," he whispered.

Oh, but what magnificent people they were! Before her stood a lady in a satin gown of deep magenta studded with pearls, with an ermine-trimmed train so long that Amy was forced to stand ten feet behind her. She turned to peek at a lady wearing a splendid gown of rich turquoise with a silver lace overlay, then spun back and clapped a hand to her open mouth. Why, the woman's bosom was all but falling out of her low neckline, which made Amy's neckline look demure!

Beside her, Colin chuckled. He raised her hand and pressed his warm lips to the back in a soft kiss.

Amy looked up at him, offering a shaky smile. She was surrounded by men in long, elaborate crimped periwigs. Their satin and velvet clothing dripped with ribbons and lace in such profusion as to rival the ladies. Their fingers were bedecked with garish gemstones, their necks adorned with ropes of huge, costly pearls. Still, she was certain that Colin was the most stunning male specimen within twenty miles of Whitehall.

They advanced slowly, until suddenly it was their turn to be announced. The usher puffed out his chest and took a deep breath. "The Earl of Greystone! The Countess of Greystone!"

As they entered the Presence Chamber, the throng of spectators in the gallery above leaned forward en masse. Heads turned to ogle the new arrivals. Amy heard a distinct murmur from the lords and ladies lining the walkway.

Gliding down the endless aisle on Colin's arm, she stared straight ahead. "What are they all saying?" she asked low, trying to keep her lips from moving.

With an easy smile, Colin inclined his head toward hers. "They're saying, 'Ah…the rumors are true. Lord Greystone jilted Lady Priscilla for an uncommon beauty.'"

"Shh!" Amy blushed and giggled. "They're all looking at us."

"Of course they are. See those ladies talking behind their fans? They're saying, 'Such a shame the earl is no longer available. But at least his gorgeous lady is taken and therefore out of the competition.'"

Amy nearly tripped. "I was never *in* the competition," she chided. "I was only a merchant's daughter."

"Tsk. They're deluding themselves, anyway. You may be out of the competition for marriage, but at Charles's court, it's assumed one is always available for an *affaire d'amour*. It's taken for granted that wives are as unfaithful as husbands; the men here demand fidelity only from their mistresses."

"Not all the men, I'm hoping." She looked up at Colin with a sparkle in her eye.

He raised one brow wickedly. "Oh, there might be one or two holdouts."

In spite of her anxiety, Amy grinned, but the smile faded as her attention was drawn ahead, to where Their Majesties sat awaiting her.

Their thrones were set side-by-side on a raised platform, framed with a swagged canopy of crimson velvet bedecked in silver and gold. But it wasn't the magnificence of the setting that awed Amy.

It was the king himself.

The most compelling figure she'd ever seen, His Majesty sat tall on his throne, dwarfing his queen, his long legs sprawled carelessly before him. Though he'd already reached the advanced age of thirty-seven, his long, shiny black hair held nary a hint of gray. His face was lean, with a thin, curly black mustache over a generous mouth.

The prospect of actually meeting him was terrifying.

The magenta-garbed lady rose and moved out of the way, swishing her fur-edged train behind her. When Charles looked up, his heavy-lidded black eyes settled on Amy. A small smile twitched at his lips, and Amy's heart clenched in her chest.

Colin drew her forward. He walked with the sure steps of a man greeting an old friend, while Amy's feet hesitated along the carpeted approach. When they reached the dais and Colin knelt down, Amy tore her gaze from King Charles and dipped into a deep curtsy.

She looked back up into the large, liquid brown eyes of Queen Catharine of Braganza.

Queen Catharine's olive-tinted features were pleasant rather than pretty. Tiny and dark, with a long nose and high forehead, she looked very, very foreign. She smiled at Amy, revealing small teeth that protruded slightly.

"Lady Greystone," she said, her Portuguese-accented voice beautiful and melodious. Her eyes were compassionate, as though she understood Amy's nervousness. They flickered toward the king and back; though theirs was an arranged marriage, Amy thought she looked very much in love with her husband.

Catharine was dressed in soft yellow, an unfortunate choice of color that did nothing for her naturally sallow complexion. She proffered a slim hand for Amy's kiss, smiling graciously at her and down to her rounded belly. Was that a trace of envy that fluttered in Catharine's welcoming expression? Sadly, in five years of marriage, the queen had not proven able to present Charles with any royal children. There was constant talk of Charles setting her aside to replace her with a queen who wasn't barren.

She was brave and kind, and Amy decided she liked her very much.

"Ah, the new Countess of Greystone," she heard King

Charles say. "It's a pleasure to finally meet you, my dear." He held out a shapely hand, and Amy moved closer to kiss it. "A pleasure," he repeated, holding on to her hand a bit longer than was necessary.

"It...is *my* pleasure, Your Majesty," Amy replied after she found her voice. Charles's eyes locked with hers, signaling a warm welcome, and she decided he wasn't frightening after all.

"You've done well for yourself, Greystone," Charles drawled with a wink in Colin's direction.

"Then you're not...displeased?"

"Displeased, Colin?"

"I assumed, when I received the summons..."

"Od's fish! What an idea. No, I asked you here for quite another reason altogether. Later, when all this"—he gestured impatiently—"rigmarole is dispensed with, we'll discuss it."

Amy smiled to herself. Colin had told her that Charles was notoriously intolerant of court ceremony, considering it a waste of time. He much preferred to be out among his people, and made it a point to be available to them casually as often as possible, in public places such as parks.

Their exchange left Amy curious, but at least reassured as to Colin's relationship with the king. It didn't sound as though Charles were perturbed with him in any way. With another curtsy and a quick bow, Amy and Colin relinquished their positions to the next in line.

Colin drew her into the crowd. "That wasn't so hard now, was it?"

"I expect I survived." Amy turned in a slow circle, taking in the splendor of her surroundings. The Presence Chamber was lit by hundreds of candles in wall sconces and liveried yeomen holding flaming torches. Dressed in every color of the rainbow, lords and ladies shimmered in the blazing light. "Look at everyone! Sequins, fur, pearls, gems, ribbon, braid, embroidery...on men and women alike!"

"You can tell which are the ladies, though. They're the ones fanning themselves with those absurd painted creations."

Amy laughed. "You surely cannot judge gender by who is wearing the gems." Ornaments of every description glittered from necks, wrists, waists, fingers, and ears. Seeing it all, Amy's fists tightened against her ever-present longing for a jeweler's bench.

One tall, pale lady emerged from the throng to tap Colin on the arm with her folded fan. He started and turned to her, wondering briefly why he was surprised to see her there. Thankful that Amy was engrossed in watching the extravaganza, he pulled the girl a few feet away.

"Priscilla."

"Greystone," she said coolly. "To what do we owe the honor of your presence at court? I was under the impression you abhorred this type of gathering."

"I was summoned by Charles," he said smoothly, refusing to rise to her bait. "Did you receive my letter of apology? I regret—"

"Well, *I* do not," she interrupted. "Buckhurst is courting me now—though I've yet to decide whether I want him."

As though she were the one who did the deciding, Colin thought. Her father would never accept Lord Buckhurst.

A handsome rogue, and popular—Priscilla doubtless basked in reflected celebrity—Buckhurst was one of the "Wits" or "Merry Gang," as they were called. These high-spirited gentlemen enlivened society with their sardonic and often vulgar poetry, plays, and literature. They were tolerated at court because Charles found them amusing, but they wielded no power. Buckhurst was most certainly *not* what Lord Hobbs was looking for in a son-in-law.

"I wish you every happiness with him," he told her.

She smiled smugly.

Amy glanced around, having finally noticed that Colin was no longer by her side. She recognized Priscilla with a jolt of surprise, and was even more surprised to find herself not worried or jealous in the least. Seeing them together, she was quite sure Colin didn't love Priscilla and never had.

She glided up to where they faced each other, and with a warm smile, Colin moved aside to include her.

"Lady Priscilla, may I present my wife, Amethyst—"

"Amethyst," Priscilla repeated under her breath, her eyes

narrowing as she struggled to remember something. "Amethyst." Suddenly, her gray eyes snapped open wide. "You!" she exclaimed.

"A pleasure to see you again, Lady Priscilla."

Colin's brow furrowed in a frown of puzzlement. "You're... acquainted with each other?"

Priscilla didn't answer. Her beautiful mouth was slack with disbelief.

"We met once, at Madame Beaumont's," Amy explained, clutching Colin's arm in a silent statement of possession. "Before we were wed."

Priscilla finally found her voice. "I don't believe this," she spat.

Colin laid a hand over Amy's where it rested on his arm. "You don't believe what, Priscilla?"

"I don't believe you broke *our* betrothal to wed *her*," she burst out as though Amy weren't there.

She had a nasty habit of doing that, Amy thought.

"Why, she's not—" Priscilla sputtered, "she's only—she's—"

"My wife," Colin supplied. "And a countess. The Countess of Greystone. A smallish estate, with a charming medieval castle. You'll remember it, I'm sure?"

Priscilla stared at him for a moment, her eyes so cold that Amy half-expected Colin's arm to turn to ice under her fingers. Then Priscilla lifted her perfect chin, turned, and walked away.

She hadn't taken more than three ladylike steps when Amy and Colin convulsed in laughter. Amy was sure Priscilla could hear them, but she didn't care.

"I do believe she'll be asking Buckhurst to send for the carriage forthwith," Colin said with more than a little satisfaction. "She's certain to have a headache this evening."

"Is she, now?"

"Based on my experience, I'd wager on it. And this time, I find myself perversely pleased to be the cause of it." He took her hand. "Come, the dancing is about to begin."

The musicians were tuning up at one end of the chamber, and the presentations were complete. King Charles stepped down from the dais and gave the signal for the music to start.

He danced the first dance with Catharine, as was only proper. It was a courante, slow and grave, a pantomimic dance suggesting courtship.

Amy watched in awe, unable to believe she was in this place, at this time, watching the King of England dance with his queen. He moved with a rare grace for so large a man and cut a dashing figure indeed. In fact, he was put together in quite a pleasing fashion and, being a man who enjoyed and excelled at all types of sports, hadn't an ounce of spare fat on his well-formed frame.

The next tune was an English country dance, a few simple steps executed by many couples in a double line. Colin pulled Amy into the queue, and there she was—dancing at Whitehall Palace. Amethyst Goldsmith, merchant's daughter. Incredible.

When the ladies' line passed the men's, she could feel Charles's gaze on her.

Following the country dance was a branle, a group dance featuring pendulum-like movements combined with much running, gliding, and skipping. It was a bit too energetic for Amy in her present condition, so Colin led her off to the side.

"Greystone!" The voice was light and self-assured, and Amy turned to see its owner. The lady's deep blue eyes were set in a classical face framed by auburn curls.

"My Lady Castlemaine." Pleasure at meeting her was evident on Colin's expressive features. "Amy, this is Barbara, the Countess of Castlemaine. Barbara, my wife, Amethyst."

So this was the king's longtime mistress! "I'm glad of your acquaintance," Amy said with a little bow, perfectly mimicking the behavior of the lords and ladies around her.

Colin watched Barbara look Amy up and down, nod her approval, then lean forward for the obligatory casual kiss. "I'm glad of your acquaintance, also," she returned with, to her credit, as much warmth as she allotted to any female.

Colin smiled to himself. A natural predator, Barbara's charms were mainly reserved for men.

"Where is your rival tonight, Barbara?" He took advantage of his excessive height to give the chamber a sweeping glance.

"My *rival*?" Barbara's tone bordered on offended, as though she thought it absurd that anyone could rival the celebrated

Countess of Castlemaine. But she wore a broad smile on her face, attesting to her good humor.

"Frances. *La Belle* Stewart."

"Frances? Have you not heard? My word, Greystone, whyever do you hide yourself away in the countryside like that? You miss all the fun."

"Heard what? Is she ill?"

"Only in the head. The ninny up and married Richmond in April—eloped, they did. Charles is livid. He won't stand to see her, at court or anywhere else."

"But why?" Colin asked dryly. "Certainly so inconsequential a matter as marriage wouldn't affect his pursuit of her." At the same time, he put an arm around Amy's shoulders to draw her near.

"If it were anyone else, you'd be right." Barbara looked from Colin to Amy and back. "*Almost* anyone else," she amended pointedly.

Colin's lips quirked in a half-smile. "But not Frances?"

"Not Frances. She's behaved with nauseating correctness—to the extent of returning all the jewels Charles had given her. Can you *imagine*?"

Of all people, Colin reflected, Barbara would have a hard time imagining *that*. "Perhaps she simply values a wedding ring over the benefits of being a royal mistress," he suggested.

"Hmmph!" Only Barbara could snort so regally. "As though she couldn't have both!" Barbara's voice dropped suddenly. "Do you want to know the real reason Frances has never graced the king's bed?" She motioned them closer, and the three huddled together as she revealed conspiratorially, "She doesn't like it. She was reluctant before she was married, and now that she is, she finds it unpleasant. So much for the Duke of Richmond's prowess!"

Amy's eyes widened in disbelief as this tidbit was revealed, and Barbara burst into laughter. "From the look on your bride's face, Greystone, I would wager you share none of Richmond's shortcomings!"

Try as he might, Colin couldn't help but laugh at Barbara's

vulgarity, and after taking a moment to digest Barbara's meaning, a red-cheeked Amy joined in.

"Ah, Colin." Barbara's blue eyes danced with mischief. "I see you finally found someone with a sense of humor."

Amy cocked her head, and a slightly bewildered look overcame her features.

"It's old history, my dear," Barbara explained with a wave of her elegant hand. "But let me be the first to welcome you to court. So refreshing to have a new face in the crowd. We're all so blasted bored of one another!"

Colin was inordinately pleased. It was the most ringing endorsement he'd ever heard Barbara give another lady, and it boded well indeed for Amy's acceptance into society.

Just then a courtier came up to curry favor with Barbara, and with a roll of her eyes, she departed.

Amy turned to Colin. "I didn't know you were friends with Lady Castlemaine."

"As Barbara said, love, it's a small circle. Everyone knows everyone else."

"But you seem to know her *especially* well," Amy pointed out, her voice tinged with an unmistakable touch of jealousy.

"Is *that* what you're thinking?" It warmed his heart to find Amy so covetous of his person. "Me? With Barbara Palmer?" He shuddered expressively. "Why, she's five years older than I am!"

Amy laughed. "That's not so great a difference! How long have you known her?"

"We knew each other in exile, and she was all of fifteen when she took up with Lord Chesterfield. She went straight from him to Charles—with some overlap, I suspect, since her oldest daughter, although recognized by His Majesty, bears a striking resemblance to Chesterfield." Colin's voice took on a melodramatic tone. "So, you see, I never got my chance with her." He sighed theatrically.

"Oh, my," Amy said. "What shocking scandals are to be discovered by attending court!"

"Enjoying yourself, my dear?"

The voice was resonant and impressive—it was King Charles, talking to *her*. She turned and gazed up at him in disbelief. As tall as Colin, or perhaps an inch higher, he was even more extraordinary standing beside her than he had been upon his throne. She grinned and nodded, the only reply she was capable of at the moment.

"Amy is a bit overwhelmed, I'm afraid," Colin answered for her.

"I am *not*," she retorted, finding her voice again. "I'm having a splendid time, Your Majesty."

Charles smiled down at her, his even white teeth flashing beneath his black mustache. "We're so pleased to have you here, Lady Greystone. A new face, and such a lovely one at that."

Amy colored—becomingly, she hoped. However, to her great consternation, she seemed to have lost her ready wit. "Thank you, sire" was all she could manage.

"The next dance is a minuet. Might you know it?"

She remembered Robert scoffing at her dancing lessons. The elegant minuet was staid enough even for a pregnant cow. "Oh, yes. It's one of my favorites."

Colin discreetly elbowed her in the ribs. Before coming to court, he'd explained that ladies were supposed to ask the king to dance, not vice versa, and she had duly noted the information. But she hadn't expected to make use of it.

Was His Majesty hinting that he wished to dance the minuet with *her*?

She looked up at Colin, and he nodded circumspectly.

"Would—would you care to dance the minuet with me, Your Majesty?" she stammered out.

King Charles proved a superb dancer. As he gazed into her eyes, Amy realized with a start that although his looks were far from the classic English standard, he was the most blatantly sensual man she'd ever met. She supposed she shouldn't be surprised he'd already sired eight acknowledged royal bastards, plus, most assumed, an undetermined number of unacknowledged children as well.

Charles possessed many talents, not the least of which was an uncanny ability to put his companions at ease. By the time he returned Amy to Colin, she was laughing along with him as though they'd been the best of friends for years.

"Don't tell me you've fallen in love with him, too?" Colin teased. Turning her so they were both facing Charles, he wrapped his arms around her from behind. "You won't be the first, and you certainly won't be the last," he warned.

Bright color flooded Amy's cheeks, for he spoke a partial truth: She was halfway in love with King Charles already, and there was nothing for it. His charm was too powerful to resist, and the prospect of a friendship with the King of England, albeit platonic, was too exciting to pass up.

Charles laughed in response. "Don't worry on that account, Greystone. Your prowess with a sword is legendary, and something tells me you wouldn't wear a cuckold's horns gracefully."

Colin dropped a kiss on the top of Amy's head. "Neither," he said pointedly, "would Lady Castlemaine."

Charles threw back his head, and a rumble of laughter poured forth. "You're quite right about that. And I've no wish to be skewered by either of you!"

Though no one would dare challenge the king for any slight either real or imagined, they shared a laugh at the absurd scenario. Then the king sobered, took Colin by the arm, and pulled him aside. "Will you come into my laboratory with me? I've something important to show you."

"Of course. Amy?"

"I'll be fine, Colin." In fact, the Duke of Buckingham was already making his way toward her.

It seemed Barbara was right. The courtiers were dying for a diversion, and having danced with Charles, Amy's popularity was a *fait accompli.*

SEVENTY-THREE

*H*ANDS BEHIND his back, the king paced determinedly through the Long Gallery, a dozen of his beloved spaniels yapping at his and Colin's heels.

"I need to beg a favor from you, Greystone."

"Anything, Charles. You know you need only to ask. What is it?"

His Majesty eyed the busy passage. "Wait till we're in the laboratory; it's the only chamber in all of Whitehall where I'm afforded privacy." Frowning, he paused on the threshold to the Royal Bedchamber. "Od's fish, how did they get here before me?"

With a sigh, he shouldered his way through the cluster of courtiers who gathered there day and night, competing shamelessly to do him the smallest personal favors.

"Would you like your slippers, sire?"

"A warming brick for your bed?"

"A cup of chocolate?"

"No. No, thank you. No." Charles beckoned Colin after him, the spaniels darting in their wake. "Quick, into the laboratory before someone offers to hold my chamber pot for me."

Colin laughed as they shut the door behind them, the clamoring courtiers and barking dogs safely on the other side. "And why not? I hear tell the French court obliges Louis so."

"Louis the Fourteenth I'm not," Charles said dryly.

After the confusion of the public areas, the laboratory seemed eerily quiet. Colin's gaze swept over the profusion of paraphernalia. "Ford would have the time of his life in here," he said, making a mental note to secure him an invitation.

King Charles only nodded distractedly. The ill-synchronized chiming of his clock collection accentuated the expectant silence. Colin leaned back against a counter, nearly knocking over a telescope in the process. As he whirled to right it, Charles drew a deep breath.

"I'm certain you've heard about our embarrassment at the hands of the Dutch."

"I've been out *in* the country, not out *of* the country," Colin replied in an attempt at wry humor.

The king seemed so very serious.

Just two days earlier, the Dutch War had escalated, with disastrous results. Aided by a lack of defense funding and interest from the English government, the Dutch had cruised right up the River Thames, burned three of the largest vessels of the Royal Navy, and sailed back out to sea with the pride of the English fleet, the flagship the *Royal Charles*, towed behind them as a prize. It was, so far, the most humiliating moment of Charles's reign.

Yesterday, Charles and his brother James had been on the scene, supervising the sinking of ships in the Thames and its creeks to block a second attack. But it had been too little, too late.

Nobody commented upon Charles's hard work in defense of the Thames. To the contrary, the talk in London was about how he'd spent the night of the catastrophe dining with his son Monmouth, in the company of his mistress Castlemaine, where they all passed a merry evening hunting a moth around the chamber. He was suffering mightily for his exaggerated reputation of pursuing pleasure over responsibility. The Dutch War had to come to a conclusion, and soon.

"The first step towards peace is to detach Louis from the Dutch," Charles explained, revealing his plan. "With the French as our ally, the Dutch will be forced to negotiate a treaty."

"Why should Louis want to side with us?" Colin asked. "Because he's your cousin?"

Charles shook his head. "One cannot rely on family relationships in foreign policy. At present, Louis covets their territory more than he desires our colonies." He picked at some lint on his velvet surcoat. "Louis has no real quarrel with England. Indeed, my reign has seen only one battle between us, and he emerged such a clear victor that he must be inclined to cooperate now."

Colin frowned, confused. "I've heard of no fighting with France," he ventured cautiously. He walked around the chamber, skimming a hand over microscopes, magnets, and air pumps.

"It was a social battle," Charles conceded with a sigh. He began pacing. "Since the fire, I've grown weary of the complicated fripperies we adorn ourselves with here at court. Plumes, periwigs, lace, ruffles, ribbons, chains...it's all quite ridiculous, don't you agree?"

Colin couldn't have agreed more, as evidenced by his pared-down version of court apparel. Still, as Charles himself had brought the dandified fashions from the Continent, a prudent courtier wouldn't be too quick to assent. "One could look at it that way," he said guardedly.

"Last October, I designed for myself a more reserved costume. A long black coat, slashed here and there to show a white shirt, with a close-fitting waistcoat to match. Quite practical, I thought."

"And?" Colin failed to see what this had to do with the Dutch War, or a supposed French War, or any war at all.

"Well, Louis heard about it and promptly dressed all his footmen in my new uniform. I'm afraid the new style was blown out of existence by a gale of laughter," Charles lamented. He stopped pacing and turned to Colin. "A surprise attack, and a clean victory."

Colin had to choke back laughter. Louis XIV, the so-called "Sun King," had pulled off a prank of such unmitigated virtuosity, it turned Colin green with envy.

What a coup!

"I suppose it's just as well," King Charles added mournfully.

"Even though the court, naturally, followed my lead, I heard later that they all felt like blasted penguins."

They both shared a laugh over that, which was a relief to Colin, since he was about to explode anyway.

When the last chuckles had died away and the king's face had settled back into worried lines, Colin asked carefully, "And what is it that I can do for you?"

Charles took a step closer. "I need you to carry a letter to my mother in Paris. I cannot correspond with Louis directly; it would raise suspicion."

The last thing Colin wanted to do was leave Amy, pregnant and vulnerable, to travel to France, a place full of sad childhood memories. He hated France. And there was the debt—what would happen to the estate's productivity without him there to oversee it?

He took a slow, deep breath and looked up from the pendulum he was playing with. "Why me? Why not Buckingham, or Arlington or Lauderdale? Such missions are part of their positions. I'm not involved in royal intelligence."

"Exactly. If I sent any of them to the Continent, they'd be followed. It's imperative these negotiations remain secret—if the Dutch suspect my designs, they'll present counterarguments to Louis before he even considers my plan."

"But there must be someone else. Someone with a lower government appointment, whom no one would notice."

"Why so reluctant?" Charles flashed a teasing grin. "The Chases have never hesitated to do my bidding before." Serious now, he put a hand on Colin's arm. "I'm sorry, but I've considered this carefully, and you're the perfect candidate. No one will question your visit to my mother; you were always close to Henrietta Maria, almost like a foster son. And no one will question when she visits Louis, her favorite nephew, afterwards."

The plan was flawless, except that Colin wanted no part of it. He swallowed hard and moved away, rearranging some bottles of chemicals. "This is a bad time to leave Amy."

She'd seemed so melancholy of late, but she always claimed everything was fine.

"Ah, I see," Charles responded with the sort of genuine

sympathy that was an integral part of his charm. "You needn't stay long; no one would expect it, with a child due soon. Just across the Channel, a short visit, and back. Three weeks—a month at the most."

Colin lifted a bottle of cloudy green fluid. A month. A month of the precious time he had left before he'd be forced to fail Amy…before everything would fall apart.

"Your wife will be fine," Charles said. "I'll send her to Greystone with a royal escort. I want you to leave tomorrow."

The bottle clinked to the counter as Colin's head shot up. "Tomorrow?"

"This is very important," Charles said gravely.

"What about Jason?" Colin asked wildly, casting about for any possible replacement.

"Jason would never holiday in France without taking the twins. Everyone knows he takes them everywhere—trying to be the father they never had, I suppose. To leave them home would be out of character, and to bring them along, too visible."

"Ford, then."

"Ford was but a child at the Restoration. My mother wouldn't even recognize him at, what, sixteen?"

"Don't you think people will find my leaving Amy at this time a mite suspicious?"

"No one who'd be watching knows you well. You must admit: for a courtier, you keep a low profile. Your reluctance surely took me by surprise. A happy marriage is the exception these days, after all."

Colin was silent. Defeated. His family had always been there when the Stuarts had needed them, and vice versa. When Colin had asked him, King Charles had granted Lord Hobbs's license without so much as a blink of his royal eye.

But he was torn apart inside. He couldn't take Amy on a sea journey, seven-and-a-half months pregnant, and he couldn't leave her home…he just couldn't…

Charles put a hand on his shoulder and said quietly, "I'm asking you, Colin, as your monarch and *as your friend*, to do this thing for me."

He had no choice.

SEVENTY-FOUR

*B*ENCHLEY LOOKED down his beak nose at Amy standing at the edge of Greystone's quarry.

"My lady, do you not think you've seen enough?"

She scanned the site once more, smiling at the view of the quarrymen dotting the stepped-down ledges. The blows of their hammers rang through the air as they toiled in the hot sun. She watched a huge slab of dimension stone begin to crack away from the face, mentally adding its value to Greystone's ledgers.

"It's doing well," she murmured, satisfied. Treading carefully on the uneven ground, she made her way down the rise and back to the two-seater caleche.

Benchley trailed behind. "In your condition, I cannot imagine why you insist on dragging yourself all over the estate. I shall take you home now."

"Nonsense—I'm with child, not ill. I haven't yet inspected the sheep."

She tried to hoist herself onto the seat, then convulsed in laughter, holding out a hand for his help. "Gad, I think my girth has doubled since Colin left for France. I've been wondering if he'll recognize me upon his return." At Benchley's wide-eyed look, she couldn't resist shocking him more. "I've also been wondering how a babe this size can possibly fit out of me, but Lydia assures me it will work."

The tips of Benchley's ears turned red. He picked up the reins and clucked at the horse.

"I try not to think about it too much," Amy added brightly.

"Excellent plan," he choked out, staring straight ahead.

During the thirty-minute drive from the quarry perched on one side of Greystone to the grazing fields bordering the other end, Amy digested what she'd seen. Though but a small portion of Greystone's income, the tiny quarry it was named for was producing well. Sky-high stacks of newly cut wood from the estate's abundant forests waited to be sold. The crops were coming in nicely, though she was glad Colin would be home for the harvest—she hadn't a clue what to do about that.

She'd brought the ledgers up to date, delighted to discover that Greystone had become self-supporting and then some. There looked to be a small profit due in the fall. She wondered why Colin had seemed so worried; did he not realize that?

She could hardly wait for him to come home so she could tell him. She missed him fiercely, his reassuring smile and the heavenly feel of his arms around her, especially when she lay alone at night in their big bed. She missed him more than she missed working with gold and diamonds.

Marry come up, she loved him. When he made it home, she'd tell him so—a million times. Maybe he would have missed her, too. Maybe he'd be truly happy then.

The caleche rolled to a halt. While Benchley went off to hail a shepherd, Amy lowered her ungainly body to the ground. She perched carefully on the low fence and swung her legs over.

As she ambled through the pasture, the long summer grasses seemed to undulate on the rolling hills. Their fresh scent tickled her nose. It was quiet out here, the silence broken only by the occasional bleat of the sheep. When a lamb came toddling up and butted his head against her skirts, she reached down to let him lick her hand.

"Lady Greystone?"

"Yes." She turned and smiled at the shepherd; no apple-cheeked nursery rhyme boy, but a grown man much older than she. "I trust the sheep are doing well?"

"I…" Lifting one weathered hand, he removed his cap and

rubbed his bald head. "Do you know anything of sheep, my lady?"

"No. No, I don't. But—"

"That youngster there has bluetongue." He kicked a pebble and pulled the cap back over his brow. "I'm sorry, my lady."

"Sorry?" She looked down at the fluffy animal nuzzling her hand. "Bluetongue?"

"An illness. Swelling of the nose and lips, bleeding in the mouth, and—"

"Mucous," she finished for him, wiping her palm on her skirt.

"My lady!" Benchley rushed to unearth a handkerchief and thrust it into her hands.

The shepherd knelt to pry open the lamb's mouth. "See?"

"Bluetongue." Amy took a deep breath and wadded up the sticky handkerchief. "Or bluish-tongue, anyway. What does it mean?" She ran her fingers through the animal's thick wool. "Are they all ill? Surely we can still shear them come time?"

The man rose slowly. "Those that still live." With a sad smile, he patted the lamb on the head. "More than half of the ill ones have died already, and more fall sick every day."

"What?" Amy's heart sank. The profit she'd calculated depended on projected income from the wool. She'd assumed the production would be consistent with last year's. "Can't you make them get better?"

"I know of no treatment." He shifted on his feet, took the cap off and replaced it again. "Lord Greystone, he keeps up with the newest ideas, but he hied himself off to London and has yet to return."

"Did he know of this?" Perhaps this was why Colin had seemed so melancholy.

"No. He left before it started. It spreads very quickly."

"Oh," Amy said blankly. "Thank you."

"My lady." The shepherd bowed and touched his cap. She would never get used to that deference, she thought vaguely as she watched him walk away, the lamb following at his heels.

"Dear heavens," she breathed, making her way back to the caleche. "Colin will really be unhappy now."

"Pardon, my lady?" Benchley raised a hand to help her up.

"Nothing, Benchley. Just talking to myself."

Her stomach felt leaden at the thought of Colin's homecoming. Now instead of greeting him with good news, she'd be reporting a sure loss of income and the need to replace expensive livestock.

She couldn't stand it, she thought as she plopped onto the seat. She really couldn't stand it. After all the work he'd put into this land, now to be saddled with her and a baby on the way, plus unexpected monetary problems…well, it just wasn't fair.

Colin deserved better than this. After all he'd done for her, was there nothing she could do for him?

She folded her hands over the mound of her stomach.

Yes, there certainly was.

SEVENTY-FIVE

*C*OLIN LOOKED again at the crumpled paper, then up at the street sign. Quai de la Tournelle. And there was the shop, Talbot Joaillerie.

For people driven out of England, the Talbots had certainly managed to land in a luxurious location. A plaque with Louis XIV's warrant was prominently displayed in the window.

"This is it," he said, stuffing the paper back into his pocket. At the cabbie's blank look, he uttered a quick *"Merci"* and thrust a few coins into his hand.

He pushed on the door, but the shop was locked. Was it past six o'clock already? Colin absently patted his surcoat, looking for his pocket watch, then froze as he remembered.

The accursed highwaymen had taken it. What a journey this had been—one disaster after another. He should never have returned to this loathsome country.

He plucked the sleeve of a passing pedestrian. *"Excusez-moi, monsieur. Avez-vous l'heure exacte?"*

The man walked past as though he hadn't seen him. Accursed Parisians literally wouldn't give you the time of day. Colin couldn't wait to get home. No matter if the crossing were as rough on the return as it had been on the way here—he could puke his guts out and be happy for it.

He pounded on the door. And pounded. And pounded. Five

minutes passed before a petite, attractive middle-aged woman pressed her nose against the window.

"*Il est six heures et quart, Monsieur,*" she scolded, pointing to the sign that listed their business hours.

"I wish to speak with you," Colin called through the glass.

"Good heavens, you're English!" she exclaimed, moving to unlock the door. She ushered him inside. "Come in, come in! I've nothing on display, but—"

"It's you I wish to see, not jewelry, madame. You're Elizabeth Talbot, I presume?" She nodded her dark head, clearly puzzled. "I'm Colin Chase—"

"Earl of Greystone and my Amy's husband," she finished for him. Delight lit her blue eyes. "I should have guessed. She described you in her letters as devastatingly handsome."

Colin felt his face heat. "Madame Talbot—"

"You must call me Aunt Elizabeth," she said, wrapping him into an embrace.

Following an awkward moment, Colin hugged her back, feeling a personal connection for the first time in weeks.

She smiled when she pulled away. "Will you come upstairs and have a cup of tea?"

"Tea?"

"Oh, I know it's a frightfully expensive delicacy, but a stuffy marquis gifted me with a supply after we designed a diamond collar for his poodle. These French!" she added with a laugh as he followed her up the staircase.

~

"*J*'M SO GLAD you saw fit to call on me," Elizabeth said after she'd hung a kettle of water over the fire. "But you didn't bring my Amy, did you?" She said it with mock disapproval, craning her neck as though he might have hidden her niece behind his back. "No, I can see you did not. I shall have to make do with you." She collected two porcelain cups, studying him with a sidelong glance as she set them on a tray. "My, but you're nice to look at. I think you'll do fine, after all."

Colin laughed, favoring her with one of his grins. He would swear she was flirting.

"Come into the sitting room, will you?" She handed him the tray, sailing past him with a swish of her skirts. A soft jasmine scent swirled after her. "You're here on king's business?"

Trailing behind her, he nearly dropped the tray. "How…"

Her musical laugh filled the air. "You'd be surprised what I know of you, my boy." Her lips twitched in amusement as she took the tray from him and set it on a table, waving him into a chair. "How did it go?"

"Not well, at first," he said carefully. How much could she know? "On the ride from Calais, my stagecoach was beset by highwaymen."

Gracefully seating herself, she raised a brow at him. "Not an auspicious start."

"To say the least." He hitched himself forward. "As I was carrying little cash, the felons took my ring—the ring Amy made for me." He rubbed the spot where it used to be, more angry every time he thought of it. "I would have run them through with my sword, but there were three of them, bearing pistols, and just one of me—"

"Amy would think you could handle them."

"She might at that." Her teasing expression coaxed a smile. "In any case, I know better, and none of the other victims seemed inclined to help."

An expectant silence filled the room. Elizabeth smoothed her skirts. "And Henrietta Maria? How did it go with her?"

Colin's jaw dropped open. "What has Amy written to you?"

"Not to worry." She waved a hand. "Only that you were visiting the king's mother on king's business. No details." Elizabeth cocked her head. "Does she know any?"

Colin nodded.

"Then she knows how to keep her mouth shut. As for writing of you…you know how it is when you're young and in love, and you look for excuses to say—or write—your loved one's name."

"I cannot say that I do," he said wryly. "I surmise circumstances forced me to grow up too quickly to be young and in love at the same time."

Elizabeth just kept on smiling.

Colin rose, pacing to the fireplace. "In any case, the Dowager Queen didn't see fit to be in residence. I cooled my heels for ten days, waiting for her return. After all that, I wouldn't have been surprised had she refused to act on her son's letter, but fortunately, that was the one thing that went right."

He toyed with a shepherdess figurine on the mantel, its frilly pink skirts reminding him of Henrietta Maria, who he trusted was on her way to Versailles to visit her nephew.

"And then?" Amy's aunt fixed him with a penetrating look. "Come on, boy, spit it out. I'm sure you wouldn't go out of your way to visit an old woman for the joy of it."

"Old woman, eh? Now you're fishing for return compliments." He laughed. "I can see right through you, Aunt Elizabeth."

"And I can see right through you. You're concerned about something, and don't try to tell me otherwise."

Uncomfortable under her knowing gaze, he walked to a window and swept aside the lace curtain. He gazed down at the bustling Parisian street. "Madame—Aunt Elizabeth—I came to ask a favor."

"Anything, my boy."

"If you could see your way clear to accompany me to Greystone for a visit, I'd be more than grateful." His hand dropped, and the lace fell back to shroud the window. "As I'm sure you know, Amy is due to bear our first child soon, and your presence would make it much easier."

He turned toward her slowly, surprising himself with a sudden wish to confide in someone for the first time in his memory. But he couldn't find the words to begin.

Elizabeth rose and came near. Her jasmine scent reminded him of someone...

His mother?

She smiled. "I suspect you may need something stronger than tea for this discussion. May I prevail on you to squire me out for supper? With William away in Antwerp, I find myself weary of dining alone." Her hand brushed his arm, and she raised a brow. "What say you to La Tour d'Argent?"

"*Restaurant* La Tour d'Argent? With no notice? I hear tell duels are fought to obtain a table there."

"Not to worry, my boy, you won't have to fence for your supper." Elizabeth's eyes sparkled. "The owner's wife has been coveting a bracelet in my window...I'm certain we can strike a bargain."

SEVENTY-SIX

"*ANGUILLE DES bois, madame.*" With a flourish, the server set a pewter plate before Elizabeth. "*Et pour vous,* Lord Greystone"—Colin smiled at the hacked pronunciation of his name, but gave the man points for trying—"*Poule d'Afrique.*"

The savory scent of the delicacy wafted to Colin's nose, but it failed to entice him. He sighed as the server walked away. "As I was saying, Amy is unhappy. I'm sure of it, though she says otherwise. I fear it's because she broke her vow to wed me, and—"

"Her vow?" A frown appeared between Elizabeth's blue eyes.

"She promised her father—your late brother..."

She nodded, indicating she wasn't too fragile to discuss him.

"She made him promises," Colin explained. "To continue the traditions of Goldsmith and Sons. To save her inheritance for future generations. There's more, and to hear her tell of it, these vows might as well have been signed in blood. She's miserable, and there's not a deuced thing I can do about it."

"Nothing?" Her bejeweled fingers toyed with her pewter goblet. "Nothing at all?"

"Not without giving her up." His voice caught, and he looked down to his plate, slowly cutting a bite of his hen. "She cannot run a shop and live with me at Greystone. And I cannot seem to make her happy there." The delicious entree could have been boiled wood chips for all it appealed to Colin. He chewed and swallowed, then brought his gaze to Elizabeth's. "I thought love would be enough, but it doesn't seem to be. Not enough for her."

"Colin—"

"It's my fault, not hers," he said through clenched teeth. A sip of his wine failed to compose him. "I manipulated her—tricked her into marrying me because I couldn't stand to lose her." He took another gulp. "It was wrong. Terribly wrong. I knew all along someone in my position hasn't the luxury of wedding for love, but I lost my mind over your niece. Now everything's a mess."

Elizabeth took a dainty bite of her eel, waiting.

He gazed out the window by their table. The Seine glowed orange in the sunset. The last rays glinted off the spire of Nôtre-Dame, making his eyes water. "There's more…"

"Yes?" Her voice came quiet.

"Did Amy mention I'd been betrothed to someone else?"

"You'd be surprised—" Elizabeth started.

"What you know of me," Colin finished dryly, looking back to her. "Well, I'd wager you don't know that I owe the lady's father a fortune—even Amy doesn't know that. Due at the end of the year."

Her delicate eyebrows rose. "And…"

"I cannot pay it." He shook his head, his hands fisting under the table. "I cannot pay it. I'll be forced to use Amy's inheritance to avoid losing Greystone." His breath came hard and fast. "She'll *really* hate me then."

"Will she?" Elizabeth murmured. He watched her graceful hands as she rearranged her cutlery. Jeweler's hands, like Amy's. "You're asking Amy to give up everything that made her what she is—that made her the girl you love. Would you give up everything for her?"

"Give up Greystone? If it were Greystone or Amy?" Had the pewter goblet been glass instead, it would have broken in his grip. He set it down, lest he spill on the snow-white cloth. "There are expectations in my world. For heaven's sake, the *king* granted me this property, this title. How can I fail him? What could I offer my children? I grew up without a home. I know what that feels like."

"From what Amy has told me, you grew up without love as well…and which was the greater loss?"

Below the window, a boat drifted lazily by. Its passengers' lighthearted laughter swirled through the open shutters, melding with the conversational buzz that filled the elegant candlelit room.

Had he ever been so carefree?

If it were Greystone or Amy, which would he choose?

His stomach clenched. It *was* Greystone or Amy.

He had to choose.

"I won't take Amy's gold," he blurted, vaguely wondering if he looked more surprised than Elizabeth. He drew a deep breath. "If I do, I'll lose her. Emotionally, even should she choose to stay. So I won't take it. I just won't." With a motion that spoke of finality, he speared a bite of chicken and forked it into his mouth. "There."

Elizabeth's response was quiet and thoughtful. "Do you reckon it must come to that?"

"Yes. I gave her my word. I cannot betray her." He shifted on his chair, meeting her gaze. "Yes."

She just looked at him for a long moment, her expression unreadable. Then her features softened with a gentle smile, and she raised her goblet in a toast.

"Well, my boy, when do we leave for England?"

SEVENTY-SEVEN

*C*OLIN POKED his head out of the carriage, frowning at the unmistakable sounds of construction. His gaze followed the circular drive as he slowly stepped to the gravel.

Atop the great hall, a new slate roof glistened in the sunshine.

Suddenly weak in the knees, he leaned against the carriage. Criminy, if she'd spent his small savings on a new roof, thinking to surprise him...

But no, it didn't matter. Not now that he'd decided to forfeit Greystone, regardless.

His attention was diverted as Amy slammed out the front door and bounded toward him, as fast as her swollen girth would allow.

"Colin! I'm so glad you're home!"

She threw herself at him, the mound of her stomach bouncing off his solid form. With a shaky laugh, he reached to set her aright, then crushed her against himself, burying his nose in her rose-scented hair. "Heavens, I missed you."

She pulled back, a radiant smile on her face, then lunged at him again, as though to convince herself he was really there.

He half-laughed, half-groaned, the gravel crunching beneath his feet as he shifted. "What is going on here?" he asked, gesturing at the roof.

Her smiled widened, then she gasped when she looked past him. "Aunt Elizabeth?"

As her aunt stepped down from the carriage, Colin ventured a small smile of his own. "It seems we both had surprises for each other."

"Oh, Colin! Aunt Elizabeth!" As she let out a cry of pleasure, enclosing her aunt in an enthusiastic embrace, Colin's smile turned genuine.

She was such a joy...how could he have ever considered betraying her, even for a moment? Any sacrifice was worth it, so long as he retained her trust. And her love.

All at once, the old fear started melting away. Here with Amy again, it seemed marrying for love was the best thing he could have done for himself and his children, no matter the consequences.

Wherever they ended up living, they'd be happy, because they'd be together.

Amy tugged on his hand. "Wait till you see the inside! Did you notice the new windows as you drove up? The downstairs chambers are ready for furniture, and our suite upstairs is nearly—"

She stopped when he didn't budge.

He *couldn't* budge.

He felt rooted to the ground. He didn't want to see all the improvements, his home restored like he'd dreamed, only to hand it all over to Hobbs.

The buzzard.

He backed up and sat on the carriage step. "Amy, love...just give me a minute to get used to this."

"There's more! I bought more sheep, and the thresher. And the mill is fixed."

He squeezed his eyes shut.

"Colin?" She jiggled his arm. "Colin, are you all right?" She gave a nervous giggle. "I'm the one who's supposed to feel faint these days."

"I'm fine," he whispered. "Did you spend it all?"

"Spend it all?" Her laugh rang through the courtyard. "Have

you any idea what those diamonds are worth? Or how much gold a trunk will hold?"

His eyes flew open. "Diamonds? Gold?"

Why did she always make him feel so dense?

Her laughter tapered off into the heavy summer air. "Did you think I would spend Greystone's accounts?" she asked slowly. "Without asking?"

"I..." He rose, but his knees still felt weak. "Are you saying, then—"

"I want you to have it, Colin. I want you to be happy." Her hand moved to the bulge of their child. "The gold was meant as security for my son, was it not?" Her amethyst eyes glistened with tears as she gazed up at him. "What could be more secure than an earldom and acres of land? The fortune will be there, in the crops planted in the fertile soil, in the stone walls of the castle and the shingles on the great hall's roof. I should have realized it months ago." One tear escaped and traced a path down her cheek. "I'm sorry."

"You're sorry...?" His hand came up to wipe away that single tear, warm against the pad of his fingertip. A peculiar grayness crept to fog his vision. He gathered her against him, holding her tight.

Holding himself up.

She was the pregnant one—he was *not* going to faint.

SEVENTY-EIGHT

*H*IS **EXPRESSION** unreadable, Colin approached their bed the next morning and handed Amy a letter decorated with an all-too-familiar red seal. A pain clenched her middle as her eyes scanned down the page, past lines of neat, flourished script, the product of many years of tutoring, to the bottom, where it was signed, "Your very loving friend, Charles R."

"Dear heavens," she groaned. The parchment rustled as she dropped it to the bed. "Not another summons, another favor."

Colin's laugh boomed through the chamber. "Read it, lazy-bones." He stalked to the window and pushed open the drapes. "It's only a letter saying a treaty with the Dutch was signed three days ago at Breda, and thanking me for service performed on behalf of England."

She blinked against the sunshine flooding the chamber. "Thank heavens for small favors." When he came to kiss her on the forehead, she flashed him a teasing smile. "I would have thrown you into the oubliette before I let you go this time. Six weeks you were gone!" She made a half-hearted attempt to sit up, then fell back against her pillows, defeated. She sighed. "I don't remember going to bed last night."

"You fell asleep in the middle of a sentence. Been lying awake missing me all those weeks?"

He sat on the bed and leaned to kiss her again, his teeth nibbling at her bottom lip, sending her pulse racing. He smiled against her mouth. "I never got the chance to thank you for sharing your inheritance—"

"There's no need—"

"—and for saving Greystone."

"Saving Greystone?" She brushed her fingertips over his scratchy cheeks. "Perhaps I made things a bit easier for you, but Greystone would have done well in the long run, regardless. It's a fine estate."

"A fine estate, yes." He took her hands. "But it would have been Lord Hobbs's fine estate."

"Lord Hobbs's?"

"I owe him money. From Priscilla's dowry, due at the close of the year. It would have been Newgate Prison for me, or Greystone for him." He gave a rueful laugh. "Coward that I am, I'm afraid he would have ended up with Greystone."

"But there was always the gold—"

He quieted her with a kiss. "I promised you I'd never take it, love."

He'd been willing to give up everything for her.

Sudden tears flooded her eyes. "A Chase promise is not given lightly," she murmured, hearing Jason say so in her head. Back at Cainewood, nearly a year ago.

It seemed like a lifetime had passed.

"No, it's never given lightly," Colin agreed. "Most especially to those we love. Now, get some rest while I tour the estate."

One more kiss, his lips soft, lingering on hers.

A hand on the doorjamb, he paused on his way out. "Are you happy?"

"Happy?" she asked in a daze. "I've never been happier in my life."

At that moment, it was true. The smile transformed her face long after Colin's footsteps had faded down the corridor.

He loved her.

SEVENTY-NINE

"**YOU SHOULD** be resting, child." Aunt Elizabeth entered the study and settled herself on the couch. "Your time is near."

"I felt a sudden urge to straighten this desk." Amy sorted through the heap of yellowed receipts she'd found crammed in the bottom drawer, then held one up. "This is dated 1660, the year King Charles granted Greystone to Colin. My husband is a secret sluggard." She grinned. "Besides, I'm not made for resting; you know that."

"Your Uncle William says the same thing about me. The Goldsmith curse, he calls it."

The paper fluttered to the desk. "The Goldsmith curse," Amy repeated in a whisper, thinking not of the work ethic, but her cursed promise.

The Goldsmith curse.

"What did you say, dear?"

"Nothing. It's nothing."

The room fell quiet except for the rustle of paper. Amy felt Aunt Elizabeth's gaze following her as she moved back and forth, filing the receipts.

"What's wrong, child?" Aunt Elizabeth asked at last, her voice heavy with loving sympathy.

Amy's eyes filled with tears. Her emotions were so close to the surface these days; she was either violently happy or in the depths of despair; there seemed to be no middle ground.

"I don't know, Aunty." She leaned both palms on the desk, staring down, studying the grain in the wood. "I was so happy this morning."

"This wouldn't have something to do with a vow to your father, would it?"

Amy watched a tear splash onto the scarred surface of Colin's desk. "How did you know?"

"Colin." A long sigh escaped Aunt Elizabeth's lips. "But you haven't discussed this with him, have you?"

Amy shook her head.

"For heaven's sake, child, how can you let a promise to a dead man stand in the way of your happiness?"

"He told me I cannot have everything," Amy said in a tiny voice.

"Colin said that?" Aunt Elizabeth sounded incredulous.

"No, Papa said it."

"Oh, balderdash. My brother was a lot of things, but open-minded wasn't one of them."

Amy flinched with a sudden cramp in her middle. "Yet it's true, isn't it?" she said when the pain eased. "I'm with Colin now, and I have so much. I must learn to live with the fact that I cannot have everything."

"Poppycock. Hugh couldn't possibly have foreseen your future. He's dead, Amy. The shop is gone." Her voice gentled. "You're a countess, child. Were your father here today, do you honestly think he'd withhold his blessing?"

"I don't know." Amy dropped onto Colin's chair. "Goldsmith and Sons was everything to Papa."

Sighing, Aunt Elizabeth stood up. "You *can* have everything, if you'll but listen to your heart. You need only speak with Colin—"

"About this? He's already told me—"

"He's not your father. Talk to him. You can live up to your vow—perhaps not literally, but the spirit, child. You can live up to the spirit of your vow, if you'll only approach your husband with open trust. He deserves that much, Amy."

She walked around the desk and leaned to kiss Amy on both cheeks. "Think about it. Now, I'm an old woman who has traveled many miles, and I think I need a nap."

Sniffling, Amy ventured a shaky smile. "Good heavens, Aunty. An old woman, indeed!"

Another cramp shot through Amy, but that didn't mean the baby was coming. He couldn't be coming—Colin had left to spend the whole day inspecting the estate.

Besides, she'd been having cramps for nearly eight weeks now, and they'd never meant anything before.

~

GREYSTONE HUMMED with productivity. Colin rode toward the fields at the far end of the property, certain the sheep and crops would prove as well maintained as the timber operation and quarry already had. Amy was a talented estate manager. Almost as talented as she'd been a jeweler.

A jeweler...

He looked down to his hands on Ebony's reins, at the band of white skin that marked where his signet ring used to rest. After all these months, he felt almost naked without it. And Amy...

Amy could make him another.

He smiled to himself, remembering her pride in her craft, the glow in her eyes when she shared the treasures in her trunk. Her joy at discovering the origin of her wedding ring. Her fingers absently caressing the necklace she'd worn to Whitehall Palace.

For certain, she'd enjoy making him another ring.

He reined in as the realization stole his breath away.

Hang it, what an idiot he'd been! She missed her craft—it was in her blood, as much a part of her as her amethyst eyes and her quick smile. She'd make him another ring, and then...

He knew how to make her happy.

Colin wheeled round toward the castle. The rest of the estate could wait for an inspection. He couldn't wait to see Amy's face when he told her. The distracted, sad look would leave her eyes. She'd throw her arms around him, kissing him all over his face in that exuberant way of hers.

He dug in his heels, urging Ebony into a gallop.

EIGHTY

"**M**Y LADY,**"** Lydia called from the study door. "Dinner is ready."

With a fierce effort, Amy opened her eyes and unclenched her fists.

"Milady?" Lydia's eyes widened until they were round blue circles. "Is it the baby?"

"No." Amy leaned against the desk. "It's only another one of those little cramps I've been having."

"Are you quite certain?" Lydia walked closer. "This looks… rather different."

"Yes, I'm quite certain," Amy snapped, her face impassive although her middle knotted in the most painful cramp yet.

Dear heavens, it felt like a steel band were squeezing the very life out of her.

"I'm quite certain," she repeated through gritted teeth. "But I believe I'll take dinner in my bedchamber. I could use a nap." She began to walk from the chamber.

"Milady," Lydia called, alarm in her voice. "You're *waddling*."

Amy whirled around. "I am *not* waddling. There's nothing wrong with my legs. Waddling is for pitiful pregnant ninnies who want to draw sympathetic attention to themselves."

She was glad no one was in the corridor to see her, because it was rather impossible to make it to the bedchamber without waddling. She fell awkwardly onto the bed, but before she could get comfortable, a pale straw-colored, sweetish fluid gushed out of her.

She knew what that meant. Lydia had related every detail of her previous five ladies' birth experiences with maximum drama, leaving Amy in a wild state of alarm. Then, last night, Aunt Elizabeth had explained everything in a very calm, informative manner. Amy didn't quite know what to believe, but one thing was clear: When the bag of waters burst, the babe was coming.

No question about that.

Hot tears squeezed from beneath her closed lids as she curled herself into a ball. The babe couldn't come now. Colin wouldn't be here for hours. And she hadn't talked to him yet; Aunt Elizabeth was right—she had to talk to him. She had to trust him.

She wasn't ready for this baby.

The fact that her son was ready, that Aunt Elizabeth had said he'd come this week or next, was beside the point entirely.

When another white-hot spasm clenched her insides, she moaned in pain and frustration. All at once, Lydia barged into the bedchamber, a dinner tray in her hands.

"I knew it!" she exclaimed, staring at the sopping mass of sheets. She dropped the tray forthwith, and Amy would have laughed had she been able.

But her womb tightened more. "He isn't coming out now," she forced through clenched teeth. "I won't let him. I'll keep my legs stuck together."

"But, my lady—"

"My body wouldn't betray me this way," Amy snapped. She'd never felt so out of control. Determined to put an end to this madness, she struggled halfway up as the pain subsided.

Then the truth dawned in a burst of anger and inevitability, and she fell back to the pillows.

"This child is coming whether I want him to or not," she wailed. "There's nothing I can do to stop him. Nothing!"

Lydia's face looked blurry through Amy's fresh onslaught of burning tears. "Send Benchley to find Colin," she said weakly, closing her eyes. "And wake Aunt Elizabeth from her nap. Wake her *now*."

"I already did," Lydia said, kneeling to gather everything back onto the tray. When Amy forced her heavy eyelids open, Lydia amended with, "Wake your aunt, I mean."

Aunt Elizabeth arrived then, stepping over the broken crockery and taking charge.

"I'm hot and sweaty," Amy complained, and Aunt Elizabeth peeled back the covers.

"I'm chilled," she said, shivering, and Aunt Elizabeth piled them back on.

Amy felt nauseated, certain she was going to vomit, then she forgot her queasy stomach as waves of drowsiness overwhelmed her. She jerked awake when the next pain seized her, and the cycle started again. Through it all, Aunt Elizabeth kept up a knowledgeable, reassuring patter.

"You're so nice and helpful, Mrs. Talbot," Lydia said frantically. "Lady Greystone is lucky."

Amy opened her eyes long enough to glare at her.

"Oh, heavens," Lydia breathed, her eyes widening. "Milady, I can see it!" She moved closer and stared between Amy's thighs, but Amy didn't care enough to be embarrassed. "It's a shilling-size circle, covered with slimy black hair."

Amy grimaced, half in pain, half because she'd never heard anything sound quite so disgusting.

"Hush, Lydia!" Aunt Elizabeth admonished. She craned her neck to see Amy's face over the mound of her belly. "It's your baby's head, dear. He's ready to be born."

Aunt Elizabeth signaled Lydia closer and instructed her to hold Amy's hand.

"Push now, Amy," she encouraged. "Push as hard as you can."

Amy took her words to heart. She pushed with all the might she could muster, wanting nothing more than to get this horrible business over with.

"Ouch!" Lydia tried to jerk her hand away, but Amy tightened her grip.

When the pain ended and Lydia reclaimed and massaged her

fingers, Amy felt guilty. Then it started again, and Lydia leaned over her, sweeping the hair off her forehead and clucking sympathetically.

"Will you stop touching me," Amy spat. She seemed trapped on a seesaw of emotions, unable to control herself. As the pain peaked, she squeezed Lydia's hand again, and she couldn't care less if she were hurting her. A tiny part of her was shocked at her behavior, but not enough to change it.

She rested, panting, then pushed, then rested and pushed again. She pushed until she was certain her insides would spill out onto the sheets, but still her son remained stubbornly stuck in her womb.

When the urge to push subsided, she closed her eyes, but the tears were leaking out all over again.

"Push, Amy, push," Aunt Elizabeth yelled.

Oh, no, it was coming again, so soon. Amy's frustrated tears flowed faster. This was so unfair! Her nails dug into the palm of her hand that wasn't clenching Lydia's.

"This isn't the place for you," she heard Aunt Elizabeth say firmly. "Pour yourself a brandy and wait in the study."

The words were more than confusing, but Amy's eyes were shut tight, and she was concentrating on the pushing.

"No," a deep voice countered. "I must speak with Amy."

Her eyes flew open. "Colin?" she moaned through the pain.

He hesitated, his breath coming heavy as though he'd been running. He glanced from Amy to Aunt Elizabeth and back again.

"I just want you to be happy, love." His fingers drumming against one thigh, he looked to where Lydia's gaze was rooted. His eyes widened before he refocused on Amy's face. "I have something I need to ask you, tell you. This is important to me."

When the pain waned, Amy nodded. "Come here. Tell me."

"I miss my ring." He moved toward her, smiling, absently rubbing the spot where it used to be. "Do you suppose you could make me another one?"

"Colin, not now," Aunt Elizabeth growled.

Though the pain had ended for the moment, Amy feared her

heart had stopped instead. "You...you want me to make you a ring?"

"We can build a workshop. I was thinking by the kitchen—"

"Oh, Colin!" Tears sprang to her eyes for the countless time that day. "How did you know? It's just—"

A pain ripped through her, and she grabbed his hand, shutting her eyes, pushing, pushing, pushing. Her son was coming; she could feel his head stretching the entrance to her body.

It was a miracle.

"Will you teach our children your craft?" Colin asked. "Your blood—your jeweler's blood—it runs in this child's veins as much as mine."

"*Your* blood will be running if you don't leave," Aunt Elizabeth warned.

"No, don't leave!" Amy panted, squeezing his hand.

"And if you don't mind living simply—"

"I don't! I've told you that," she wailed as the pain subsided.

"Then we'll save to replace your inheritance. And someday, a younger son who cannot inherit will open the finest shop in London."

"A younger son?" Lydia scoffed, mopping Amy's brow. "Cuds bobs, d'ye think she'll have another after going through this?"

"If you can all shut up for one minute," Aunt Elizabeth interjected, "this baby is about to arrive."

"Colin," Amy breathed.

She had so much she wanted to say, but the urge to push distracted her.

"Amy, it's time," Aunt Elizabeth encouraged. "Push."

Amy pushed hard then, harder, harder still—and her babe slipped out into the world.

"It's a miracle," she managed to choke out. "Everything." Then laughter bubbled up from her throat, even as tears flowed down her cheeks. And their babe's cries added the sweetest sound to the emotional confusion.

Colin moved toward the foot of the bed, his eyes registering sheer disbelief as his child was wiped off and wrapped in a blanket. Aunt Elizabeth set the wriggling bundle on Amy's abdomen, opened the blanket halfway, and used clean linen strips to tie the cord in two places.

Then Colin touched his offspring for the first time, holding the child still while the pulsing lifeline was severed.

"It's a miracle," Amy whispered to herself. Her precious son. Colin's wonderful plan to assure Goldsmith & Sons would rise again. Her love for Colin and—the biggest miracle of all—his for her.

All of it—a miracle.

She held her wailing babe snug to her chest, afraid to crush him, but afraid to let him go. Ever.

She gazed into Colin's eyes, fresh tears of joy flowing from her own. "Would you mind very much," she said tremulously, "if we called him Hugh, after my father?"

The warm sound of Colin's laughter brought a smile to her lips. "If it's very important to you, we will, love," he choked out, "but I'm afraid the other little girls might tease her."

"The other little girls?" She blinked, confused. "It's a girl? *A girl?* Impossible." She opened the blanket a bit, slipping Colin a sidelong glance. "It would be just like you to play a prank like this."

But there she was, pink-toed and perfect. Amy tore off the blankets and cradled her sniffling daughter against her own skin, rocking her instinctively.

"How could I ever have thought she was a boy?" she wondered of a sudden. "She's been a girl all along. This infinitely precious girl is mine."

Her daughter quieted then, cuddled against Amy's familiar body, her ear on Amy's chest, listening to the heartbeat that had sustained her for nine long months.

Aunt Elizabeth beckoned to Lydia, and they slipped from the room.

"I can teach her to make jewelry?" Amy asked, gazing up at Colin.

His answer was in his eyes. They bore into hers, unblinking.

"Will it not appear...unseemly?"

He smiled, that old mischievous smile that made her heart turn over. "Are you trying to talk me out of it?"

"No." She took a deep breath. "It's just...too good to be true. Papa said I couldn't have everything, but I do. I have everything."

Just then, their daughter opened her eyes to gaze unfocused at her parents for the very first time.

Her emerald eyes mirrored Colin's own. He reached out to touch one little hand, his heart in his eyes as her tiny fingers wrapped around his big one.

"What a precious jewel," he murmured.

Amy met his gaze, her heart swelling in the shared moment. He was right. Of all the jewels she'd ever made, their daughter was the most precious.

"Jewel," they whispered together.

EPILOGUE

Six years later

JEWEL CLIMBED down the ladder and set it against the wall. Quietly, so her mother wouldn't hear. Then she squeezed through the door—carefully, carefully —since it was open only a tiny bit, just enough for a slip of a six-year-old pixie to fit through.

She skipped through the kitchen, pausing to grab a warm tart from a fresh-baked pile, then across the great hall and down the corridor to the study. Hesitating, she wiped the crumbs from her rosebud mouth and swept the disheveled ebony hair back from her heart-shaped face. Then she placed a delicate hand on the latch and pushed, bursting into the chamber.

"Papa, come quick! Mama's burned herself!"

Papa jumped up from behind his desk. "The workshop?" he called out as he darted past her, and Jewel nodded, then retraced her steps, this time at a run at her father's heels. She hurried to keep up.

"Let it not be bad," Colin whispered. The blast furnace in the workshop could rise to such incredibly high temperatures. "Please let it not be bad."

The workshop door was slightly ajar. He pushed it open

—*scrape, bang*—and a deluge of frigid water poured down on him.

Behind him, Jewel dissolved into hysterical giggles. Colin's wife turned around from her workbench, a knife and wax ring model in her hands.

"She got you," Amy said. "Again." Seeing Colin standing there, drenched, his hair plastered to his head and hanging to his shoulders in thick wet tendrils, she burst into laughter.

Colin reached back to pull his still-giggling daughter into the room. With a violent shake of his head, he sprayed droplets of cold water onto her small head and shoulders. "Jewel Edith Chase," he said with mock severity, "this is getting way out of hand."

"I owed you. For the lemonade."

The previous week, Colin had promised Jewel a cool mug of lemonade after a vigorous fencing lesson, but the concoction he'd given her had been double-strength, no sugar. The pucker on her face had been priceless.

He chuckled now, savoring the memory. "*That* was for the hay," he protested. "How did you do that hay thing, anyway?"

"I'm not telling. We're even now."

"Oh, no, we're not." Colin smiled to himself, then narrowed his eyes at Jewel. "Is it not past your bedtime, young lady?"

"Mama said I could cast my ring tonight."

Amy laughed. "Good try, Jewel, but you spent the evening balancing a bucket of water."

Colin knelt and hugged his daughter to his side. "You can cast your ring tomorrow."

"If I go to bed now, will you tell me a story?"

Colin groaned. "What is this, a negotiation?"

"What's a negotayshun?"

He ruffled her hair. "A negotiation is when—"

"It's when you bat your pretty eyes at your father"—Amy's own eyes glittered with mischief—"and he gives you what you want."

"Amy!" Colin protested.

"Tell me a story, please," Jewel begged, her eyes sparkling with hope. Those emerald eyes that were exactly like his. Amy was right; he could never deny his daughter when she gazed at him like that. "Please, Papa. Tell me the one about when you were in France for the king, and your coach was stopped by hackneymen."

"Highwaymen."

"Whatever. Tell me, *please*."

Those eyes. "As you wish. Go get ready for bed, and I'll come up in a while and tell you the story."

"Can Hugh hear it, too?"

Jewel's brother Hugh was a strapping boy of four who followed his father around like a shadow. The next Earl of Greystone.

And then, of course, there was Aidan. Colin glanced at the sleeping child snuggled in the corner of the workshop. At six months, he still needed Amy near. And he would learn his trade here; his future was here.

"Papa..." His gaze moved from the cradle back to Jewel. "Please, Papa. Hugh loves your stories—you know he does."

"Very well, sweetheart." Emerald eyes sparkled again, and Colin's heart melted a bit more. Would he never get over the wonder of these precious beings entrusted to his care? "Now, go. I'll be along directly," he told her with a sigh.

She went, skipping out into the kitchen as though she hadn't a care in the world. Which was true. And Colin hoped he could keep it that way for a long, long time.

Closing the door, he turned to his wife. "Did you see how ingenious that was?" he asked, amazed at his daughter's creativity. "Look how she connected the bucket's handle to the door latch with a rope, so it wouldn't hit me on the head when it fell off the top of the door. Brilliant. Just brilliant." He shook his head slowly in admiration. "Our daughter is so incredible."

Trust Colin to equate intelligence with a well executed prank, Amy mused, rising from her workbench. She too was convinced their daughter was a genius, but her opinion stemmed from Jewel's reading ability and thirst for knowledge.

"I know what she did." Amy pushed the wet hair off Colin's face and wrapped her arms around his waist. "I was here, working."

"And you let her do it, anyway."

"Of course—you deserved it after the lemonade. Besides, she thinks she went unnoticed. She was quiet as a mouse, and I kept my back to her the whole time."

"So you're an accessory to the crime," Colin accused, with that devastating smile that made Amy's heart turn over, even after all these years.

"I suppose one could conclude that."

"Which reminds me: How did she manage that hay trick? You must know."

Amy did know. Jewel and Benchley, whom she'd long ago charmed into acting as her willing accomplice, had placed a board against the open wardrobe and stuffed hay behind it, then closed the door most of the way, pulled the board, and slammed the wardrobe shut. When Colin opened it to hang his shirt on a peg, he'd turned into a human haystack.

Watching from their bed, Amy had laughed herself sick. Jewel had run in, crowing with delight, prompting Colin to initiate a wrestling match that resulted in an explosion of sweet-smelling hay spread all about the chamber. And after Jewel returned to bed, Colin had picked the strands of hay from Amy's hair, one by one...

Amy shook her head to clear it. No, she hadn't the right to give away Jewel's secrets. "I have no idea," she said coyly. "Jewel doesn't confide in me."

But Benchley does, she amended to herself. Benchley was forever boasting about Lady Jewel's accomplishments. To everyone but Jewel's father, that was.

Benchley was loyal to a fault.

"Are you quite certain?" Colin asked, his mouth against hers.

"Quite."

His arms tightened around her, and his lips pressed closer. Amy's knees turned to pudding, and she felt her pulse quicken. His kiss intensified, claiming her as his alone. Her senses whirled, and her heart pounded so loudly she was certain he could hear it.

She vaguely wondered how she could feel this way—she, a grown lady of twenty-four, with three children. But inside, she felt no older than when Colin first kissed her, so many years ago. And his kisses still affected her the same way, only more so.

"Amy…" Colin murmured into her mouth.

"Hmm?"

He pulled his lips from hers. But he pressed her even closer to him. "How did Jewel pull off the hay trick?"

His lips brushed hers teasingly. And she almost told him…

"Lord Greystone?" A sharp knock came at the door.

Colin jumped away with a groan. "Yes?"

Lydia opened the door and stuck her head in just as Amy smoothed her skirts, her cheeks hot with embarrassment.

"Lady Jewel says you were supposed to tell her a story?"

"Oh…yes…I did promise her a story…didn't I?" Colin groaned again, but Amy knew he would follow—he'd never disappoint his precious Jewel.

A Chase promise was not given lightly.

"This will be continued," Colin vowed before going to his daughter. His deep, husky voice held a challenge, and Amy knew he was referring to the hay episode and what he doubtless considered an ingenious, delicious method of inducing her to confess what she knew about it.

But she chose to interpret his words in an entirely different context.

This will be continued. For a long, long, long time.

Forever.

AUTHOR'S NOTE

∼

DEAR READER,

When I read a historical novel, I always find myself wondering what and who (besides obvious people like the king and queen) might actually be real. In case any of my readers share this curiosity, I thought a bit of information might be welcome.

The king's mistress, Barbara Villiers Palmer, Countess of Castlemaine (and later, after this story takes place, the Duchess of Cleveland), was indeed real. As King Charles's mistress on and off for at least ten years, she bore him four sons—all of which he created dukes—and a daughter. Charles granted lifetime annuities of £6000 a year for Barbara and £3000 for each of their sons. These were amazing sums at the time and more than he granted any other mistresses or children, yet he must have known Barbara had other lovers—a vast string of them, including not only many English and French courtiers, but also actors, a playwright, a Groom of the King's Bedchamber, and even a rope dancer.

I tried my best to recreate Barbara's vibrant personality from contemporary accounts of her life. I'll never forget the first time I read one of her early biographies, as a college student in the library at UC Irvine. The book, almost 300 years old, was much too valuable and brittle for them to lend out, but (unbelievably!) they did let me touch and read it. I remember my hands shaking —I found it so incredible that someone's words had come down to me through all that time. Years have passed, and I now have several very old books in my own library, but I still touch them reverently—such is the power and endurance of the written word.

Barbara Palmer was not the king's only mistress, though she presented him with more children than any other. He eventually acknowledged nine sons and five daughters, and it's assumed that he had more. Sadly, Queen Catharine never did bear Charles any legitimate offspring, but nearly four centuries later, a descendant of his is poised to sit on the throne: Princess Diana's sons are descended from Charles II and Barbara, through their son Charles Fitzroy, Duke of Grafton, born in 1663.

As for Frances Stewart, the gorgeous but empty-headed courtier that Barbara and Colin were gossiping about, Charles decided to forgive her for marrying the Duke of Richmond. Though he did eventually succeed in wooing her as well, shortly thereafter she fell ill of smallpox, and the resulting facial disfigurement seems to have cooled Charles's passions. Before Frances succumbed to the dreaded disease, Charles's sister described her as "the prettiest girl in the world," and Charles immortalized that famous beauty when he had her pose as Britannia: Frances Stewart's face and torso still grace English coins.

Cainewood Castle is loosely modeled on Arundel Castle in West Sussex. It has been home to the Dukes of Norfolk and their family, the Fitzalan Howards, since 1243, save for a short period during the Civil War. Although the family still resides there, portions of their magnificent home are open to visitors and more than worth a detour, should you ever find yourself in the area.

Greystone was inspired by Amberley Castle, also in West Sussex. Charles II visited the castle in 1651 and 1685. The then tenant, Sir John Brisco, commemorated the second visit by commissioning a mural of Charles and Queen Catharine, which can still be seen in the Queen's Room, now a gourmet restaurant. The castle has passed through many hands and is now run as a luxurious country house hotel. The walls exude the spirit of dreams and legends, and a stay there is the stuff memories are made of, well worth the splurge.

For their London town house, the Chases have borrowed Lindsey House bordering Lincoln's Inn Fields. Attributed to the esteemed architect Inigo Jones, it is the only original house left in the square. The house takes its name from Robert, third Earl of Lindsey, who purchased the property in the 1660s from the family of Sir Theodore Mayerne, who had been doctor to James I and Charles I. There have been various distinguished occupants since, including James Whistler, who painted the famous portrait of his mother there.

I hope you enjoyed *The Earl's Unsuitable Bride!* Next up is Jason's story in *The Marquess's Scottish Bride.* Please read on for an excerpt!

Always,

Lauren Royal

Read on for an excerpt from

The Marquess's Scottish Bride

Book 2 of the
Sweet Chase Brides series
by Lauren & Devon Royal

Jason Chase, the Marquess of Cainewood, is on the road to bring a blackguard to justice when he crosses paths with a woeful Scottish lad—who turns out to be a lovely Scottish lass.

∽

England, 1667

HEARING A VOICE, Caithren shifted on the bed, her head in a painful fog.

The voice had been a dark, harsh whisper. She wasn't sure whether she'd actually heard it or if it had been part of her disturbing dream. She tried to move, but her head hurt. She moaned, struggling against the nausea.

Swift footsteps approached. "You're awake, then?" It was the same male voice, but rich, comforting, and laced with relief.

Cait tried to roll closer to the sound.

He held her in place with a large, warm hand. "For heaven's sake, be still." Tinged with worry, his voice wasn't quite as nice. "You bumped your head but good."

She was lying facedown with her nose mashed into the pillow. She couldn't breathe properly.

The man's hands gripped her shoulders, gently helping her turn. "Are you dizzy?" he asked, moving to arrange her aching head on the pillow.

She intended to say aye, but when he came into view, her answer got lost somewhere between her mind and her mouth. Clear green eyes—too beautiful for a man—were studying her. He had a slim black mustache that reminded her of the one King Charles wore in a picture she'd once seen. But the man's shadowed jaw and fine tanned features were framed by glorious, long raven hair that was wavy and prettier than her own. Bent over her as he was, the ends tickled her cheeks.

He looked frustrated and concerned. And she had no idea who he was.

"Can you talk? Emerald, are you all right?"

"Emerald?" she echoed. She supposed she was all right, if she didn't take her aching head into account. But she couldn't say for sure, distracted as she was by a faint dimple in the stranger's chin. There was only one thing she was certain of in that moment. "I-I'm not Emerald," she managed.

"Oh?" Beneath the silly English mustache, his lips curved, but not in humor. "You're Scottish," he said, as though that explained everything.

"You're English," she countered, batting his hair from her face. He straightened, and his spicy scent wafted away, leaving her head a little clearer.

The room swam into view. She lay beneath not the dusky rose canopy of her bed at home, but a utilitarian beamed ceiling, the plaster cracked and at least a century older than Leslie Castle.

She was somewhere in England, and Da was dead.

Disoriented, she raised herself to her elbows, then flopped back to the pillow. A fresh burst of pain detonated inside her head, forcing a moan out through her lips.

"I told you to keep still." With a gentle hand, the man swept her hair off her face.

She pushed his hand away and fingered the ends of her hair, confused. He'd unraveled her plaits. Her other hand drifted up to touch the side of her head where the pain was the sharpest. "I'm not Emerald."

"You're Scottish"—he held up a palm to stop her words from tumbling out—"you're wearing men's clothes, you're carrying a pistol, and you're after a wanted outlaw. Now tell me you're not Emerald MacCallum."

"I'm not Emerald MacCallum."

His mouth curved as though he were amused. "Did the knock on your head damage your memory?"

"My memory is intact, thank you. But my name isn't Emerald." Despite her strong denial, her brain seemed impossibly muddled by the throbbing pain. "It's Caithren," she managed finally. "Caithren Leslie. Not Emerald."

"Hmm…" The man raised one black brow. "You do seem rather *young* to be an infamous bounty hunter. If you're not Emerald, then can you explain what you're doing here?"

"Why shouldn't I be here?" she asked on a huff. "Is there some law against my visiting your country? England and Scotland share a king, last I heard. Though not for long, saints willing."

Looking less than satisfied, he crossed his arms while one booted foot tapped against the wooden floor. Obviously he was waiting for her to explain herself.

Arrogant cur.

She wouldn't look at him, then. Her gaze swept the room, taking in the plain whitewashed walls, a simple wood cabinet, a utilitarian washstand, a small tub full of dirty bathwater that should have been carried away.

Pontefract. She was in her room at the inn in Pontefract. She was here in Pontefract...

She squeezed her eyes shut tight, blocking out the man so she could concentrate. "I've come to find my brother," she said at last, opening them in relief.

"Hmm, is that so?" he challenged in a calm voice laced with a touch of irony. "Then I suppose you can explain to me how you know Gothard."

She stared at him blankly. "Gothard?"

"Geoffrey Gothard. The man you tried to shoot in order to collect the reward. I'm not a half-wit, Emerald."

"I'm not Emerald. And I'm not a half-wit, either, but you're certainly making me feel so, since I haven't the slightest notion what you're blethering about."

He sat at the edge of the bed and studied her for a while, as though trying to gauge her sincerity. The mattress sagged beneath his weight, rolling her too close to him for her comfort. The queasiness clawed at her stomach again.

She was alone with a strange man. A strange *English* man. Her mouth went dry, and she licked her lips.

His eyes darkened, making her nervous. With a sigh, she reached up to fiddle with a plait, then remembered her hair was loose. Her hands curled into fists atop the bedcovers. "It's the truth I'm telling you, Mr...."

His mouth twisted up in a hint of a smile. "Chase. But you may call me Jason."

"I may, may I?" Stuffy, these English. Well, she *had* been warned. She took a deep breath and decided to try again. "Do you believe me?"

"Would you believe you?" His sarcastic tone irked her. "What is your brother's name?"

She struggled against the pain in her head. "…Adam."

"And why do you have cause to think he'd be here?"

"He was invited by…"

As she strained to come up with the name, he shook his head, sending the glorious hair swinging. "You'll have to invent these lies more quickly if you expect them to sound believable."

"Scarborough," she gritted out.

"The *Earl* of Scarborough?" A sparkle came into his eyes, as though he were entertained by the thought of someone related to her being invited anywhere by an earl.

Just like the innkeeper downstairs.

Did she look that provincial? Her clothes were in decent condition. Her father had been a baronet.

"I'm surprised at you, Emerald." His mocking voice interrupted her musings. "You've a reputation for being the cunning sort. Surely you can come up with a better story than that. It must be the knock on the head."

Exasperated, she slammed her hand against the mattress, wincing when it jarred her. "Bile *yer* heid!"

"Pardon?" He raised a single, amused brow. "Are you suggesting I boil my head?"

Clenching her teeth, she looked away. Her plaid was tossed over a chair, her shoes and stockings on the floor. Alarm shot through her. "Did you undress me as well, then?" She thrust her hands under the bedclothes to see what else he might have taken off of her.

That brow went up again. "I reckon you'll find you're still decent. What do you take me for?"

"An Englishman." Her clothing was all in place, although the laces on her shirt had been loosened. She gave them a vicious tug, then looked down and gasped. "There's blood on my shirt." She felt for the source, though it didn't really hurt much.

"You were cut. Nothing serious."

Slackening the laces, she peeked beneath. He was right. The meadow rue she'd picked would heal it in no time.

"That's why your shirt was unlaced," he continued. "I...checked."

When she looked up, his face was red. A proper gentleman he was, then, but he was still an Englishman. And he was staring at her. Caithren bit her lip and felt for her good-luck charm.

Her hands closed on air.

"Where's my amulet?" she squeaked in a panic. She struggled up on her elbows again and felt the dizziness rush back.

"I have it right here." He reached to the bedside table, lifted the amulet, and dangled it over her head by its chain. The emerald swung in a hypnotizing pattern. "I'm hardly the type who'd steal from an unconscious maiden."

"Well, I don't know you, do I?" She snatched it to her chest.

His mouth tightened with annoyance. "But you know Geoffrey Gothard, don't you?"

Crivvens, the man was bullheaded. She shot him a peevish look and slipped the chain back over her head, feeling better when the amulet was settled in place. She wrapped a hand around it.

That Geoffrey he was talking about, she remembered who he was now—the murdering cur she'd overheard at Scarborough's and met again on the inn's staircase. That terrible, horrible man and his scum of a brother.

Englishmen.

She shivered and tugged up on the thin quilt. Well, at least *this* Englishman was looking out for her, even if she didn't care for him badgering her with questions. And though he was plainly cross, he'd yet to raise his voice to her.

"Thank you for your help," she said softly by way of apology. She tried to smile.

His eyes softened in response. All at once he seemed very close to her, though he had not moved. And he was staring at her mouth, the same way that bampot Duncan had stared right before he tried to kiss her at the village dance.

Was this strange man going to kiss her, then?

Nay, she was daft! She must have truly knocked herself silly.

What would a mustached, pretty-haired, bullheaded Englishman want with a girl like her? Besides, he was still cross with her: his mouth remained pressed into that thin, tight line.

She couldn't help noticing it spoiled the dimple.

"Why are you so cross?" she heard herself asking.

"I had a job to do, Emerald," he said with a sigh that, if she didn't know better, she might take to be apologetic. "And you got in the way. No fault of yours." He waved a dismissive hand. "Stay away from Geoffrey Gothard. He's a dangerous man."

"I quite agree. But he's unlikely to be a danger to me, seeing as he's on his way to London."

"London?" She saw his body tense. "How come you to know this?"

"I...overheard him and—his brother, aye? When I went out to Scarborough's to find Adam." Because he seemed concerned for her welfare, she added, "They didn't see me."

The Englishman's clear green eyes narrowed on hers suspiciously. "Why are you telling me this? To send me off in the wrong direction?"

"Pardon me?"

He stood abruptly. "Just stay away from Gothard. Find yourself another reward to collect." The candle flames flickered as he strode to the door, disturbing the room's musty air. His gaze settled on her emerald amulet for a moment before he pierced her with those incredible eyes. "I admire your persistence—it puts me in mind of my family—but I cannot see why you refuse to admit who you are."

"You know what my mam would have said?" Caithren crossed her arms beneath the quilt. "Telling it true, pits ain in a stew."

He paused with his hand on the latch. "I cannot understand you."

"Then permit me to translate. Telling the truth confuses your enemies."

"I'm not your enemy." He blinked several times. "Why of a sudden does everyone think me his enemy?"

He said it to no one in particular, his gaze aimed toward the blackened beamed ceiling, as though he were looking for the heavens to send down an answer.

"I should be on the road after Gothard," he mused to himself. Then he sighed and looked back to her. "But hang it if I don't feel responsible for you."

"Well, you needn't be," Cait said. "I can take care of myself."

"Not from what I've seen. And now, thanks to me, you're injured and even more vulnerable to men like the Gothards."

"What do you mean, thanks to you?"

"You fell down the stairs after I intervened. And it was my sword that cut you. Accidentally—I wasn't even holding it—but it's my responsibility nonetheless." She heard a click when he pushed down on the door latch. "I insist you accept my help."

"I'd say you've helped me quite enough already." Was this man out of his mind? "Your kind of help I don't need."

He didn't seem to hear her. "Get some sleep," he said, "but make sure you awaken. The last thing I need is another Mary."

Mary? Who on earth was Mary?

He opened the door. "I'll check on you in the morning. If your head still aches, we'll have a doctor in to examine it."

Caithren was so confused and frustrated that if she'd had the energy, she'd have kicked the door shut behind him. As it was, it closed softly.

Did he think he could order her about as he pleased?

I'll check on you in the morning.

Not if she had anything to say about it.

∿

AVAILABLE NOW!
Learn more about *The Marquess's Scottish Bride* at
www.DevonAndLaurenRoyal.com

ENTER FOR A CHANCE TO WIN
a replica of the sterling silver locket
Amy gives Mary for Christmas in this book!*

Visit the Contest page on Lauren & Devon's website
at www.LaurenandDevonRoyal.com
and answer a question to be
entered in the monthly drawing.

No purchase necessary. See complete rules on the site.

*Please note: Depending on when you enter, the prize may be another piece of jewelry associated with one of Lauren & Devon's books. The authors reserve the right to discontinue this promotion at any time.

ABOUT LAUREN & DEVON ROYAL

LAUREN ROYAL decided to become a writer in the third grade, after winning a "Why My Mother is the Greatest" essay contest. Now she's a *New York Times* and *USA Today* bestselling author of humorous historical romance novels. Lauren lives in Southern California with her family and their constantly shedding cat. She still thinks her mother is the greatest.

DEVON ROYAL is the daughter of romance novelist Lauren Royal. After attending film school, she wrote an award-winning TV comedy pilot and worked in digital video production before turning her focus to fiction writing. Devon lives in Southern California with her husband and son. She also thinks her mother is the greatest.

ACKNOWLEDGMENTS

~

OUR HEARTFELT THANKS:

To Elise Misiorowski, from the Gemological Institute of America, for her wonderful insight into old jewelry manufacturing techniques.

To Mark Zana, for exhaustive research into England's confusing monetary history.

To Herb Royal, for explaining all about obsolete guns and the resulting wounds in excruciating detail.

To Teri Royal, Becca Royal-Gordon, and Blake Royal-Gordon, for invaluable firsthand experience in the mechanics of sibling rivalry.

To all the honorary Chase cousins in our Chase Family Readers Group, for their enthusiastic support.

And to all of our readers.

Thank you, one and all!

CONTACT INFORMATION

∼

Newsletter

littl.ink/News

Facebook Readers Group

facebook.com/groups/ChaseFamilyReaders

Website

www.DevonAndLaurenRoyal.com

Email

royall.ink/Email